CLASSIC Adventure STORIES

DERRYDALE BOOKS
New York

© 1974 Presseburo Junior

English Language Edition, designed and produced by
Autumn Publishing Limited, Chichester, England

This 1987 edition published by Derrydale Books
distributed by Crown Publishers, Inc.
225 Park Avenue South
New York, New York 10003

Derrydale Books
New York

Library of Congress Cataloging-in-Publication Data
Classic adventure stories.
Contents: Treasure island — Oliver Twist — Moby
Dick — The call of the wild — [etc.]
1. Adventure stories. [1. Adventure and
adventurers — Fiction]
PZ5.C557   1987   [Fic]   86-19790
ISBN 0-517-60127-3 (Crown)

ISBN 0 517 60127 3
h g f e d c b a

Printed in Czechoslovakia

CONTENTS

ALEXANDRE DUMAS

The Three Musketeers

ALEXANDRE DUMAS
The Three Musketeers

The stranger and the lady

It was 1st April 1625. The young man who leapt from his saddle outside the coach-stage at Meung did not seem in the least concerned by the astonished stares of those around him, although he knew very well that they were directed at his appearance and that of his horse.

Neither the large, fluttering feather on his hat nor the lengthy sword could disguise the fact that the stranger was poorly clad and that his steed, by virtue of its age, colouring and spindly frame, was anything but a noble war-horse. And yet the newcomer gave off such an air of self-assurance that any mockery was out of the question.

In fact, the young man was ready to take on anyone who failed to pay him the respect he felt he deserved. After all, he was not just anybody, but the latest in the long line of the d'Artagnans, that noble family whose name had proved its worth in countless battles over the centuries in the defence of France's honour. But no amount of fame could alter the fact that the d'Artagnans were now reduced to poverty. They were left with one small estate in the Béarn region, deep in the heart of Gascony, where the people had been noted since time immemorial for a special kind of haughty pride.

"Never allow yourself to be tainted with even a hint of offence," his father had said by way of farewell.

"You can only make a name for yourself by the sword in a duel, but duelling is now forbidden by order of the King. Should you ever be wounded, this ointment from your mother will heal all injury. Apart from this advice, all I can give you is this horse and fifteen talers, and a letter to my old friend, Monsieur de Treville. Like you he is a Gascon; he too had to fight his

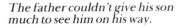

The father couldn't give his son much to see him on his way.

D'Artagnan lunged forward, but in a flash the other had also drawn his sword.

way up from the bottom, but today he is Captain of the Royal Musketeers. Therefore after His Majesty and the Cardinal he is the third most powerful man in France. Approach him with respect but do not tolerate any injustice from him. Only from the King and his chancellor, the Cardinal, must you suffer injustice if it so pleases them."

The young d'Artagnan recalled these very words as he caught sight of a nobleman at the window of an inn, talking to someone inside. He spoke in a tone of voice which made the sensitive Gascon prick up his ears.

Without a moment's hesitation, he grasped his sword and called to the stranger, "What is there to laugh about, sir? Out with it, so that we can both be amused!"

The astonished stranger turned around. "Are you addressing me? Then first tell me, what is your name?"

"And you tell me yours!"

The other shrugged his shoulders somewhat indecisively, before pointing to d'Artagnan's horse. "You will not deny that the colouring of your horse is remarkable, to say the least."

"Ah, so it's my horse which causes you to laugh. Do not dare to laugh at its rider!"

"I seldom laugh," replied the stranger, coldly, "but I laugh when it pleases me."

"Not, however, when it displeases me," cried the Gascon, rashly.

"Do as you wish," replied the other and turned away, obviously bored. "And leave me in peace."

"Turn back so that the point of my sword does not pierce you from behind!"

The stranger turned his head, unable to believe what he had just heard. His face, already grey, turned even greyer and a scar on his forehead glowed deep red. "Are you mad, young man? You would dare to strike me . . ."

Just then, d'Artagnan lunged forward in a rage. Only a nimble jump to one side saved the nobleman from being struck. In a flash he also drew his sword. But before the blades had time to clash, the innkeeper and several of his servants pounced on the Gascon. He hit out wildly but was no match for their numbers. A cudgel blow brought him down to the ground.

"Those damned Gascons," mumbled the nobleman and ordered the innkeeper to take the wounded man indoors. He then ordered his carriage.

The innkeeper hurriedly obeyed, but returned after only a few minutes. He sidled up to the guest, bowing all the while.

"Beware of him," he whispered excitedly. "He has just come round cursing like a madman and has sworn to kill you, my Lord."

The aristocrat laughed contemptuously and merely asked, "Who does the fellow think he is?"

"No idea," replied the innkeeper and pulled a sly face. "I had to make sure he had some money on him and I found this letter."

"Addressed to Treville?" The nobleman grabbed it and became pensive. "What business can the Gascon have with Treville? Has he set him on my trail? Strange . . . by the way, has Milady driven up yet?" A nod from the innkeeper sent him hurrying outside.

In front of the inn a coach was waiting, the curtains drawn. He dashed up to it. The curtains were pulled back to reveal the face of a fair-haired lady of extraordinary beauty.

"His Eminence wishes you to return to England without delay, Milady," the nobleman said to the passenger. "And to inform him immediately as soon as the Duke leaves London. You will find your further instructions here in this case."

At that very moment d'Artagnan burst out of the inn, barely restrained by his makeshift bonds. He had heard everything and roared, "So you want to depart, do you, without giving me satisfaction? Are you too cowardly, you with . . . " His words faded to a murmur as he collapsed to the ground, faint from loss of blood.

The coach carrying the lady drove off. A few minutes later, the nobleman also left Meung, but in the opposite direction.

After two days d'Artagnan had recovered enough to continue his ride to Paris. He was determined to get back the letter of recommendation to Monsieur de Treville.

A roundabout friendship

D'Artagnan was in no doubt that Paris was not only a large city, it was also very expensive. To make ends meet, he sold his horse to a pedlar. Although he had to surrender his steed for a measly sum, he still had enough money to replace the blade of his sword, which had been smashed in the brawl at Meung. He had enough left over to pay for a small garret in the Rue de Fossoyeurs. Only a short distance away lived Monsieur de Treville, in a palatial mansion on Rue du Vieux Colombier.

In accordance with custom, the Gascon had his arrival announced by a footman and was summoned for the following afternoon. He turned up punctually. The fact that there were other people waiting for an audience with Monsieur de Treville was unmistakable proof to the young man from the provinces that old d'Artagnan had been absolutely right when he described Treville as a powerful and influential man.

While the Gascon was waiting in the guardroom, he had the time and leisure to

He was finally led in to see Monsieur de Treville.

D'Artagnan arrived on time at the appointed place. The musketeer was already waiting.

observe some musketeers on duty there and to listen to their conversation. The mere fact that they belonged to the King's bodyguard filled him with admiration. The free and relaxed manner in which they spoke of high-ranking people, courteous ladies and money difficulties made him regard them with even greater awe. They had already achieved what he had long aimed for, one of the peaks of his burning ambition.

He was especially struck by a tall, bold musketeer, better dressed than the rest, who wore a golden sword-belt with unconcealed pride. When the other musketeers enquired which beauty he had to thank for it, he furiously appealed to a rather young, modest companion to be his witness. "Tell them, Aramis, you know that the belt cost me 12 gold pistols!"

"And one day your vanity will cost you everlasting bliss, Porthos," replied Aramis.

"Never fear," Porthos cried merrily, "by that time you'll be the Abbot of some beautiful monastery and you'll be able to pray for my salvation!"

Everyone roared with laughter, with the exception of Aramis, until one musketeer chimed in, "Old Rochefort, the traitor, has been spreading another nasty rumour about the Queen."

"Rochefort?" exclaimed another, doubtfully. "You can bet your life it's the Cardinal who is at the bottom of it. He and his pack of spies! I would . . . "

The rest was lost on d'Artagnan for just at that moment he was summoned to Monsieur de Treville.

The Captain of the Musketeers was obviously not in the best of moods. True, he received the young Gascon in a friendly enough fashion but he seemed to be only half listening to what he was saying. Something else appeared to be troubling him. Suddenly, in the middle of d'Artagnan's speech, he shouted to his adjutant, "Bring in the Three Musketeers!"

15

D'Artagnan was about to witness an un-forgettable scene. Through the door came Porthos and Aramis who snapped to attention.

Treville frowned at them severely. "What did I hear today at court? Yet another brawl with the Cardinal's guard? You had to be restrained by guardsmen – Royal Musketeers arrested by guardsmen!"

"By your leave, sir," ventured Porthos, "we fell into a trap. And there were too many of them. When Athos . . . "

"Ah, yes, Athos!" Treville's temper flared up again. "Where is the damned fellow?"

"He's ill. With chickenpox," blurted out Aramis.

"Chickenpox?" Treville raised his eyebrows quizzically. "So some of the guardsmen might go down with it now, I suppose?"

"There is that danger," answered Porthos.

"So that's why the Cardinal was so incensed." Treville had stopped shaking so much with anger and turned to Aramis. "You do know, I take it, that the King has forbidden all duels . . . "

A sudden commotion in the guardroom interrupted him. The door crashed open and a musketeer of about 30 years of age, with a strikingly aristocratic look, stormed into the room, stood to attention and raised his feathered cap respectfully. "You summoned me, sir? Here I am!"

"Athos! So your illness doesn't seem so . . . or does it? You look so pale!"

"You haven't seen the guards yet," growled the musketeer. "They are all as white as ghosts. And if another scoundrel like that gets in my way again . . . oh . . . "

Athos had collapsed.

"He is badly wounded in the shoulder!" Porthos was already bent over his companion. "He took on three guardsmen single-handed!"

"Call a doctor! Either mine or the King's!" roared Treville to the adjutant. "Be off with you and hurry! My Athos is dying! Quick, get going!"

Athos was carried unconscious to the guardroom. Only after the doctor reassured

In a matter of seconds, a fierce fight had broken out between the musketeers and the Cardinal's guards. The Gascon joined in readily.

them that he was in no serious danger and that it had been the heavy loss of blood which caused him to pass out did Treville finally return to the reception room, where d'Artagnan was still waiting.

"So you want to be a musketeer?" resumed Treville. "That's not a simple matter; you must first prove yourself. I shall recommend your name to the Director of the Academy, who will first train you in all the courtly arts. Don't hang your head like that. When I first came to Paris I was even poorer than you. Believe me, I can do no more for you at the moment. Now, if you had been able to produce a letter of recommendation, well . . . "

"I had one – it was stolen from me," interrupted d'Artagnan passionately and told the story of what happened to him at Meung.

Treville listened with increasing interest. He asked d'Artagnan to repeat the description of the beautiful lady and the strange nobleman.

17

"Are you sure about the scar on his forehead?" he demanded to know. When the Gascon nodded, Treville murmured, "It is he! And I thought he was in Brussels . . . I must . . ." Abruptly, he stretched out his hand to the young man. "You have done me and the King a great service. Call on me whenever you wish. You are free to visit at any time and I shall help you in whatever way I can. Oh yes, wait, the letter of recomm . . ."

Just then d'Artagnan rushed to the window and cried, "There! On the street below! That's the fellow! This time he won't escape!"

Monsieur de Treville shook his head, more bewildered than surprised, and turned to greet his next visitor. D'Artagnan, meanwhile, had not got very far.

In his rush to leave he nearly knocked down Porthos, the musketeer.

"Sorry!" exclaimed the Gascon but this apology did not satisfy the musketeer and an altercation ensued in which each felt offended by the other. They did not part until they had agreed on a duel at twelve o'clock sharp behind the Franciscan convent.

By the time d'Artagnan managed to get away there was no sign of the stranger. He searched every alley and tavern, but all he succeeded in doing was to step on the toes of the musketeer Athos, who happened to be resting in a nearby inn, recovering from his loss of blood.

Athos was not satisfied with a short, if polite, apology either. He would not let the Gascon go until he had promised to fight a duel at one o'clock sharp in the park behind the Luxembourg Palace.

Enraged, d'Artagnan resumed his search. He suddenly found himself in front of the Palais d'Anguillon where he saw the musketeer Aramis in conversation with some other soldiers. A delicately embroidered handkerchief fell from the royal musketeer's cloak. The Gascon dashed to pick it up and returned it to him, without, however, earning any thanks for his pains. On the contrary, Aramis denied being the owner and in such an obstinate manner

Instead of reprimanding them, the King summoned all four and paid tribute to their bravery.

that one of the soldiers remarked, with a twinkle in his eyes, "I bet it wasn't in church that you got it, Aramis. No, don't tell me, one of your nieces gave it you as a present . . . "

"Shut up!" thundered Aramis, blushing and then barked at the Gascon, "Take your handkerchief and get out of my sight!"

The tone of voice infuriated d'Artagnan. All the more so since Aramis was publicly accusing him of being a liar. Yet again an argument ensued, followed by the inevitable challenge to a duel. In front of Monsieur de Treville's house, declared Aramis, where one was safest from spying eyes. At two o'clock in the afternoon, sharp.

D'Artagnan hurried on, still on the trail of the stranger. But once again in vain. He suddenly realized with a shock that he only had a few minutes before his meeting with Porthos. Panting, he finally reached the convent. The musketeer was already waiting.

"What about your second?" he asked.

D'Artagnan replied regretfully that he still knew no-one whom he could trust, but that he would be happy to do without a second since Porthos was undoubtedly a man of honour. These words flattered the musketeer but he remained adamant, "Then permit one of my seconds to defend your rights!"

It was only then that the Gascon noticed two men, hitherto hidden in the shadows. Athos and Aramis! There was general amazement at this. Nevertheless all three paid the young man from Béarn their greatest respects, expressing a regret that he was unlikely to survive to see another day.

"Do not be too sure of that, gentlemen!" cried d'Artagnan somewhat recklessly and took the guard position. "Let us begin, Monsieur Porthos!"

"As you wish." Porthos drew his sword too, but then asked by way of precaution, "Whom are we to notify of your death?"

The question remained unanswered be- cause of an unexpected turn of events. Suddenly, out of nowhere, appeared seven heavily armed sentinels of the Cardinal's guard. They faced the duellists. Their commander, a certain Jussac, whose sword was feared far and wide, exclaimed scornfully, "So the gentlemen are about to fight an illegal duel, are they? This will greatly displease His Majesty. Not to mention His Eminence, the Cardinal. Be so good as to hand over your swords." He gave d'Artagnan a look of sheer contempt. "As for you, get out of here, as fast as you can!"

"Yes, get away, quick," advised Aramis, softly. "What is about to take place concerns only us."

"Does it now? I think differently!" declared the Gascon and then shouted at Jussac, "We shall soon see who takes the sword from whom! Take that!" He let fly with his sword. "And that!"

In a matter of seconds a bitter fight had broken out between the musketeers, their

19

young helper and the guards. Seven against four. The Cardinal's men seemed sure of victory, but rather too soon. Before they knew it, Jussac was writhing on the ground, pierced by d'Artagnan's blade. Porthos had taken on two of them and Athos, whose shoulder injury was causing him trouble, managed to hold one at bay until Aramis could relieve him, but only after he had put yet another out of action. The sixth had the misfortune to run into the point of d'Artagnan's sword when making a cut at Porthos. Just as the Gascon was about to tackle the seventh, who was already taking to his heels, Athos roared, "Let him flee! Someone has to let the others know how they made fools of themselves! Quickly now, put the wounded in the shadows so that no-one can accuse us of abandoning them in their misery. Their companions will soon be here. We had better withdraw."

"But not before we have thanked you!" Porthos bowed respectfully before d'Artagnan. "Are we still going to fight that duel, or shall we be friends?"

"Friends!" cried d'Artagnan with delight and, laughing, all four fell into each other's arms.

"In that case we must celebrate victory together!" Porthos hammered a leather pouch with his fist. "I still have a few ducats which want changing into wine!"

A few hours later, when Monsieur de Treville appeared at his daily audience before the King, he was angrily reproached for the unruly behaviour of the musketeers. "I have promised the Cardinal that the wrongdoers will be severely punished," concluded Louis XIII bluntly.

And yet the King's anger turned to amazement and admiration when he heard that the guards had outnumbered the musketeers by almost two to one. And when he learnt that an unknown Gascon had overpowered the feared Jussac, he summoned the four to his presence and paid tribute to their bravery. He even gave young d'Artagnan a purse of gold and ordered Monsieur de Treville to place him in the Compagnie d'Essart, a famous and trusted body of knights.

A secret abduction

The next few days and weeks flew by for d'Artagnan and he soon realized that a soldier's life required a great deal of skill. The meagre wages scarcely paid the rent, to say nothing of suitable apparel and the cost of a servant. Nonetheless the three musketeers who, together with their new friend, had quickly got through the King's gold, insisted that d'Artagnan took on a not altogether clever but good-natured peasant lad from Picardy, by the name of Planchet. Athos had found him on a bridge where he had been passing the time seeing how far he could spit into the water. As for himself, Athos preferred a servant called Grimaud, who hardly ever opened his mouth. The very opposite, in fact, of Mousqueton who liked to behave just as grandly as his master, Porthos. The most unusual of all, however, was Bazin. He was not content with looking after Aramis' physical well-being; he felt equally obliged to see to his master's spiritual salvation. He never gave up the hope that one day Aramis would leave the rough trade of a soldier and devote himself to the Church. In accordance with this pious outlook Bazin would always solemnly dress in black.

The friends' living quarters were as different as their servants. Athos rented two modest rooms in the Rue de Frou which he had furnished with great taste. Porthos, meanwhile, lived with a lot of mostly empty bottles in a house near Monsieur de Treville. Aramis even boasted a garden, in which he was wont to stroll about, philosophizing and composing poetry. The smallest dwelling of all belonged to d'Artagnan. It consisted of nothing more than a garret, which meant that trusty Planchet was forced to sleep outside, by the door.

The friends saw each other almost every day. Most of the time they spent thinking up ways of getting food and drink. As they had no money, their suggestions were always inventive. They were just as inventive when it came to playing tricks on Richelieu's guards.

They were musketeers of the King and even d'Artagnan felt as much. At first he failed to appreciate that the King and Cardinal, who always behaved as though they were trusted friends, were in fact at odds with one another. France's nobility was correspondingly split into two camps. The first were faithful followers of the royal family, mostly landed gentry and the military, who could thank the King for their positions and privileges. The others were supporters of the Cardinal, a man who craftily exploited his growing power, and whose smooth diplomacy earned him great respect; especially since he always appeared to have only France's interests at heart, even in the most difficult of situations.

In reality, however, it was fear rather than honour which had made Richelieu the most powerful man in the country. He had spies and informers everywhere. Even the King lived in constant fear of them. He relied more and more on the loyalty and devotion of his musketeers and their Captain, Treville. Under the circumstances it was hardly surprising that a heartfelt loathing existed between the Cardinal and the Captain. And consequently between the Cardinal's guards and the King's musketeers.

The tense relationship between musketeers and guards was an open secret, but d'Artagnan was still somewhat taken aback when he received a visit one day from a very portly stranger, who peered around anxiously several times before he finally nervously blurted out why he had come.

"Help me, noble sir! My wife has been abducted. I shall reward you highly if you can get her back. I . . . I'm afraid I'm no hero like you."

"Abducted? Your wife?" The Gascon shook his head in disbelief. "Who are you, my good fellow? And who is your wife?"

To d'Artagnan's surprise, the fat man introduced himself as Monsieur Bonacieux, the owner of the house. He did not omit to mention that the Gascon owed the rent for the last three months. However, he would be willing to overlook this if d'Artagnan was prepared to save Madame Bonacieux.

The prospect of reward *and* adventure

The portly fellow asked for his help.

made the Gascon agree. Yet it took a lot of coaxing to worm the most important details out of the agitated man. Madame Bonacieux was the godchild of a certain Monsieur de la Porte, a chamberlain and intimate of the Queen.

Three years ago he got the young woman a job as linen maid with the Queen. It was not long before Madame Bonacieux was part of that small, select circle of servants in whom the Queen confided all her secrets. No doubt d'Artagnan knew only too well that the Queen always had to be on her guard for fear of being reported for improper conduct by the Cardinal to His Majesty.

Although this was news to the Gascon, he nodded sagely before learning how the Cardinal distrusted the Queen simply because she was Spanish by birth, a fact of which no true Frenchman could approve. There was also the story concerning the English Duke of Buckingham, one of France's most dangerous arch-enemies.

"That story was never proved," interjected d'Artagnan for good measure, since he felt duty-bound to defend the honour of his Queen.

"No," agreed Bonacieux hastily, "but there's no doubt that the Cardinal wants to find proof and has lured the Duke to Paris by means of a forged letter, supposedly written by the Queen. My wife told me all this. He's now hoping to surprise the Queen at a meeting with Buckingham and so . . . "

"Your wife seems to know a great deal, Monsieur!"

"That's why she was abducted! By a nobleman I've never seen before with a scar just here, on his forehead. A confidant of the Cardinal, I'll be bound, because the accomplices he had with him are known to be henchmen of His Eminence."

Queen, Cardinal and the man with the scar – reasons enough to make d'Artagnan declare his mind was made up. "You can depend on me, Monsieur. But now leave me be so that I can think it over in peace."

No sooner had Bonacieux made his exit,

bowing as he went, than Porthos was clattering up the stairs to the garret. He was followed by Athos and Aramis.

D'Artagnan quickly told them of the promise he had made. After only a few moments' pause for thought, all three friends pledged their support.

"Even though old Bonacieux doesn't deserve his pretty, young wife!" grumbled Porthos. "What a repulsive, mercenary blackguard to think that money can buy everything. He would even sell his own soul for money."

"And the Queen," added Aramis. "We ought to pray for him."

"You might be right there," said Athos, for at that moment cries were heard from the stairs and the door flew open. In the doorway stood Bonacieux, trembling and wailing. "Help, the informers want to arrest me!"

In a flash, the musketeers had reached for their swords. The Gascon, however, simply shook his head and, with exquisite politeness, greeted the leader of the guards who appeared at that moment behind Bonacieux. "You wish to arrest this man? Please, attend to your duties. I'm sure he deserves all he gets. And remember us to His Eminence!"

Rather bewildered, the guards withdrew, holding fast to their writhing prisoner. Porthos immediately turned on the Gascon and bellowed, "How could you be so deceitful?"

"And how can you be so foolish," grinned Athos, before d'Artagnan had a chance to reply. "Do we want to help the Queen? Yes, we do! In which case we must, under no circumstances, appear to be accomplices of Bonacieux. Don't worry, he'll soon talk his way to freedom again. We, on the other hand, need to be free right from the start."

"Got it, Porthos?" added Aramis.

Porthos' face was working feverishly, until he, too, laughed. "D'Artagnan, take my hand! You are the cleverest of us all!"

The friends stayed together a while longer and enjoyed a few bottles of wine from the landlord's cellar. When they finally parted they were still none the wiser. Until they knew where Madame Bonacieux was imprisoned they could do nothing to set her free. Time will tell, they finally decided by way of consolation.

Time told sooner than they expected. The following afternoon d'Artagnan had just settled down for a nap when he suddenly heard loud cries from the dwelling below. He tore up one of the planks in the floor and peered through the hole, just in time to see three guards violently dragging a very pretty young woman from the room. Madame Bonacieux!

"Fetch the others!" roared d'Artagnan through the closed door at a startled Planchet, before leaping through the window with one bound on to the street below. He had drawn his sword almost before touching the ground. And not a moment too soon! Out of the door came the sentinels with their prisoner.

"Get back! Miserable scoundrels!" shouted d'Artagnan before throwing himself at the Cardinal's surprised guards. The first he simply ran through, while he knocked the sword out of the second guard's hand. The third was quicker off the mark and ran as fast as his legs could carry him.

Semi-conscious, the young woman sank into the Gascon's arms. He shook her gently. "Quick, we must get away from here before

The young woman tried to resist the guards but her entreaties were all in vain.

When Athos was led in, Bonacieux let out a scream on seeing him.

reinforcements arrive! I shall take you to a safer place."

"But where?" whispered Madame Bonacieux.

"To a friend's house."

"It's wrong that you should risk your life for me!" remonstrated the former captive, but d'Artagnan stubbornly ignored this and took her to Athos' house which he found empty. He tried in vain to make Madame Bonacieux say why she had been abducted in her own house, in broad daylight.

"Please do not ask me!" implored the young woman, before asking him to secretly inform Monsieur de la Porte at the Court what had happened. He was then to come and collect her as quickly as possible.

"Depend on me!" promised d'Artagnan, who had not failed to notice the fear in Madame Bonacieux's eyes. After carrying out this request, he returned to his room. Another surprise was in store for him there: Planchet had only been able to find one of the mus-

keteers, Athos. He had come immediately. Once there, a large contingent of informers had arrested him in the belief that he was d'Artagnan. Athos had let them believe this.

A secret errand

Monsieur Bonacieux was haggard, deathly pale and shivering all over when he was led off for interrogation. He had spent the night in the Bastille, that terrible prison from which there was no escape.

"Confess that you are guilty of high treason!" demanded a grim-looking commissioner.

Bonacieux's knees were shaking. "High treason? Me? Don't you know, Your Grace, that my wife is one of the most trusted confidants of the . . . "

"Exactly!" interrupted the other, icily. "That is why you dared to plot her release with d'Artagnan! Come on, out with it! Where is she?"

"Upon my soul, I know nothing of any plot or of my wife," howled Bonacieux. "Ask Monsieur d'Artagnan!"

The commissioner surprised him by nodding, albeit scornfully, in the direction of the door. "I'd like nothing better!"

Two soldiers led Athos inside. With a disdainful glance at Bonacieux, he exclaimed, "Who is that supposed to be? What has he to do with me?"

"I could say the same!" shrieked the fat landlord. "That's not d'Artagnan! That's a musketeer! Can't you see? D'Artagnan wears the uniform of the Compagnie d'Essart!"

For a moment the commissioner looked perplexed, before bellowing at Athos, "Who are *you* then?"

Grinning, Athos gave his name and added, "You have only your bloodhounds to blame – they wouldn't let me utter a word!"

"Back to the cells!" The commissioner's face was burning a fiery red. "You're in for some surprises!"

With this threat still ringing in his ears, Bonacieux looked even more wretched when, the following day, he was dragged into a heavily guarded palace where he found himself face to face with a man in distinguished dress. This man looked down at him long and piercingly before finally ordering the guards to leave the room. Bonacieux hardly dared look up from the floor. He knew instinctively whom he was facing – the most powerful man in France, Prince Armand Jean Duplessis, Cardinal de Richelieu.

"How could you conspire against me?" asked the Cardinal, coldly. "Do you not know that my only concern, day and night, is for France? Did your commonsense not tell you that there were good reasons for taking your wife away for a short time . . . "

"Yes, yes, yes," interrupted Bonacieux, beseechingly. "I would never have dared to doubt if I had known that Your Eminence was involved in the abduction of my wife."

"Blockhead!" exploded Richelieu. "How

The Gascon had heard everything through the hole in the floor

dare you blame me for an abduction!"

Bathed in sweat, Bonacieux lost no time trying to make good his error. "Now you see, Your Grace, how my wife has deceived me! What have I done to deserve that? I, whose only desire was to revere Your Eminence and the King. But was I not to trust my wife when she daily had dealings with the Queen?"

The Cardinal smiled slyly. "The Queen ... who knows how she is led astray, ill-advised by false friends? That would indeed be a bad thing and one which must be prevented at all costs. Don't you agree, Monsieur?"

"Of course!" assured the fat landlord with passion.

"Fine, I can trust you. You seem to be an honest fellow." Richelieu nodded benevolently. "Will you inform me in future of everything you learn from your wife? Everything that concerns the Queen? France expects your help and you won't regret it."

The greedy flicker in the fat man's eyes was proof that the statesman had assessed Bonacieux correctly. For money this man would sell his own soul.

"For Your Eminence I would have myself torn to pieces!" he swore somewhat dramatically and accepted, with profuse thanks, a purse full of gold pistols which the Cardinal contemptuously threw his way. "I shall tell you everything as soon as I get wind of it."

"Fine, now go!" ordered the Cardinal and sat down at a writing desk, paying no further heed to the fat landlord.

The latter bowed so deeply as he made for the door that he failed to notice the man who entered from the other side. It was the man with the scar.

"My dear Rochefort," was the Cardinal's good-natured greeting, "everything seems to be going just as we wish. I have new orders for you." He asked the Count to be seated before enlightening him. "It is immaterial that Bonacieux has got away. I have just bought off the spineless creature. But now listen: my agents at Court have informed me that Buckingham was actually here as a result of the letter and has met the Queen in secret. He is completely infatuated with her and I fear she is using her influence over him to harm France. That means she wants to compel him, the most powerful adviser to the English court, to declare war on us again. Unlike Buckingham, she is thinking less of England's gain than about her own Austro-Spanish relations. Presumably in order to make him even more disposed towards her, she has given the Duke the precious brooch with the twelve diamond studs, which ... "

"Surely not that," interrupted the Count in disbelief, "the one she received as a present from His Majesty, after his flirtation with the Comtesse ... "

"The very same," confirmed Richelieu with satisfaction, "and by doing so she has set her own trap in which I intend to catch her. Or rather, His Majesty will do it on my behalf. I've asked the King to organize a Ball for 3rd October, two weeks from now, when she will be expected to wear the brooch. The Queen will try anything to get the diamond studs back from Buckingham. But there will be only ten of them."

"How do you mean?" marvelled Rochefort.

"Because I instructed Milady to approach Buckingham at a Court Ball in London and to ... well, shall we say ... remove two of the studs. She has succeeded. It is now up to you to ensure that Milady in London gets the reward I promised her and that she gets back to Paris, unharmed, with the diamond studs, as soon as possible."

A devilish grin flitted across Rochefort's sallow face, before he bowed deeply and, taking his leave, assured, "Your Eminence can always depend on me."

The Cardinal's plan seemed to be going better than he had dared hope.

Madame Bonacieux, meanwhile, had been instructed by the unhappy Queen to find an unsuspicious messenger to collect the brooch from the Duke of Buckingham. She turned to her husband of all people.

"That strikes me as being against the wishes of my close friend, His Eminence," declared Bonacieux and when his wife stared at him uncomprehendingly, he ostentatiously pointed to the purse containing the gold coins. "He and I have seen through the intrigues of that Spanish woman. Beware of acting against France's best interests!"

This said, he stood up and left the house, leaving his pretty wife stricken with terror.

"Don't lose heart!" The words came from above. D'Artagnan, who had heard everything through the hole in the floorboards and whose heart was aflame with love for the young woman, hurried downstairs and volunteered to take up the Queen's request.

"It might cost you your head," warned Madame Bonacieux. "The Cardinal will . . ."

"My life belongs to the King and Queen!" D'Artagnan caught hold of the beautiful woman's hand, which she did not pull away. "And to you!"

At last Madame Bonacieux relented. "The Queen's destiny lies in your hands. And mine too," she added softly, as she finally handed over a sealed letter addressed to the Duke. She then smiled, "You will need money for travelling. There!" She took the purse containing the gold pistols. "No, don't fuss – the Cardinal can pay. It's only right."

"Indeed!" nodded d'Artagnan. That same evening he asked Monsieur de Treville for leave and when the latter heard that it concerned a secret which would hardly please the Cardinal, he insisted that the three musketeers

The man fawned on them so obviously that they saw through him immediately.

The Ball began.

must accompany the Gascon on his mission.

"I have no idea what you are planning, d'Artagnan," declared the Captain, earnestly, "but when you are up against Richelieu, as it seems, then four men are better than one. May God go with you!"

A race against time

Although the three musketeers were greatly puzzled at their unexpected leave, they did not press their young friend, who only told them as much as they definitely needed to know.

"Never fear," Athos finally declared – he had, meanwhile, been released from the Bastille, thanks to Monsieur de Treville – "we will follow you through thick and thin. The important thing is that the letter reaches its destination; it matters not which of us delivers it. As far as I'm concerned, we can move off!"

Shortly after the four friends were riding along the road to Calais, heavily armed and accompanied by their servants. They arrived safe and sound at Chantilly, where they rested at an inn.

A self-styled traveller there crudely tried to become friendly with them. They immediately saw through him as one of the many informers in the Cardinal's service. In fact, he so enraged Porthos that the latter fell into an ugly brawl with him.

"That's your business!" shouted d'Artagnan, calmly. "Fight it out yourself. We must be off!" Mousqueton stayed behind with his master.

The Gascon, Aramis and Athos, however, galloped off in the direction of Amiens. On the way they were ambushed by highwaymen. Although they managed to escape, Aramis and his faithful Bazin were so badly wounded that they had to stop at Crèvecoeur, where an innkeeper looked after them.

The following morning, after d'Artagnan and Athos had spent the night in a none-too-pleasant inn, the keeper claimed that Athos had tried to pay with counterfeit money. The Gascon agreed to leave his friend behind to settle this difference of opinion alone. He and Planchet only stayed long enough to see four ruffians hurl themselves on Athos and his servant, but they could not stay for the outcome. Their mission had to continue!

It was about noon when they finally reached Calais. To their horror d'Artagnan was told by a boatman that no-one could be ferried across the Channel unless they had a special travel permit from the Cardinal.

Fortunately, the Gascon's despondency did not last long. Another traveller and his servant leapt from a carriage, went up to the seaman and cried, "We have a pass!"

"Good," nodded the captain, "but first it has to be checked by the Governor. You'll find him at his summer residence to the south of the town."

The stranger climbed back into the coach and headed off. "Now it's our turn," whispered d'Artagnan. "After them!"

They overtook the carriage in an empty avenue and the Gascon did not find it difficult to pick a fight with the passenger, a young man. The traveller and his servant fought like tigers. In the end, though, the young man lay unconscious on the ground. Planchet, meanwhile, tied up the servant.

D'Artagnan seized the pass, which was made out to a certain Count de Warde and his servant, Lubin, and signed by Richelieu himself. D'Artagnan played the part of the Count when they reached the Governor's residence. The latter issued the necessary authentication and expressed his deepest gratitude when the false Count informed him that back in the avenue leading to the harbour, he could arrest a certain d'Artagnan and his servant. In fact, said the Gascon, it was on their account that the Cardinal had ordered the harbour blockade.

Early the next morning, the ship docked into Dover and after a bumpy ride with the mail-horses they arrived in London at about noon. But they still had to get to Windsor where the Duke was staying and amusing himself with falconry.

The Duke stared at the Frenchman with a

mixture of distrust and amazement. But he had no sooner read the Queen's words than he turned pale and cried, "Quick! Back to London! I'll do anything for Anna!"

At the Duke's palace, he led the Gascon through a secret door into a room where he kept the small box containing the precious brooch in a cabinet. To their horror two of the diamond studs were missing!

"I wore it only once!" gasped Buckingham. "And only one person came near me. The Countess de Winter! Of course, she is known to be an agent of Richelieu. And she left this morning! But Buckingham doesn't give up that easily, especially when his lady love is at stake!"

D'Artagnan now witnessed the extent of the Duke's power. Although it virtually amounted to a declaration of war, he immediately ordered all ports to be sealed off. No ship could leave for France! He then summoned the best jeweller in London, locked him in the palace with his tools and promised him £6000 if, in two days, he could make exact replicas of the missing studs, even though they cost only £1000. The goldsmith did a brilliant job and after two days d'Artagnan was able to take charge of all twelve diamond studs.

"A ship awaits you in the harbour," the Duke said by way of farewell, "and once you reach France, a friend will be waiting for you with four splendid horses. Take them as a token of my gratitude."

At Dover, as d'Artagnan sailed past in the Duke's ship, he thought he recognized the lady traveller from Meung on a ship waiting for permission to sail. But he could not be sure.

Without further mishap, d'Artagnan arrived back in Paris on the eve of the glittering Ball and immediately reported to Monsieur de Treville.

Meanwhile, the Cardinal, thanks to his agents, had in his possession the studs stolen from the Duke. He presented them to the King just before the Ball was due to start, hypocritically remarking that the Queen must have mislaid them.

Yet when the Queen arrived at the Ball an

Aramis suddenly threw aside the dish of vegetables and tore off the cassock he was wearing.

hour later, all twelve studs were sparkling on her robe. "And I thought the Cardinal had found two of them," stammered Louis, with a mixture of confusion and relief.

Richelieu was quick to rally his thoughts. "These two studs were meant to be a surprise for Her Majesty. But I dared not present them as a gift and took the liberty of engaging Your Majesty, so to speak, as the go-between."

"So to speak," smiled the Queen suspiciously. "I accept the two studs as a gift, which, I fear, may have cost you dearer than the twelve did His Majesty."

Richelieu bowed low and forced a polite smile. "Possibly, Madame."

The friends meet up again

That same evening Treville summoned the Gascon and said, grimly, "I don't know exactly what you've been up to in the past two weeks,

but one thing I do know – the Cardinal is in an evil humour and he won't easily forget the dirty trick you publicly played on him. Take my advice and get out of Paris for a few days. It's about time you contacted your friends again. Ride off and fetch them. Do not waste a second. I can't settle until I know you are outside the walls of the city."

"I'll be gone within the hour," promised d'Artagnan, but no sooner had he reached his room, intending to pack, than Planchet surprised him with some news that made him forget all his plans.

An unknown messenger had delivered a letter from Madame Bonacieux. With pounding heart, d'Artagnan read how much she thanked him for his great service and how she would do her best to meet him in secret at ten o'clock that evening in a pavilion near St. Cloud.

"Constance, my Constance," muttered the

infatuated Gascon and, as it was already getting late, he was up and away. In his excitement he left the letter lying on the table and paid no heed on the stairs to Monsieur Bonacieux, standing in the hall and glowering after him.

It was a few minutes before ten o'clock when he arrived at the outskirts of the village. The pavilion was not difficult to find. It stood in a park, illuminated in the moonlight, and the Gascon slowed his pace a little when he fancied he saw shadows flitting fast through the trees.

As soon as all fell still again he approached the small building. Nothing stirred. And then d'Artagnan noticed the smashed door. A terrible suspicion overcame him. He rushed inside only to have his worst fears confirmed. Furniture was tipped over, a window broken, and on the floor lay a ripped handkerchief. The delicately embroidered initials C.B. were the final proof. His beloved had been abducted!

Just then the Gascon remembered the letter and the treacherous landlord, who, as he knew only too well, was one of the Cardinal's stool-pigeons!

D'Artagnan made a desperate dash back to Paris and Monsieur de Treville. The latter gave him a very frosty reception and insisted that d'Artagnan's fate was far more important than that of Madame Bonacieux. For the moment, no-one could help her. Her life, however, was not at risk even if she was in the hands of Count Rochefort.

D'Artagnan only agreed to go when Monsieur de Treville had assured him that he would do all in his power to discover where the young lady was being held in custody.

He succeeded in leaving Paris unseen at daybreak, accompanied by Planchet. He reached Chantilly without any trouble. To the landlord's great annoyance, Porthos and Mousqueton were still ensconced at the inn. When asked whether they had fully recovered from the scuffle, the landlord threw up his hands in exasperation.

"Anyone who guzzles and sups like those two, without paying, must be all right. Otherwise they wouldn't throw us out every time we present them with the bill!"

D'Artagnan laughed, settled Porthos' debts, and went up to his room. Porthos greeted him joyfully. But then it emerged that he and Mousqueton had sustained some nasty sword wounds.

"Apart from that I have had an excellent time here," admitted Porthos. "Go and fetch the others and let's celebrate your return!"

The Gascon agreed and shortly after he set off for Crèvecoeur with Planchet, where Aramis and his servant Bazin had stayed behind because of *their* injuries. By now both were restored to glowing health, but to d'Artagnan's horror, Aramis had finally made up his mind – he was going to give up the King's robe and become a priest, as he had always wanted.

"A warrior of God," explained Bazin with pious glee and served up, not meat, but a dish of vegetables, and instead of red wine, a carafe of clear water.

The Gascon tried all his powers of persuasion but to no avail. "Fine, I now see that we shall have to conquer England without you," he concluded regretfully. "The war can no longer be avoided, I'm afraid."

"What? War?" Aramis jumped to his feet. "Why didn't you say so before?" He ripped off his black cassock. "Bazin, my sword! My uniform! And get some wine and roast meat before we ride! War! Theology can wait!"

It proved considerably more difficult to lure Athos from the inn at Amiens, when d'Artagnan arrived late in the evening. After over-powering the ruffians with the help of his servant Grimaud, they had barricaded themselves in the wine cellar. Neither could have been described as sober.

"Do you know," said Athos, drunkenly lying between two barrels and embracing d'Artagnan, "I want to forget, forget. Like the Count, who married a lovely girl, chastity embodied she was, or so he thought. He soon had to admit he'd fallen into a witch's snare, denounced by everyone . . . but who'd escaped the hangman's noose . . . the shame of it made the Count ill . . . he lost his estate, assumed another name. Oh yes, oh yes . . . but first, first

Grimaud had made himself comfortable underneath the barrel.

he hanged the witch . . . "

"Hanged her? By the neck? But that was murder!" gasped the Gascon.

"Murder . . . yes, I . . . the Count is a murderer . . . and she was a witch . . . come on, drink up, my friend! We must drink to forget women!"

The following morning Athos had recovered enough for them to think about returning. First though, d'Artagnan took the landlord severely to task over the business of the alleged counterfeit money. He had obviously bribed the ruffians to help, and more than likely had succeeded in the past with more gullible travellers.

"As punishment we shan't pay one sou for the wine my friends have supped," the Gascon decided and then laughed when he saw Grimaud lying underneath the running tap of a barrel. "Or for any they're still supping!"

"Fine, agreed, no charge," whimpered the scared landlord and crossed himself three times as the riders disappeared around a bend in the road.

Back in Chantilly, the three friends saw

Porthos in the distance, sitting in front of the inn, consuming a huge roast in company with Mousqueton. They merrily joined in, but the merriest of all was the landlord when they finally left. He too made the sign of the cross three times.

It was at dead of night when they rode into Paris through a city gate guarded by soldiers of the Compagnie d'Essart. When they saw a light still burning in the palace of Monsieur de Treville, they reported to him immediately.

The Captain visibly heaved a sigh of relief, shook each hand in turn and then cried joyfully, "I would have been sorry for His Majesty to have lost even one of you. Especially now when the call to arms might be sounded at any time. Return to your quarters, gentlemen, and await further orders. As for you, d'Artagnan, report to my friend, d'Essart."

He then took the Gascon to one side. "I have heard that Madame Bonacieux was taken to a convent where she is being well treated."

"Thank you, thank you, sir," murmured d'Artagnan.

The Cardinal nodded thoughtfully.

Danger from ambush

The next day, before d'Artagnan had a chance to set off for his meeting with d'Essart, Planchet excitedly announced a visitor, "Count de Rochefort."

The man who entered was the stranger with the scar. The Gascon immediately reached for his sword.

"No, please, sir," he said politely, "I am here on behalf of His Eminence. The Cardinal asks to see you straightaway. I shall accompany you to his palace."

A trap, wondered d'Artagnan, but nodded anyway. He had never side-stepped danger before; why should he start to fear it now?

Some fifteen minutes later he was standing before the mysterious Chancellor, who silently beckoned him to take a seat. So this was the man about whom they whispered the most incongruous things, before whose eyes apparently nothing could be hidden and in whose heart no-one knew what really went on.

"I value men of your calibre," said Richelieu, to d'Artagnan's utter surprise. "Courage, honesty, initiative, all rare qualities. You have proved your mettle in all these things. But they are dangerous qualities and can all too easily make powerful enemies. Don't you agree?"

D'Artagnan was on his guard: he had grasped the hidden threat in the Cardinal's words. "Many enemies, much honour," he replied, "no-one can pick his own enemies."

"Well put." The Cardinal nodded. "But your friends . . . " he reflected. "The right friends could do a lot for you."

As the Gascon remained silent, Richelieu broke the silence by saying, "What would you say about joining my bodyguard? As a cadet?"

D'Artagnan looked at his questioner with surprise. "Do you really mean it, Your Eminence? That would be an undeserved honour. And besides," he declared decisively, "I have devoted myself to serving the King. I want to be a musketeer. First I must prove my worth on the battlefield."

"An honourable point of view. But the King is France, our Fatherland. We all serve him. Believe me, my only concern is how I can be of use to France, how I can protect our country from harm. Do you wish to help me in this?"

"As always my role for France is by the side of the King," insisted d'Artagnan and saw all too clearly the dangerous glint in Richelieu's eyes. "Please do not misunderstand me," he quickly added. "It is in the interest of Your Eminence too. The musketeers would think me disloyal and ungrateful, whilst your friends would regard me as an ambitious opportunist, interested only in furthering his own career. They would shun me. What use would I be to you then?"

The Cardinal became thoughtful before finally stretching out his hand in farewell. "We shall speak again, when you return from the battlefield, covered with glory. I hope you return," he added, in an undertone.

"So do I!" growled d'Artagnan, more than once to himself, as he hurried away to his regiment which was already preparing for battle.

It was necessary to win back the port of La Rochelle. There had been a revolt against the King there and the rebels had managed to seize the town and the fortifications, with help from the English navy. True, to start with, Buckingham had hesitated before endangering the short-lived peace with France again on account of a domestic conflict. But the blind, hopeless love he felt for the French King's consort had robbed him of his usual statesmanlike wisdom. He was prepared to sacrifice the lives of thousands, simply in order to gain revenge on Richelieu, especially now after the affair of the diamond studs, even though it had misfired.

Milady had only just succeeded in getting back to France and was not likely to forget whom she had to thank for her misfortune. D'Artagnan was to discover this when he was least prepared for it.

The Compagnie d'Essart had set up camp right outside the fortifications of the beleaguered town. To begin with, however, there was just the occasional skirmish, as the bulk of the French army, including Treville's musketeers, were still stationed near Villeroi until the King, who had assumed supreme command, recovered from a none too grave illness.

During a reconnaissance trip, the Gascon came under fire from enemy gunners. He threw himself to the ground and thought no more about it until it suddenly occurred to him

The wounded man pleaded for his life.

that the shots had come from the wrong direction. The enemies were in the other direction! He tensed himself and cautiously peered around on all sides and noticed two rifle barrels jutting from a hollow.

Shots rang out again. He struggled up and then froze. Two French soldiers leapt from their hiding-place and ran towards him. The first he finished off with his heavy riding pistol and furiously lashed out at the second with his sword, injuring him. He grabbed hold of him, dragged him away from the fire which had opened up on the besieged town, bent over him threateningly and shouted, "Out with it! Who talked you into this wicked act? Come on, tell the truth!"

The wounded soldier whimpered piteously for mercy and confessed that a stunningly beautiful lady in Paris had promised him and his comrade 100 gold pieces if they got rid of d'Artagnan without too much fuss. She had told them he was an English spy.

"Milady," murmured the Gascon, "so she has managed to get back into France." Grim-faced, he turned back to the soldier. "I shall spare your life. But you must stay by me as my servant. Woe be . . . "

"I'll do anything for you," swore the soldier, hastily, overjoyed to have escaped so lightly. "My life is yours."

Two days later Planchet welcomed his master outside their tent and, laughing, pointed to a letter and a very promising-looking small barrel.

The letter was from the landlord of the inn at Villeroi, where Louis XIII was recuperating from his illness. "Your friends, the Royal Musketeers, Athos, Porthos and Aramis," read d'Artagnan, "have asked me to send you a small barrel of the wine they are supping every evening at my hostelry with such pleasure. They seem convinced it will tickle your palate too. In the next few days, they will accompany His Majesty to join the troops already assembled outside the gates of La Rochelle."

D'Artagnan immediately decided to keep the barrel unopened until his friends arrived. "A reunion drink!"

The final secret

Athos, Porthos and Aramis were slowly riding in the darkness through a mist-soaked wood which stretched far to the north-east of La Rochelle. They were the vanguard of the royal troops and were ahead of them by some three hours. Suddenly, a commanding voice rang out at them from the gloom. A man on horseback appeared. They immediately reached for their swords.

"Let us see your face!" ordered Athos. The man bent forward, his dark eyes flashing. "Good, musketeers," he said, coolly. "Your names?"

To their surprise, the friends recognized the Cardinal. They sprang to attention and introduced themselves.

"I have heard speak of you as trusty, courageous soldiers," said Richelieu. "I would be grateful if you could accompany me and keep guard so that no-one disturbs me when, in a few minutes, I hold a very important discussion about the future of France. I am relying on your discretion!"

He rode on, silently followed by the musketeers, to a tavern on the edge of the wood, in front of which a carriage and four was waiting. The landlord whispered to the Cardinal before disappearing back into the kitchen that he was already expected. The musketeers were ordered to wait in the empty bar room, while Richelieu proceeded up a narrow staircase to the top floor. There sat, showing every sign of impatience, the mysterious beauty who called herself 'Milady' or 'Lady Winter'.

"I have ensured that you can return to London without any fear of molestation," the Cardinal said, without further ado. "You know your mission. How you manage to stop the war against France is now up to you."

"In other words," smiled Milady, sarcastically, "if all goes well, the fame is yours. If it doesn't, I face the music alone."

"You are wrong on both counts, Milady. Success serves only to further the honour of France. As for failure, I shall do all in my power to protect you. Whatever happens, my name must never be mentioned."

The secret agent shook her head. "I'm afraid that doesn't satisfy me. What, God forbid, if anything befalls you? No, I must have a better guarantee than that!"

Without a word, the Cardinal sat down at the table, picked up quill and paper and began to write. After carefully blotting the note, he handed it to Milady. "That should put your mind at rest," he exclaimed, coldly.

With equal coldness, she read it out, half to herself. "Whatever this person has done, this pass proves that they did it in the interests of France. No-one ought to call them to account because of this. Richelieu."

The Cardinal stood up and made a token bow. "I wish you every success, Milady. You should be on your way in half an hour. I now take leave of you. Adieu."

A few minutes later he set off for La Rochelle, accompanied by the three musketeers. He was so immersed in his own thoughts that he failed to notice Athos' deathly pale face or the slight tremble in the latter's voice when the musketeer asked permission to ride on ahead to see how the land lay.

Richelieu praised Athos for his prudence. He immediately galloped off into the darkness of the wood. Even his companions did not notice how he turned back in the direction of the tavern.

The driver in the coach-box was snoring away, the landlord was pottering about in the kitchen. Unseen, Athos rushed upstairs, tore open the door and gagged Milady with his hand before she had a chance to scream out in terror. Slowly, he removed his iron-hard fin-

gers from over her mouth. Lady Winter gazed at him in horror as if she was seeing a ghost. "You . . . Count de la Fère?" she stammered, quaking with fear. "I . . . I thought you were dead."

"No, God has been merciful with me," said Athos, softly. "But the Devil himself has been good to you! Otherwise the rope I hanged you with wouldn't have snapped. But this time you won't escape me, miserable traitor! You have already brought terrible misfortune on countless honest fellows; their blood still sticks to your delicate hands! You were already wanted by the executioner in Lille for terrible crimes when you managed to creep into my trust and became my wife. But you were not content with demolishing my life – you went on to destroy others. Your last victim was Lord Winter. He died from poisoning, even if a bribed doctor diagnosed otherwise! You don't even stop at our own dear Queen, or the Duke of Buckingham who is an honourable man even though he's our enemy. Now what filthy tricks are you taking back with you to London, eh? Ah, so you grow pale. How could you possibly guess that I could hear up the chimney and know every word you said; as I sat downstairs by the stove, every word you exchanged with the one who gives you orders . . . I knew you by your voice. Believe me, it was a shock for me too when a suspicion I've harboured for a long time was suddenly confirmed! However, I don't intend to harm you now. I simply want to warn you: one more foul deed and it's death for you, as sure as I'm standing here. Now hand over the letter the Cardinal wrote for you up here!"

Milady's entire body was shaking as she obeyed, her eyes flashing with deadly hate. Athos pocketed the letter and without paying further heed to the woman, left. When he finally caught up with the Cardinal again, he announced calmly, "All clear, Your Eminence. Not an enemy in sight."

The next morning they had the pleasure of meeting up with d'Artagnan again. "Planchet! Broach that barrel!" he shouted to his servant. "We've waited long enough for it." He then turned to the musketeers and said, "Let's drink the wine you donated so nobly!"

He failed to notice the astonished looks of all three, or the puzzled question put by Athos, "Wine? That we donated?"

But a horrible cry made him stop short. The soldier who had once tried to shoot him down was writhing on the ground in the throes of death. "He . . . he tasted the wine," stammered Planchet, growing pale.

"Poison! A cowardly blow!" D'Artagnan bent down over the dead man. "I don't think we need puzzle our heads over this one, do you?"

"Milady." The word seemed to come from all three at once, the three who had just narrowly escaped death.

"Milady," repeated Athos, faintly. No more, no less.

He remained curiously silent for the next few weeks. Then, one day, an inexplicable commotion broke out behind enemy lines and Athos called to his friends to join him.

"Do you know what it means? I have just heard from Monsieur de Treville – Buckingham has been murdered in London! Don't ask me who did it, I don't know, although I've got my suspicions. What is more important now is that we should take advantage of the enemy's uncertainty. Do you want to help me?" When they all nodded decisively, he proceeded to tell them his plan.

The next morning both sides were treated to an almost unbelievable spectacle. On the

highest plateau of one of the most important enemy bastions sat the three musketeers and d'Artagnan, calmly eating their breakfast as if they were in the safest place in the world.

During the night they had scaled the walls, overpowered the garrison and were now loudly jeering at the enemy. When they had recovered from their surprise and took to arms, the fate of the four friends seemed sealed. But, quite calmly, the Gascon lit a slow fuse and like a will-o'-the-wisp the flame flitted over to a high wall, to be abruptly followed by a violent explosion. Giant chunks of stone were tossed into the air, crashing down on the charging enemy. The shrill screams of dying men filled the air. Confusion reigned. The royal troops saw their moment had come at last and trumpets sounded the attack. The final battle blazed up and a few hours later the town was taken, without the English navy intervening. Instead, their ships hurriedly sailed away.

Neither side could believe their eyes when they saw the three musketeers and their friend from Gascony having breakfast on the bastion as if it was the safest place in the world.

Indescribable jubilation ensued among the victors. Everyone rushed to shake the hands and clap the shoulders of the three musketeers and d'Artagnan.

Later that same evening, Monsieur de Treville took all four to one side, "I know where Constance Bonacieux is being held." He named a convent near Lille. "Be off with you, d'Artagnan. Your friends will accompany you. And another thing: be careful, Milady is back from England!"

A few minutes later they set off and rode through the night. But they arrived too late. The young lady lay dead in the arms of the Abbess. Poisoned by a female visitor. From the description, the four had no difficulty recognizing Milady.

"She can't have got far yet," declared Athos in a furious voice and galloped off. "I'll be back soon," he shouted.

Hours later he returned to the convent where d'Artagnan was grieving for his dead sweetheart. The musketeer gave his friend a grave look. "Milady was my wife. She won't harm another soul. I have seen to that. Now come back to Paris with me. You've got your whole life ahead of you."

Although d'Artagnan believed he would never get over the pain, as each day passed he felt more and more as if he had been chasing unattainable happiness anyway. and by the time the roofs of the capital came into view, he already seemed his old self again. He was suddenly more concerned about Athos. "The Cardinal is sure to take you to account because of Milady. Even though he despised her, she was still his best spy."

Unmoved, Athos took the letter of guarantee out of his pocket and gave it to d'Artagnan to read. "He didn't have me in mind," he smiled, "but Richelieu usually keeps his word."

Athos was right. Richelieu had achieved his aim, victory over England, and he lost no time in praising the part played by the musketeers in it, even before the King.

"I have just heard from Count Rochefort," said Monsieur de Treville to the friends when they reported to him. "He came to deliver a message from the King. Kneel down, Gascon!" Covered in confusion, d'Artagnan obeyed the command. Monsieur de Treville brought down the sword on to his shoulder. "And now arise, Royal Musketeer d'Artagnan! At last you are one of us!"

Monsieur de Treville touched d'Artagnan's shoulder with the sword three times.

CHARLES DICKENS

Oliver Twist

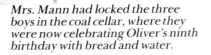

Mrs. Mann had locked the three boys in the coal cellar, where they were now celebrating Oliver's ninth birthday with bread and water.

A birthday in the coal cellar and an unexpected ending

Oliver Twist was obliged to celebrate his ninth birthday in the coal cellar. Mrs. Mann had locked him in with three other boys because the three had dared to assert that they were hungry. Mrs. Mann ran the house which accommodated some of the orphan children of a certain English town, which had best be nameless. In this respect it must be said that Mrs. Mann regarded eating and drinking as a bad habit to which man and beast had merely grown accustomed. To break this bad habit in the children entrusted to her, she simply allowed the greater part of the money destined for housekeeping to flow into her own pocket. Naturally this caused the children to become weaker and weaker, many became seriously ill and some even died. If Oliver, a slight and not very tall boy, had survived thus far with Mrs. Mann it must be concluded that he had a particularly tough constitution.

Even now as the boys crouched in the coal cellar, Mr. Bumble the parish officer (beadle) was striking angrily with his boot against the locked garden door. He was a fat, rather boisterous man and was already reproaching Mrs. Mann for taking so long to open up. She took care not to tell him that

she had first quickly taken the boys out of the cellar. Sanctimoniously she affirmed she had been getting the children he was so fond of ready for his arrival. At this Mr. Bumble forgot his anger and nodded complacently. "I am pleased to hear that, and now let me in at last for I have something to say to you." Mrs. Mann led him into the red-brick paved parlour and offering him a stool, placed his cane and cocked hat on the table nearby. Mr. Bumble wiped the perspiration from his plump face and glanced proud and pleased at the cocked hat and cane, the signs of his rank, and smiled. Indeed his smile was quite human. Mrs. Mann straightaway gave him a large glass of hot grog to keep him in a good mood. "Otherwise I keep the rum for the dear little ones when they don't feel well," she lied without blushing.

"Touching, the way you care for your charges," praised Mr. Bumble. "I will make this known in higher places." And when he had emptied the glass nearly to the dregs he began to explain the reason for his visit. Oliver was now nine years' old, and although a reward of first ten and later even twenty pounds had been offered, still no one knew from whence he came nor even his proper name. "His name?" interrupted Mrs. Mann, amazed, "he has a name!" But Mr. Bumble disclosed that he himself had invented that name in accordance with the established custom of naming foundlings in alphabetical order. When Oliver was born, the letter T had come round again and so Mr. Bumble had decided on Twist. "How clever, how ingenious!" cried Mrs. Mann, and Mr. Bumble replied, flattered, "Quite so, quite so."

At last he announced that he had come on the orders of the parish council to take Oliver away. He was now old enough for proper work and no longer needed Mrs. Mann's loving care. Oliver was apprehensive as, freshly washed and dressed, he was pushed into the parlour by Mrs. Mann. Nevertheless when Mr. Bumble invited him to go with him, he was ready to accept with enthusiasm. But just in time, he saw from Mrs. Mann's grim expression what answer she was expecting and hypocritically, he cried, "Can she come too?"

"That would not be possible," regretted Mr. Bumble, "but she will certainly visit you often."

As Oliver was now crying bitterly, more from hunger than from sorrow at parting, Mrs. Mann hugged him several times and even put a thick slice of bread and butter in his hand before he left the house at Mr. Bumble's side.

They were not happy memories of the house and Mrs. Mann that Oliver took with him into an unknown future. On the way, there came over him an overpowering feeling of emptiness and loneliness. He would now be quite alone in the midst of a frighteningly huge and hostile world!

After Mr. Bumble had delivered him to the parish poor house, it was not long before he was led before the orphan board. This consisted of from eight to ten staring, corpulent men who immediately asked him a lot of questions.

Oliver slowly lost his shyness, but his answers did not please them. In particular, one of the men, who had a rather larger stomach curving out of his white waistcoat, took him for a complete idiot. It was therefore quickly decided that he should unravel threads from old rags and clothes. That was about all he was capable of. He was to start work early next morning.

He was then brought to a large dirty room where many boys, just as poor and parentless as he, were accommodated, rather for worse than for better. Above all they were suffering from extreme hunger, as Oliver was now to do, for in spite of the hard work, they only received a few spoonfuls of watery soup and oatmeal gruel daily. Sickness and death were constant guests and things did not get better even after one of the boys, whose father had kept a small shop, threatened in his despair to kill his sleeping neighbour and eat him.

Oliver is entrusted to Mr. Sowerberry

As Oliver had not developed the required skill in rag unravelling, and one day had dared to ask the overseer for another bowl of soup, he was, after a sound thrashing, locked in a dark room. He had already spent a week there when Mr. Bumble suddenly arrived and fetched him out – not out of kindness or generosity, but because the chimney-sweep Gamfield, widely renowned for his brutality, was looking for a cheap apprentice. Mr. Bumble therefore brought Oliver to the magistrate who must give his consent for the indentures. On the way there he was strongly exhorted by Mr. Bumble to show great pleasure and gratitude before the gentlemen because he was now able to become a chimneysweep.

After waiting about half an hour in an anteroom at the parish office, they were called into a large room where two trustees sat in front of a high window, at a writing desk covered with documents. They wore white powdered wigs, and next to them stood the chimneysweep, his face half washed. Before Oliver could reply to the magistrate's question as to whether he wished to learn the chimney-sweep's trade, Mr. Bumble quickly assured him that Oliver was most anxious to do so. Thereupon, the magistrate, who was half blind in one eye and apart from that already quite decrepit, declared in a loud voice that he took Mr. Gamfield for an honest and law-abiding citizen. Meanwhile he tried several times to dip the quill in the narrow neck of the inkwell. During these efforts, his glance fell quite by chance on Oliver, who was staring at him, his face white and anxious.

"Is something the matter?" croaked the magistrate astonished. "Speak up, my boy!" Oliver fell on his knees and, raising his hands imploringly, told him that he would rather go back in the dark room and die there from hunger or beating than be handed over to this brutal man. Mr. Bumble immediately began to criticize the unheard-of behaviour of his charge, but the other magistrate told him brusquely to be quiet and gave his colleague a meaningful look. He nodded and declared in a short and decisive manner, "We decline to give our consent!" He then told Mr. Bumble to take the boy back to the poor house and to see that he was treated kindly there.

On the next day, the poor house made it known once more that anyone who wanted to take Oliver would receive sufficient fees and living allowance every month. Since no one reported, however, Mr. Bumble was instructed by the orphan board to enquire in the shipping companies if somewhere an inexpensive ordinary seaman was not required.

Oliver raised his hands, imploring,
"I want to go back in the dark room.
I would rather die there than . . ."

However, it happened just in time that an old friend by the name of Sowerberry crossed Mr. Bumble's path.

Mr. Sowerberry was a large, fat man and was also the parish undertaker. In keeping with his position he was always dressed in dignified black. After a short discussion he declared that he was willing to take the boy "on trial", and it only took five minutes for the orphan board to give their approval. Contrary to the opinion of the board, Oliver was a very alert and sensitive boy, who had suffered more from the ill treatment meted out to him than from hunger. He heard the news of his new destiny in silence, packed his few possessions in a paper bag, put his cap on and taking Mr. Bumble's hand set out. Before they came to the undertaker's house the official had enough time to heap reproaches on Oliver, who allowed his tears to flow freely. At Mr. Bumble's bidding he set his cap straight and held himself erect, but Mr. Bumble was still not quite satisfied and raised his stick angrily. "God knows, of all the perverse boys I have had to deal with, you are the . . ." In despair Oliver grasped the hand with the stick and sobbed, "I . . . I am such a small boy . . . and so . . ." "So what?" enquired Mr. Bumble involuntarily. "So lonely . . ." stuttered Oliver, tears streaming. Nobody loved him, he was just pushed around by everybody, and clutching at Mr. Bumble's waistcoat with his hands Oliver implored him not to be so hard. Mr. Bumble was so surprised that he clapped Oliver several times on the back reassur-

ingly and even told him that he took him for a good fellow. Then he pushed him into the coffin-maker's shop and entrusted him to Mrs. Sowerberry. She raised her hands to her head and complained that she had been sent such a skinny dwarf, who would now have to be fattened up at her expense. "Get down there," she shouted to Oliver, and pushed him over some steep steps into a narrow, damp kitchen just in front of the coal cellar. A girl called Charlotte, dressed like the mistress in dark clothes, pushed Oliver a bowl of left-over meat scraps, which had been rejected by the dog. Extremely hungry, Oliver wolfed this down. Mrs. Sowerberry called him back into the workshop and showed him a rough bench as his sleeping place among the finished and half-finished coffins. Bathed in sweat and wishing that he could simply die at last, Oliver finally fell asleep.

He whom good fortune has abandoned has no need to worry about further misfortune. Oliver was soon to be reminded of this old saying by Noah Claypole who also lived and worked with Mr. Sowerberry. Noah was the child of a washerwoman and a soldier who had been discharged for habitual drunkenness. He had come to the undertaker from a charitable institution. He also had an unhappy childhood when he was frequently the object of the merciless scorn of the neighbours' children. However, the sight of a boy obviously even more miserable, awakened in Noah not the least sympathy, but rather a spiteful feeling of malicious pleasure so that at every opportunity he made Oliver compensate for the humiliations he himself had suffered. Nevertheless, despite all the unfriendliness he had to endure from the mistress, her foster-daughter and above all from Noah, Oliver recovered visibly, because at last he received enough to eat, even if it was only fit for a dog. However, he still retained the dead look in his eyes. Mr. Sowerberry, a practical and thinking man, determined to make use of this. At children's burials Oliver was to accompany the coffin to the grave. The first death to which Mr. Sowerberry took him was that of old Mrs. Bayton who had been carried off, not by illness nor by age, but presumably by hunger. The memories of despair, and the misery of the relatives were a great shock to Oliver. Mr. Sowerberry felt that he would soon get used to it. Death was no more than a trade like any other. Indeed from one funeral procession to the next Oliver gradually lost his fear and took pride in doing everything correctly.

In time he became so skilled that many unhappy parents specifically asked Mr. Sowerberry for Oliver to accompany their prematurely departed dear ones on the last journey. The mothers were particularly moved by his appearance, for he carried a staff with a black flower and wore a black top hat.

Mr. Sowerberry noted this development with pleasure, and after only a few months made Oliver his apprentice. As an outward sign of this recognition he was allowed permanently to wear clothes just as dark as those of Mrs. Sowerberry and Charlotte. Noah, who as before had to go around in a coloured cap and yellow stockings, nearly exploded from jealousy, and his envy made him even more disagreeable towards Oliver. But one day, as Noah suggested that Oliver's mother had not been a respectable woman but a dishonest slut, Oliver's patience came to an end. In an uncontrollable rage he struck out at Noah and the screams of Charlotte and Mrs. Sowerberry, who hurried to Noah's aid, only made him more angry. He was finally overcome by the three who managed to drag him into the coal cellar and bolt the door from outside. In a powerless rage Oliver beat on the boards with fist and boot, while Charlotte screamed, "He'll murder us all!" Whereupon Mrs. Sowerberry cried, "We must fetch Mr. Bumble!" "I'll do that," offered Noah full of spite, and hurried away. Mr. Bumble believed the tale all too readily that Noah sanctimoniously poured out. As he heard for himself in the workshop Oliver's banging on the door, and was unable to calm him, he nodded seriously and said in a troubled voice, "Yes, yes, I always knew this boy had bad blood in his veins. Probably inherited from his mother. No other woman would have managed, in the state she was in at the time, to drag herself to the poor house where she bore this boy before she

One day, Oliver's patience came to an end. In an uncontrollable rage he struck out at Noah, whose roaring only made him angrier.

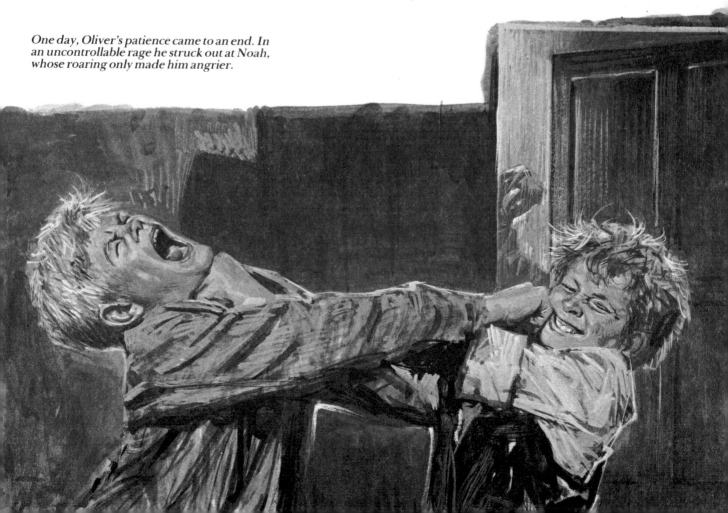

died." And then he recommended that Oliver's rage should be allowed to abate and he should then be given short rations. Above all no more meat, only meal soup, that would soon tame him.

Meanwhile Mr. Sowerberry had returned home and was pleased to agree with these recommendations and confirmed that he would consider them for the entire apprenticeship. Late that evening he took Oliver, completely exhausted, from the cellar, pushèd him into the workshop and then left him alone.

Tears of despair overcame Oliver. He saw no other way out of his hopeless situation but to run away. Silently he tied up his few belongings in a bundle and slipped out of the door.

Oliver comes to London and meets Fagin

Aimlessly Oliver wandered through the narrow and presently silent streets, and in the light of dawn he recognized the house of Mrs. Mann. Against the front garden gate leaned little Dick, one of his former companions, and he stared at him from hollow eyes like a ghost. "I am going away, a long way from here," whispered Oliver. Dick hugged him over the fence. "Good luck, Oliver . . . God keep you!" he whispered scarcely audibly. "I . . . I'm too ill to run away. I know I must soon die." Trembling, Oliver tore himself away and ran off. Never before had anyone wished him well.

He reached a wide street that took him out of town. He followed it for several hours, forced into the ditch many times by wagons and farmers, until he came to a milestone on which was inscribed the distance from London – one hundred miles. In the poor house he had often heard the old people speak of this great and wonderful town where a determined youngster could easily make his fortune. He was not long therefore in deciding to make his way to London. It was more than a week before tired, hungry and footsore he came to the suburb Barnet. He could scarcely have reached his goal without the help of certain sympathetic people he met on the way. Sometimes a kind-hearted caretaker or, on one occasion, a woman whose son was missing at sea and who hoped that somewhere in the world someone would repay what she was doing for Oliver.

Covered with dust, his feet bleeding and his stomach rumbling, he crouched early one morning on the doorstep of a house, feeling lost as never before. After a while a boy approached him, about the same age, but very confident and wearing a coat

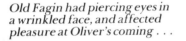

Old Fagin had piercing eyes in a wrinkled face, and affected pleasure at Oliver's coming . . .

that was much too long. He had penetrating eyes and began to speak to Oliver with a strong dialect. "You want to go to London? Have you anywhere to stay?" As Oliver shook his head, he went on, "I'll take you to an old friend. By the way, my name is Jack Dawkins. My friends call me the Dodger." This nickname belonged to a particularly wily, cunning fellow, but Oliver was far too exhausted to notice. Almost automatically he stumbled along with the Dodger, past houses and people, through narrow alleys and dirty squares, and it was only as they came at last to a delapidated, small-fronted house, that he even noticed night had fallen.

This house stood in Field Lane, a particularly rough area, and belonged to an old Jew who lived there with several boys. He was known simply as Fagin. He had piercing eyes and an avaricious expression on his wrinkled face. He seemed to be pleased at Oliver's appearance. The other boys, none of whom gave a particularly trustworthy impression, immediately wanted to take charge of Oliver's bundle, whereupon one by the name of Charley Bates came forward. However, Fagin told them brusquely to leave the new guest in peace. From a dirty dish Oliver was given something to eat. Dodger gave him a beaker full of brandy and hot water and, astonished, Oliver then noticed in a corner a pile of fine lace handkerchiefs.

"They have to be washed," explained Fagin at Oliver's questioning glance, and Oliver could not understand why Dodger and his friends grinned maliciously. He did not question further and was overjoyed as he was allowed to lie down on a dirty bunk. Fagin threw him a blanket every bit as dirty and a few minutes later he sank into a deathlike, dreamless sleep.

Next day Oliver had to stay in the house. He passed the time unpicking the embroidered initials from the handkerchiefs. Every evening the Dodger and Charley brought new ones in from their walks, but Oliver began gradually to wonder about this, nor did he understand the strange game Fagin played with them before they left the house late in the morning. Fagin tucked handkerchiefs into the many pockets of his much too large overcoat and the two boys tried to take them out, as quick as lightning, without the old man noticing. If successful they were praised, if not their ears were boxed.

At last, after a week, the Dodger invited Oliver to accompany him and Charley. Happily Oliver strolled between them to the market, but as they pilfered fruit and sweet-things from the stalls unperturbed, he was horrified and thought he knew now why Fagin often called them a dirty and useless pack, hit them and on occasion even let them go hungry. He therefore reproached the two himself, but they only laughed at him, and suddenly the

Dodger drew him into a corner and pointed to a small book stall opposite. "There. That's a cinch!" In front of the shop stood a well-dressed elderly gentleman engrossed in a book.

An ugly sneer came over Charley Bates' pimply face. "I like that too!" And straightaway the two crept up on the gentleman. Dodger pushed him as if by mistake and at the same time Charley, as quick as lightning, prised the lace kerchief from the gentleman's breast pocket. Bewildered, the gentleman looked up and shaking his head, watched the two boys running away. He then realized that he had been robbed, and as now Oliver also began to run (having looked on till now as if paralysed), the gentleman set off in pursuit shouting, "Thief! Thief!" Everything went black before Oliver as he tore along the uneven pavements, frightened to death.

Now he knew where the lace handkerchiefs, watches and the many jewels he had seen at Fagin's came from . . . only now it was too late . . . more and more people, alarmed by the cries of the old gentleman, were running after him and it was not very long before he was caught by them. All his expressions of innocence were of no avail as a policeman seized him by the collar and took him to the district magistrate, who had his office right next to a small prison. He did not notice that one of the men in the street stared long and hard after him.

Meanwhile the gentleman who had been robbed had also gone to the court and, unlike the ill-mannered magistrate, took the time to listen to Oliver's explanation. "That's true," he declared thoughtfully, "the boy cannot be the thief." The magistrate however glared at Oliver, but, as the bookseller now came and insisted that he had clearly seen that two other boys were guilty, the magistrate was finally obliged to let Oliver go free. A police officer was ordered to do this, and he simply threw the already half-conscious boy out of the courtyard, where he now lost his senses completely.

In Mr. Brownlow's house

The elderly gentleman who had at first taken Oliver for a thief and had then arranged his release, saw with indignation how this release was carried out. With great compassion he bent over Oliver, murmured several times, "The poor boy!" and bade an onlooker fetch a cab. Together with the bookseller he lifted the unconscious Oliver into the vehicle and gave the driver an address in Pentonville, one of the most elegant districts in London. There the old gentleman, whose name was Brownlow, lived in a large house. He handed Oliver over to the care of the housekeeper, Mrs. Bedwin, who eagerly looked after him. Besides this, there was a maid who watch-

*Only now did Oliver also take flight.
The gentleman who had been
robbed set off after him shouting,
"Thief! Stop, thief!"*

ed over him at night on the orders of the doctor who had been called immediately.

It was several days before Oliver regained consciousness and his weakened body no longer shook with fever. And as he was at last strong enough to sit up in bed, Mrs. Bedwin had him brought into her own room where she could attend to him the whole time.

She was a little uneasy, however, at the way Oliver, from the very first moment, stared steadfastly as if transfixed, at the portrait of a lady hanging on one of the walls. She asked him if he was frightened of the picture. "Oh no, quite the opposite!" Oliver assured her hastily. "It . . . is only because the lady seems to be so sad." And then he added so as scarcely to be heard, "I feel she is always looking at me . . . it really makes my heart beat."

"For God's sake, don't say that!" cried Mrs. Bedwin and immediately turned the bed round so that Oliver could no longer see the picture. Not to upset the good soul he left it at that, and shortly afterwards, his attention was taken up with Mr. Brownlow who came to visit him for the first time in that room. Mr. Brownlow chatted a while in a friendly manner with him, but suddenly he turned to Mrs. Bedwin. "That . . . that's just not possible! Just look." He pointed to the picture and then looked in disbelief at Oliver. No doubt about it, Oliver resembled the portrait of the woman as if cut out from it. And for a moment the same sad expression appeared on both their faces. Oliver was so disturbed by Mr. Brownlow's sudden loss of self-control that he was again overcome by weakness and then sank into a deep sleep.

Let us leave him in peace and concern ourselves rather with Dodger Dawkins and Charley Bates. As Oliver was being followed as a suspected thief by Mr. Brownlow, they had not been slow to distract attention from themselves by shouting the most loudly, "Stop thief!" When their mean trick was in fact successful they laughed unperturbed at Oliver's misfortune and returned to Fagin. He immediately asked threateningly, "Where's Oliver? Where have you left him?" But only as he became more and more angry did Dodger tell him that Oliver had been arrested. Only the appearance of Bill Sikes saved the two from Fagin's beating. Sikes was about thirty-five years old and had conspicuously large, coarse features. Fagin calmed down quite quickly so that the four rogues were able to quarrel even more loudly as to whether Oliver's arrest spelt danger for them, and what they should do about it. They had not yet come to a decision when Nancy and Beth joined the party. These two

48

ambitious young ladies were extraordinarily well suited to the company of thieves, both great and small, and other such rascals.

They were all agreed that they must first find out what had happened to Oliver, and whether he had said anything incriminating. Nancy unwillingly agreed, after threats from Sikes, to spy out the answers to these questions. She was still hardly known in the district or by the county court and was soon back with the news that the victim of the theft had taken Oliver to the Pentonville district.

Immediately Fagin ordered her with Dodger and Charley to find out the details of Oliver's stay, gave them a few coins and chased them out of the house. As Sikes and Beth had already gone, he was now alone in the musty room and was pleased to spread out in the candle-light the day's stolen booty – rings, watches, purses and lace handkerchiefs. As he counted it all and then hid it in a hole under the floorboards, he murmured, "He has apparently not yet said anything, good, good. And he will also keep quiet later, I'll make sure of that!"

A little later Fagin went out of the door, locked up and slipped out into the night.

Sikes and Nancy bring Oliver back to Fagin

About a month after the incident with the picture Mr. Brownlow asked Oliver to come into his study. He wanted to hear from him the whole story of his life, for so far, despite many attempts, he had not been able to ascertain anything. When Oliver saw the serious expression on his benefactor's face, he was deeply perturbed, for he thought he was now once again to be left alone. He begged Mr. Brownlow to let him stay, be it only to perform the most menial tasks. But Mr. Brownlow stroked Oliver's hair soothingly and said, more to himself, "No, no. How could I shut my heart to this child, whose pain and anxiety move me so deeply . . ."

Stuttering at first, and then more coherently, Oliver told his sad story and he had just got to the day when Mr. Bumble took him away from Mrs. Mann, when the maid announced Mr. Grimwig. He was an old friend of the master of the house, well nourished and well dressed, but always only too ready to complain at the slightest cause. Now he was

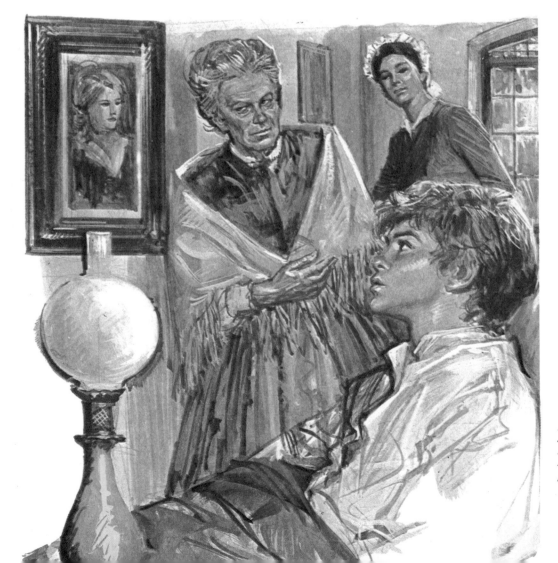

Mrs. Bedwin was alarmed by the boy's look, as he gazed steadfastly at the picture on the wall.

Nancy had been lying in wait for days. Now she approached Oliver from behind.

complaining about some orange peel on the step, and described almost with pleasure how a thoughtlessly discarded orange peel would be the death of him. "You will see that I am right," he declared in conclusion turning to Mr. Brownlow and looking reproachfully at Oliver, as if he wanted to make him responsible for all the fruit peelings lying around in London. Feeling the boy's embarrassment Mr. Brownlow sent him out of the room with the suggestion he should bring the tea. Scarcely were the two friends alone when Mr. Grimwig reiterated his mistrust of Brownlow's small charge. "The boy will only use you," he grumbled, less from conviction than from basic contrariness. If the truth be known, Mr. Grimwig also had a very soft heart and it would never have occurred to him to upset his friend Brownlow, but he liked to hide his good heart under a seemingly rough exterior.

While the two friends were still arguing about Oliver's good or bad character, Mrs. Bedwin came in to remind Mr. Brownlow that several long overdue books should finally be returned to the lending library nearby. Mr. Grimwig immediately suggested Oliver for this errand. It would then soon be apparent whether he was worthy of Mr. Brownlow's trust or, as Mr. Grimwig feared, would disappear together with the valuable books and the money.

Oliver, pleased to be able to do his benefactor a favour, took the books under his arm and putting the money, nearly £5, carefully away he set out. Satisfied, Mr. Brownlow watched him go and laid his watch on the table. "It will soon be dark. But he will be back at the latest within half an hour."

"Or else not," growled Mr. Grimwig contrarily. Then the two gentlemen fell silent and watched the hand go slowly round.

Meanwhile, Oliver went happily on his way not thinking of anything unpleasant. Suddenly he heard a familiar voice behind him calling, "There you are, dear brother! What luck, that I have found you at last!" At that moment he felt two arms clinging fast round his neck almost taking his breath away. Frightened he cried out, then he recognized Nancy. For days she had lain in wait for him, and now, with a cunning worthy of better things, she took the opportunity to overpower Oliver. "Come straight home to your parents and brother and sisters, you ungrateful little rascal!" she scolded loudly, with well-acted indignation, and held Oliver's mouth tighter and tighter shut, stifling his cries for help.

A few people were already taking notice, among them a man who looked closely several times at Oliver. But with great presence of mind Nancy called to him, "Don't worry, this is my young brother who has run away from home and got himself into bad company." The people nodded, some uncaring, and some almost enraged over the "lousy boy who no longer wanted to be with his parents". No one was surprised when a young man with a dog came from a dark doorway, tore the books from beneath Oliver's arm and shouted, "You have stolen these!" It was Bill Sikes, who had first watched Nancy from a safe distance and now, as Oliver struck out in despair, brought the heavy books down so hard on his head that he was almost knocked unconscious, and fell down, quite overcome, between Sikes and Nancy. None of the casual witnesses bothered themselves further with the three, who now rapidly disappeared down a dark alleyway. Oliver only came to again as the two pushed him inside a gloomy house. There it seemed as if all those whom he had hoped never to see again were waiting for him. Fagin grinned at him with feigned pleasure, the Dodger looked at him reproachfully, and Charley wanted to go through Oliver's pockets without delay. But Nancy was quicker. With a single grasp she found the money, which Sikes immediately took over. The books were given to Fagin and everyone got something from the new clothes.

Meanwhile Oliver had recovered somewhat. He suddenly rushed to the window and leaned out, but his cries for help were suffocated in Sikes' iron grip. Fagin then dragged him into a room where,

Oliver was near to despair.

mad with rage, the old man set about him. Rescue, at least for the present, came from a quite unexpected quarter. With a shout, Nancy fell on Fagin's arm. "Stop, that's enough. I won't go along with that," she cried angrily. "I have brought him to you, but I don't mind him at all and will not have him beaten. It's bad enough for him that he's here again with you!" With this outburst she had reached such a pitch of excitement that she began to tremble all over and fell whimpering to the floor.

"One of her stupid turns," hissed Sikes scornfully. Fagin let the stick fall and gave Oliver a push so that he fell full length onto a bunk which was just as dirty as the one in Fagin's house in Field Lane. For a while still he cried softly to himself before he finally went to sleep.

The two friends in Mr. Brownlow's house were still sitting at the table looking at the watch. The hands had long passed over the half hour.

Parish officer Bumble reads a newspaper advertisement and visits Mr. Brownlow

We had almost forgotten Mr. Bumble. Quite unjustifiably, since it was not long before his path crossed Oliver's again. One day Mr. Bumble was instructed to bring two of the parish wards to London. Having installed them properly in a home there, he ordered a substantial supper in an inn and called for the newspapers. He was reading them in comfort during the meal when suddenly a large advertisement so surprised him that his food nearly stuck in his throat. A large reward was promised to anyone who had news of a boy called Oliver Twist. Mr. Bumble immediately made his way to the address given and was soon sitting opposite Mr. Brownlow and Mr. Grimwig. He described to them the disagreeable experience he had had with Oliver. But Mr. Brownlow still did not want to believe the hair-raising tales of Oliver's wickedness. Mr. Grimwig on the other hand saw his worst fears confirmed. The only one to be pleased was Mr. Bumble. He had earned a considerable reward, and with much bowing made his way out.

As soon as the parish officer had left the house, Mr. Brownlow called Mrs. Bedwin and told her that she must realize that Oliver was apparently nothing but a pernicious hypocrite. But here, both he and Mr. Grimwig (who in any case was a batchelor and knew nothing of children) came up against Mrs. Bedwin, who as before remained convinced that Oliver was a good fellow, and she only brought her speech to an end when Mr. Brownlow declared emphatically that he wished to hear no more of the

"Away from here!" shouted Bill Sikes. Oliver recoiled in fright. He heard a bang and fell backwards down the stairs.

A night out with Sikes

business. He could not guess that Oliver had tried to get back the property entrusted to him and come back to Pentonville. No, he could not know that Oliver remained for days locked in a damp room, troubled and in despair because Mr. Brownlow must take him for a thief.

When at last Oliver was allowed to leave his prison for a little while, he immediately considered his escape, but all doors and windows were shut and no one would have heard his cries for help. He was left to his misery, completely alone. At last he could no longer bear this emptiness both around and within him. He longed, whatever the price, for human voices and human company. Fagin's poison was having its effect on Oliver's soul. The old man's plan to destroy Oliver's character and so to bring him down for ever, seemed to be working slowly but surely.

It was a particularly cold night as Fagin crept along to Sikes to speak with him about a robbery in a rich lady's house. Since, as Fagin had suspected, the servants were not to be bribed, Sikes finally declared he was prepared to risk the burglary in his own way, but only on two conditions. He wanted much more than the usual portion, and also one of Fagin's boys as an assistant. He was thinking of Oliver who was the right size. Fagin was pleased to agree. He hoped thus to achieve Oliver's irrevocable dependence upon him, and then to be able to persuade him to further dishonest tricks. And to Sikes' question as to what would happen if Oliver were to lose his life in the undertaking, since it was not without danger, Fagin simply shrugged his shoulders and said, "The main thing is that you bring the booty back safely!"

When Oliver found a pair of new shoes with his things in the morning he thought for a moment that he was to be set free at last. However, Fagin soon dashed his hopes. "In a few days I will take you to Bill Sikes, and my advice to you is to listen carefully to his every word!"

Left alone again Oliver worried over what he

was to do at Sikes' place. Probably keep his house in order, he thought, and waited patiently to be fetched. To pass the time he leafed through an old book that, as if by chance, was lying on a chair. It never occurred to him that Fagin had put it there intentionally. It contained reports of horrible crimes and the no less frightful punishments with which the criminals had to atone for their evil deeds. It made Oliver feel quite ill. He let the book fall and sank to his knees. His white lips stammered helplessly a prayer to God to save him, and he did not hear Nancy coming into the house. The girl tried to encourage him, although she herself was very pale with a feverish light in her eyes. She reminded him that she had already helped him and promised she would not desert him. However, the moment was not favourable for his escape and, on the contrary, it would cost Nancy her life if he did not follow her now. Without speaking Oliver followed her outside where a cab was waiting to take them quickly to Sikes' house.

In a voice which was not so rough as usual, and therefore even more threatening, Sikes gave Oliver to understand that he would blow his brains out of his skull with a pistol if he did not listen carefully. Then he asked Nancy to kindly get something to eat, since he and Oliver had to sleep for a few hours to be rested for the work. Towards half past five the next morning Nancy woke them and gave them breakfast. Shortly afterwards Sikes and Oliver went out into the fog and rain. Oliver wore a much too large rough jacket, and on his head a handkerchief. Shyly he turned round once more to catch a glance from Nancy, but the shivering girl had gone back into the house to the stove. There she crouched down and remained without moving as if paralysed.

Sikes and Oliver walked quite quickly through the still silent town to Hyde Park and took the way towards Kensington. A carrier then took them to Isleworth with him. From there they again had to go on foot. Before they reached Hampton they spent a short time in the district and then quickly had something to eat in a cheap tavern. Then further on to Shepperton, and it was already dark when Sikes stopped in front of a decaying house that stood alone by a river. In the dark water the lights of a distant town were reflected like stars. In the house a man called Toby Crackit sat on a tattered sofa, smoking a pipe. He lived by theft, and there was also a certain Barney there, a fellow from Fagin's gang, whom Oliver already knew. Toby immediately wanted to know who the boy was. Sikes whispered something to him and informed them all of the purpose of their visit. They then all sat down at a rickety table to eat, but Oliver was so tired that, after several mouthfuls, he slid off the chair. He was troubled by unpleasant dreams and turned restlessly to and fro. Just before midnight he was pleased to

be roughly woken up. Sikes and Toby told him to follow them. Outside it was pitch black and damp with mist.

They crossed a village and came at last to a house standing alone surrounded by a high wall. With a jump Toby was up and, with help from him and Sikes, Oliver found himself a few seconds later on the wet lawn between the wall and the house. And now finally he realized that he was to be an accomplice to a burglary: indeed he already was! He flung himself on the ground, clasped Sikes round the knees and begged him to let him go. Beside himself with rage Sikes held the muzzle of his pistol to Oliver's head and wanted to shoot, but Toby tore him away, whilst at the same time clamping Oliver's mouth shut with the other hand. Threatening to kill him, the two bandits dragged him to a small window, from which Sikes, in just a few minutes, prised away the grille with a crowbar.

Now came Oliver's task. He had to climb through the opening, which was too narrow for the other two, and when Sikes had handed him a lantern and shown him the way, he had to creep to the front door and draw the bolts.

Oliver nodded, speechless. However, although he knew that Sikes would shoot him without thinking, he was quite determined not to go to the front door but instead to hurry to the floor above and

He simply left the boy lying there and disappeared into the mist . . .

warn the owners. But he had only climbed a few steps when he heard Sikes shouting quite loudly, "Come back, quick, quick, let's get out of here!" Oliver was so frightened that he took a false step and tripped, and the lamp fell. Suddenly he was dazzled by several flashes of light. He saw the silhouette of two men on the steps, heard a dull bang and felt a sharp pain in his arm. Oliver felt Sikes and Toby pulling him through the window into the open air, then Sikes, breathing heavily, carried him away on his shoulders. But after a while Sikes stopped. The voices of their pursuers could clearly be heard, and dogs were barking dangerously near. Then he simply threw the boy, bleeding and by now unconscious, into a ditch. Hurrying after Toby Crackit, he disappeared into the all-enveloping mist.

Old Sally makes a confession

For a better understanding of the subsequent and sometimes most significant events, we must again turn to Mr. Bumble, who was now visiting a Mrs. Corney. This lady was the matron of the poor house to which Oliver's mother had dragged herself shortly before his birth and her own death. Whilst the two were having a discussion there was a loud knocking at the door. In the winter cold stood a woman urging, "Hurry Mrs. Corney! Old Sally is dying. She insists she has something to tell you." Mrs. Corney was most put out by this interruption because she guessed that Mr. Bumble had come to declare his love. But her curiosity got the better of her and she asked him to be sure to wait for her. Warmly wrapped up, she then hurried over to the hospital. There lay the dying woman in a dark corner, staring absent-mindedly at Mrs. Corney, who remained close to the bed. At last her patience ran out and she turned to go. At that moment old Sally came to again and groaned wearily, "Stay . . . come nearer . . . I must whisper something in your ear . . ." Mrs. Corney sent the two attendants who were waiting in

At that moment old Sally came to herself again and moaned with difficulty, "I . . . a secret . . ."

the background out of the room so that they could not overhear, and then bent over the old woman who began to recount an interesting tale.

Many years ago in that same bed, a young and beautiful woman had died after giving birth to a baby boy. Blood on her feet showed that she had wandered far. "I . . . I took from the dead woman something she had always carried with her hidden under her blouse," explained Sally. "She had parted with everything for food to keep from starving, except this . . . this little thing of pure gold . . . gold . . . that could have saved her life." The word gold caused Mrs. Corney to listen enviously and she demanded more details. But the old woman rambled on remorsefully that only she was to blame if the child perhaps had also died in the meantime. "It . . . it would surely have been better treated . . . if I had told what I knew . . ." she sighed, her voice choked with tears. "Such . . . such a handsome boy . . . he was the image of his mother . . . Yes, I've always thought that . . . when I sometimes met him later . . . and his looks reminded me every time of the theft I had committed . . ." Sally fell silent once more, while Mrs. Corney's agitation grew visibly. "Who was the boy? Do I know him?" she shouted in the old woman's ear.

At last the faded lips stammered out a few more words. "Perhaps . . . perhaps he will find out one day who his mother was and . . . that he has no need to be ashamed of her." Suddenly a heavy perspiration broke out on Sally's brow, and her breathing became more and more difficult. With a weak movement she raised her head in a last effort. "His . . . his name is Oliver . . . and the gold object I stole . . . was . . . was . . ." Slowly she sank back into the cushions, her eyes closed for ever. Speechless and deep in thought Mrs. Corney made her way home.

A man called Monks speaks with old Fagin

Fagin was already waiting impatiently in the gang's hideout as Toby Crackit finally returned. Alone. He and Sikes had split up as a precaution during their escape, he explained. And Oliver? Toby shrugged his shoulders. Probably he was dead by now, he suggested unperturbed. He had been shot during the unsuccessful burglary. Why had he not brought him with him? shouted Fagin. "Be glad that I and Sikes have come out of it unharmed!" fumed Toby angrily. "And besides . . ." What he thought besides, Fagin did not want to know. "Such bad luck," he howled, and tearing his hair, slammed the door furiously behind him and stamped out of the house.

Under cover of busy streets he slipped through dark alleyways and secluded backyards into the district around Field Lane where he felt really safe.

The landlord shook his head.

Suddenly a man was standing next to him.

There in the neighbourhood of thieves and receivers, disreputable dealers and tavern keepers, he felt at home. There the people greeted each other with a mutual wink and everyone knew immediately when danger threatened from whatever quarter. Fagin was not going home, but spoke one after another with a series of dark figures to find out the whereabouts of Bill Sikes. But no one knew where he was hiding, not even in his usual tavern had anyone heard news of him. "Barney has also disappeared," whispered the landlord, whom Fagin had fetched from the taproom into the stairway where they were undisturbed. "He'll wait till the grass has grown over a thing or two." "And how is it with him? If only he would come this evening," whispered Fagin, stressing the 'him' and 'he' meaningfully. "Oh, Monks?" returned the landlord hesitantly. "Ssh! no names!" hissed the old man, almost anxiously. The landlord confirmed that he was expecting 'him'. He must be spoken to urgently said Fagin. The landlord should tell him to come to Field Lane that night or at the latest the next day.

Then Fagin wanted to go, but the landlord held him back. Was it not time, he asked, to give up a certain Phil Barker to the police? There were more and more doubts as to his dependability. Not yet, decided Fagin, Barker must first do another job before he was dispensed with. Oliver had heard such talk often enough, and must have realized that Fagin and his accomplices did not shrink from giving up to the police anyone who did not carry out their orders without reservation.

In the street the old man looked carefully around several times before he hailed a cab and was taken to Bethnal Green. Near Sikes' place he paid the cab and went the last stretch on foot. He hesitated a while outside before he pushed open the door and went into the living room. Nancy was crouched over the table and looked at him glassy-eyed. Her head was slumped forward and her hair hung untidily on all sides. Either she's drunk or else she has one of her unpredictable fits of world-weariness again, thought Fagin with indifference. He asked the girl in a flat voice if she knew anything of Sikes. When he had assured himself that she really was alone and had no idea where Sikes was, Fagin quickly told his news. The conversation began rather cautiously since neither of the two entirely trusted the other. But, as Fagin mentioned in passing that Oliver lay wounded in a ditch somewhere, Nancy was shaken out of her complacency and cried, "The boy is better off in a ditch than with us! And so long as Bill is not blamed, I hope that he has died in peace!"

At this, Fagin lost his former reticence. For a while he lost all control of himself and his rage drove him to make remarks that he would never have made in his right mind. He threatened to call Sikes to account because he had not brought the boy back, be it alive or dead. The boy was worth more than a mere few hundred pounds, and it was unthinkable, he fumed, to lose such a fortune just because of a drunkard, and above all to be dependent on a deceitful devil in human form who only had him in the hand because . . . Fagin came suddenly to a halt in mid-sentence. Shocked, he realized he had given away far too many of his carefully guarded secrets, and he took great pains to cover up his mistake. Nancy, however, seemed to understand nothing of his explanation and did not participate, but only babbled to herself, scarcely comprehensible, that the boy had only been overtaken by the fate that they must all expect one day. Taking no notice of Fagin's questions and exhortations, she quietly fell asleep. Reassured, the old man left the house about an hour after midnight.

An ice-cold wind made him shiver as he made for his house in Field Lane. He was just a few steps from the door when suddenly a man appeared from a niche, and like a shadow, silently approached him. Fagin recoiled, but then snorted, breathing heavily, "Monks!"

Silently the man accompanied him into the house, where in an untidy room on the first floor, he took a seat opposite Fagin. "Are we alone?" he asked. Fagin nodded and told him of the unsuccessful burglary and Oliver's fate. Shaking with anger, Monks reproached the old man bitterly.

It would have been much cleverer to have kept the boy with him and made a pickpocket of him as quickly as possible. Afterwards it would not have been difficult to hand him over to the police and arrange his life-long exile in a far-off penal colony. Fagin disagreed. With two partners each has an equal claim to the profit. He had not succeeded in making a criminal of Oliver, but his arrest following the theft near the bookstall had turned out to be an incredible stroke of luck for Monks. As a chance witness, he had noticed for the first time Oliver's great resemblance to someone. Oh yes, the likeness was noticeable. "And besides," added Fagin, "with Nancy's help I have got the boy back. Who could have guessed that the hussy would suddenly have assumed the role of his protector?" "Throttle her!" fumed Monks. But Fagin thought this premature. She would in any case soon lose her sympathy for Oliver. "Naturally, when the boy is no longer alive," hissed Monks. He had not wanted his death. Fagin was responsible for that. "And . . ." Monks stopped. "Something moved! Like a shadow."

Fagin laughed at him. He nevertheless searched the house with him from top to bottom, but found nothing. Reassured, Monks agreed that he had been mistaken and went on his way disgruntled.

Neither he nor Fagin guessed that there had indeed been an eavesdropper. It was Nancy, who had followed the old man home.

Seriously wounded, Oliver is taken in by Mrs. Maylie

Cold and pain roused Oliver from his unconscious state. He recognized the ditch where Sikes had thrown him and saw with fright that it was gradually filling with muddy water. Only then did he become aware of the rain falling monotonously from a grey sky. Gathering all his strength he managed to crawl out of the water and painfully stood up. He found himself in a marshy meadow. He stumbled forward like a drunken man without knowing where he was going. At last he came to a road, and his only hope

now was to be allowed to die amongst people instead of all alone. Relentlessly the rain came down as he dragged himself along. Finally he saw a house. Breathing heavily he drew near, and then shrank back horrified as he recognized the wall of the previous night's burglary. For a moment he thought of turning back, but then a feeling of indifference came over him. What could happen to him that was worse than before? He opened the outer gate. Crawling rather than walking, he reached the door and knocked weakly several times before losing consciousness.

At that very moment the servants were sitting in the kitchen discussing the unsuccessful burglary at great length. There was the house steward, Giles, and then the house boy, Brittles, and a day-labourer who had also taken part in the chase the previous night. In spite of all their bragging, the three were

They bent over the boy and recognized him immediately. He was one of the burglars of the previous night.

not great heroes and cowered together, just as frightened as the two house maids, when they suddenly heard the muffled knocking. Finally they all went together to the door. When they saw only a small boy lying as if lifeless before them, they at once recognized him as the burglar who had been shot, and their courage returned.

Giles took him somewhat roughly and dragged him into the hall where he let him fall onto the cold tiles. One of the maids hurried with the news upstairs to Mrs. Maylie, the mistress of the house. She was quite an elderly lady but very energetic, and with her was an extremely pretty and charming girl of about seventeen, called Rose. She told the servants to be sure to make no noise, and then, at Mrs. Maylie's request, had the injured boy brought into Giles' room. She then ordered the servants to ride to Chertsey to fetch the police and the doctor. But despite the continued bragging of Giles, who made out that this important event was due to his prudence and courage alone, she did not at first even glance at the apparently very dangerous fellow. In fact she requested, before she withdrew, that he was at all costs to be treated kindly whilst he remained in the house.

Dr. Losberne arrived shortly afterwards. For a long time now he had been a good friend of the Maylies, and he was first informed by Giles exactly what had happened. He then went up to the attic floor to see the injured boy. When he had treated the wound he reported to the two ladies. The boy's life was not in danger, and therefore he thought it was time they got to know their uninvited guest. Somewhat hesitantly the two followed the doctor upstairs, and they were completely speechless when, instead of a rough burglar, they saw a child sleeping soundly. His thin body showed signs of hunger and many beatings, and the girl was so shaken by the sight that she bent protectively over the bed and shed tears of sympathy over Oliver's face. He sighed as if, even in his sleep, he felt a previously unknown human warmth around him.

From this first moment Rose was convinced that this poor little fellow could only be the much misused victim of unscrupulous brutes. "Perhaps he has been deprived from birth of mother love and the security of a family circle, dear Aunt," she said to Mrs. Maylie, and begged her earnestly to take in the boy. Rose felt he should be treated with as much love as had been shown to her, for she was also an orphan. The old lady was not unwilling, but wanted first to hear Dr. Losberne's opinion. The doctor was a just man, and declared that he was willing to see that the boy was not given up to the authorities, provided he really deserved this magnanimity. They should therefore first of all hear what the patient had to say. Shortly afterwards Oliver came

to his senses and, constantly interrupted by tears, recounted his sad life. When he had finished he stared, speechless, at his audience for a long while. Finally, Mrs. Maylie stroked him gently on his thin cheek, nodded encouragingly and said, "Don't trouble yourself, my child. You need not worry any more. In my house you will find a good home." Oliver could not speak for gratitude, he thought he must be dreaming, but his eyes showed how he felt.

Dr. Losberne kept his word. He had a serious talk with the servants, who were naturally very surprised at the unexpected turn of events, and could only be convinced of its justice after many persuasive arguments. However, with their help, Dr. Losberne managed to persuade the police and the court that Oliver could not possibly be the burglar whom Giles had shot. His injury came rather from careless play with neighbours' children who were exploring unfamiliar and forbidden ground, as children often do. And when Giles went to chase them off, Oliver, because of his injury, was the only one of the little rascals who could not escape him. The authorities could not deny this statement, and did not bother any more about the boy who had at first caused such a stir.

Henry and Oliver were soon good friends.

The stranger made as if to strike Oliver, but at that moment . . .

During his convalescence under the loving care of Mrs. Maylie, Rose and Dr. Losberne and, indeed, also the servants, Oliver was only able to express his gratitude in words, but he longed also to be able to show it in deeds. "Don't worry," comforted Rose, with whom he was particularly friendly. "You will soon have plenty of opportunity. We will be spending the next few months in the country, where Mrs. Maylie also has a nice house."

Oliver kept thinking of Mr. Brownlow and Mrs. Bedwin, who had been so good to him. Dr. Losberne also felt they should be told what had happened, and as soon as Oliver had recovered completely he took the boy to London with him. But the journey, undertaken with such high hopes, ended in disappointment. The house where Oliver had been kept after his abduction was empty, apart from an unkempt beggar. This they could bear, but it was upsetting to see that Mr. Brownlow's house was also abandoned. They learnt that he had gone to the West Indies with Mrs. Bedwin and his friend Grimwig and it was not known when they would return. Downcast, Oliver returned from the journey, but he did not give up hope that one day he would be able to thank Mr. Brownlow.

Only his stay in the country with Mrs. Maylie and Rose succeeded in making him a little more cheerful. These were happy weeks. In the mornings he learned to read and write, and most afternoons he spent walking with the ladies. In the evenings they sat on the terrace, or Rose played the piano and sang old well-known songs. Oliver carried out all the little tasks he was given, such as gathering fresh food for Rose's birds, or helping Mrs. Maylie to water the flowers. Sometimes, however, he stole into the nearby graveyard, where at the sight of the graves, he would begin to cry as he thought of his mother who had died in such misery.

In a few weeks the relationship between the two ladies and their charge was so affectionate that it seemed as if he had always been a member of the family, and slowly Oliver began to forget the fearful experiences that lay behind him.

Rose becomes ill, and Oliver has a strange experience

One evening, when it was already summer, Mrs. Maylie's foster-daughter began to feel sharp pains. As her condition did not improve overnight, Oliver was sent early next morning to the post with an express letter for Dr. Losberne. He arrived in good time before the departure of the mailcoach in the village. On the way back, in front of a guesthouse, he accidentally bumped into a rather tall man who, after a quick penetrating look, began to shout at him in a most unpleasant manner. Then he cursed vulgarly and finally called himself a fool because he had not had the courage to speak the word that in one night would have rid him of the spectre for ever. Then suddenly he fumed, "The devil take you. Whatever are you doing here?" and made as if to strike the astonished boy. But at that moment an epileptic fit threw him full-length into the road. Oliver ran immediately into the inn to get help for the unfortunate man. He waited till some guests carried him into the house, then set off hurriedly on his way, and in his anxiety over Rose soon forgot the unpleasant incident.

Indeed, Rose's condition had become even more worrying. Pains and fever-fantasies troubled her constantly, and the country doctor treating her could only hope for a miracle. The following night the illness reached a climax. Oliver felt a terrible anxiety which was in no way lessened by the arrival of Dr. Losberne, who only confirmed his colleague's worst fears. The next few days were terrible for all concerned, but then the doctor, breathing more freely, declared that the worst was over.

As Oliver had flown out of the house to give his worries over Rose free reign in the open air, he only learned the good news much later from Giles. He had gone to fetch Mrs. Maylie's son from the mail coach. Henry was a young man of twenty-five years and of unaffected simplicity, who dearly loved his mother's foster-daughter, but seldom saw her because he was studying in London. He was soon friends with Oliver, and now the two rejoiced together over the good fortune that had saved Rose from almost certain death. They hurried home so fast that Giles could hardly keep up with them.

Over the next weeks Oliver competed daily with Henry to see which of them could find the most beautiful flowers for the convalescent. From Henry, Oliver learnt more about Rose. Although her parents were not known, which in the eyes of many people was a disgrace, this could not influence the love which Mrs. Maylie and her son felt for her. However, as the disapproval of so-called polite society regarding unknown parentage could obviously not be concealed from Rose, she continued to refuse to become Henry's wife. Out of love she wanted to save him from being avoided or even despised by his equals because of a marriage, which, according to the custom of the time, was not appropriate to his class. Henry, however, was now more than ever determined to convince her of the steadfastness of his love, and was only waiting for a suitable opportunity to pour out his heart.

One evening Oliver was so tired that he fell asleep at his writing desk. Dreams overcame him and he thought he was again in Fagin's house. He heard someone say, "That's the boy," whereat Fagin whispered, "And if it's him I would recognize him even if he lay five yards under the earth." Bathed in perspiration, Oliver awoke, but what he saw frightened him even more. Two men were pressing their faces against the window panes. Although they disappeared immediately, he had recognized them. It was Fagin and the stranger who had shouted and cursed at him in front of the mail station. Calling loudly for help Oliver rushed from the room.

Although Henry, Dr. Losberne and Giles immediately made a search, their efforts met with no more success than later by daylight, and although no one doubted Oliver's observation, as the weeks went by the mysterious incident was forgotten.

Mr. Bumble goes to the tavern and there reveals certain recollections

Whilst Oliver grew accustomed to a new life in peaceful surroundings, time naturally did not stand still for the acquaintances of his less happy days. Mr. Bumble, for instance, could not otherwise have courted Mrs. Corney. She allowed him to take her to

At last there was again hope.

In a dream Oliver thought he heard voices.

the altar, and as she was a very energetic and determined lady with influential connections, it was not long before her husband was promoted from parish officer to supervisor in the men's workhouse. He came even more quickly, however, under the thumb of his power-hungry, nagging wife. More and more frequently he sought refuge and solace in alcohol, and so, after a particularly unpleasant quarrel with his wife, he made his way once again to the tavern. Apart from himself, there was only one other guest in the smoky bar, who, Bumble remembered, had formerly come there more often. After a while the stranger sat next to him at the table, and now Bumble also remembered the name – Monks! He needed certain information, he explained, holding out his hand, and would pay well for it. Where could he find the old witch who had been present at the birth of Oliver Twist and the death of his mother, he wanted to know.

The prospect of a reward immediately touched Mr. Bumble's greed. Old Sally was dead, he informed him, but added with satisfaction, as he saw the other's disappointment, that he knew a woman to whom Sally had entrusted something just before she died. He did not say that it was his own wife. Monks gave him a penetrating look, then scrawled an address on a greasy bit of paper and said, in a voice that brooked no argument, that Bumble should bring the woman at a certain time to the place indicated on the paper. And woe betide him if he told anyone else of the rendezvous!

It was lucky for Mr. Bumble that his wife was not only greedier than he, but above all seemed to fear neither death nor the devil. Indeed, he would have preferred to turn back as the two made their way, one stormy night, through an utterly desolate area reputed to be a hide-out for all manner of rabble. The house noted on the paper stood inaccessibly on a river, and several of the decaying rooms were built on tall piles far out in the water. Monks was already waiting and led them into one of these. There in a threatening voice he bade the woman say what she knew. But he had spoken to the wrong woman, for neither Monks nor the raging storm could shake her. First the money, she demanded in an unmistakable tone. Gnashing his teeth, Monks threw several gold pieces onto the dusty table. Mrs. Bumble tested each one before she began her story. Yes, she had been the only witness at Sally's death, and the old woman had briefly told her that she had robbed Oliver Twist's mother. In Sally's stiffened hand she had then found a pawn ticket. This she had redeemed a few days later. "And what was it?" breathed Monks.

"This here!" Mrs. Bumble took a leather purse from her pocket, which, besides two locks of a child's hair fastened in a gold locket, held also a wedding ring. On the inside the name 'Agnes' and a year was inscribed. The space between, for a family name, was empty. "That's the year before Oliver's birth," explained Mr. Bumble meaningfully. Monks nodded absentmindedly, and put the locket and the ring back in the purse. He also put in a piece of lead. Then, without uttering a word, he opened a trapdoor, under which the river gurgled darkly. For a moment he seemed to hesitate. Then he let the purse fall, listened for the splash and suddenly gave a shrill laugh, whilst his face took on a satanic grimace. But he was soon in full control of himself, and led the perspiring Bumble and his wife to the door. But before he let them out into the stormy night he turned to Bumble with a fearsome expression, "I'm sure that your wife, . . . she is your wife? Ah, I see you don't deny it . . . can and will keep quiet. And I advise you to do the same, otherwise . . ." He did not need to be more specific, Mr. Bumble had well understood the threat.

That, then, was the news of the Bumbles. We must now take a look at Sikes. He had been lucky in his flight from the unsuccessful burglary. He did not risk returning to his home, however, although as a result of the night spent in the rain, he was

"Write to me often," begged Henry.

Monks raised his voice threateningly, "Tell no one of our meeting. Otherwise . . ."

shivering with a high fever. Just in time, he found cover in another part of London, where Nancy, after a long search, eventually found him, and for many weeks devotedly nursed him. Bill Sikes gave her small thanks for this labour of love. He ill-treated her as before, and only when she collapsed from exhaustion did he become anxious.

Cautiously he left the house hoping to find help somewhere. Thereby he fell straight into Fagin's arms. The old Jew, who was accompanied by the Dodger and Charley Bates, was just as surprised as Sikes. He followed him, and took care of Nancy, who soon regained consciousness. Sikes then demanded to know why the old man had not been seen. Did he want to swindle him out of his share of their business together? Excitedly Fagin professed his innocence, let Charley fetch a good meal from a tavern nearby, and gave the excuse that he had not had time to look for Sikes, for reasons which he could only explain to him alone. But Sikes was still angry and distrustful, and only when his stomach was full did he take Fagin into an adjacent room. There, the old man spoke to him at great length. Finally, Sikes, who needed money badly, agreed that Nancy should go to Fagin to live for a certain time. The girl herself was not even asked. Nancy's move to the house in Field Lane had unexpected consequences for Oliver Twist. It came about that

one day, as the old man went to get money once more from the hiding place under the floorboards, Monks suddenly appeared. "You will now work only for me!" he told Fagin, and glanced upstairs. "Come with me, I have important news!" and turning to Nancy who was suffering from a bad headache, he hissed, "You will not move from the spot until I allow you to!" He then disappeared with Fagin upstairs. Neither he nor the old man noticed that the girl slipped after them.

When Monks had gone, Fagin became alarmed at Nancy's white face. To his questions she replied that she had been shut up too long in this fusty house and he should let her go back to Sikes. Fagin called her an ungrateful wretch who did not know what was good for her, angrily threw her a few coins and let her go. Instead of taking the shortest way back to Sikes, however, Nancy wandered aimlessly for a long time. She needed time to overcome, at least outwardly, the uneasiness that had overtaken her ever since she had secretly overheard Monks and Fagin planning a certain villainous business.

When she finally came to Sikes, he did not notice her anxiety. It was not until the next day when she did not answer his questions, that his suspicions were roused. Did she plan to betray him to the police and so be rid of him forever? But then he blamed her behaviour on her ill-health, which reminded him of his own sickness, from which he had not quite recovered. Feeling quite sorry for himself, he let Nancy give him medicine, without even noticing what she was actually administering, and fell quietly asleep.

Nancy decides on a dangerous move

Impatiently, Nancy waited for the sleeping draught to take effect. Then she slipped out of the house and hurried through the dark streets to Hyde Park which was surrounded by many elegant houses. After a quick search she approached one of these and asked the woman in the porter's lodge to take her to Miss Maylie. She must first ask the man-servant, replied the woman, who had recognized Nancy's dubious profession. He refused disdainfully. It was only thanks to the cook, who felt sorry for the street girl, that she finally came to Rose. Rose was spending several days in London with Oliver after her convalescence, and was naturally astonished at the late visit, but felt it must be something very important. She learned that Nancy was the person who had abducted Oliver from Mr. Brownlow's charge. In a friendly manner she invited the girl to speak. Tearfully, Nancy acknowledged the unworthy life she led, the shame into which she had sunk beyond recall. She hoped now at least to be able to make amends in a small way.

Then she told of the conversation she had overheard between Fagin and Monks. Monks had once promised a large reward for the further abduction of the boy, which he would double if Fagin succeeded in making a scoundrel out of him. "But," continued Nancy, "there's worse to come. Listen to what I found out yesterday!" In that conversation Monks had triumphantly told the old man that all the evidence which could have explained Oliver's parentage was lost for ever in a river. However, although he now had indisputably at his disposal the money intended for Oliver, Monks would have much preferred, if he could have managed it, simply to have taken revenge on Oliver's father over the cursed will, by bringing Oliver one day to the gallows. Then Monks reproached Fagin angrily for his failure. For the old man, the execution of these evil plans should, with a little more discretion, have been child's play. By exploiting the boy appropriately he could have made a great deal of good business for himself. Now Monks' hatred went even further. Only fear for his own neck had kept him from taking the boy's life already. But he would never tire of pursuing him, for all time and in all places, and if Oliver let fall a single false word, then Monks would catch his little brother out, in a way that even Fagin, with his black soul, could not imagine!

"His brother?" interrupted Rose, amazed and disbelieving. "Yes, he has spoken of Oliver as his brother," confirmed Nancy earnestly. "And then he cursed the chance that had let the boy find refuge with the Maylies." On the other hand this encounter gave him a certain evil satisfaction, for he knew only too well how much it was worth to the Maylies to find out what two-legged mongrel they had taken in.

Neither Fagin nor Monks noticed that they were secretly followed by Nancy . . .

Rose was furious at what she heard, but she was no less upset by Nancy's hopeless misery. "Stay with us," she cried without hesitating, and took Nancy's hand. "Mrs. Maylie and I will do everything we can to bring you back to an existence more consistent with human dignity."

Sobbing, Nancy shook her head. For her there was no going back, she declared stubbornly. She had not deserved a better lot, and did not want to desert Sikes, even though he would kill her if he ever found out about her visit there, for without her help he would surely soon die.

Perplexed, Rose asked what she should do. "Tell no one of my confidence, which above all things must be kept secret," cried Nancy. "But how shall I find you again?" "I am every Sunday evening from eleven to midnight on London Bridge. But I must go now, or Sikes will wake up before I get back," replied Nancy. Rose thanked her once more from her heart and hugged her, then Nancy quickly left the house.

Alone again, Rose found no peace. Whom could she confide in? As the whole family wanted to go to the sea within the next few days, there was the utmost urgency. Dr. Losberne? No, he was not cool-headed enough. Mrs. Maylie? Also no, she would go straight to Losberne. Finally she decided it would be best to write to Henry. However, next morning as she was about to begin the letter, Oliver rushed into her room in great excitement. He had seen Mr. Brownlow from a distance and also knew where he was living.

This surprise made Rose forget everything else for a moment. She called for the carriage to be harnessed, and in a few minutes she was on her way with Oliver.

Oliver meets Mr. Brownlow again

On his return from the West Indies, Mr. Brownlow had moved into a large house again. Rose was first announced alone, and received a warm welcome from the old gentleman and his friend Grimwig. As soon as Mr. Brownlow understood that Oliver was sitting outside in the coach, he could not contain himself. He rushed out, tore open the coach door and seized the boy in his arms. Mr. Grimwig, who had remained behind alone with Rose, gave the girl, much to her surprise, a kiss on the cheek from sheer joy, and stammered, "I am so happy that, with your help, everything has turned out well!" Mrs. Bedwin was quite beside herself with delight when she saw Oliver, and kept repeating that she had always known he was innocent.

Rose was so impressed with Mr. Brownlow's worthy conduct that she asked to speak with him in private, and then confided to him her experience with Nancy. Brownlow at once recognized the significance of this news. Oliver should not be troubled yet, but the old gentleman considered it imperative to let Mrs. Maylie and Dr. Losberne (and naturally Mr. Grimwig) into the secret as soon as possible. Thereupon, they all travelled to Chertsey that day, where Rose's news also caused great excitement. Dr. Losberne would have preferred to have Fagin's whole gang apprehended on the spot, but finally saw that this was premature. First, with Nancy's help, but without endangering her, this Monks must be seized and made to speak before the court, for it seemed that he alone knew the whole secret of Oliver's parentage. Under these circumstances, Mrs. Maylie was naturally prepared to put off the trip, and finally it was agreed that Mr. Brownlow would accompany Rose to London Bridge where she would meet Nancy.

Sikes commits another crime and Mr. Brownlow solves a mystery

Certainly Fagin's efforts to make a criminal out of Oliver had failed completely, but that had not prevented him from successfully enlarging his gang with new members. Among these was a particularly intelligent pupil called Noah Claypole, of whom we have unpleasant memories from Oliver's unhappy days with the undertaker. Accompanied by the dirty and unscrupulous Charlotte, he had simply run away from his master one evening and made his way to London. In a low tavern, which was a meeting place for all manner of daylight-shy rabble, Fagin spotted the two, and recognized immediately their suitability for his questionable trade. Indeed his hopes were not disappointed, either by Noah or by Charlotte. For risks that required personal courage, Noah was at any rate too cowardly, but on the other hand he had shown himself to be a clever trickster. With pride he now called himself "Bolter" to indicate that he knew how to open any type of door bolt. And from Charlotte, Fagin cashed daily a fair sum, which she had taken from wealthy men. So Fagin's knowledge of human nature served him well. Although Sikes laughed at his mistrust, Fagin's suspicions had been roused by Nancy's recent strange behaviour. He could not believe that it was due to a slight fever, as the girl always pretended.

As Fagin once again visited Sikes, late one Sunday evening, he witnessed a scene which caused him to reflect deeply. Just before eleven o'clock Nancy put on her hat and coat, and although she had been complaining all day of shivering and fever, insisted on going out. Sikes, however, stopped her and asked in an ugly mood what she intended to do. "To get some fresh air," replied Nancy. "Not now!" affirmed Sikes, who had been drinking heavily. As Nancy insisted, he dragged her back from the door with some force and tore the coat from her shoulders. White as a ghost Nancy cowered in a corner, staring at the floor and said not another word. "She often behaves like that these days," said Sikes to Fagin, unperturbed. But the clever Jew was not satisfied with this answer.

Probably she has a new lover, he thought on his way home, whom she meets in secret, and certainly plans to leave Sikes. Good, good, if it's a rich fellow then something can be made of it! I must find out, and then my silence will pay something. Either Nancy pays, or I threaten to tell Sikes of her treachery. He will strike her dead, yes, that he will! Just wait, my little dove, I will soon have you in the hand!

Next day Fagin began to lay the traps with which he hoped to ensnare Nancy. The Bolter seemed to him just right for this. "I will give you a whole pound if you carry this out to my satisfaction!" he promised him. "A pound? But without any risk?" repeated Noah cautiously. "Child's play!" Fagin assured him. "You only have to watch someone, whom I will point out to you. I want to know who she meets."

It was a week, however, before Fagin took Bolter, who was dressed as a carter, into a notorious inn, and pointed to Nancy through a hole in the

"Stay," Rose begged the street girl.

At this surprising news, Rose immediately had the carriage harnessed.

Nancy led the gentleman and the lady down some steep steps to the river below, without any of them being aware of the secret eavesdropper.

wall. "When she goes, follow her secretly!" They did not have to wait long. Towards eleven o'clock Nancy went out. Unnoticed, Bolter followed her steps as they echoed on the pavements.

The girl hurried along the Thames embankment to London Bridge. Here she walked slowly to and fro, and Bolter, who was hiding in the shadow of a house, was already bored, when exactly at midnight, horses' hooves could be heard approaching. A carriage came onto the bridge, stopped, and an elegant young lady and a distinguished gentleman stepped out and went straight over to Nancy. The girl, looking anxiously around all the while, led them down some steps which ended on the river bank. "No one must see us," Bolter heard her say. Hidden behind a mooring post very near to the three, he was able to understand nearly every word of the following conversation.

Why was she so frightened, asked the gentleman. The whole day she had been troubled by frightful visions, replied Nancy shivering, and in them she always saw a coffin. The gentleman tried to calm her, and assured her that he was completely trustworthy. He and his friends were determined to force Monks to give up his secret. Should this ex-

pectation not succeed, however, then she must tell them where Fagin and his gang were hiding, to bring them before the court. Horrified, the girl drew back. No, no, she would never betray her companions, even if they richly deserved punishment. She had shared her life with them till now, and although she had sunk so low that it was not possible to sink lower, still these unfortunate people belonged to her, as she to them. This applied also to Bill Sikes whom she would never leave, regardless of how badly he had treated her, and would still treat her. On hearing these words, the gentleman abandoned his request. But Monks was not one of her friends, if he had understood her correctly? He had, confirmed Nancy, and she above all wanted to help Oliver, whose misfortune was partly her fault. She told them where Monks' usual tavern was and when he usually went there, and finally, she gave them an exact description of him. He was about forty-five years old, she said, and had remarkably deep-set eyes. As she then described the many scars on Monks' hands and arms, which showed how he bit himself like a madman during his sudden fits, the gentleman looked up surprised. To a question from the lady he replied that similar strange things did sometimes occur.

Nancy was becoming more and more agitated. She must be home before Sikes returned. In vain the lady and gentleman invited her to go with them. They would smooth the way to a new and honest life, and help her to forget the unhappy past. It was too late, sobbed Nancy. She also refused a gift of money. In the end, the only thing she accepted was the young lady's white lace handkerchief. It would remind her always of Oliver and of the people to whom his good fortune had led him. She hurried away, whilst the other two, whom we have of course recognized as Rose Maylie and Mr. Brownlow, slowly returned to the carriage.

Neither they nor Nancy had noticed the hidden eavesdropper. He waited a few minutes until it was again quiet on the bridge, then hurried off to Fagin.

That same night Sikes had not been idle. Pleased with the success of his 'work', he knocked at Fagin's door about two hours before dawn. The old scoundrel did not withhold his appreciation as he received a sack filled with stolen goods. But Sikes noticed immediately the curious expression on the deeply lined and wrinkled face. His suspicions were suddenly aroused as he saw Noah asleep at the table. "What is the matter?" asked Sikes sharply. Fagin was some time with his answer, to give it more weight. "We are lost, someone has betrayed us!" With a rough push he woke Bolter up. "Here, tell Bill what you heard!" Noah did not need to be asked twice, and described the eavesdropping incident with such conceit that it sounded like a heroic deed. Sikes' anger increased at every word, the veins in his forehead swelled up alarmingly and suddenly he let out a terrible oath and rushed out.

As if the devil were after him, he tore home, where Nancy, unsuspecting, lay sleeping in bed. With a wild cry he tore her out of bed and squeezed her round the neck. "You'll be sorry for this, you miserable traitor," he fumed as if out of his mind. Nancy defended herself in despair and entreated him to believe her. If someone had really been listening, they must also know that she had absolutely refused to allow either Sikes or Fagin's gang to be brought to justice. Choked by tears, she implored Sikes to give up his former life. The lady and gentleman would certainly help him also to go to a faraway

"Ah! How pale you are! Yes, no one but I knew till now that, at that time, my unhappy friend handed over to me this portrait of a girl . . ."

land where no one would know his past, and where they could live a decent life without fear.

But her pleading only increased his rage. He raised his pistol and struck her with the stock, with all his force, in the face. Nancy fell bleeding to the floor. Mad with rage, Sikes now took a cudgel and let it fall several times onto the quivering body. With her last remaining strength Nancy held up the lace handkerchief, and in her dying voice asked God to be merciful to her. Then Sikes returned to his senses. But it was too late. The pitiful creature had passed away. Only for a short while did horror and fear paralyse the murderer. Then he whistled for his dog and fled the scene of his infamous deed. At about the same time, and not far from there, Mr. Brownlow and his friends had succeeded, thanks to Nancy's clear directions, in seizing Monks. A single word whispered in his ear in a quiet side-street had taken him so by surprise that, from sheer fright, he offered no resistance, as guarded by two strong men, he was driven in a closed coach to Mr. Brownlow's house and brought into the study there.

When the master of the house had sent his helpers from the room, he gazed at Monks for a while in silence, full of contempt. Although Monks could not hide the fear in his voice he asked insolently, "What exactly do you want from me? To charge me with some unlawful act? Don't make me laugh!" "You will soon stop laughing," returned Mr. Brownlow. "You know quite well what it's about. It is only the memory of an old friend and the recollection of the happy time of my engagement to his sister, that prevents me from handing you over to the authorities. Instead, you have the opportunity, through a frank confession, to make amends, at least in part, for what you have done wrong." Unrelenting, Monks returned, "I am curious to know what I am supposed to have done."

"As you wish. Let us therefore begin at the beginning," said Mr. Brownlow, "although you know this part of the story very well." He paused for a moment before he continued, "My bride-to-be died shortly before the wedding. However, I still had my friendship with her brother, your father, Mr. Edward Leeford! Obviously you were yourself aware of the disgrace you would bring on this honourable name through your dissolute life, and therefore you decided to pander to your depravity under another name. Let us leave it then as Monks!"

"Have it as you will," growled Monks. This did not alter the fact that he was a Leeford and the only person with the right to bear that name. "Wait!" answered Mr. Brownlow sharply, before he took up the thread again. "Your father was unfortunately obliged, for family considerations, to marry a girl who was not only much older than he, but in addition, loved him no more than he loved her. She was

your mother, but because of their very different characters, your parents were very soon living apart, and your father finally went his own way. He then became friendly with a retired naval officer who had two charming daughters. One was only three years old, the other was about nineteen. He formed a deep attachment for her, which was returned. Your father, married already, saw himself in a situation which could not very quickly be changed in his favour. During these weeks, filled with happiness but without hope, the news arrived that one of his wealthiest relatives, who at the time had particularly insisted on the marriage with your mother, had now died in Rome, and named him as his only heir – perhaps out of remorse for something, which even with so much money, could not be made good. Despite a debilitating sickness, your father travelled to Rome, but as he was arranging the inheritance, he himself met with a sudden death. Immediately your mother also travelled to Rome, and as there was no will, she inherited the whole fortune, which, apart from several bank accounts, included large estates in our West Indian colonies."

"A very nice inheritance!" laughed Monks bluntly, "which has rightly passed down to me at my mother's death. What luck!"

"Luck can run out," returned Mr. Brownlow. "You will soon see. Your father came to visit me before his departure. Ah, I see from your face that you did not know this. No one but he and I knew it. He was greatly troubled by his conscience because, as he explained to me, full of self-reproach, he had abused the trust of the girl who loved him. She was expecting a child. Immediately upon his return he would speak with her father and above all make sure that mother and child never went in need. As soon as he had the inherited fortune at his disposal he would pay his wife and his son Edward a fixed income. The main portion, however, should go to the girl and their child. He himself would leave the country for ever. Whether alone . . ? He left this question unanswered but I could guess the reply. Then he entrusted to my care a picture that he had painted of his young and beautiful beloved, and took his leave of me. He never returned, and when I learned of his death, I wanted to concern myself with the retired officer's family and the unfortunate girl. My efforts came to nothing, however, because the household had moved away to an unknown destination."

Monks' eyes lit up in triumph. This did not escape Mr. Brownlow, and he warned, "You rejoice too soon, for now comes the most important part of my story that you do not yet know. Good luck, or let us say rather, Providence, brought this child precisely to me. We know him as Oliver Twist, and, as you long suspected, he is your half-brother!" As if startled by thunder, Monks stared at the speaker, his eyes wide with horror. Now he had found out what Fagin had always kept secret: the name of the man with whom Oliver had first taken refuge. This was a severe blow to the self-assurance he had affected till now.

After a while Mr. Brownlow continued, "I noticed straight away the great likeness between the boy and the girl's portrait left with me. Unfortunately further steps were made difficult by the capture of the child, in whom only you could have had such an interest. But I did not give up. My enquiries even went as far as your unlawfully inherited estates in the West Indies." Monks' eyes flickered. "And how will you prove this fairy-tale of a brother, eh? With the alleged confession of a dead person? Or simply on the grounds of a chance resemblance? No," he mocked, "you have no real proof against me, absolutely none!"

"Wrong!" returned Mr. Brownlow calmly. "In Oliver you yourself recognized your half-brother beyond all doubt, and for that reason followed him so relentlessly. And," he continued, "furthermore, your recent conversations with Fagin in Field Lane and in Sikes' home, would be sufficient. A girl, who was not so depraved as you thought, has in her remorse, revealed the truth to us. Or will you also deny that you know Nancy?"

At this Monks went white, and his whole body began to shake. Without pity, Mr. Brownlow threw the next accusation in his ever paler face. "Do you deny that your father did leave a will, in which he provided for the girl and the child she would bear him, even though she was not his wife? Your mother found it and secretly destroyed it, and you knew this many years ago. But instead of taking your innocent younger brother to you with love, you hoped that with your help, he would degenerate in misery and poverty. That the child's soul remained pure and courageous despite your disgraceful conduct, is a miracle for which I cannot thank God enough." Under the weight of these accusations Monks' resistance finally broke down. "What do you intend to do with me?" he groaned. The fear of being forever banished behind prison walls brought a cold sweat out on his brow.

"You admit everything then," admonished Mr. Brownlow. Monks nodded weakly, and even admitted what he had learnt from Mr. and Mrs. Bumble, and how he had thrown the only evidence of Oliver's parentage into the river. "I should really deliver you up to the justice of this world," declared Mr. Brownlow, "but that would only bring more disgrace on the name of Leeford. Therefore, under the following conditions I will refrain from denouncing you. You will accompany me to a notary and there give your written statement regarding Oliver's parentage and the will. Moreover, you will also undertake to share with Oliver the remaining fortune, in accordance with the stipulations of the will. And when all is in order you will never again

"You admit everything then."

The eyes of those listening grew wide with horror and disgust.

. . ." At this point Dr. Losberne burst into the room without knocking, and shouted in great excitement, "Poor Nancy has been murdered! By Sikes. The police are looking for him everywhere!"

"And Fagin?" enquired Mr. Brownlow, very shaken by Nancy's death. "He is still free, but certainly not for long," Dr. Losberne assured him. Then Mr. Brownlow bade the doctor guard Monks, and hurried to the police station, where he put up a £50 reward for the capture of Sikes. However, three days passed before the murderer was tracked down on the so-called Jacob's Island.

This was a piece of land in a Thames creek near Rotherhithe where there had formerly been mills and small factories. The old buildings had long since rotted away. Dangerous water ditches and swamps could render any stay there fatal. Since Toby Crackit, Charley Bates and other accomplices had taken their spoils to the island, Sikes thought he would also be safe there. But his old friends would have nothing more to do with a murderer. The arguments got worse and worse and finally became so violent that the police were alerted. Sikes was recognized, and immediately the police and an angry crowd, incited by the large reward, set off in pursuit.

Sikes came near to escaping. On the edge of a steep ditch he began to climb down a long rope to the water and to safety. But suddenly he thought he saw Nancy's lifeless eyes gazing at him reproachfully. In fright he missed the rope and plunged with a ghastly last cry into the depths, while the rope fastened itself tighter and tighter, like a noose round his neck.

The last veils fall from the mystery

A few days after Sikes' just punishment had overtaken him, Mr. Brownlow invited Mrs. Maylie, Rose, Dr. Losberne and naturally Oliver, to visit with him and Mrs. Bedwin the little town where the boy had first seen the light of this world. As Mr. Brownlow had cautiously told Oliver and Rose much of what first Nancy and then Monks had said, they both felt this journey had special significance. Oliver in particular showed a steadily increasing uneasiness as the carriage drew nearer to the places he knew only too well. In the town they went straight to the best hotel where Mr. Grimwig was already waiting for them. He led them into a large room where a man with a sinister face was sitting. Shocked, Oliver drew back. He had recognized Monks.

"I could not spare you this further meeting," regretted Mr. Brownlow, "but he is your half-brother, whom I have already told you about. Now, at the end of all this unhappiness, he must repeat his testimony so that it can finally be verified."

"The devil take you!" hissed Monks, without attempting to hide his hatred of Oliver. "And if I don't want?"

"You will want!" said Mr. Brownlow, threateningly, and although swearing the while, Monks agreed.

He confirmed that in Oliver he recognized his half-brother, offspring of the union between his father Edwin Leeford and Agnes, the daughter of the naval officer Fleming. He then told how his, Monks', mother had found the will in Rome, and so discovered the stipulations favourable to Agnes and her child. For himself and his mother only a yearly income of £800 was provided, whereas the large remainder of the fortune was to fall to Agnes and the other half to the child, but only when it had shown that it would not disgrace the name of Leeford. Monks' mother had done what he felt any mother in her right mind would have done, and destroyed the wretched will immediately.

Scarcely back in England, she told Mr. Fleming of his daughter's relationship with Leeford. The old gentleman felt his officer's and his family honour so deeply affected that, out of shame before his neighbours and friends, he went with his daughters to live under a false name in a remote part of Wales. Then, secretly, Agnes left her father and sister, to spare them more shame. Worn out by hunger and heartache, she died after Oliver's birth in the poor house of this town. Her father, who had sought her in vain, and heard from somebody that she had committed suicide, was also snatched away by death soon afterwards. "That ought to suffice," said Monks angrily as he finished his tale, to which Oliver and the others had been listening amazed.

"Only for the moment," said Mr. Brownlow icily, "while I explain what happened to the surreptitiously obtained fortune. Just as your mother had swindled Oliver and Agnes, you now swindled her out of money and goods. Yes, you were not ashamed to steal your mother's jewellery and to waste and gamble the money in bad company! Only on her deathbed did you again trouble about your mother, whose bad character you inherited. How else could she have taken an oath from you that if, in fact, Agnes had brought a child into the world, you would find it and destroy it!" Monks shrugged his shoulders, unperturbed. As Mr. Brownlow told him to his face that Agnes had carried with her till her death, a ring and a locket, Monks explained unmoved, how, with the help of the Bumbles, he had first acquired and then got rid of them. At a sign from Mr. Brownlow, his friend Mr. Grimwig ushered Mr. and Mrs. Bumble into the room. The former parish officer was completely taken aback, but his wife recommended him to remember nothing, and she energetically denied that they had ever seen Monks before. However, Mr. Grimwig called in the two old attendants who had been present at Sally's death. To Mrs. Bumble's horror they said that they had seen through a crack in the door, how she had prised a ticket from the dead woman's fingers. Neither had it escaped them that she had

later taken it to the pawn shop. At this, Mrs. Bumble reluctantly admitted everything. She and her husband should consider themselves lucky that Mr. Brownlow did not insist on their dismissal from the parish service, or on any further punishment.

When the two had departed very subdued, Mr. Brownlow turned to Rose and Mrs. Maylie. "Now you must be very brave, Rose." The girl went white as she heard, as if from afar, the question put to Monks, "You know that Agnes Fleming had a small sister. What happened to her?"

"You know that yourself," growled Monks, but then condescended to give an answer. "It was not only Fleming's relatives who were looking for him, but also my mother. She found the place to which he had withdrawn under a false name. But he was already dead, and Agnes was apparently dead also. Hatred made my mother follow the other daughter, who had been put into the care of a poor farming family. My mother did everything to set these people against the girl. She told them it was the illegitimate child of a drunkard and his drinking companion, who had both ended up in prison as criminals. But before her lies could bear fruit, a wealthy woman had seen the girl and taken her in. And there they are: Rose, the younger sister of Agnes Fleming, and Mrs. Maylie, ostensibly her aunt! Anyone who does not believe me should ask Fagin. I have given him for safekeeping several of my mother's letters which show that my assertions are correct." But no one doubted his word. Mrs. Maylie took Rose in her arms and said sweetly, her whole body shaking, "I will also be a good mother now, my entire love is for you." And then came Oliver, who also put his arm round Rose and said, "Rose, you are in fact my aunt, but you mean much, much more to me. You are, and will always be, my heart's sister!"

All this time Mr. Grimwig was beaming with joy that so much human suffering had found a happy ending. He stood at the door and waited till the general excitement had died down somewhat. He then reminded them that even happy people could not live without food and drink, and that supper was served.

Monks had to take his in another room alone, but first he was instructed by Mr. Brownlow that he was to go with him next day to the notary.

On the following day also, Oliver returned with the Maylies and Dr. Losberne to the house in Chertsey. To everyone's delight Henry arrived from London shortly afterwards. He was deeply moved by all the news. In a quiet moment he asked Rose if, now that she knew who her parents were, she would consider becoming his wife. A kiss from her lips was the long hoped for reply. He then told her, and his mother, that in a small but pretty village nearby, a house was already waiting for him, for he was to take up the post of clergyman there. With this, the Maylies' happiness seemed to be complete.

For Oliver, however, there was still a hard task. He had to accompany Mr. Brownlow to the prison where Fagin sat in the death-cell. Neither he nor the other members of the gang had escaped the police. The judge had made Fagin's trial particularly short. But since he stubbornly refused to reveal the whereabouts of the letters from Monks' mother, which were of such importance as evidence, Mr. Brownlow hoped that, at the sight of the boy, Fagin would relent. Indeed the old man recognized his former victim, but only talked to himself in a confused way about gold and jewels. Mr. Brownlow wanted to terminate the unfruitful visit, so painful to him and to Oliver, but suddenly Fagin pulled Oliver's head near to his lips and whispered, "You must look in a hole in the ceiling above the fireplace." For once, at least, he had spoken the truth. The letters were taken from their hiding place at the very hour when Fagin was stepping under the gallows.

And so our tale comes to an end

We have already heard that Rose and Henry were a happy couple. Let us leave them then, content in their ivy-clad vicarage, where they were often visited by Mrs. Maylie and also by Giles and Brittles. Let us turn our attention for a while to London. There, Oliver now lives with Mr. Brownlow, taking the place of a son. The old gentleman, as also his friend Grimwig and the good Mrs. Bedwin, watches with pride as his charge, industrious and thirsty for knowledge, takes every opportunity to learn, in order to become a capable man in life one day. And Monks? He received, as we understand it, much better treatment than he deserved. Mr. Brownlow, in his efforts to bring him to a respectable life, went so far as to persuade Oliver to share his father's inheritance with Monks, although he alone had claim to it. In any case there was not much left. After his mother's death, Monks had squandered it down to a relatively miserable remainder. Nevertheless,

there was still about £3,000, of which he might have half. This had been just enough to make a new and honest beginning, even in America, where Monks emigrated. But he soon returned to his dissolute life, keeping dubious company, and, as he finally had not a cent left in his pocket, he again tried his luck with fraud and other crimes. Naturally this did not go well. He was put in prison, became ill, and died behind bars.

Things went better for Charley Bates. From the death of his friend Dodger, who met his end in a swamp whilst on the run, and above all from the fate of Sikes and Fagin, he drew the moral, and became an honest man. In Northamptonshire, where no one knew of his former life, he earned his living as a hard-working and widely respected cattle breeder.

Noah Claypole had also taken up a profession, although it would not have suited everybody. As he had turned King's evidence against Fagin, he had come off without punishment, and had then become an informer in the service of the police. His chief work was, either he or Charlotte, who had remained with him, would affect a fainting fit. They would let themselves be taken by passers-by to the nearest public house, where the landlord, anxious to help, would usually given them a brandy to recuperate. This they would drink, say thankyou, and then later, inform on those who had helped them, regarding the bar licence. As we said, not everyone is suited to such a profession.

There remains now only Dr. Losberne and Mr. Grimwig. The doctor sold his practice, and settled down peacefully in Henry's parish. Mr. Grimwig also moved to the country, where he grows flowers and vegetables. At least twice a year, however, he goes on his travels, and on the way home he visits his friends, who usually all meet at Rose and Henry's house. Everything goes well then in this circle of contented people, and not one of them cares to remember the bad times of the past. Only a gold rimmed tablet over a lovingly-tended grave in the churchyard at Oliver's birthplace, recalls them. The inscription reads simply 'Agnes'.

"Rose is willing to be my wife, Mother," beamed the young man.

JACK LONDON

The Call of the Wild

JACK LONDON
The Call of the Wild

Buck gets a nasty surprise

Buck did not read newspapers. If he did, he would have known that they were full of announcements of enormous discoveries of gold in the Klondike high up in the North, just the other side of the Canadian border. He would also have known that the prospectors of this area were in urgent need of powerful dogs, which could pull their sledges over the snowy, icy wastes. However, since there were more prospectors than dogs in the Klondike, dog trading developed into a flourishing business and stretched deep down into the southern United States. In the areas where there were no more dogs to buy, unscrupulous catchers would simply steal them and dealers, who did not research too deeply into where the dogs came from, would pack them off to the North, making a handsome profit.

Manuel put the rope round Buck's neck.

Buck would have known all this, if he read the newspapers. But this he could not do, for he himself was a dog. A splendid specimen, big and powerful with a white spot on his muzzle and under his neck, and the long-haired brown coat that he had inherited from his father, a St. Bernard. He owed his intelligence and perseverance to his mother, a Scottish sheepdog. He was now four years old and undisputed master of the dogs on Richter Miller's extensive plantations in sunny California.

Buck respected his master. Yet dignity and an innate pride prevented him from expressing this esteem in subservient behaviour, as the other dogs did. And if he listened to Richter and his servants, this was only because it was a mark of good breeding.

So when Manuel whistled to him one evening and went for a walk with him, he obeyed. Manuel was the gardener. He had gambling debts and was in urgent need of money.

Buck snapped at him in an uncontrollable fury.

In the twilight, they walked to the small station building. A man stepped out of an engine house and Manuel spoke softly to him. Then he stretched out his hand, and the other man dropped several gold coins into it and grunted, "After that, you can wrap up the goods!" Manuel sneered, got a thick rope out of his pocket and tied it round Buck's neck, who by this time was totally bewildered.

Up till now Buck had endured everything with a calm dignity, relying on his experience that although men often did things that were remarkable, they were never crazy. Yet when the man now suddenly and powerfully tugged on the rope and an unaccustomed pain shot through Buck's neck, he felt deeply insulted. He growled resentfully.

The man was frightened and leapt back, but at the same moment he jerked the noose even tighter. Buck desperately panted for air and pressed his forelegs into the ground. This was all in vain. He fainted.

Buck has to change his views

The shrill whistle of a locomotive roused Buck from his unconsciousness. He sensed the vibration of the train, heard the familiar hiss, which he recalled from earlier journeys, but before he had time to ponder on this, he saw a stranger's arm getting nearer. In an excessive explosion of fury, Buck snapped at it, the man shouted and then came that dreadful blow on the neck and darkness swam again before Buck's eyes.

When he came round again, he found himself in a narrow crate, and the only sound he heard was the monotonous rattle of iron wheels on rails. The journey lasted for many days. Now and again the strange man would appear, or a train official. Since Buck rejected every approach by furiously growling, he had only himself to blame that lack of food, and especially water, had rendered him half-mad

Buck looked round unbelievingly. He had never seen snow.

by the time the journey ended in Seattle. Several men carried the crate out of the truck and took it to a horsebox, which drove through the town and finally turned into a back yard. A boorish man was already waiting there. The most striking thing about him was his red jacket and an axe. He ripped the packing slats apart. With one leap Buck bounded into freedom and shakily took the offensive.

Silently, the man crashed a thick cudgel down on Buck's head. As Buck dizzily staggered to his feet, a second blow followed. Buck did not grasp where the abrupt pains were coming from. It was only when his next attempt to spring at Redjacket's throat failed, and even more violent and sharp pains followed, that he realized that they were caused by the cudgel. Now he had learnt that a dog was powerless against a flailing cudgel. Totally exhausted, he sank to the ground and lay there trembling.

The man bent down over him, gently stroked the fur round his neck, and murmured, "You know now who's the master round here. Just do as you're told, and we'll get along fine."

Indeed the man straightaway brought him a bowl of water and a large hunk of meat. Buck did not hesitate for an instant to take both out of the man's hands. He perceived that misplaced pride would be of little use to him. The only important thing now was to concentrate all his intelligence so as to master this new life, which threatened to not be easy.

In spite of his resentment of the blows, during the next few days Buck had to admit that Redjacket looked after the other dogs and himself properly. Dogs were brought time after time to his yard.

But it was not only dogs that came. All sorts of people came too. Some carried on long conversations with the man, pressed money into his hand and then went off with one or more dogs. One day a rather small man turned up, his face was as wrinkled as a prune. He glanced at the pack of dogs and then pointed at Buck. "How much?" he asked.

"Three hundred dollars, Perrault," replied the man with the red jacket and he laughed. "At last we've got a dog with brains. You know very well that the dog is worth a lot more!"

Perrault smoothed down Buck's coat, nodded and counted. Then he bought another dog: a good-tempered Newfoundland hound with a woolly coat, called Flock.

Redjacket did not say much. Perrault was acting on behalf of the Canadian government on this contract. He used the dogs to transport dispatches and letters to the far-flung settlements and camps, and his years of experience had taught him how to recognize a good dog straightaway.

He took the dogs to a freighter. There, they were locked in a cabin between decks where there were already other dogs. When the steamer's hooter sounded, and the ship got under way, Buck had the unbearable sensation that the last link with his sunny homeland of California was being broken.

One other man, apart from Perrault, cared for the dogs. His skin was dark and he was called Francois. Buck did not take a particular shine to either him or Perrault, but he could not deny Francois' care. He had to admit that both men regularly and punctually provided meat and drinking water. And most important of all, they were fair. This was proved when they met Spitz on the first day.

Spitz was a big, powerful, white-haired Eskimo hound and came from Spitzbergen. His clever face did not blind Buck to the fact that he was extremely malicious. And indeed, when Buck was momentarily diverted by Taff, a sullen and eccentric travelling companion whose pedigree was questionable, Spitz gobbled down the largest piece of meat from Buck's portion. Yet before Buck could bring the thief to justice, Francois' whip crashed down on the rascal's back. Jolly good, thought Buck, that was decent of that man.

The journey lasted for many days and the air which filtered through the numerous cracks was perceptibly cooler. At last the ship put into a port, its engines silent. Perrault and Francois coupled the dogs to each other and led them out on deck. Buck blinked incredulously at the planks; they were white and soft. And this white stuff was also falling slowly out of the sky. Buck snapped at it. For a second it burned his tongue, and cooled it at the same time, then it was gone. Buck growled uncomprehendingly, the people around him laughed, and Perrault shouted contentedly, "It's the first time he's seen snow, ha! ha!"

Buck quickly learned that snow held no further dangers. But this was not the case with the pack of dogs that he briefly met later in the yard of an inn. He had never seen such rough animals. They were unknown to Flock too, and he greeted the dog next to him in a friendly way. Then something inconceivable happened: the dog bit him and blood flowed down over Flock's shoulder.

Flock immediately put up a fight. A battle began which Buck realized would be fought to the death. He was unable to go to Flock's aid because the other dogs, who numbered about forty, formed themselves into a narrow circle around the combatants, growling threateningly. Flock defended himself despairingly, but to

They leapt on poor Flock.

no avail. Bleeding profusely from his several wounds, he stumbled and at that very moment all the other dogs were on him. Even before Perrault and Francois were able to separate the dogs by cracking their whips, Flock had been torn to shreds.

Buck found it hard to grasp that from now on he would be subject to new laws, laws which were very different from those in the middle-class south, where there were no packs of wild dogs. As he glanced back yet again at the remains of poor Flock, Spitz slunk past. A sneer played around his jowls. From this moment on, Buck hated the white dog.

Early on the following day there came the next unpleasant surprise. Buck was coupled to a sledge along with half a dozen dogs, like a horse. His pride was deeply offended; it did

79

Spitz headed the team as leading dog, and Buck quickly grasped what it was all about.

"Good Lord," stuttered Perrault and petted him approvingly. "Buck's a good dog and learns everything verrrry fast. A real devil of a dog."

In spite of this praise, Buck was full of animosity. It annoyed him that Spitz, of all dogs, should be the leader; he certainly would not dream of allowing himself to be punished by him. So he was thinking of something quite different, but this he very prudently kept to himself.

Buck succeeds

In the evening of the same day, Francois brought another dog to the tent. He had bought the dog for a very good price at a settlement. The dog was called Sollek and was a veteran sledge puller. However, he was blind in his left eye. For this reason, he found it intolerable when anyone approached him from the left side. Spitz was unaware of this. He became painfully aware of it when he tried, fawningly, to chum up with the newcomer. Sollek just gave a short growl and then snapped. Terrified,

not occur to him that he would have to work. His masters, however, did not give him long to ponder this humiliation.

With a crack of the whip and "Gee up, gee up!" they drove the team forward, and Buck quickly learned from the other dogs how and when to run or when to stop, so that the rope was always kept taut, and when climbing slopes, he had to be careful not to be slower than the shafts of the sledge. Taff, Billy, and Billy's brother Jerry were used to this kind of work already and would give him a quick but unmistakable nip, if he did something wrong. And as a last resort, if Buck made as if to snap back, Perrault or Francois would intervene with the whip. Buck did not resent this instruction, and gave no further grounds for complaint before evening.

A dog peered happily out of the hole.

The quarrel was suddenly interrupted as a pack of wild dogs greedily overran the camp which resulted in a dreadful confusion.

Spitz sprang back. But the spiteful gleam in his eyes revealed that from now on, Sollek had better keep his distance from him.

Night was falling and Buck looked for a warm sleeping place for himself in the tent. He was quite perplexed when Francois deliberately chased him out into the open air. It was bitterly cold outside. The other dogs had to go out as well and Buck wondered how he and the others would survive spending the night in the freezing cold. Shivering, he squeezed into a niche between two crates. After a short time, however, he left the draughty spot and went to see what the other dogs were doing. There was no sign of them. All the dogs had disappeared.

Somewhat at a loss, Buck ran over the frozen snow. Suddenly he trod on something white and soft and he heard an irritated growl-

ing. He immediately adopted an aggressive stance. Then he observed something quite remarkable. Billy was lying in front of him, in the snow, looking cheerfully up at him.

Buck's surprise lasted for only a few minutes. When he discovered Sollek in a similar hole a few metres away, he then knew how the other dogs were surviving the icy cold. All you had to do was simply to dig a hole in the snow and crawl in.

Everything went quite smoothly. After only a few minutes, his powerful claws had dug deep down into the covering of snow and he worked himself down so that there was barely anything of him to be seen. He curled up and could actually feel the warmth of his body spreading throughout the walls of snow. Content at last, he gave a short bark and fell asleep.

It snowed during the night and when Buck woke up in the morning, he saw only a dull darkness all around, although his eyes were wide open. He was extremely frightened but suddenly the feeling came over him that he was sitting in a trap, without knowing what a trap was. Instinctively, he tensed his muscles and then with a sudden spring, he leapt upwards. Snow sprayed everywhere, light flooded in and he caught sight of the dogs, the tent, the sledges and heard Perrault laughing out loud. At the same time, he remembered the night and the snow hole and immediately calmed down.

Perrault gave him a friendly slap on the back before he stammered to Francois, "Verrry clever dog! Learrrns quickly. Much quicker than the other dogs. Good! Good!"

The tent was dismantled and after all the

The men made moccasins to cover the dogs' paws which were painful and covered with wounds.

pieces of luggage had been stowed on the sledges, the journey continued. The team now comprised nine dogs and Perrault and Francois were therefore hopeful that they would reach their next destination, Dyea Canon, without further delay.

Every day, for days on end it was the same thing – hauling, rushing along, crack of the whip, curses, and on and on from morning to evening – pitching tents, eating, sleeping, dismantling tents, hauling, rushing along . . .

To begin with, the worst thing for Buck was the constant hunger. The animals were fed only once a day, and that was in the evenings. They were thrown pieces of frozen meat, and although Perrault or Francois threw nearly twice as much to Buck every time, because he was the biggest and most powerful, he quickly lost all his superfluous fat. His body became wiry and slender, his muscles hardened and definite changes permeated his thoughts, emotions and indeed his whole behaviour. Pride and good breeding quickly fell into oblivion. They counted for nothing vis-à-vis the hungry mob, none of whom would think twice about stealing the others' food. They did this out of pure self-preservation, and put up with the fact

Often they would be on the point of falling into the dangerously cracking ice. Then Perrault and Francois would set about the dogs furiously, spurring them on with curses, and coaxing them so as to save the precious cargo.

that their food would be stolen if they did not keep their wits about them.

Cunning was the order of the day in a situation where the cudgel, whip and law of the strongest formed the laws and in which the canine was dominant.

Over a long period of time, Buck had got used to eating things which previously he would have disdainfully declined, and he savoured the fine moment when he managed to steal a side of bacon from the tent without the theft being suspected. In contrast to this, he was justifiably proud of his ability to sense the slightest movements in the air, hours before midnight. Thus he always knew precisely where to dig his snow hole, in order to have the maximum shelter against the wind which blew up later and which frequently developed into a storm. He began to develop instincts which had lain dormant in his veins and of which he had previously been unaware. He was gradually being transformed into a beast of prey.

This was discernible in his relationship with Spitz, which was becoming tenser from day to day. The white dog only had to come near Buck and the latter felt his blood beginning to boil. He experienced an overpowering yearning to sink his teeth into the villain's neck.

The opportunity finally presented itself at La Barge Lake. Buck had dug his snow hole as soon as he was unharnessed and then prowled round Perrault, to get his portion of fish. He returned to his hole with the fish, only to find that Spitz had made himself comfortable in it, and was baring his teeth at him.

Buck crouched down, but just in time he remembered the fish. Since he could be sure Spitz would keep his distance, he devoted himself to his food but hardly had he wolfed down the last morsel, when he hurled himself, without any warning, at the intruder's flank and sank his sharp teeth into his neck. Spitz reared up, wriggled out of the hole, and both dogs immediately became entangled in an inextricable knot on the hard, frozen snow.

Now or never! flickered through Buck's mind, as his bloodshot eyes sought the other's flank. And then something totally unexpected happened which caused him to forget his fight with Spitz instantly. A huge shadow flew over the brawling dogs and at the same time a raucous barking began. Jerry howled and Francois and Perrault ran into the open, cursing and swinging their cudgels. The place was

*Buck listened to the huskies'
howling as if spellbound. They
had moved into the town when it
was full moon.*

suddenly swarming with strange dogs that
hurled themselves at everything they could get
their teeth into – supplies, leather bags, dogs
and humans.

"Damned creatures!" roared Francois and
crashed his cudgel down on one of the animals.
"Dogs! Blasted dogs!" shouted Perrault, and
his axe smashed down on the skull of a big, grey
animal who bore only a remote resemblance to
a dog, he was so emaciated and covered with
scars.

There were at least fifty or sixty such dogs,
starved to the bones. Madness seemed to glow
from their eyes and a battle for life or death
began. Yet however bravely the sledge hounds
defended themselves, they were no match for
the majority, and one after the other, they fled
across the iced-over lake, bleeding and yelping
with pain.

Buck stayed until the end, but when a
dozen wild dogs assailed him, it would have
been the end of him, had not Francois inter-

vened in the nick of time. Panting, Buck took
refuge by the tent and sank down in front of it,
totally exhausted. Spitz made the most of this
opportunity, and sprang at his neck. Buck was
gasping for breath. Yet before he could stand
up, Francois' cudgel rained down on the white
dog's head, and he sidled off, yelping.

The sledge dogs did not return before
morning. Jerry had lost an eye, others were
limping and only Sollek had emerged relatively
unscathed.

Perrault and Francois spent the whole
morning treating the dogs' wounds, and
assembling the strewn luggage. Leather thongs
had been gnawed, awnings torn to pieces, and
most of the provisions had disappeared.

The next stage of the journey to Dawson
was a unique ordeal. Perrault and Francois had
no alternative but to drive the dogs pitilessly on
as this was their only chance of survival. Dobby
had to be put down after only a few days. He
had developed rabies which he probably con-

tracted from the wild dogs.

For several miles, the route lay over the courses of iced-up rivers and the sledges fell in many times. Thanks in particular to Buck, they were always able to retrieve them. From day to day it became increasingly apparent that Spitz's authority in the other dogs' eyes was diminishing. They were becoming rebellious towards him and listened to him sullenly.

At last they reached Dawson and for nearly two weeks the animals were able to recuperate in the busy commercial town, with good food. Their torn paws, which Perrault and Francois had only been able to protect with moccasins made of leather rags, healed at last.

For Buck the rest brought a special experience. For the first time he encountered huskies, the descendants of wild dogs, who had not lost their original characteristics. At night, in the glow of the midnight sun, they would

The pack chased the hare, barking loudly. Buck raced immediately to the fore.

Again and again he tried to seize Spitz by the throat.

group together and join in a loud, complaining howl. This would have disconcerted Buck in earlier times, but now he listened to it spellbound and one evening he joined in. By doing this, he felt happier than he had for a long time.

Then it was time to make the return journey. The tension between Buck and Spitz became increasingly unbearable. It came to a head at Thakeena River. The dogs had unearthed an arctic hare and together with another pack from the nearby rural police station, had chased it over the iced-up river and into the woods. Buck led the chase.

As soon as he had come within leaping range of it, Spitz shot out of a bush, where he had been lying in wait for the quarry and bit Buck through the neck. The impertinence of this action made Buck see red. Baring his teeth, he threw himself on the white dog.

A relentless battle immediately broke out. Spitz was an experienced warrior. He had always beaten off any challenge to his leadership, but he knew that he had never encountered such an opponent as Buck. There was no mercy in this battle – there would not be two survivors. All his hatred for Buck, who had so often humiliated him and which he had kept pent up, now exploded. The same went for Buck, who was determined to pay the white dog back for his many treacherous actions, and above all for the scorn he showed when poor Flock died.

The other dogs sensed the drama unfolding before them. Silently and cowering, they gathered in a circle round the two rivals and followed every stage in the inexorable struggle.

Once Spitz fell to the floor, then it was Buck's turn. Each dog attempted to seize the other so that he could not bite him. Buck's shoulder was bleeding but he paid no attention to the pain. He managed to overturn Spitz and

in so doing, broke his left front paw. Yet the white dog would not give in. Growling, he sprang at Buck, but the leap fell short, he missed him and simultaneously felt Buck's jaw closing on his neck. Buck was oblivious to the sound of crunching bones. Still panting, but full of pride, he straightened up. Holding his head high, he turned back to the camp without even glancing at the dead white dog. Why should he? Why worry about a loser?

A record journey to Skagway

When Morgen Perrault coupled up the dogs on the following morning, and noticed that Spitz was missing, he grasped at once the significance of this. "Buck's like a couple of devils, Spitz was no match for him. He'll not be back! Damn and blast!"

Although the situation seemed to be cleared up, Buck was in for a considerable dis-

appointment: Francois put Sollek in as leading dog. This was absolutely intolerable and Buck expressed his opinion in no uncertain manner. With a mighty push, he jolted Sollek to one side. Sollek, for his part, did not have the slightest ambition to occupy the leading place. But Buck had reckoned without Francois and Perrault. Neither man seemed to realize that this place belonged to Buck alone. They kept trying to harness Buck to his old place, and when coaxing and curses failed, they tried the whip.

Now they realized just how much Buck had learnt. He skilfully dodged every lash and then pushed his way back to the leading place. At last the men gave up, as they could not afford to waste any more precious time. Perrault threw the whip into the snow and cursed in his anger and bewilderment, "That devil of a dog will have his way! Well, come here, Buck."

From this moment Buck set the pace in the team. The men and dogs both learned quickly that it was a good pace. Buck would not put up

At last they reached Skagway.

Buck kept pushing against Sollek and made it clear to him that his place was at the front, and that the position of team leader belonged to him alone.

with any breaches of discipline. Even lazy Piko, who hitherto had avoided anything strenuous, and feigned illness on many occasions, had to recognize that things were different. Buck dismissed all his tired excuses in the first hour with a fierce bite and Piko hauled as he had never hauled before.

Not only was there a new influence on the team, but the weather was good; still bitterly cold but no blizzards or squalls. The journey was accomplished in record time. In the camps and isolated police stations which they called at on the journey back, the team aroused considerable astonishment each time. People whispered to each other that this would be a record journey.

Their feelings were not misplaced. When Perrault and Francois finally brought their sledge and cargo into Skagway, the last hundred metres before the post office was transformed into a triumphal procession for the two popular carriers and their dogs. Never before

Summoning up all his remaining strength, Taff carried out his work, although he must have suffered agonizing pains.

had a team achieved the difficult and long journey from Dawson to their destination in such a short time. The rejoicing was understandable.

The dogs felt that they had accomplished something too. They were praised on all sides. Perrault and Francois and even complete strangers threw them titbits. Suddenly life seemed good. But this was short lived: quite unexpectedly the two men received a new assignment from the government but were not able to use the dogs. With tears in their eyes, they sold the team to a half-breed.

Buck was pleased that at least the four-footed chums were staying together, and since the half-breed and his men behaved decently to the dogs, Buck was determined that every animal should do his duty.

Although the work comprised an ordinary postal cargo, with no express goods involved, Buck found it very difficult as it required a good deal of care. The journey to Dawson became sheer agony for men and animals. The snow fell, almost without interruption, for

weeks on end.

The dogs' paws could scarcely grip in the soft snow, the runners would sink down to the bottom of the sledge, and ice formed on coats and harness. It seemed that the men suffered more than the dogs, nevertheless they looked after the dogs extremely well. They rubbed them down regularly, tended their wounds and often went without their own food so that they could give more to the dogs.

In spite of all this the dogs grew increasingly indifferent. They constantly felt ready to drop, and it was plain that every movement hurt them. Taff suffered the worst. Once when the sledge had got stuck again, he had strained himself while pulling it out and suffered internal injuries. He grew weaker from day to day, then suddenly he would howl, then whimper quietly to himself until the men finally knew that they had no alternative but to uncouple him and prevent him from working.

The faithful animal's behaviour changed in a most remarkable way. Mustering his last remaining strength in a supreme effort, he pushed his way to his usual place, which Sollek was now to occupy, and bit through the reins. As he did so there was such an imploring expression in his eyes, that they harnessed the dying animal again and he carried out his usual work until he collapsed. In the evening he sank down whimpering, and deeply moved, the half-breed put him out of his misery with a pistol.

A nightmare journey into spring

Buck underwent another traumatic experience during this journey. At night while asleep, he would imagine himself lying in a hole by a fire and next to him there would be a man crouching, dressed only in rags and staring down at the cudgel in his hairy hands, his tiny

Buck had only contempt for the three of them.

The half-breed put him out of his misery.

eyes glowering beneath his mean brow. Everything struck Buck as strangely familiar. Yet as soon as he began to reflect on it, the hole, the man and the crackling flames would vanish into the thick, grey mist.

When the team returned to Skagway after more than a month away, the dogs were barely recognizable as the journey had taken so much out of them. They were all reduced to skin and bones. They could hardly stand, and they felt weak and miserable. Piko hobbled on three legs, and Bud had dislocated his shoulder. Buck was completely exhausted too; he longed for peace and sleep. The dogs could not be used for top speed carrier deliveries for the time being, and so the men decided to sell the team as it stood, together with the sledge, as quickly as possible.

Early on the fourth day, two interested parties came forward. As soon as Buck saw them, he knew they had not the faintest idea of

Slowly, winter turned to spring.

place, the woman pulled out one at the bottom and declared that she must have that one close at hand and that it would have to go on top. At last, the dogs were made to haul. But the runners would not budge an inch. Charles and Hal seized their whips and heartlessly threatened the animals. This attracted more and more spectators.

One of them could stand it no longer and bellowed, "Can't you numbskulls see that the rockers are frozen solid?"

A few of the bystanders helped to shake the runners free but the dogs made no headway and, faced with the woman's nagging and the bystanders' scorn, the men unloaded the parcels, one after the other.

Whilst all this was going on, the dogs stood silent. They sensed that the days ahead would not be easy ones. Then a lash of the whip urged them on and they jerked violently. They chased down the steep slopes to the sea with the

life in the North. One, called Charles, was about forty years old, and had cold, watery blue eyes. The other was a good twenty years younger, and carried à revolver and long knife in his belt. He was named Hal.

They bought the team for a song and took it to a tent where a young, somewhat plump but fairly pretty woman was busily running about without actually achieving anything very sensible. Buck inspected the inside of the tent and his suspicions were confirmed; everywhere was untidy and he noticed a profusion of junk which might have been suitable in civilized towns but certainly was not appropriate in the raw North.

The woman was called Mercedes, she was Hal's sister and was married to Charles. All three began straightaway to put the sledge to the test. When he saw how clumsily they worked, Buck could only shake his head glumly. Awkwardly, they strapped on the inexpertly packed parcels and when these were all in

The man shook his head when Hal asked him about supplies.

sledge, and rushed on because the runners had long since overturned and scattered the freight wildly over a wide area.

Although the relationship between the dogs and their new owners had never been exactly cordial, it now became so much worse that Charles and Hal brought in six new dogs: five terriers and a newfoundland. They were as ignorant of life in the North as their masters. Buck had no end of trouble teaching them even a few of the basic rules of behaviour.

When it was time to leave on the following morning, Charles, his wife and brother-in-law strutted round boasting that with fourteen dogs, they had the biggest team for miles around. This being so, they should have carried the bulk of their provisions as food, but they had not thought of that.

Buck and his old companions were used to getting by with little food. But when they had to stand by and see the new dogs wolfing down two or three portions of food, with no understanding of rations, they grew angrier day by day. Mercedes, especially, would throw out food galore. It was not long before food became scarce. Furthermore the prospect of reaching Dawson City on schedule became increasingly unlikely. Nothing went right for the three humans. In the mornings they would waste precious time wrangling and quarrelling over who should do what work, and this would continue well into the night, with the tent only half assembled. The arguments usually ended up with Charles or Hal taking out their fury on the dogs.

So, instead of food, the dogs got beaten every day, either with the whip or cudgel. But the dogs had become so indifferent and hardened that they did their work until they dropped. Only Buck had a burning iron will to survive. He would not be broken. The lessons he learnt with Redjacket were too deeply ingrained and they had hardened him for ever.

Bud was the first victim of the agonizing journey. His dislocated shoulder caused him appalling pain. Although the freight was properly loaded, he, more than the others, felt the runners were getting more and more difficult

A punch knocked him down.

to haul. In the day time, the warmth of approaching spring was melting the snow and the runners would sink down into it. Bud had come to the end of his tether and one morning Hal shot him.

A few hours later, the vehicle encountered a very old Red Indian. After much bargaining, they exchanged Hal's revolver for an ancient horse skin. Cut into strips, this provided food for the animals over the next few days. As a result they all became ill and the terriers died.

The good-natured Billy succumbed to it a few days later. Hunger and misery had reduced him to hobbling around on three legs, yet he remained faithful and courageous until his strength failed him. Hal killed him pitilessly with an axe.

And when Krona simply collapsed and died shortly afterwards, Buck, Jerry, Kid, Piko and Sollek were the sorry remains of the team. They dragged the sledge, with the little

The sledge rolled upwards almost vertically, then sank into the ice.

strength left them, through the awakening spring, onto the suspiciously cracking ice of the Milky River as far as John Thornton's settlement.

Thornton was a weatherbeaten giant who had been trying his luck gold-prospecting at the river for some time, with fluctuating success. He shrugged his shoulders sympathetically when the strangers asked for provisions. He had almost run out himself.

"And you'll hardly get to Dawson with the dogs," he warned. "It's still a good few days away, over land."

Charles and Hal laughed in a superior way. "Over land? But we're going over the ice. We'll be there by morning."

Thornton shook his head. "It's too late to go over the ice. Just be glad you got this far. You must go over land."

"You worry too much!" sneered Hal, and cracked the whip around the dogs, who lay as if dead on the ground.

It was only after several more lashes that the dogs struggled to their feet. Except for Buck. He had grown accustomed to the pain, indifferent to everything.

An overwhelming fury seized Hal. He thrashed the animal like a madman and when this achieved nothing, he clutched at his axe. But he never managed to use it – Thornton's punch knocked him down.

He picked himself up with a roar, but then he saw the giant's expression. Without a word he turned away and Charles, Mercedes and the other four dogs followed him just as silently up the frozen river. The sound of whips cracking rang out again as Buck lay beside his saviour, exhausted, panting and so tired that he did not even raise his head when the air was filled with the sudden noise of creaking, cracking and screaming.

The sledge had been about half way to the other bank, when it had suddenly rolled. It had remained vertical for a few seconds, as if suspended, then it sank with men and animals into the cracking ice.

Buck becomes famous

The warm spring weather, together with the peaceful life in John Thornton's camp, made Buck quickly recover from the strains of the previous months. His coat regained its gleam, he put on weight again and most importantly he recovered his good temper and former spirit of adventure. He enjoyed life more than ever he had done in California.

Nobody forced him to work and he could romp around the paths and along the bank as much as he wanted. There were two other dogs, apart from him: the lovable setter bitch, Skit, who loved and mothered him from the outset, and the large, shaggy Nick who was a mongrel. Nick never challenged his authority; moreover he adored games, which usually took the form of a running race or a romp.

Actually, for the first time in his life, Buck felt really happy. And he experienced something which he had previously never felt – love. He had felt obliged to his previous masters in accordance with how correctly and sensibly they behaved, Perrault and Francois for example and even Redjacket, but this obligation had never gone beyond fellowship and friendship. But he loved John Thornton. Not violently or begging for affection, as Skit and Nick did, but with all his innate dignity. He would have gone through fire for Thornton. He knew just by looking at him what Thornton wanted, and it would never have occurred to him to deceive him or steal from him. The Scandinavian's mere presence had caused all the characteristics of the domestic dog, which had so nearly been obliterated in him, to come to the fore again.

Nevertheless he was no longer the same dog as before. From the hard life up in the North, where only the law of the canine counted and that consisted of simply killing in order not to be killed, he had developed certain

Only at the last moment did they manage to stop them falling into the menacing depths.

A mighty shadow flew up at the man and he screamed.

instincts which had aroused his almost forgotten role as a beast of prey, and these instincts would continue to influence his behaviour. He would not hesitate to steal things in the most underhand way if they appealed to him, unless they belonged to Thornton, Skit or Nick. He would tear any strange dog to pieces quite mercilessly if it threatened his authority in any way, and if he caught sight of any wild animal he would savagely chase it away.

One day two men arrived on a raft, having waved to Thornton from some distance. Buck observed them suspiciously and only when he ascertained that they were friends of his master who had been expecting them for a long time, did Buck generously tolerate their presence and permit them to stroke him.

But his whole affection belonged as always to John Thornton. He obeyed him unquestioningly. How unquestioningly would be shown in totally unexpected ways after the men had dismantled the camp and were making their way on the raft to Dawson.

One day, because of the wolves, they camped on the top of a steep cliff, one side of which was a perpendicular drop of almost a hundred metres down to the river. In the night the sound of the howling wolves floated up from the nearby woods. Buck stayed awake for hours, listening to the distant voices, the whining and moaning that was as familiar now as if he had grown up with it. If it had not been for Thornton, he would have rejected the last comfortable vestiges of civilization long ago and followed unhesitatingly the call of the wild. But he would not leave Thornton in the lurch under any circumstances. At the same time, his yearning for total freedom was getting more and more acute. Thornton sensed nothing of Buck's frame of mind; he only knew that he could count on the animal unconditionally. He was suddenly seized with the desire to put this absolute obedience to the test.

He leapt up abruptly, pointed over the edge of the cliff, towards the setting sun and called, "Buck! Jump!"

Buck did not hesitate for even a second. He crouched down, made ready to jump and leapt high into the air . . . and it was only at the last moment that Thornton just managed to grab him by his harness. They would both have plunged down into the abyss if Pete and Jack had not had the presence of mind to clutch them.

All colour drained from his face, Thornton petted the dog and whispered unintelligible words of apology, while Jack and Pete admiringly shouted at almost the same moment, "That dog's a miracle! Heaven help the man who falls out with him!"

They had the opportunity to get to know more about this side of Buck's nature a few days later in Circle City, a camping town which consisted of tents and which had sprung up only recently. It was actually a stranger who helped them to broaden their knowledge.

Nobody knew his real name – he was simply called Black Bert because of his black beard. When the three friends walked into the store, he was rolling drunk, bawling and setting about several harmless bystanders. Thornton, who towered above all of them by almost a head, went to some pains to settle the argument during the course of which he deliberately pushed Black Bert to one side.

It actually looked as if Black Bert was going to give in, but the very moment that Thornton turned away from him, he picked up a chair, and hit Thornton with it from behind. Before Thornton, who was only half conscious, was able to defend himself, Black Bert prepared to hit him again.

He didn't get that far. Like a shadow, Buck suddenly flew up at him, his teeth aimed at his throat. The man shouted and raised his arm to protect himself. It was this action that saved his life, for Buck's teeth now sank into the man's arm. Only on Thornton's command did he reluctantly release him.

Buck had done his duty. Proudly, he gazed at his master, but he still had a lot to learn about humans. Instead of understanding, as any intelligent animal would, that he had been entitled to injure the attacker, and instead of leaving it at that, people started shouting for an enquiry. He, Buck, who had only defended his master, was to be the accused. Blankly, he followed the strange proceedings in a dull room which was packed with people. Black Bert described angrily how he had been knocked to the ground for no apparent reason. Then it was John Thornton's turn and he described events in their true light, and then a stream of witnesses spoke and confirmed Thornton's account.

Much to the joy of the audience, Buck was pronounced by the judge to be free and from this day on, he became famous throughout Circle City and many other gold prospecting towns.

Over the next few days, the melting ice transformed rivers and brooks into mighty torrents. Travelling along the river by raft was becoming an increasingly dangerous adventure. The three friends kept their spirits up however and took short cuts here and there across narrower streams. But this often in-

Thornton managed to grasp the rope.

volved pulling the raft against the current.

Pete and Jack usually wound the rope round their shoulders and, accompanied by Buck, made their way, panting, to the bank, while Thornton would stand up on the raft and, by using a long pole, would steer clear of rocks and boulders.

In a gorge with a particularly dangerous current, Thornton lost his balance and lurched into the raging water. Desperately he fought for his life. All his friends' efforts to throw him a life-saving rope fell short; he was being irresistibly dragged towards a thundering waterfall.

Buck watched, whimpering with fear. And then, before Jack and Pete could grasp what he had in mind, Buck seized a rope, ran towards the waterfall and a little distance in front of it, leapt into the foaming river. He swam as if possessed against the current, and actually managed to reach Thornton, who grasped the rope with the little strength he had left. He was semi-conscious when Jack and Pete dragged him to the bank, and Buck had broken three ribs on the rocks. But his pain was nothing compared with the joy of having done something for Thornton.

The rest of the journey to Dawson City was accomplished without further incident. Almost the entire town was on the move. Every man wanted to try his luck during the short summer months and now the gold rush to the potential fortunes of the North was coming to an end. Some had already been tempted to go East, where it was rumoured that new veins were being discovered.

Thornton and his friends would also have preferred to go East because the region was less overcrowded, but they did not have enough money to undertake such a journey.

Then Thornton happened to be present when a dealer was boasting about what his team could do. "Any one of my dogs can pull two hundred kilos with no trouble at all!"

"Mine can pull five hundred!" countered Thornton.

A huge crowd of people had assembled and Buck felt that some great effort was expected of him.

The three friends worked for days on end, the gold making them happy.

Yet before he had time to regret this senseless statement, the bystanders took him at his word. "Five hundred? How much will you bet?" The roar spread wildly through the crowd and soon somebody was collecting coins, notes and nuggets. "A thousand dollars! Or do you want to back down, Mister?"

Thornton took a deep breath, glanced round at the challenging faces, petted Buck somewhat shakily and nodded, "It's a bet!"

The sledge stood in front of the saloon. The dealer had loaded it a short time before and, including its freight, it weighed five hundred kilos. Ten dogs were supposed to pull this heavy load but now, as the crowd steadily increased and men stood round shaking their heads, Buck alone stood harnessed to it. He seemed to feel that now everything was at stake. And when Thornton shouted, "Pull!" he jerked twice as powerfully, the runners which were frozen solid, broke out of the ice and the sledge began to move centimetre by centimetre, slowly at first and then faster and faster until it reached its goal.

A shout of joy went up. Thornton fell round the trusty animal's neck and Buck, still panting, became from that hour onwards the most famous dog in the whole of Alaska.

The lonely valley

The rumours that there was a lot more gold 'in the East' than had been hitherto discovered in the North grew stronger. But nobody knew exactly where in the East. People talked of an almost inexhaustible vein, but its secret had disappeared with the violent death of its finder. John Thornton and his friends dreamed of re-discovering it.

Using the money they gained from Buck's wonderful achievement, they set out with plenty of provisions. Firstly up the Yukon, then eastwards to the source of the Stewart River. It was a leisurely journey, with plenty of stops and as far as the dogs were concerned, it was a pleasure to pull the sledge or go hunting with their masters or stand by them for hours, watching them fish.

There was always plenty of game and they always found marvellous camping sites, but they did not find the mysterious mine, nor the log cabin which was supposed to be near it. And there was certainly no sign of the much longed for gold.

Spring turned to summer, the last snow was melting and the loads had to be transferred from the sledge to the men's shoulders. The trek led over hazy, blue mountains, through dark woods and green valleys, along bubbling brooks and silver lakes. They never encountered any other human. But they did discover a track which began abruptly in the wood and after a few metres petered out, just as abruptly.

Another time they came across a tumble-down cabin in a hidden clearing. On the table which lay covered in dust, was an ancient and totally rusty rifle, but there was no sign of its owner, who had certainly died a long time ago.

Thornton, Jack and Pete repaired the cabin in a few days and the small party spent the winter in it. Yet as soon as the first birdsong heralded the forthcoming spring, Thornton was eager to be off again.

For weeks on end they wandered again through the virgin countryside, in vain they searched the mountains and rivers which promised gold, and gradually they began to lose hope.

One evening they were camping by a crystal clear lake, which lay, surrounded by a thick forest, in the middle of a valley. It was here that

As Buck circled around him, the wolf gradually lost his fear.

the barely hoped-for miracle took place: in the morning when the three men were bathing in the cool water, they noticed, almost simultaneously, something glistening on the stony lake bed. Quick as lightning, Thornton dived. When he stood up again, spluttering, he kept shouting one word, "Gold! Gold! Gold!" The sand and gravel in his hands were interspersed with numerous yellow grains, some as big as the tip of a thumb.

The men roared with joy, danced like children, sang and laughed and could barely contain themselves, so great was their happiness.

In fact, they had not discovered the legendary mine, but the lake proved to be just as precious a goldmine over the next few weeks. Day after day they tirelessly washed away the sand and gravel and filled up little bags with about a thousand dollars' worth of the precious metal. In time they stacked up the little bags beside the tent and they formed a handsome pile. The lake's treasure seemed inexhaustible.

Those were wonderful weeks for Buck. Nobody bothered him when he lay at the edge of the wood or by the lake and daydreamed. Then he suddenly became increasingly aware of the presence of a ragged, thick-haired figure. It accompanied him hunting and since the stocky and muscular figure crept silently and stoopingly through the woods, Buck moved just as quietly. Each time that happened, a mysterious, arousing sound reached Buck's pricked ears. It was an eerie cry, which remained indelibly imprinted on his mind. He never succeeded in tracing its origin, it was simply there.

One night, however, when Buck had again been listening to this unfathomable note for hours on end, he suddenly felt his coat instinctively bristling, and his nerves stretched to breaking point. The call came nearer and nearer, the uncanny howling was now tangibly close.

Cautiously, Buck stalked into the wood, followed the noise and then stopped as if spellbound: in the gleaming moonlight a fully adult and lean wolf sat under a tree, its mouth wide open and pointing upwards to create the

Buck rushed at John Thornton impetuously, nearly knocked him over and refused to let him out of his sight for days.

penetrating call.

Buck stared at it without moving and he knew straightaway that the wolf had seen him too. With his body almost blending with the ground, and his tail fully extended, he crept gradually closer, at once friendly and threatening. Then the wolf leapt up suddenly and ran off. Buck was more excited than he had ever been before and chased after him.

The wolf finally turned round, and bared his teeth. But Buck led him to understand, through his behaviour, that he had no intention of starting a fight. Nevertheless the wolf, who was significantly smaller, worried for some time and always ran off until he eventually started a playful and friendly romp.

The wolf suddenly ran deeper into the wood and Buck followed him as if this were the natural thing to do. Hours went by. Buck thought that he had stepped back into a far distant time, which was opening up to him like an ever-clearing mist.

Towards midday they came to a river and as far as the eye could see, countless waves were mirrored against the sun. Buck suddenly remembered John Thornton. Without a moment's thought, he turned round. Whimpering and howling, the wolf ran beside him for over an hour, but Buck would not be put off. A longing drove him back to the camp. When the wolf realized that there was nothing he could do, he howled again loudly, and sat down.

When he got back to the camp, Buck smothered his friend with affection and would not let him out of his sight for a minute during the next few days. Full of love and remorse, he followed John Thornton's every movement.

But it was not long before he again felt very restless. He could no longer ignore his yearning to return to the land of the dark woods and glistening waves. He stayed away from the camp for days, running after the mysterious call, but however hard he searched he never saw the wolf.

This fruitless search made Buck wilder, and when he came across a bear that had been blinded by bees and was all the more dangerous as a result of this, he attacked him unhesitatingly. The battle lasted for hours and Buck finally emerged the victor. There was now nothing more to be frightened of. His authority was supreme. Large, strong and bloodthirsty, with a gleaming coat: a beast of prey who would only acknowledge another master for John Thornton's sake.

Of course the three gold prospectors noticed that each time Buck returned from one of his roving expeditions, he was more proud and self-confident. But they did not perceive how he was changing inwardly.

"He's a unique animal," Pete and Nick would nod admiringly. "There'll never be another like him in Alaska!"

Meanwhile Thornton said hardly a word. Yet when his hand stroked Buck's head and back, it was more than an acknowledgement. Thornton loved Buck as much as the dog loved Thornton. In such moments Buck forgot even the mysterious call, which soon afterwards made him wander restlessly through the woods again.

Soon it would be autumn and the time came when the elks began to migrate to warmer areas. These massive animals would stand self-confidently in the meadows, cropping peacefully and remaining imperturbable even when they drank. Their powerful hooves and mighty antlers were a protection which even the wolves and bears respected. They knew this, so when Buck dared to approach a gigantic buck, he remained quite calm. But after a short time the animal had fully realized that he had come up against an opponent that was as tenacious as any wolf and more cunning and powerful than a bear.

Buck immediately adopted an aggressive stance without getting anywhere near those huge antlers. He chased off the herd, without giving them time to breathe and when he had managed to separate the old elk from the herd in the evening, both knew who would be the final loser.

The elk fought for survival for days, but Buck remained merciless and remorseless. Again and again he circled his opponent, allowed him no rest, leapt at him as soon as he lowered his head to graze, chased him away from the rivers and growling and baring his teeth, he dogged his every footstep.

This continued for four days until that evening the elk lowered his head and sank to his knees. Seconds later, Buck dragged him down and immediately emitted his howl of victory, feeling more triumphant than ever before.

He felt that compared with many other victims, this elk had been a really worthy opponent. Indeed men had failed to catch him as was

Bees had blinded the bear and made him an even more dangerous opponent, and not to be under-estimated in his present fury.

At last Buck had found a truly worthy opponent.

proved by the broken Indian arrow which lay in his flank. Buck returned with the utmost pride and satisfaction. His directional instincts were as unerring as a compass needle. He ran faster and faster and as he did so, a remarkable unease came over him.

The nearer he got to the camp, the stronger he felt that something had changed. Even the song of the birds, the scolding of the squirrels, and the whispering wind seemed different. And when he suddenly came across an unknown track, every one of his nerves was stretched taut. He sensed a deathly stillness around him; every noise in the wood had suddenly faded and everything was absolutely silent.

Buck stopped dead in his tracks, sniffed in all directions and as the silence seemed threatening, he sensed that something terrible had happened. Silently and cautiously he followed the track.

It came to an end in a bush. Dear old Nick was lying quite still in a massive pool of blood, under a blackberry bush. Many arrows were sticking out of his shaggy coat. He must have suffered appalling agonies as he died.

A terrible anxiety swept over Buck as well as anger, which drove every thought from his mind. He ran on.

A little way on he found one of the sledge dogs which John Thornton had bought for the team in Dawson. He was bleeding from many wounds, he too was dead.

Buck lay down beside him and listened.

He had not been wrong. He heard voices coming from the direction of the camp, and a strange chant. Human voices, but those of John Thornton or Pete or Jack were not among them.

Buck crept slowly forwards. He did not get

As Buck leapt at the chief, his fury
knew no bounds.

The call of the wild

About a dozen Indians were squatting in a tight circle in front of the tent. Their half-naked bodies were swaying, they were singing and one of them, probably the chief, was dancing in the middle. They were Yeehats, and belonged to a tribe from Alaska.

Suddenly they moved together. They heard a howling which was more ghastly and gruesome than they had ever heard before. At the same moment a gigantic shadow flew over the squatting Indians and leapt at the chief. With a single bite, he ripped out his throat.

Buck had already whipped round and seized a nearby Indian, killed him in the same way and motivated by uncontrollable blood-lust, leapt at a third. Only now did the Indians begin to grasp that this was a matter of life or death.

The scent led into the lake, but did
not re-emerge from it.

far before he discovered Jack. He was lying crookedly under a tree with two arrows in his back, and his eyes gazed lifelessly out of a face, distorted with pain, into the deep blue sky.

Something died in Buck. Instinctively he hurried forward until he came to the edge of the wood and could see the lake and the camp. The monotonous song rang endlessly in his ears. Every clear thought he had was destroyed by the beating of countless hammers, which penetrated every fibre of his being.

For some seconds, Buck stared at the tent and at the whole area, which he knew so well. A boundless fury, a rage such as he had never before experienced overwhelmed him. A burning hatred and this passion became so intense that he did not realize when he suddenly express-ed all his love for John Thornton in a terrifying and bloodcurdling howl. Then he lost his head and without reflecting any longer, he charged out of the protective wood.

But they were sitting too closely together to be able to seize their weapons. They shouted, screamed with fear and terror while the mighty animal raged in their midst, crunching, biting and tearing necks, arms and legs. One of them managed to throw his spear but in the confusion of flesh and blood, he pierced one of his own men.

Only a few managed to run off, quivering with panic and terror, but even fewer managed to escape. Pitilessly, Buck chased them, harassed them and when he had got them down, he tore them to pieces. The rest scattered in all directions and it was many days before they found each other again.

When Buck had given up the chase, he went back to the lake. He went into the tent and found Pete. The Indians had smashed his skull. And then he picked up a scent, which bore the marks of John Thornton.

He followed it, his muzzle pressed close to the ground, whimpering quietly. It led him far away from the bank to an area where mud and swamp made it dangerous to go any further. Skit, the brave setter bitch lay among the reeds, her bleeding forepaws dangling lifelessly into the water. Beside her John Thornton's scent disappeared into the lake. Into the lake, not out of it. Now Buck finally knew that he would never see his friend again.

He felt an inconsolable emptiness inside him, a hunger which ached because it was not the kind to be appeased with food. It was the hunger for revenge and Buck drove himself on as if following an unwritten law. During the weeks to come, Buck chased restlessly through the woods and woe betide any Yeehats he came across. Buck showed no mercy. He had finished with humans forever.

After each hunting trip, he came back to the lake with the slowly decaying tent. And then he would listen again to the mysterious call which came to him from far away. Yet when, one moonlit night, a pack of hungry wolves appeared on the spot, he sprang among them recklessly, tore out the throat of the largest and broke the necks of two more. For a moment the wolves were paralysed with fear.

Buck stared only briefly at the place which he knew so well.

Then they all fell on him. It was a fight to the death. Buck had to summon up all his cunning, speed and intelligence to fend off the savage animals who were motivated by a frenzied hunger and bloodlust. Finally he emerged as the victor. The survivors retreated, yelping and whimpering and bleeding from numerous wounds. They formed a wide circle around the mighty animal who was so like them, but much bigger and stronger and wilder.

Baring his teeth, Buck confronted each of them. At last a lean wolf crept slowly nearer to him, on all fours as a sign of submission. Buck listened and suddenly remembered something; in this gaunt wolf he recognized the companion with whom he strayed, so long ago, to the land of the silver waves. He squatted down on his back legs, opened his terrible jaws and began to howl. The gaunt wolf immediately joined in and then the whole pack produced the eerie call, that all-pervasive call of the wild.

The Yeehats still whisper about the time that the wolves suddenly grew bigger and about their ancestor, who was stronger than any wolf there had ever been and who had a white spot on his muzzle and on his chest.

Sometimes he was seen in the moonlight, a distant, unreal and eerily gigantic shadow. He was known as the "phantom wolf".

The Indians would only speak in whispers about the 'phantom wolf', who was so different from all previous wolves.

ROBERT LOUIS STEVENSON

Treasure Island

TO THE
HESITATING PURCHASER

If sailor tales to sailor tunes,
Storm and adventure, heat and cold,
If schooners, islands and maroons
And Buccaneers and buried Gold,
And all the old romance, retold
Exactly in the ancient way,
Can please, as me they pleased of old,
The wiser youngsters of to-day:

– So be it, and fall on! If not,
If studious youth no longer crave,
His ancient appetites forgot,
Kingston, or Ballantyne the brave,
Or Cooper of the wood and wave:
So be it also! And may I
And all my pirates share the grave
Where these and their creations lie!

ROBERT LOUIS STEVENSON
Treasure Island

The old buccaneer

Squire Trelawney, the lord of the manor, Dr. Livesey and the other men have asked me, now that we have returned safe and sound from our adventures, to write down everything that happened, without omitting anything. So I will begin with the day in 1743 when the man with the sabre-cut scar appeared at our door.

At that time my father was running the inn called *The Admiral Benbow* and since he was ill, my mother and I had to do most of the work. It was a cold morning when a tall, rough-looking man came up the road. His tarred pig-tail hung down below his blue sailor's jacket, his face was disfigured by a scar and his hands were as broad as shovels.

The man stopped in front of the door, glanced inquiringly around the small, quiet cove, then turned back to my father. "Nice place here, I like it. Many people staying, friend?"

"I'm afraid not," admitted my father.

"Suits me. Hoy!" He called to the man who had accompanied him, pushing a handcart with a heavy seaman's chest on it. "Have yourself shown up to my room and take up the trunk. I'll stay here in front of the anchor." Again he turned to my father: "You won't have much work to do with me here, friend. I'm a simple soul, always happy with bacon, eggs and a swig of rum. The main thing is that I'm left in peace. Take this to start with," he threw four gold coins carelessly on the counter, "and tell me when it's been used up. My name? Nothing to do with you, just call me Cap'n. Understand?" The sailor had spoken in such a commanding way, obviously used to being obeyed, that my father could only nod in agreement. While our new guest was inspecting his room, the man who had brought him here explained to us: "He came yesterday by mail coach from Bristol and stayed overnight in the *King George*. He made enquiries about all the ale-houses along the coast and finally settled for this one, apparently because it is so isolated."

During the next few weeks we had plenty of time to get used to the Captain. We soon noticed that he did not actually want to see anybody. It was clear that he wanted to be seen even less. Every time an unknown traveller came along the road, he disappeared into the darkest corner so that he could carefully study the newcomer. I had also got used to observing the comings and goings of the tavern much more attentively than before. It was not just that I sensed, I knew that something secret cloaked the Captain. Only a few days after he arrived, he beckoned me over to him one evening when nobody else was paying attention and whispered: "You seem to be a bright boy. What was your name again? Ah yes, Jim, Jim Hawkins. Listen here, I'll reward you. You'll get a fourpenny bit every month if you tell me as soon as you see a sailor with only one leg approaching. Do you understand? A man with a crutch because his left leg is missing."

The Captain seemed worried about this one-legged sailor. I noticed that he consoled himself more often with increasingly large glasses of rum. He could sit silently for hours, always with a bottle in front of him, huddled in a corner from which he used to stare unswervingly at the street and cove through a narrow window. Yet in the evenings when the regular customers who were local fishermen and builders came in, he would boast of his adventures all over the world and throughout the seven seas. If all his dreadful tales were to be believed, he had spent his entire life among bandits and murderers. Robbery, looting and the most infamous deeds of violence sounded like normal events when he described them, and woe betide us if we did not all heartily laugh with him as soon as he felt moved to laughter. Since this was usually the case when he recalled all those who had come to a shameful end on the gallows, the customers refrained from shuddering.

Yet they always came back. The Captain

What struck me most was the heavy seaman's chest, with its welded iron bands.

livened up their humdrum lives. So they would meekly accept the insults and ghastly curses which he would hurl at them if they did not loudly join in his songs, which he would bawl to himself at the most inappropriate times:

"Fifteen men on the Dead Man's Chest –
Yo-ho-ho and a bottle of rum!
Drink and the devil had done for the rest –
Yo-ho-ho and a bottle of rum."

But one evening when he was carrying on particularly badly, and my mother and I were very afraid that our customers would leave us once and for all, Dr. Livesey arrived. He wanted to see my father, whose health had deteriorated alarmingly in the previous few days. After the Doctor had treated my father, he sat down in the public bar with an old acquaintance and began conversing with him. He paid no attention to the bawling Captain until he suddenly roared, "Silence on deck." All the customers fell silent, only Dr. Livesey went on talking as if he had not heard anything. Furiously the old man leapt at him, drew out his knife and staggered towards the doctor.

Our doctor gazed at him icily, and equally icily, his lips barely open, said to him, "If you don't sit down calmly and immediately, I'll have you hanged! This I swear in my capacity as a public official. And remember this! If the slightest complaint reaches my ears, I'll have you thrown in the local stocks. I won't tolerate riff-raff here!"

For a moment it seemed as if the Captain would rush at Dr. Livesey and plunge his dagger into his breast. Yet he suddenly turned and, without saying a word, he stamped out of the room.

From that day on, the Captain grew more and more sullen. He also seemed to come down more frequently. Moreover he did not make any arrangements to pay us anything towards board and lodgings and so my mother and I hoped that he might at last be moving on. But this was wishful thinking. On the contrary, something happened that as I now know was only the harmless beginning of the worst ex-

I heard the noise of a stool being thrown and then I saw both men rush at each other.

periences that have ever befallen me.

One bitterly cold morning in January, an ailing, sallow-skinned man rode up to the door. I noticed immediately that two fingers of his left hand were missing. His grappling knife revealed him to be a seaman. He demanded rum and then pointed to the table which was laid for the Captain and asked, his eyes glittering, "Is that for my mate Bill, then? Where's he hiding?"

"If you mean the Cap'n, he's gone down to the cove and will be back soon."

"Then I'll just wait. My old Bill will be pleased," declared the stranger and I dared not voice my doubts. Now I'll make it short: the Captain was certainly not pleased; naked fear glittered in his eyes when he caught sight of the customer and he simply muttered, "It's you, Black Dog. So you've found me then. What do you want?"

Unfortunately the two men sent me out of the room at that point and I did not manage to catch anything of their conversation until I suddenly heard the Captain roar, "No, no. And if you're talking about hanging already, then we may as well all hang!" At the same moment a chair crashed against the wall, Black Dog screamed, I rushed into the room and saw exactly how the old man with the knife flew at the seaman who for his part was trying to stab the Captain. But the old man, in a towering rage, was more than a match for him, and when Black Dog realized this, he cursed hideously, then sought his safety in flight.

The Black Spot

The Captain was a terrible sight as he stood at the open door, his arm wildly thrashing as he shouted appalling threats after the fugitive. Then he turned round, reeled somewhat and gasped, "Rum, Jim, rum!"

Yet before I could get him a glass, I heard a muffled crash. The Captain lay gasping on the floor, his eyes rolling strangely.

110

"He's dying," my mother moaned. "What a disgrace for our house, and your poor father is ill!"

Fortunately at that moment, Dr. Livesey rode up the snowy road. He merely glanced at the unconscious man, helped us to carry him upstairs, and said, "Don't worry, Mrs. Hawkins, he's not dying. Not yet. It was just a stroke, he'll be over it in a week. But the very next glass of rum could cause his death." Then he went to see my father who was lying in a deep fever. But before he left he pointed to the tattoos which covered the old man's arms. One was of a girl's head. Below it was written 'Billy Bones' Sweetheart'. Dr. Livesey was disturbed. "There was once a dreaded buccaneer, a pirate called that," he murmured. "Pirate riff-raff; even the gallows are too good for them."

Shortly after the doctor's departure, I took the Captain his medicine. He had regained consciousness, was rolling his eyes in a terrifying way and asked, "How long do I have to lie here?"

"For a week at least, in Dr. Livesey's opinion."

"A week! Quickly Jim, bring me a glass of rum and I'll show you how soon I can be back on my legs."

"Rum would kill you."

"To hell with that quackery! I'm the only one that knows what's the best thing for me." He struggled to his feet and winked at me confidentially. "Just a little glassful, Jim, a little glassful. You'll see, it'll help me."

I was not convinced of this but since I was worried that he might begin to rage, I let myself be persuaded. After he had greedily emptied the glass, he sank back in the pillows and groaned, "A week? In that time they'll have long since brought me the Black Spot. But it won't do them any good, I'll fool them again."

"The Black Spot? What's that?" I wanted to know.

The Captain shook his head. "I'll explain that to you when the time is right. Did you see Black Dog?" he asked suddenly. When I nodded, he went on quietly and urgently, "Now listen to me carefully, Jim, I'll tell you a secret

The Captain allowed me to put his hand in the blind man's.

and woe betide you if you don't keep your mouth shut. They're going to slip me the Black Spot. Well, that's something of a warning. You know they're after me here. Black Dog and One-Leg and all those left from the old gang, from Flint's crew. Yes, I was his coxswain on the *Walrus* and I was the only one there when he died." He gasped, panting for breath. "Jim, listen to every word that I say to you. They saw it on my trunk. They already know why they want it. But you've got to help me so that they never get it. Now listen, keep a good look out, Jim, and if you see Black Dog or even the one-legged man coming, or if they slip me the

*My mother and I
opened the trunk.*

Black Spot, Lord knows how, then jump on your horse – you can ride, can't you? – and ride hell for leather to that quack."

"To Doctor Livesey?" I gasped unbelievingly.

"Are there any others? He must get everyone together; bailiffs, court officials, customs guards, and come with them straightaway here to the anchor. All Old Flint's accursed crew, unless they've fetched the devil, will fall into their hands. Have you understood all this, Jim?"

I was so confused that I could only nod dumbly. He clutched my hand. "Mind, not a word yet, to anyone! Promise me!" His voice was growing steadily fainter.

"Yes, yes," I said uneasily and he finally

fell asleep.

During the next few hours I became increasingly worried that I had shared in a secret which was bound to hold great danger for us all, and about which I was not allowed to tell anybody. But when my beloved father died that same evening, in the grief of his death and all the disruption which befell my mother and myself, I forgot about the conversation with the Captain. He did not mention it again, although on the day after the funeral, he had recovered so well that he was able to sit in the public bar and in spite of all the Doctor's warnings, drank copious amounts of rum.

Half-drunk, he stared in front of him and kept on singing his favourite song about fifteen men on a Dead Man's Chest. He would not be distracted from this when outside could be heard fumbling footsteps crunching along in the snow and then a piteous voice called out, "Won't anyone help a poor blind man, who lost his sight in the service of the King?"

Sympathetically I hurried out and saw a pitifully ragged person, who immediately clutched my arm and held it in an iron grasp. "Hey now," he said, "you're a fine lad. And now take me to my friend Bill!" He seemed to sense the hesitation and continued angrily, "Or shall I break your arm, friendly like?"

What else could I do but take him over to the Captain's table. The old man stared at him glassy-eyed, and meekly allowed me to put his hand in the blind man's as the latter had ordered me to do. And almost in the same instant the blind man tore himself free and hastened to the door with an assuredness which would have done a sighted person credit.

"The Black Spot! Jim, they've slipped me the Black Spot!" exclaimed the Captain, and flushed angrily. "But they'll make a mistake. We've still got six hours left. Go and fetch the qua. . ." The Captain suddenly clasped his neck, gasped and slumped to the floor where he lay motionless! A heart attack had brought his life to an end.

For a few minutes I was paralysed but then I thought about the men who had so terrified the Captain. They were bound to come soon and might murder us to seize the trunk. I called my mother. She listened to everything much more calmly than I had anticipated and decided: "Fetch the village people, they'll protect us. And as for the trunk – never mind what happens to it. I'll just get the money owing to us out of it."

It was already dark when I got to the village inn and asked the men there for help. But nobody would come with me. They were plainly scared, though some offered to go and warn Dr. Livesey. Furiously I went back and helped my mother to break open the chest. It contained a lot of worthless rubbish but also some gold and silver coins. My mother took only what was owing to us, but while she was still counting out the amount, I heard voices outside, the blind man's among them, and wild

blows on the door. "We must run!" I shouted to my mother and hurriedly clutched a pouch which was lying at the bottom of the trunk. "Quickly, the back door!"

I do not know what would have become of us if Dr. Livesey and our Squire had not arrived at the last minute with several armed men. There was much wild shooting but all the bandits managed to escape, except one: the blind man. He lay dead in the snow.

"I'd just like to know what they were really doing here," considered Squire Trelawney, after we had recovered a little from the terrible ordeal. The answer was found in the pouch from the trunk. It contained a map of an island in the South Seas, with all the necessary information. On the map itself, mountains, valleys and inlets were drawn in. Several were labelled with names and strange signs.

We gazed, full of curiosity, at the sketch.

Suddenly Dr. Livesey shouted, "This map shows where that pirate Flint buried his treasure! A huge fortune!"

The voyage of the *Hispaniola*

Dr. Livesey and the Squire pored over the map until late into the night, studying the notes on the front and back. They became more and more excited about the map's value and did not doubt its authenticity for a moment. Then at last Squire Trelawney stood up as straight as a ram-rod, glanced at the Doctor and declared, "I'll buy a ship in Bristol, have it fitted out there and in three, no, two weeks' time at the latest, we'll be on our way to Treasure Island! Livesey, you'll come along as ship's doctor, and you, Jim, will make a fine cabin boy."

I was struck dumb by this surprising news. Dr. Livesey raised some objections but Squire Trelawney dismissed them all with a sweeping movement of his hand. "Close your practice,

Doctor, I'll stand the cost of any possible loss. I'll have *The Admiral Benbow* redecorated from top to bottom, Jim. And I'll find a capable boy to help your mother. There, it's settled. Early tomorrow I'll set off for Bristol to get everything moving. Dr. Livesey, you'll have things to do in London," the Doctor nodded, "and Jim will live in the manor until we leave and make all the arrangements with Redruth, Joyce and Hunter, my loyal servants, whom we'll take with us on the voyage, of course. And remember, absolute secrecy!"

"You're the one who should remember that," grumbled Dr. Livesey in rather an irreverent way. He was not the only one who knew about Squire Trelawney's tendency to gossip. But he was not paying much attention to what we were saying. He was thinking of some new idea every other moment and would tolerate no opposition. So, the following day he travelled to Bristol, the Doctor took himself off to London and I waited impatiently in the manor for the final orders to leave.

"Black Dog!" I shouted.

At last the Hispaniola set sail from Bristol; the sea adventure was beginning.

Considerably more than three weeks had passed when a letter arrived. The servants and I were ordered to go to Bristol. I took my leave of my mother, for whom Squire Trelawney had found a hard-working boy, and after a few days the Squire and the Doctor welcomed us in the area of the town by the docks.

"I managed to buy a magnificent ship called the *Hispaniola*," gushed Squire Trelawney. "It was much more difficult to find a good crew, but I had some luck there, too. I met an old sailor, who now runs a tavern by the port, because one of his legs was shot off. A first-class chap, and with his help, I quickly got a fearless crew together. And I took him on as ship's cook. He's called John Silver. Then I bumped into Mr. Smollett, an experienced Captain, and an equally capable Mate called Arrow. We're off to sea tomorrow!" His whole face was beaming as he handed me a letter. "Take this to John Silver. His tavern is easy to find."

His inn was right by the port and was called 'The Spy-glass'. But when I saw John Silver, I was terrified. Not because of the crutch with which he walked as nimbly as a healthy man, but because of the fact that the whole of his left leg was missing. Could this be the man so feared by the deceased Captain? When one of the customers hurriedly disappeared, I was even more startled. "Black Dog! After him!" I shouted.

"Black Dog," said John Silver in a puzzled voice, "I don't know anyone of that name." But he immediately sent two sailors after the fugitive and in a threatening voice, he took the sailor who had been sitting next to Black Dog to task. "Who was that fellow? Speak up, Morgan!"

The other protested, "No idea. I've never seen him before."

"Is that so? Darn! But I've seen him before with that blind beggar," Silver remembered

*I was so frightened
of being discovered,
that I was shaking.*

angrily. "And now I'd better look after my precious gold."

His suspicions were justified. Black Dog had escaped his pursuers. "He'd better stay well away from me," snarled John Silver and when I saw his face, any lingering doubts as to his integrity were dispelled. No, this man was all right. He read the letter and nodded to me in a friendly way. "All right, Jim, tell Squire Trelawney I'll be on board tomorrow in good time with all the men."

I spent the night on board the *Hispaniola*. Beforehand, however, I went along to the cabin where the Captain was also visiting Squire Trelawney and Dr. Livesey. He was a gaunt, stern-looking man and was explaining in rather a cross way, "If I'm to be Captain, I would have expected that the choice of crew be left to me. It is scandalous that I had to undertake to be responsible for the ship, sail under sealed orders, only to hear from the *sailors* that

we're off on a treasure hunt, to an island whose latitude and longitude are known in every tavern. Do you realize that this could mean murder and manslaughter?"

"None of us has talked," objected Squire Trelawney, unconvincingly, while Dr. Livesey wanted to know, "What would you advise then, Mr. Smollett?"

"Who can you vouch for?" was his question.

"Us four here in the cabin and my three servants," replied the Squire.

"Good, then you, the servants and the boy will take the cabins on the quarterdeck. And of course, weapons, powder and ammunition will have to disappear from the crew's quarters. They can all be stored aft, first thing tomorrow morning."

The Captain was not an easy customer to deal with; he could read our feelings from our faces, and added harshly, "Either I give the orders or you can look for another man." Squire Trelawney was furious but gave way and the following morning saw the beginning of the move to which I actually had no objections, as well as the reloading. While this work was in progress, John Silver arrived on a jolly-boat and he shouted harshly, "Who ordered this?"

"The Captain," replied a sailor.

"That's all right then," nodded Silver. He reported to Squire Trelawney and took himself straight up to the crow's nest. Then he beckoned to me, "Come up and help me, Jim. You're a smart fellow, I saw that straightaway. I'll make a useful seaman out of you."

I have to admit that I liked Silver. Even the sailors who were rough, bold souls would obey him instantly and would tell each other the most fantastic yarns about his bravery and fearlessness. On these occasions, Long John Silver always exhibited the appropriate modesty owed to his seniors. He seemed to know their every wish and was always on the spot when he was needed.

Even Captain Smollett had to admit, after a few days on the high seas, that he was "a fine man, quite different from that constantly drunken Mate, Arrow. I've been watching him the whole time and can't discover where he's getting his rum from."

"Land, land," shouted the man in the crow's nest, and everybody ran to the rail.

Nobody discovered that, because Arrow was swept overboard in the first storm and never seen again. "That saves me having to put him in irons," was Captain Smollett's only comment on the disaster.

We managed fairly well without a Mate, because Squire Trelawney had served in the Navy and was quite capable of taking the helm, and two of the ship's crew, Anderson and Israel Hands, were excellent at the job.

Thanks to Captain Smollett's efficiency and to the first-class facilities of the *Hispaniola*, our voyage proceeded with no further incidents and whenever I could, I would sit up in the crow's nest with John Silver and listen to his stories. He was a clever and well-read man and was adept at choosing the right words when conversing with me or the 'gentlemen'. Quite the opposite to Cap'n Flint!

This was the name of Silver's parrot, reputed to be many, many years old, who mostly perched on his shoulder, and who screeched the filthiest abuse in many different languages. He would scream "All hands stand by to fight!" or "Pieces of Eight! Pieces of Eight!" which he probably picked up from some pirates who had just stumbled upon treasure. "Scoundrels, idle riff-raff!" and "I'll have 'e tarred and feathered!" also formed part of Cap'n Flint's seemingly inexhaustible vocabulary.

We were approaching the area in which the island lay, when I went to fetch an apple from the cask which stood on deck and from which anybody could help themselves. Since it was almost empty, I climbed right into it. I was just on the point of getting out when I heard Silver's voice. He sat down beside the cask and, thereafter, I overheard a conversation in which almost the entire crew took part, and which made my blood run cold.

"Listen now," said Long John Silver, "you know that I was Old Flint's quartermaster and I know he never had a better crew than you, and we all know that we're the last of Old Flint's gang, and if you don't control your damned impatience, you'll end up on the gallows one day. We've only got to pick up the treasure and everything'll be just dandy. But have you numbskulls just considered how we get back? No, of course not. I reckon we'll just behave ourselves 'till the treasure's safely on board. And I might not attack until Smollett's brought us into the trade winds. But I can tell by your faces that you're not really serious. Well, as soon as they've found the treasure and brought it back on board, we'll take over the ship. We'll be able to steer into the trade winds by ourselves."

"And what'll happen to Trelawney and the others?" asked Israel Hands.

John Silver laughed. "What do you mean? Dead men don't talk, that's what Old Flint always said and I took good note of it. And you listen to this, Captain Smollett is mine!"

At that very moment, the look-out in the crow's nest shouted, "Land ahoy! Land!"

A loud clattering of footsteps told me that everyone had rushed over to the railing. Shaking from head to toe, I clambered, unnoticed, from the cask.

Dangerous landing

The outlines of the island lay before us in the white moonlight, rising blackly out of the shimmering sea. In the general excitement, I remembered that we were in mortal danger and it was not long before I made my way to Squire Trelawney's cabin, to tell him, Dr. Livesey and Captain Smollett about Silver's infamous plot. My words caused the greatest consternation, of course, especially in Squire Trelawney's case. But he was the first to pull himself together. "Captain Smollett," he turned back to the captain, "I'm sorry that I didn't pay enough attention to your doubts. I confess that only your experience can get us out of this situation."

"Thank you," replied Captain Smollett abruptly, and after reflecting, he declared, "As long as they don't know which of us has the map and where he's hiding it – and I don't want to know either – Silver will risk anything to suppress the planned mutiny. But I doubt he'll succeed. Gold lust makes men unpredictable. One false word or one false move from us which might arouse Silver's suspicions and we're done for. I propose that as soon as we drop anchor, we let the whole crew go ashore, however contradictory that may sound. That'll give Silver (our best ally at present) the chance to persuade his bandits to bide their time. They still need us to find the treasure. And while they're ashore, we'll stay on board. If the wind is right, we might even manage to simply sail away."

So none of us betrayed our feelings while Captain Smollett spent the next few hours, helped by the zealous Silver, trying to locate a suitable anchorage. We found it marked on the map as Kidd's Anchorage, in a cove, enclosed to the west by Haulbowline Head, and to the east by White Rock. To the south, a barren island (the so-called Skeleton Island), pro-

tected the natural harbour against even the wildest storms.

As soon as we had dropped anchor, Captain Smollett ordered Long John to assemble the crew on deck. He then delivered a short speech to them, in which he praised everyone's efficiency. "As a token of thanks for your services," he called at last, "Squire Trelawney is presenting you with a small barrel of rum, and whoever wants to, can go ashore and have a look round. If you hear a cannon fired this evening, you will be warned that you should return on board."

"Three cheers for our Captain, three cheers for Squire Trelawney!" shouted John Silver hypocritically, and the men joined in loudly.

A few minutes later, two boats with thirteen men under Silver's command, cast off with the little cask of rum. Six men had prefer-

I leapt to the shore and ran headlong into the undergrowth.

red to stay on board. They were lolling around the forecastle. Captain Smollett, Squire Trelawney, Dr. Livesey and the servants, Hunter, Joyce and Redruth had moved inconspicuously back to their cabins. I was the seventh, who could be relied on by law-abiding souls, yet I, of all people, was suddenly motivated by a reckless idea.

At the last minute, I leapt into one of the boats, which had cast off. I had to go with them to the shore. Why, I did not know. Perhaps God was the guiding force.

It was only as the boat was approaching the shore that I became aware of the danger into which I had so thoughtlessly leapt. What if Long John Silver used me as a hostage? What a triumph for him if I were to fall into his hands. I'd have to prevent that. So before the men in the boat could realize what was wrong, I ran away from the beach and threw myself into the undergrowth. They roared after me but after a little time I no longer heard them.

But suddenly I became aware of Long John Silver. In the nick of time I crouched

"Have you got any cheese?" implored the man.

down behind the trunk of a huge evergreen oak and saw him standing with one of our sailors on an open slope. I could hear every word both men said. I gathered, to my astonishment, that the sailor apparently would not take part in the mutiny. Long John tried in vain to persuade him, but amidst his cajoling, threatening tones, I heard, coming from the coast, the sudden, shrill death cries of a man.

"He wouldn't join in either," laughed Silver sneeringly and when the sailor desperately tried to run away, Silver stabbed him, in cold blood. He then whistled loudly. I was seized with horror, and rushed deeper into the wood.

Up to this point the ground had been fairly marshy. The higher I climbed, the fresher and drier the air became. Gradually the trees were receding, a hill-top rose before me and behind it I saw towering like a flattened skittle, the mighty rock which had been labelled "Spye-Glass Hill" on the map. Totally exhausted, I sat down on a stone and with a sinking heart, reflected on my hopeless situation. I was startled by a curious sound.

But it was too late. I could neither run away, nor hide. From the slope a man was walking rather hesitatingly towards me. He looked completely wild; a long beard covered his animal-skin clothes and curiosity jostled with fear in his eyes. When he was a few yards away from me, he sank to his knees, wrung his hands and begged, "Do you have a piece of cheese, young man? I've been dreaming of a piece of cheese for three years. Any cheese for poor Ben Gunn?"

Although I had no cheese, I breathed a sigh of relief. This man was certainly not after my life. On the contrary, he listened with growing sympathy as I described my fate to him. Finally he gave me a confidential poke in the ribs.

"Don't worry Jim," he whispered excitedly. "If you and your friends help me, I'll help you. I've got a boat hidden down there, under the white cliff. Promise me that your Squire Trelawney will take me with you? I'll reward you handsomely. And promise me you won't

The stockade and fence provided a good protection against all possible attackers.

tell Silver and the other blackguards about me. Do you understand – not a word!"

I nodded dumbly, although frankly I grasped very little. However Ben Gunn chattered on. He had been part of Captain Flint's crew and was present when the pirate had himself rowed to the island with chests full of gold and coins. John Silver, the helmsman and Bill Bones, the quartermaster of the *Walrus*, had remained on board with most of the crew. Flint had only taken seven men with him. He returned alone, having murdered the others after the treasure had been buried. "When Flint died in Savannah later on, I transferred to another ship," continued the unfortunate man, "and persuaded the Captain and his crew to look for the treasure. But we found nothing except the skeletons of our former friends. Then the others left me behind on the island, so furious and disappointed were they. Do you know what it's like to be marooned on an island for three years? You may well shake your head. No, you can't have any idea. But come on now,

we'll get the boat and . . ."

At that moment cannon fire thundered from the sea and immediately afterwards we heard distinct gunshots. "They're fighting!" I yelled and leapt up. Ben Gunn became pale but remained calm. "Perhaps your friends are safe behind the fence," he shouted and dragged me into the wood.

I ran beside him through the thicket and we reached the marshy valley, some way away from the shore. Ben Gunn pointed to the left. And there I saw on top of an easily defendable hill, a stockade with a strong fence. The Union Jack fluttered from the stockade's flagpole and I could clearly make out my friends behind the railings.

"Run!" Ben Gunn told me. "The blackguards will be attacking soon. Run while you can and don't forget your promise. Just look for me where I met you today!"

He was gone before I could answer and since I saw the murderers coming, I ran to the stockade.

*"Fire!" ordered the
Captain, in an icy
tone.*

Silver's offer

Of course it would have been very foolish to
run across the open slopes, so I made my way
through the protective undergrowth until I
reached the back of the stockade. I climbed
over the fence and my friends, who were visibly
relieved, welcomed me and listened eagerly to
my adventures. It seemed that they thought my
encounter with Ben Gunn the most significant.
However, I had to endure much reproach on
the subject of my rash actions. "Just be thankful
that we couldn't contemplate overpowering
the mutineers on board and simply sailing
away," Dr. Livesey said to me later. "The
adverse wind put paid to that." Then I learned
from him everything that had happened during my absence.

My friends managed to lock the mutineers
in the forward hold and persuade one of them,
Tom Gray, to join them. Then, unnoticed by
the mutineers on land, my friends had rowed
themselves across to the island in five trips,
using the only remaining boat. Previously the

Doctor had established that the stockade on the
map still existed. Unfortunately, the last trip
came to grief. The mutineers in the bow of the
ship broke free, and manned the cannon. They
hit the boat and it sank, together with most of
the provisions. For all that, my friends were
able to get to the safety of the stockade just in
time, and staved off the attack which followed.

"So with you we number seven, as Gray
stayed with us, seven against . . ." Dr. Livesey
counted up the mutineers' casualties on his
fingers. "They killed two themselves, Squire
Trelawney shot one of them from the boat . . .
against fifteen, two of whom are certainly
wounded. And they're all sitting in the middle
of a fever swamp. That'll make them move very
soon. It's lucky that they couldn't get the cannon ashore, and we're also lucky in having a
spring running through the stockade."

But that was all the luck we had, as Captain
Smollett explained shortly afterwards. "Our
provisions will only last for a week at the most,"

he announced. "The ammunition should last a little longer."

Then he assigned the night watches and although cannon fire from the *Hispaniola* crashed around us, he could not be persuaded to haul down the flag, which he had hoisted, and which the sailors were using as a target. "I've never hauled down a flag in my life," he declared. "It stays there!"

The night passed without further incident and if the glow of the fire on the shore had not reminded us of the men besieging us, we might have thought ourselves in the friendliest place in the world.

The cry "Flag of truce!" roused me from my sleep. The others were already awake, and stood at the fence, their muskets cocked. In the haze of the cold morning mist, we saw an ill-defined shape, and as it got nearer, we recognized John Silver. He was carrying a white flag and was roaring from a good way away: "I want to talk with you."

After a brief delay, Captain Smollett allowed him to climb over the fence. He met him halfway and brusquely ordered, "Sit down and make it short!"

Silver sank gasping to the ground and came straight to the point. "You're at our mercy, gentlemen, and you know it. My lads aren't just out for the gold, they're after your blood as well. So be reasonable. Hand over the map and as soon as we've found the treasure, I'll give you free passage. In writing if you don't believe me. You can then choose whether you stay here with provisions or come with us and we'll put you ashore in some safe port. Well?"

Silver's parrot perched on his shoulder, but remained absolutely still during the entire discussion.

Cautiously, I carried the boat to the water.

"Fine words!" Captain Smollett barked at him. "And now you listen to me. Give yourselves up and I'll guarantee you a fair trial in England before you all swing. If you don't give yourselves up, you'll either rot here with us or die of fever first. None of you can get the ship out of the bay, you're on a lee shore. So think it over and now get out!"

For a long time afterwards we could hear John Silver's curses as he stumbled back to his gang.

My adventure at sea

It was clear to us that the mutineers would not delay in attacking the stockade and pitilessly killing us. In spite of this, our morale was high.

"They'll come at us from all sides," presumed Captain Smollett, whose command even Squire Trelawney had unquestioningly accepted, "so we must stand by on all sides. Jim, you stay here in the cabin and keep the muskets loaded. Gray will help you. Squire Trelawney, as our best marksman, you'll man the south fence, overlooking the slope. That's probably where the main attack will be. Dr. Livesey, Hunter and Joyce will defend the other flanks. I'll step in wherever I'm most needed. Gray, before we start, give a good ration of rum to everyone to cheer us up."

For a good hour, during which our nerves were strained to breaking point, we crouched expectantly in our assigned places. The mist had cleared, the heat was unbearable, the sun burned down on the island from between the mass of threatening clouds.

And then a sudden and terrible roar could be heard on all sides, coming up the hill, and out of the edge of the wood and undergrowth to our left and right, burst the mutineers. Long John Silver's words lashed them to a fury, and his voice was almost drowned by the screeching of his parrot, perched on his shoulder, which screamed, "Stand by to attack! Pieces of eight! Pieces of eight!"

"Fire!" commanded Captain Smollett, but the order was not necessary. The volley of shots blended with the cries of wounded men, the violent roars of the attackers and the squawking of terrified birds.

Everything happened so fast and furiously that I can scarcely recall the details. But I will never forget how some of the mutineers managed to clamber over the fence. I saw one of them slaughter poor Ben Hunter, I remember that Tom Gray stabbed the bloodthirsty boatswain, Bob Anderson, with a boarding knife as the latter was stumbling towards me. I felt a blade graze my leg, saw Captain Smollett suddenly falter and heard Squire Trelawney's cry of victory, "They're running away, they're retreating!"

One last impression of the battle is stamped on my memory; that of a mutineer wearing a red night-cap, scared to death, trying to save himself by climbing up the fence. He sat briefly astride it, then dropped down and ran off to the woods screaming.

It was some time before the smoke and reek of the gunpowder cleared. It was then obvious that Hunter had breathed his last. Fortunately, Captain Smollett was not fatally wounded but Dr. Livesey ordered that he just rest for a few days. I had emerged with nothing more than a few harmless cuts. The pirates had left seven dead. "So there's only eight of them left," said Captain Smollett in a faint but contented voice.

While Gray, Joyce and I were keeping watch outside, our leaders were conferring with each other. We saw Dr. Livesey step outside, arrange his musket and powder horn, and carefully stow the map in a jacket pocket. Without a word, he made his way to the north fence, climbed over and disappeared into the wood. Gray watched him through a peephole for some time and uncomprehendingly shook his head many times. "What's he doing?'

"He's off to look for Ben Gunn," I guessed.

Meanwhile the skies grew dark and a mighty storm blew in from the sea. Since there would certainly not be an attack now, we sheltered in the cabin, and I fell to thinking about Ben Gunn's boat by the white cliff. Was it still there? Or had some of the pirates discovered its hiding place? I had to find out. The idea began to obsess me and when the storm died as suddenly as it had begun, I seized upon the plan to investigate. Since no one was paying me any attention, it all went quite smoothly.

I took bullets, a powder belt and two pistols with me and climbed over the fence facing the wood, when no one was looking. After a few minutes, I found myself in a thicket on the way

Neither of them moved.

Delightedly, I hauled the Jolly Roger, the pirates' black flag, down from the mast.

to the white cliffs. I quickly reached the beach and peered at the sea. The water was a leaden grey colour. Skeleton Island rose ghost-like above the cove and the *Hispaniola* looked like a ghost-ship with its Jolly Roger, the black flag with its skull and crossbones, which the pirates had hoisted. But then I saw two men leaning over the railing and a gig unloading. Long John Silver sat in it and then rowed back to shore.

There, the remaining pirates were lolling round a barrel of rum and the wind carried snatches of their song, which I had heard so many times before, and which made my blood run cold:

But one man of her crew alive
What put to sea with seventy-five . . .

I moved quickly onwards round the bay until I stood by the rocks of the white cliffs. I found the boat under a sail which had been weighted down with stones. It was very small, the frame was covered with goatskins and the heaviest thing was the paddle. For some time I gazed thoughtfully at my discovery which, oddly enough, seemed to be alive in the light of the sinking sun. Alive! Yes, we wanted to live and the pirates would never get the *Hispaniola*! As if compelled, I carried the boat to the water, jumped in and began to paddle. I had decided to cut through the ship's anchor cable, so that it would be wrecked on the coast or drift out to sea. The fact that we would then also be without a ship shows how short-sightedly I was thinking in my anger and confusion.

I paddled along almost noiselessly in the darkness. On the shore I could see the glimmer of a great fire with the shadowy figures of the mutineers moving around. A weak light showed me where the *Hispaniola* was lying.

At last her outline rose up before me. I heard a loud quarrel on deck; the two watches were hurling abuse at each other. This was most useful to me because I could head for the tautly stretched hawser, completely unobserved. In a few seconds I had cut through it with my boarding knife. It rebounded and almost flung me out of the boat. I managed to steady myself at the last moment and since a slight swell was blowing up, I swiftly moved away from the now dark ship. But delight at my escape proved too premature.

Unexpectedly the wind freshened and simultaneously the ebb tide began to run and my boat was being dragged out to sea like a ball. I heard the breakers rolling ever more threateningly against the cliffs of the headland, my vessel spun round in circles, a foaming breaker smashed over me and I bailed the water out of the boat with my bare hands. My strength was slipping away and I sensed another breaker, and the thundering and roaring of the waves seemed to be getting closer . . . then I fainted.

The sky above was blue, the boat bobbed calmly and close by, the island rose picturesquely out of a mirror-like sea. And as I saw the *Hispaniola* gliding past with billowing sails between me and the shore, I realized that I was not dreaming, I was still alive. I watched the ship as if spell-bound. It veered wildly, its sails slackened as it was slowly driven onto the coast. Then I knew nobody was steering the *Hispa-*

I had been so absorbed by the wheel that I had not paid attention to anything else.

niola and an audacious idea struck me. What if I could sail the ship to a hidden cove on the north of the island? I had to try. Cautiously, I rowed up to the *Hispaniola*. Nothing stirred on board. Under the bowsprit, I managed to seize hold of a loose cable, and hauled myself up. I was not unduly worried about losing my boat.

My concentration was abruptly focussed on the horrible scene on board. O'Brien, the sailor with the red night-cap, whom I had last seen sitting astride the fencing, was leaning lifeless against the ship's side with a knife in his chest. Beside him lay Israel Hands, moaning in a pool of blood and staring motionlessly at me through glassy eyes. "Rum, give me rum," he mumbled. The two men had fought to the death. An almost empty bottle of rum rolled around the forecastle. I held it to the dying man's lips. He drank it back greedily until the cask was almost empty. "Jim," he whispered, "we must save the ship. You must take the helm."

"But not to Kidd's Anchorage," I declared clearly. "I mean to get round to North Inlet."

"Do whatever you want to, Jim. Just put in a good word for me with your friends."

"We've got to get to them first," I said evasively and grasped the steering wheel, without showing how happy I was to get the right responses from the well-seasoned schooner. The strange journey began. We sailed along the west coast, round the north headland and in the late afternoon slipped gently into the inlet. A smooth white sandy shore sparkled ahead of us.

"Ebb tide's running now," gasped Israel Hands. "That suits us. We can let the ship run aground. It won't be difficult to refloat her at high tide. Now do as I tell you."

I knew what a difficult manoeuvre lay ahead of me, so I concentrated totally on the wheel and looked up for the first time when the sand crunched under the bow. Not a moment too soon, for Hands stood behind me, his dagger poised. With one bound, I leapt onto the rope ladder which led to the mizzen-mast and climbed up to the first cross-tree. He followed me, his dagger between his lips. I remembered the pistols, ripped one out, cocked it and shouted "Stop!" His hand clutched at me and I pulled the trigger. At that very instant, the ship lurched to one side, and the traitor fell into the water with a ghastly cry.

I climbed down slowly and when I saw that the ship was firmly beached I jumped down into the shallow water and waded ashore. I still had a long way to go and allowed myself hardly a moment's rest. During the moonlit night I crossed almost the whole island and finally, at first light, I found myself in the area I knew.

Not long afterwards I saw the stockade in front of me. A huge fire was burning outside it; nobody was on watch. I ran joyfully forward, climbed over the fence and threw open the door.

"Pieces of eight! Pieces of eight!" shrieked the parrot at me and then I saw the pirates.

In the pirates' clutches

They staggered sleepily to their feet and stared at me as if I were a ghost. Only Long John Silver seemed totally composed. He sat down comfortably on a brandy cask, stroked Captain Flint, who was perched on his shoulder, lit his pipe and nodded to me in an exaggeratedly friendly manner. "Come here, Jim, and forget about going back to your friends. They don't think well of you at all."

In spite of the threats I felt relieved.

"So they're still alive?"

"Of course they are," laughed Silver. "And they've struck a good deal with us. The Doctor arrived with a white flag yesterday. He offered us supplies, brandy, and firewood, in exchange for free passage for all those in the stockade. There was no mention of you. Now why shouldn't we let them leave? The ship's gone anyway and apart from that, we need someone to look after our wounded, the wound in Morgan's head, for example, or George's fever. Now make up your mind, are you with us or . . ."

"I'm still your Captain!"
roared Silver to the others and
looked at them savagely.

Or the pirates would kill me on the spot.

He did not have to go into any further detail, and my voice trembling with anger and scorn, I exclaimed, "Kill me then. What good will it do you? You've lost everything, ship and treasure, and those of you who aren't already dead soon will be. You owe me thanks. I overheard your infamous plan, I cut through the *Hispaniola*'s hawser and mark my words, it was I who had the schooner. So what are you going to do? You could kill me but you'll gain nothing by so doing. Or you can spare me and when you're standing in the docks, yes, go on laugh, but you *will* be standing there, you'll be pleased when I put in a good word for you."

"Shut up!" roared Morgan. He was the man whom I'd once seen sitting at Black Dog's table in Bristol and he made as if to rush at me when Silver, as quick as lightning, pushed him back.

"I'm still your Captain," he bawled, "none of you will lay a finger on the boy!"

"Yes, you're still our Captain, but for how long?" asked George Merry, in a slimy tone. He was a haggard lad, burning with fever and he looked around meaningfully. "Who got us into all this mess? Eh? You did, Silver! You got us shut in here. And how are we faring? No ship, no treasure. Now you know the rules. We're going to discuss your position."

"Please do," replied Silver, totally composed, and he remained that way even when the five pirates moved to the clear space in front of the cabin and began to whisper there. "Those fools," he murmured, "I'll show them yet." Then he seized my hand. "Jim, I know when the game's up. Ours is lost. I promise I'll save your life, but you must promise you'll save me from the gallows. What do you say, Jim?"

I simply nodded, for the others were coming back into the room. Morgan hesitated, then pressed something into Silver's hand. Silver looked at the black scrap of paper at once mockingly and curiously. "Aha! The Black Spot, and you've written 'Deposed' so beautifully on it. Tell me, where did you get the black paper from? It looks as if it came from a Bible, eh?" Dick turned away, shamefacedly. "It's from my Bible, John. Do you think . . .?" ". . . That it'll bring bad luck? I would never have dreamed of tearing up a Bible," confirmed Silver. "You're all up to your necks in bad luck. Now then, who's your new Captain?"

"I am," said George Merry proudly, and folded his arms.

"Congratulations, congratulations all round." Silver looked him straight in the eyes. "And have you told your new crew how you were the main objector to my plan only to open attack when the treasure was on board? You haven't told them, I can see it in your face. Did you tell them that the Doctor comes every day to look after your head wound thanks to my bargain – no you didn't. And did you tell them that the boy can only save us as long as he's alive? He is invaluable to us as a hostage. No, of course you didn't! And last of all, did you tell them," he raised his voice, "that I got the map from the Doctor?" The sailors and I watched dumbstruck as he pulled the map, which I had once seen in the Captain's trunk, out of his pocket and threw it on the floor. "Well now, Captain Merry, give your orders!"

The five men rushed at the sheet of paper and examined every aspect of it. "That's it. I can see Flint's signs," cried Morgan suddenly and leapt up. "Silver, be our Captain, you must, you must." George slunk off to a corner, looking embarrassed as Silver graciously accepted re-election. From the babble of voices, somebody shouted, "Look, the Doctor's coming!"

Dr. Livesey was indeed climbing over the fence. He stopped dead for a moment when he saw me and turned to Silver. "How are the wounded?" "Thank you for asking," replied Silver as politely as before, and then the Doctor went to treat the casualties. "I've got to keep you all safe for King George's gallows," he declared heartily. When he was ready he said to Silver, "Now I want to talk to the boy!"

"Of course," agreed Silver, but first he made me promise that I wouldn't run away. "And remember your promise," he whispered to me, "I can't restrain the men much longer."

I accompanied Dr. Livesey to the fence and quickly told him how everything had happened and where I'd hidden the *Hispaniola*. "I was going to scold you, but you seem to bring us good luck," he murmured in astonishment. "And we are in your debt for your meeting with Ben Gunn, a most useful man. Chin up, Jim! We won't desert you."

"Time up," called Silver and hobbled over.

"Has the boy told you how . . ."

"He has," interrupted Dr. Livesey and said softly to Silver, "you save him and I'll save you. And don't rush ahead with that treasure hunt. Prepare yourself for a storm to break, Silver."

"Hey, Silver, are you betraying us?" roared Morgan suspiciously, from the cabin.

"Storm," repeated the Doctor and after this mysterious warning, he left us.

The treasure hunt

Hardly had Dr. Livesey disappeared into the wood, when five sailors surrounded Silver and clamoured, "How much longer will you put off the treasure hunt? Tell us where we should start." Long John sneered in a superior fashion. "Oh yes, now you're begging me again, you've only just grasped that your heads are not good for thinking, only for swinging! How do you think I've spent the time? Working out how to save us all! What can happen to us now we've got Jim as hostage, eh? The others have nothing left to make us do as they want. We've got the map, we'll look for the treasure, and then, damn it, we'll find the ship! Friends, what more could you want than a ship under your feet and gold in your pockets – as much gold as you could waste in your lifetime! And our dear Jim," he spitefully pinched my shoulder, "will get his share, ha ha! Just as his friends will get theirs!"

Shivers ran down my spine. What sort of

I had to give Silver my word of honour, before I was finally allowed to talk to Dr. Livesey alone.

man was he! He was already thinking of betrayal again, he was only capable of double-crossing tricks. I wasn't under any illusions; my life was worth little more than a shot of powder. And any lingering doubts I may have had were dispelled by Silver's next words:

"You'll allow me, Jim, to chain you to me with a rope. It would be such a pity if you were to go missing."

Like a dancing bear on a long rope, he dragged me down to the beach where the others had already assembled bread, brandy and more importantly, choppers, pick-axes, and shovels.

Silver drew out his map and explained: "First we must go to Kidd's Anchorage and then make for a rock that lies on Skeleton Island-Anchorage-bay axis. Off, in the boats!"

The men rowed as if their lives depended on it. When we got to the spot where the *Hispaniola* had been anchored, Silver hove to. He glanced alternately at a cliff on Skeleton Island, at the compass and at the coast. Satisfied, he pointed to the mouth of a narrow river. "Over there!"

After the boats had been beached, Silver pointed to the woods and slopes behind us. "We've got to go up to the plateau. We'll find a tall tree there. Then we'll look again."

We trudged through swampy ground to start with, then upwards over sand and pebbles, through wood and thickets.

Oddly enough I became aware for a few moments of what a remarkable tableau we made: five men in tattered clothes, with terrifying faces, and into the bargain a one-legged man, armed to the teeth with muskets and pistols, a screeching parrot perched on his shoulder and a long rope round his waist with me on the other end.

At last we reached the elevated plateau. "A tall tree!" shouted Dick disappointedly, carrying his axe and Bible jammed under his arm. "There's plenty of tall trees here."

"Well, look all the same," snarled Silver and contemplated a huge fir. He dragged me towards it but Merry and Morgan were quick-er. Suddenly they stopped in front of the tree and stared at the ground terrified.

I was terrified too. A strangely distorted human skeleton lay beside the trunk. A few dark blue shreds of cloth flapped round the ribs.

Silver poked round the bones with his crutch and seemed very content. "Probably one of the six Flint took with him and then killed. But that's funny, where's his knife? Where are his belt and tobacco pouch. Murdered – that's one thing, but robbed! No that doesn't look like Flint's work at all. And why's he lying so twisted? I know. His arms and legs! They're all pointing in one direction. Exactly opposite that hill over there – Spye-Glass Hill. Let's go. The dead man is Flint's sign. A comic signpost, ha ha! Come on men, it can't be much further!"

We all trudged off again. And Silver, however incredible it might sound, was at the front in spite of only having one leg. He dragged me along like a piece of wood, gold lust and blood thirstiness glittering in his eyes. He stopped, however, in a shady hollow and waited for the others. "It's getting too hot, we'll rest awhile," he ordered.

The men listened reluctantly. They could only think of the gold that lay within their grasp. "Who could the dead man have been?" asked Dick.

"Perhaps Allardyce. He was blond, wasn't he, Tom Morgan?"

Tom nodded and peered back suspiciously in the direction of the dead man. "What if his ghost's still on the island?" Strangely, nobody laughed at him. Only Silver mumbled crossly, "Damn fool superstition." But at that very moment, we all leapt to our feet. Quite distinctly, we heard a plaintive snatch of song, borne on the wind, as if the very air were trembling. "Drink and the devil have done for the rest, Yo-ho-ho . . ."

Dick sank to his knees and clutched his Bible to him. Morgan grew pale. Merry's whole body shook and he whispered, "That's Flint, Flint's ghost!"

The song suddenly faded. But then we

*The pirates were
only thinking about
the vast store of gold.*

made out a ghostly moaning and entreaty: "Darby! Darby! Fetch . . . fetch the rum!"

Morgan blocked his ears. "Flint. His last words. I was there in Savannah when he died," he groaned.

"Damn and blast!" roared Silver. "Neither Flint nor his ghost will keep me from finding the seven thousand pounds. I wasn't afraid of Flint when he was alive, am I supposed to fear him now he's dead? Get up! The treasure is waiting for us somewhere near the cliffs over there." Without paying attention to the others he trudged off, forcing me in front of him. The five pirates followed us immediately, even overtaking us. The greed for gold was stronger than superstition and fear of ghosts. Merry ran ahead of everyone. And he was the first to discover the deep pit, in one of the bushes of the surrounding meadows.

"Over here!" his voice was almost breathless. "Here, I've found it at last!"

At last we stood in front of the pit, panting and sweating. We looked down into it unbelievingly. It was some time before we grasped what we saw: apart from two old shovels and a few smashed planks of wood, one of them plainly carrying the word 'Walrus', the pit was empty. Somebody had got to the treasure before us. Like madmen, the pirates jumped into the loose earth and began to dig. Only Long John remained expressionless.

"Come here, Jim," he whispered, cutting my rope in a lightning-fast movement, and pressing a pistol into my hand. "There'll be a storm and the Doctor knew it. I'll defend you to my dying breath. Chin up, Jim, don't worry!"

Was this the same man that was going to kill me in cold blood a few minutes ago? But I had no time to ponder. With a shout of fury, Morgan held up a gold coin.

"Is this the treasure you promised us, John Silver?" he screamed.

"You may find a few peanuts if you dig harder," jeered Silver.

On one of the planks, the name of Captain Flint's ship could still clearly be seen.

The five men emerged from the pit and Merry walked menacingly up to the Captain. "You've made us look fools long enough! You were a good Captain once, but now . . ." he drew his dagger, "your time is up."

Silver's pistol rang out and, simultaneously, shots rang out of the bushes. George Merry fell headlong into the pit and immediately afterwards, Dick fell to the ground, dead. And while Dr. Livesey, Tom Gray and Ben Gunn stepped out from behind the bushes, the three surviving pirates fled as fast as their legs would carry them. John Silver bowed to the Doctor. "You saved us at the critical time. Humble thanks." He then called, "Jim, tell him I was ready to defend you with my life, that I . . ."

"Tell us later," Dr. Livesey barked at us. "Better follow the rogues, we've got to cut them off from the boats."

Ben Gunn's secret

The Doctor hurried us relentlessly the whole way back. And Silver was forced to keep up with us, although he could scarcely hold himself up on his crutches any more. We eventually reached the beach. But there was no sign of the mutineers. Apparently they preferred to hide in the wood somewhere. Dr. Livesey himself helped to smash up one of the boats. We had to get in the other and while Silver, Gray, Ben Gunn and I rowed, Dr. Livesey at last had a chance to speak.

"Didn't I tell you, Silver, that a storm would blow up? You're indebted to Ben Gunn for that. Did you recognize him? Ah, you're nodding. He found the treasure long ago, before we came to the island. He had it in his cave above Rum Cove. When I learned that after a very detailed conversation with him, I could well afford to hand you over the map. It was much more important for us to get away from the malaria swamp. I was just worried that we would get to the pit in time to stop you killing Jim in your fury. So Ben Gunn, being the fastest, ran on ahead and had the inspired idea of terrifying you all by using Flint's voice."

"The idea wasn't that inspired," growled Silver sarcastically, "but I'm delighted that old Ben Gunn is still alive and so cheerful!"

"Not half as pleased as Ben Gunn," declared Livesey. "But to the treasure. Squire Trelawney and Captain Smollett are guarding that in Ben Gunn's cave at the moment. As soon as we've got it on board the *Hispaniola*, it's going to England."

"And what'll happen to me. And to my . . . to the three rogues?" asked Silver warily.

"You all deserve to be hung. But we'll leave the other three behind with supplies and hunting weapons. You can either stay with them or journey back to England with us. I'll hand you over to a court of law, but as I promised, I'll see that you get off with your life."

"I'll go with you," said Silver, but no one knew what was going through his mind.

Late in the evening, after we had rowed around the island, we reached the *Hispaniola*. She had righted herself during the high tide and was drifting in the bay. Tom Gray stayed back on board as guard. Then we rowed ashore and climbed up a sort of hill. Ben Gunn's cave lay under its summit. When I got there, I was heartily embraced by Squire Trelawney. Captain Smollett beckoned to me from a bed of animal skins. "You're a brave boy, Jim," he said approvingly and pointed behind him.

In the rays of the setting sun glittered gold

Captain Smollett beckoned to me joyfully.

bars, jewellery, coins and precious stones. So this was the famous treasure, for which so many good and evil people had lost their lives. And a part of it belonged to me.

Two days later, everything was on board the *Hispaniola*, and the journey home began. John Silver was as polite and obliging and eager to please as he had been in the early days. We no longer believed in his words, however. And when he secretly made off with a sack of gold at the first port we came to for supplies and a new crew, nobody shed a tear for him. We have never seen or heard of him again.

Now that I'm back in England, I often think back to our great sea adventure, which made us so rich after subjecting us to so much danger. Ben Gunn entered Squire Trelawney's service, the Doctor retired and I, God willing, will be a good host with my mother, to the fishermen and sailors in *The Admiral Benbow*, for many long years to come.

The three men whom we had left behind on the island deserved no other fate.

JULES VERNE

Captain Grant's Children

JULES VERNE
Captain Grant's Children

What could the bottle contain?

A mysterious call for help

On 26th July 1864 the yacht *Duncan*, sailing under the British flag, approached the port of Glasgow at full steam. On board were Lord Edward Glenervan, a peer from an old-established Scottish family and his young wife Lady Helen, whom he had married only a few months before. They were accompanied by a cousin of the Earl, Major MacNabbs. The *Duncan* was a magnificent ship and they were returning from sea-trials in the Atlantic. The Earl had acquired her in order to spend his belated honeymoon aboard her. She was due to be cruising in the Mediterranean shortly. Thus they were just talking about the sunny coast to which the young lady was eagerly looking forward, when in a loud voice the look-out reported an enormous fish in their wake.

Everyone was gripped by the excitement of the hunt. A sailor threw out bait on a line and it was not long before the voracious creature snapped at it.

"A dog fish. They can be dangerous," observed the Major after the huge fish had been pulled on board and killed. Then the sailors busied themselves cutting the catch into pieces suitable for the kitchen.

Suddenly there was great commotion amongst the seamen, and soon after the officer of the watch brought the Earl a bottle encrusted with barnacles, and reported, "It was inside the shark."

"French champagne!" cried the Major. But the Earl was doubtful. "Who throws champagne overboard?"

The mate removed the crust from the neck of the bottle with his knife, and finally managed to pull out the cork. "Papers," he said with astonishment, "rolled-up papers!"

"Strange!" Lord Edward checked. "They seem to be damp." With a powerful blow he broke the neck off the bottle and carefully extracted the roll. "Three sheets. I hope we don't destroy them when we unroll them."

Caution was justified. The paper had already suffered considerably from the salt water, yet finally three hand-written sheets were lying spread out on the table in the Earl's cabin. Although many words on each sheet were no longer legible, Lord Edward and Major Mac-Nabbs managed to decipher the contents, as each bore the same message but in a different language, English, French and German.

It was an S.O.S. and it said, "On the 7th June 1862 the three-master *Britannia* ran onto a reef off the coast of Patagonia. Captain Grant and two sailors are trying to reach the mainland where they will be captured by savage Indian natives. They have thrown this message in a bottle into the sea at latitude 37° 11′. If help does not come quickly they shall be lost!"

"Captain Grant, our famous fellow-countryman! He wanted to find an island which would be a new homeland for freedom-loving Scots!" MacNabbs recalled excitedly.

"Our first duty now should be to find him," said the Earl. "We must inform the Admiralty immediately!"

Hardly had the *Duncan* reached port than he set off for London while his wife and cousin returned to Malcolm Castle. Yet first he telegraphed the leading newspapers:

"If you wish to know more about the fate of the *Britannia* and Captain Grant, apply to Glenervan, Malcolm Castle, Luss, Scotland!"

Malcolm Castle at Luss was one of the oldest and proudest Scottish castles and had long been the seat of the Glenervans.

One evening, before the Earl returned from London, a young lady and gentleman were announced to Lady Helen. Rather surprised, she received them and was even more surprised when she heard their names. Mary and Robert Grant, the Captain's daughter and her younger brother. They had read about the message in the bottle in the newspapers.

Lady Helen, who was immediately impressed by the brother and sister, welcomed them cordially and invited them to stay at the

They presented themselves to Lady Helen.

*On 25th August the Duncan finally put to sea,
heading for unknown adventures.*

Castle until the Earl returned. Mary and
Robert were only too happy to accept.

They had been on their own for nearly two
years. Their mother had died young and even
the aunt who had cared for them upon the
Captain's departure had died soon after. Fear
for their father's life was reflected in the young
faces.

They were gripped by sheer despair next
morning, when the Earl, still wearing his
travelling-cloak, dashed into his wife's drawing
room. He did not notice the guests at first and,
instead of a greeting, cried out in disappointed
anger, "The Admiralty has no intention of
doing anything to rescue Grant. The most stupid excuses are not stupid enough for that
senile stay-at-home bunch. I . . ."

"My poor father!" cried Mary, horrified.

Only now did the Earl become aware of
their presence. His wife explained the situation, adding, "Well, there's always another
way."

"What am I to make of that, Helen?"

"We shall look for Captain Grant! Haven't
we bought an excellent sea-worthy ship, the
Duncan? Instead of the Mediterranean, we'll
just sail to South America. Or do you have a
better idea, Edward?"

"No!" was the determined answer.

Acting on orders, Captain Mangles spent
the next few days having the ship re-fitted and
victualled for the long journey.

When the pilot came on board at dawn on
25th August and the anchor was finally raised,
Captain Grant's children were on board,
together with Lord Edward and his wife and
cousin.

They found it quite natural that the children should be there. After all, they were going
to look for their father.

An unexpected passenger

The first day of the journey had been rather stormy, but the sea was calmer on the second and so Major MacNabbs, leaning against the ship's rail, was contentedly puffing his pipe. Thus he did not notice that a strangely-dressed man was busily trying to attract his attention.

The man was about forty years old, thin as a rake, and had a face which was enormous. In spite of his unprepossessing appearance, which was not helped by a suit with many pockets and a check-cap, intelligence and determination flashed from his eyes. Then Mr. Olbinetti, the steward, happened to cross the deck. The man turned to him.

"I'm in Cabin Six. Could you bring my breakfast there, please? I haven't eaten anything since Paris."

"Certainly, sir," answered the steward. "But . . ."

At this moment, Captain Mangles appeared and surveyed the stranger with astonishment. "You are . . . ?"

"Ah, Captain Burton, Commander of the *Scotland*. Pleased to meet you. I am Jacques Eliacin François Marie Paganel, secretary of the Geographical Society in Paris, corresponding member of the Ethnological Societies of Berlin, Bombay, Darmstadt, London, St. Petersburg, Vienna and New York, honorary member of the Royal Geographical and Ethnographical Societies of . . ."

"Et cetera, et cetera." Lord Edward, who had joined the gentlemen, interrupted him with mild amusement. "All very nice, but where are you travelling to?"

"Where to? To India – where else? My research project there . . ."

" . . . may be somewhat delayed!" growled Captain Mangles with some displeasure. "My dear sir, you have mistaken the ship. The *Scotland* was berthed alongside us!"

"Good Heavens!" gasped Mr. Paganel and turned pale. Yet he grew visibly more cheerful when the Earl promised to put him ashore at Madeira. He would have no problem in obtaining a passage to India from there.

He was Jacques Eliacin François Marie Paganel, Secretary of many famous Societies for Geography and Ethnology.

By the time they reached Madeira, Mr. Paganel had grown so accustomed to his hosts that he asked Lord and Lady Glenervan, shortly before they put in to the port, "Would you permit me to accompany you to Patagonia? The country and its people are scientifically just as attractive to me as India. Besides, I'm no stranger to expeditions. Perhaps I can be of use in the search for Captain Grant. I should so much like to help the children."

"Agreed!" said the Earl with a pleasure which was shared by all on board, since Mr. Paganel had proved himself a charming, consistently good-tempered traveller.

The journey continued westwards. On 15th September the *Duncan* crossed the Equator off the coast of Brazil. Two weeks later the Patagonian coast-line was already looming up. Yet there were no people to be seen anywhere, certainly none of giant stature and with disproportionately large feet, to which, because of an old sailor's yarn, the land at the extreme south of the American continent owed its name.

Now they had to venture the rounding of the notorious Cape Horn. Yet the *Duncan* and its crew were fortunate. The much-feared Cape showed itself in its best light and exactly forty-two days after leaving Scotland, the yacht dropped anchor outside the little Chilean port of Talcahuano.

Immediately Lord Edward called on the British Consul. "He has no idea where, when or even if Grant's *Britannia* approached the Chilean or Argentinian coast," he disappointedly reported to his companions later.

"But there's no mistake about it!" MacNabbs said with conviction. "Patagonia, 37° latitude. That was plain enough, wasn't it?"

"Perhaps," said Mr. Paganel hesitantly,

"we have misunderstood the message. Nevertheless, it is strange that it says they will be prisoners of the Indians, not they are." As they all listened attentively, he continued, "Perhaps they were transported into the interior and .."

"You can't throw a bottle into the sea from the interior," the Earl objected.

"No, but into a river!"

An astonished silence followed. Finally, Paganel continued, "If I might make a suggestion?"

"Of course," the Earl encouraged him eagerly.

The scientist spread out a large map and began to explain, "Here Latitude 37 runs across the continent from West to East, from the Pacific to the Atlantic coast. We must equip an expedition and follow it. A difficult undertaking, I know. Over the Andes, through rainforests, across the pampas. And yet . . . ."

"Well," the Earl interrupted. "I see no other possibility either. Is anyone against it?"

No-one had a better suggestion to make and so Paganel was asked to prepare the route for the search party, and pay special attention to the many rivers, one of which may have carried the bottle.

On 14th October they were ready. A long column of beasts of burden moved off. Apart from Lord Edward, the Major and Mr. Paganel, three particularly stout-hearted sailors took part in the expedition, John Austin, Wilson and Murray.

Robert Grant, on the other hand, was to return with his sister and Lady Helen to Buenos Aires aboard the *Duncan*, and await the rescuers there.

Yet the boy insisted on being allowed to participate in the search for his father and his companions.

"You're still too young," the Earl explained to him several times. Yet when reference to the great dangers made no impression on Robert, he finally nodded. "Right, you can come along. In your place I should probably have moved Heaven and Earth to be there, too!"

A long column of baggage-carrying animals set off.

A terrible tremor shook the mountain.

Rescue from dire distress

In spite of the bad roads the column made good progress. The 'peons' they had engaged in the port proved themselves excellent guides, and by 12th October the sierra, the Argentinian highland, was stretching before the eyes of the expedition.

"Well," MacNabbs rejoiced, "we have now put Chile and the Cordilleras behind us. Yet the most difficult part, over the Andes, still lies ahead."

"You're right," Paganel agreed, and pointed to distant snow-caps. "There lies the Antuco Pass, nine thousand feet high. We must go over that."

Yet when they came to the foot of the mountain range, the peons pointed to the massive mud-covered boulders which lay around everywhere. "Landslide," the eldest peon conveyed to them in broken Spanish and sign-language. "Path to Antuco buried. Change to other pass. Or very dangerous."

"Unless we want to veer too far from the 37th parallel we shall have to settle for the danger," declared Lord Edward.

No-one wanted to deviate too far from Captain Grant's presumed forced abode, and thus began a very difficult climb which demanded the utmost of the horses and mules.

The sun was already sinking over the horizon and the column had been struggling for some time through snow and ice, when the Major, who was up with the leaders, discovered a stone hut.

"An ideal place to spend the night," he suggested, and a few minutes later they had all made themselves at home in the small space as best they could.

The peons roasted some meat. No-one paid any attention to the distant murmuring which echoed from the mountains long after night had fallen.

"Only a thunderstorm," presumed the Major.

"Perhaps," said Paganel to himself. The

146

worried whispering of the peons had not escaped him. Yet as nothing could be heard now, he lay down on his side and soon fell asleep.

A tremor, so strong that all the walls of the hut shook and pieces fell from the rafters, jerked the men awake. Paganel was the first to appreciate the situation.

"Outside!" he roared. "An earthquake!"

Everyone dashed for the door. At that moment the floor began to sway. Bursting and cracking sounds filled the air, and just as the last man was through the doorway, the hut collapsed with a roar.

Yet the greatest shock was still to come. For a few seconds there was an uncanny silence and the men expectantly squinted into the first rays of the rising sun. Then they felt the earth tremble beneath them. The frozen ground burst asunder, a gigantic avalanche of boulders detached itself from the rock face and in a cloud of dust and snow thundered and boomed its way down over the top of those lying helplessly beneath it.

Then all was quite calm again.

"It should be over now," Paganel's relieved voice rang from between the boulders.

Yet when they all finally gathered round the ruins of the hut, Robert was missing.

"He was lying beside me," recalled Wilson the Mate, "and suddenly he was gone."

Immediately Lord Edward ordered a rescue operation. They searched all day. They clambered in gorges and clefts in the rock. They shouted until their throats were hoarse. Yet nowhere could they find even a trace of the missing boy.

Deeply distressed, Lord Edward gave the order to leave. Once more he turned round and let his gaze sweep the snow-capped peak.

Then he saw a mighty condor rising from a crevice. The others had also spotted the giant bird.

"He's dragging a calf in his talons," cried the Earl. "Such strength and . . ."

"No!" MacNabbs interrupted in horror, and raised his rifle. "That's Robert!"

The bird came closer, yet not very high because of his prey. The Major took careful aim. But just as he was about to pull the trigger, a shot rang out. The condor plunged into the snow like a stone.

The men ran up, dragged the heavy bird aside and bent over the boy. "Alive! He's still alive!"

While many hands tended the lad who had been saved so miraculously, the Earl asked his cousin, "Who fired the shot?"

"I didn't," replied the latter, with a shake of his head.

The answer soon came. A Patagonian was making a dignified descent down a rocky slope.

Mortally wounded, the condor crashed down, its wings folded together over its victim.

A red poncho hung over his shoulders, beneath which he wore trousers and shirt made of fox skin. From his belt dangled a lasso and bolas. In his right hand he held a rifle.

"Me Thacalve," he said. "Me know all tracks. All Indian tribes. Need me?"

The Earl stretched out his hand to him. "Heaven has sent you to us."

The first trace

The first few days had already proved how fortunate the travellers were to have met the Indian. He was not afraid of even the most impossible rocky barriers and chasms. He always knew of a way and had an unerring eye for where game was to be found.

Mr. Paganel was particularly impressed by the new companion because the latter submitted himself to the scholar's unceasing questions with the calm of one who could never be flustered.

The results came one evening at the camp-fire when Paganel excitedly announced, "Thacalve has told me of a tribe which captured a white man about three years ago."

"Grant?" asked the Major excitedly.

"Or one of his crew?" the Earl said, limiting the hope somewhat. "What else have you learned?"

"Unfortunately nothing which indicates it may be one of those we are looking for. But also nothing which proves it may not be. At present the tribe is said to be between the Rio Negro and the Rio Colorado."

"Which we want to cross anyway," Lord Edward nodded. "We must follow this first trail without fail."

This decision raised the depressed mood perceptibly, and it was not deflated again by the fact that all further attempts by Paganel to find out anything more about the mysterious prisoner were unfruitful.

By the end of October the party had finally crossed the mountain-range. Before them lay the far Argentinian Pampas, the plains which were covered with short, dried-out grass.

"We soon at Lago Salinas," Thacalve comforted them. "There fresh water and perhaps also tribe with prisoner."

But when they eventually reached Lago Salinas, the salt lake, the streams which carried drinkable water to it were completely dried up. There was no sign of the Indians. Scattered shepherds who grazed their sheep near the lake knew only that they had moved on to the north. One of them, however, knew something more. The prisoner they had with them and who was obviously treated very well, was without doubt no Briton, and certainly not a Scot, but a French merchant. The prisoner had told the shepherd so himself.

That was naturally a great disappointment. "So we carry on along the 37° Parallel," decided Lord Edward, "and as soon as we are back in civilized parts, we must inform the French representative. They will look after their fellow-countryman."

As the shortage of water became more marked from day to day, Thacalve suggested he should scout the district with a small troop in order to rest the baggage-carrying animals.

"Very sensible," MacNabbs praised him, but was not very enthusiastic when he was designated to guard the baggage-train, and Lord Edward and Robert set off shortly afterwards with the Indian in the direction of Rio Guamini.

Silently the three rode through the salt waste, hour by hour, without finding a sign of water anywhere. Yet in the late afternoon the horses suddenly went faster and Thanka, the Indian's splendid steed, even whinnied.

"What s the matter with the horses?" Robert wondered.

"Smell water," smiled Thacalve.

It was actually not long before the white salt crust gave way to a soft, then more and more luxuriant green. Single bushes and trees appeared and finally a river was reflected glittering like gold in the light of the setting sun.

"The Rio Guamini, one of the tributaries of the Rio Grande!" cried Lord Edward with relief, while Robert with the practical sense of the young just said, "Water, thank God!" Shortly after, man and beast were enjoying a long-awaited drink. They did not notice that it had meanwhile grown dark. Near the river, Thacalve discovered a deserted sheep-pen. The three made their camp inside the low enclosure. The fire shone brightly into the darkness. It was still burning cheerfully when all three were fast asleep.

In the middle of the night Thacalve woke the two Scots.

"Danger! Rifles, quick!"

The horses stamped restlessly. A large shadow appeared beside Thanka. At this moment the Indian fired.

"What was that?" whispered the Earl, and almost in the same second the answer came with a terrifying howling.

"Red wolves. Very hungry, very wild. Besiege us all night. Fear nothing but bright day."

While speaking, Thacalve fired again and immediately afterwards a bullet from the Earl smashed a wolf's skull.

Robert threw dry grass into the dying flames. Immediately the wolves drew back a little. Then they came from all sides again. For each one the men shot down two new ones seemed to appear.

"We have hardly any ammunition left!" gasped the Earl after a short time, and when the flames threatened to die away it seemed as if their fate was sealed.

Thacalve, who was already warding off the wolves with his knife, cried, "Thanka fastest horse. Me ride away and draw off wolves!"

"No!" Lord Edward's rifle-butt crashed onto a wolf's back. "They will tear you to pieces. We cannot accept that."

"No!" cried Robert. "I am lighter!"

Before the Earl and the Indian were able to prevent him, he jumped onto Thanka's back and galloped out of the pen.

"Oh God, protect him!" prayed Lord Edward when he saw the wolf-pack racing after the horse.

Thacalve remained calm. "Thanka fast horse. Robert very brave. They save us. No

The valiant horse galloped out into the night. Immediately the red wolves eagerly gave chase.

Although the enormous tree was deeply-rooted in the earth, it slowly began to sway under the force of the storm gusts and the fire spread quickly.

worry, Señor."

He was right. Next morning, when they rode back to the baggage-train, their companions were already half-way towards them. At their head galloped Robert.

The column stayed at the river only long enough to fill all the water-containers to bursting point. Then they rode back into the barren grassland. They crossed the broad plain which drops between Rio Negro and Rio Colorado, slowly down to the Atlantic coast where the heat bore down. The sky assumed an ever paler hue, and the earth seemed to exude nothing but moisture. At first just a few small puddles were formed, but soon they made way for shallow pools and ever larger lagoons. Instead of firm ground, the horses were trotting over treacherous bogs.

More and more often, Thacalve cast worried glances upwards and to all sides.

"Whatever is the matter?" the Earl asked anxiously.

"Thunderstorms from mountains."

"And what will happen then?"

"When the Negro and Colorado flood we sit in the middle of a lake. And without a ship. Clear enough?" Mr. Paganel answered in place of Thacalve.

It was clear enough and the others needed no instruction to drive the animals on in order to escape the deadly trap. But after a few hours they realized they could not win the race. With unimaginable force, Heaven opened its sluice-gates. The land round about turned into a limitless lake, and when the rain just as suddenly stopped, a tall, roaring, mud-brown wall was approaching from the south.

"A spring-tide!" roared MacNabbs. "We are lost . . . ! No! There! To the tree!"

Out of the leaden grey mist emerged the outlines of a giant native tree. Yet before the riders reached it, the enormous wave caught them. What they thought was their misfortune turned out to be their salvation. The wave threw them upwards for several feet and dropped them into the wide-spreading lower branches of the tree. While the horses were carried away by the masses of mud and water, all the companions were re-united in the dense top of the ninety-feet tall ombu, a wild nut-tree; the Earl and his friends, the sailors and the peons. Only one was missing. Thacalve! He was drifting away far out in the current on his trusty Thanka.

Under different circumstances the excursion onto the ombu would perhaps have been quite cheerful. Thanks to the many nests in its branches there was enough to eat, the strong branches made relatively comfortable seats, and its deep roots seemed safe from the current. Yet the crocodiles which the flood had washed up would not allow the men in the tree to forget reality.

Quite different thoughts were occupying Mr. Paganel's mind. "I've got it!" he suddenly cried with delight. "We must go to Australia!" Without heeding the others' astonishment he burst out to Lord Edward, "You and the Major completed the message incorrectly. '37° 11′ austral' . . . that doesn't mean southern hemisphere but Australia. And 'indi . . . ' didn't mean Indians, but indigines, that is, natives. So he was not talking about Patagonia but about ' . . . onia'. That could just as well be New Caledonia in my opinion! No, believe me, we are lying in the wrong place here."

"Sitting!" the Major corrected him sarcastically, and then became just as excited as the others about Paganel's bold assertions. So heated was the clash of pros and cons that only a bright flash of lightning suddenly ended the argument.

The lightning had struck the treetop. Immediately it burst into flame, quickly spreading through the dense foliage in spite of the damp. They had given themselves up for lost, when a sudden gust of wind swept across the surface of the water, whipping up spray and foam and uprooting the tree with one mighty jerk as though it were a sapling.

In the space of a second it crashed into the raging torrent, and the fire was extinguished. It was carried away by the current, bearing with it the men, who cheered up again. Two days later, with the sun shining once more and the water drained away, there, like a miracle, stood

For a long time they saw Thacalve standing on the cliffs and knew they would remember him all their lives.

Thacalve with almost all the horses and mules.

"Not far to coast!" he cried in place of a greeting. "Ship *Duncan* already there!"

The same evening there was a joyful reunion on the yacht. Then they took leave of Thacalve. He stood for a long time, waving on the shore as the *Duncan* set course for Australia as Mr. Paganel had suggested.

A surprising statement

The *Duncan* made good time and reached the coast of South Africa without any particular incidents. Admittedly Captain Mangles had to stop for a few days in order to take on coal. Then they were really on the way to Australia!

During the long journey the companions had lots of time to think about the slim chances of success and to discuss them at length. Yet Mr. Paganel, who was unshakable in his optimism had an illuminating answer to every objection.

"Then just tell me one thing," the Major asked him one evening at dinner. "We know for certain that the *Britannia* sailed from the Peruvian port of Callao on 30th May. How could she run aground off the coast of Australia on 7th June?"

"It wasn't the 7th," answered Paganel calmly, "but the 27th of June. Please remember, the papers were badly damaged just where the date was written. Only the 7 was legible. Does that rule out the fact that a 2 was originally written in front of it?"

"No," they all agreed with amazement. Only the Earl had a significant question, "And where do you imagine the ship-wreck took place? Off the east or west coast of Australia?"

"To the west of that part of the country which the 37th Parallel passes through, of course," Captain Mangles announced. "Because those are the only areas inhabited by Aborigines. If Grant had been stranded in the east he would hardly have needed to worry about being rescued. The coast has long since been settled by white men. Savage natives . . ."

"Cannibals!" said Mary Grant with horror.

"No, no," Paganel comforted her, "neither murderers nor cannibals. Am I right, Captain?"

"Certainly. You only have to be really afraid of escaped deportees. You know – criminals who were exiled to Australia. But certainly not to this coast."

The *Duncan*, they decided, was to head for Cape Jaffa, at the extreme south-west of Australia, from where the 37th Parallel runs eastwards right across the country to the foot of the Australian Alps by the Tasmanian Sea.

At first things did not turn out as planned. The sea, which had been calm so far, turned

For days on end the storm rocked the ship.

The farmer, his wife and their five sons welcomed the travellers like old friends.

within a very short time into a veritable witch's cauldron. For days, mighty storms rocked the ship. It often seemed as if she would disappear for ever under the roar of the mountainous waves. The sails were torn to scraps and when one of the propellers broke, the *Duncan* was at the mercy of the forces of nature.

Day and night the Captain stood upon the bridge. The sailors worked to the point of collapse, and the passengers kept to their cabins with little hope of survival. Finally the wind rent the clouds asunder and the waves ran more smoothly.

The look-out's cry of "Land ahoy" brought forth a shout of joy from everyone.

It was not long before Captain Mangles had determined their exact position. "Ladies and gentlemen," he said almost solemnly to those waiting expectantly, "it's an ill wind that blows no-one any good. Before us lies the Australian coast and in particular Cape Catastrophe and Kangaroo Island. In other words, one day's journey and we will be exactly where we want to be!"

Great as the general rejoicing at this news was, because no-one doubted the calculations, nevertheless Mary and Robert Grant could not conceal a certain depression.

"No wonder," declared Lady Helen to her husband and the Major. "They both feel very keenly that the decision is to be made now. If we don't find certain proof in a few days that the *Britannia* was wrecked somewhere round here, then our expedition has been a failure and we can do nothing but turn back without having achieved our purpose."

"We haven't reached that point yet," answered her husband confidently. "A Glenervan doesn't give up that quickly."

"And certainly not a MacNabbs!" the Major assured her stout-heartedly.

Lady Helen squeezed their hands gratefully. Thanks to a jurymast the *Duncan* reached a calm bay that very evening. As Captain Mangles wanted to lie at anchor there long enough to carry out the most urgent repairs, Edward and his friends had themselves rowed to the shore, behind which the coast rose steeply. They wanted to reconnoitre a little.

They had just climbed the comparatively easy cliff when they saw a windmill and a large farmhouse not far off. They went straight up to it and were astonished when a sturdy red-haired man greeted them as if they were long-awaited guests.

"Come in and have a meal with us. My

The blacksmith acted as if he had not heard the question, but Ayrton explained the meaning of the sign on the horse-shoe.

house is your house," he declared in a friendly voice. "This farm belongs to Paddy O'Moore. That's me."

"Irish?" Lord Edward shook the other's hand. "We're Scots." He introduced his companions and finally asked, "What brought you here?"

At lunch, at which the Irishman's wife and five sons were also present, he told them about the troubles in Ireland and that he had never regretted having emigrated. "If you work hard you can achieve something here," he concluded.

"Seems like it," replied Lord Edward, and in his turn related what had brought him and his friends to Australia. As was only to be expected, O'Moore shook his head. "The *Britannia*? She certainly didn't sink on this coast. I've never heard anything about a Captain Grant."

"Still, if he's anywhere, he can only be in Australia!" one of the farm-hands at the table said unexpectedly.

Everyone looked at him in astonishment. MacNabbs was the first to collect himself. "What makes you so sure, man?"

"I was on board the *Britannia* when it was ship-wrecked," was the answer.

For a moment a ghostly silence reigned. Then questions were hurled at the man from all sides. It took some time before he was able to give anything like a cohesive report.

"My name is Jim Ayrton. I was quartermaster on the *Britannia*, and when the ship went down I thought I was the only one to be lucky. I grabbed a beam and was carried to the shore."

"Where was that?" enquired the Earl.

"Off the east coast at Twofold Bay. It lies exactly on the 37th Parallel. If the Cap'n was able to save himself, he could only have got to the Australian shore. I'm certain of that."

MacNabbs was still taken aback by the unexpected witness. "When did the ship sink?" he wanted to know.

"On 27th June '62, sir. We had taken on supplies and cargo in Callao and were actually going home. Then this storm drove us off course. On shore I fell into the hands of Aborigines. After almost two years in the Australian Alps I was able to escape and eventually came to Mr. O'Moore. Do you want to see my papers? I managed to rescue them."

While Ayrton went to fetch them, the farmer cleared his throat. "Isn't that a miracle?

Ayrton is a good, hard-working man. We all think a lot of him."

"I don't much believe in miracles," MacNabbs confessed, but the documents Ayrton produced confirmed his story.

"At Twofold Bay?" Paganel repeated and looked at the Earl. "So we must begin on the opposite coast. We shall soon be there on the *Duncan*."

He was mistaken. They could not repair the yacht by themselves and Captain Mangles explained that they would have to take her to a shipyard in Melbourne.

"That'll take weeks," the Earl feared.

"During which we can easily go overland to the east coast!" maintained Mr. Paganel. "After all, we are in the civilized part of Australia where there's even a railway. No, I mean

that seriously, and you'll see that we can also take the ladies with us this time. What do you think, Mr. Ayrton?"

The man he asked, who had cast an expert eye over the ship and its damage, seemed to consider his answer very carefully. "Well," he said at length, "it's not just a short stroll, but if we are well-equipped we can manage it."

"We?" the Earl asked, and looked pleased. "You'd come with us? Your experiences would be a great help to us, of course!"

O'Moore was not happy to hear that his hard-working farmhand was going to leave him, but accepted the reasons and personally saw to it that the company was equipped with mounts and heavy oxcarts for the ladies.

This time Captain Mangles was also one of the party. The *Duncan* was to await further

It was a terrible sight and it soon turned out that the disaster was caused as a result of a criminal conspiracy.

The old man looked up and inspected the flock of birds.

orders in Melbourne under the command of his deputy, the First Officer Austin. If Captain Grant were found fairly soon, the voyage and the march to Twofold Bay would not be necessary after all.

On 22nd December the travellers were already setting off for the east. Along the 37th Parallel they crossed the province of Adelaide without difficulty. They spent Christmas on the plains, and one rainy day, the Wimerra had to be forded. This produced minor set-backs:

an iron hoop came off a wheel of the ox-cart and Lord Edward's horse cast a shoe.

Ayrton offered to fetch help from the nearest village. He returned a few hours later with a man who was sparing with words and inspired little confidence, yet who turned out to be an excellent blacksmith. He repaired the cart and shod the horse. MacNabbs was surprised about a clover-leaf mark which stood out clearly between the calkins.

Ayrton explained its meaning to him. "That's how you find runaway horses more easily on the huge pastures. There are many such signs."

A day later they were at Camden Bridge, an enormous railway bridge over the Murray, a terrible sight. The bridge had collapsed and the express train to Victoria had crashed into the depths below.

It soon became apparent that it was not an accident, but the work of a gang of criminals who had escaped from Perth and were terrorizing the country under the leadership of a certain Ben Joyce.

"So there's no danger from deportees here?" the Major growled at Mr. Paganel, who was rather subdued, and advised that they should say nothing of this band to the ladies. "They would only worry unnecessarily." They all agreed with this suggestion.

A terrible discovery

During the first days of January 1865 the travellers were still making good progress. The route now ran through the northern part of Victoria Province, through extensive eucalyptus forests and finally through a native reservation hardly entered by white men. It was not long before MacNabbs thought he spied a large monkey behind a tree in the midst of the undisturbed natural surroundings.

Yet in one voice Ayrton and Paganel called, "You're mistaken, Major. That's an aborigine!"

They were right. A few moments later and they were surrounded by a crowd of half-naked men, women and children, who drew back timidly at every attempt the white people made to approach them.

"They are monkeys," growled the Major, but was immediately reprimanded by Lady Helen. "You should be ashamed of yourself, Mac!"

Mary began to distribute food. Slowly the brown figures gained confidence. Yet when a swarm of cockatoos fluttered up shrieking from a tree-top they turned all their attention to the birds.

"Watch out, they'll start hunting now!" surmised Ayrton. "You'll be surprised!"

He had not exaggerated. An old man threw a flat, bent piece of wood at the birds. At first the wood whirled low over the grass, then suddenly spun almost vertically upwards, struck several birds, which crashed to the ground, and in an elegant arc returned to the old man's feet. "I've heard a lot about boomerangs," cried Paganel with enthusiasm, "but this is the first time I really believe what I've read about them."

By the door a warrant was nailed up for the arrest of Ben Joyce and his fellow-murderers, for whose capture a large reward was offered.

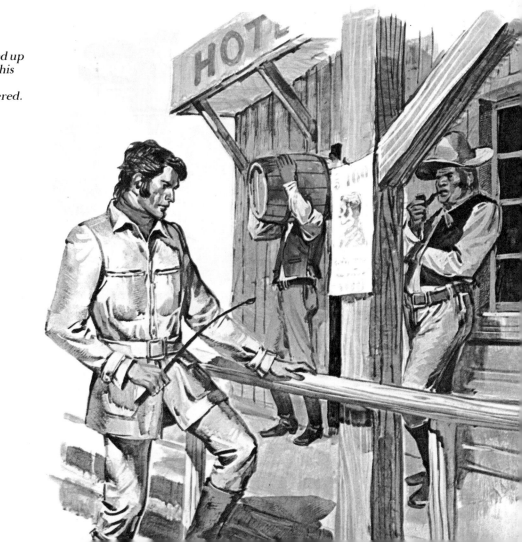

The others must have felt the same. They had found a gratifying topic for conversation during their long journey.

After a few days the column had put the plain behind them. The ascent into the Australian Alps began. It soon turned out that Paganel's optimism had been somewhat premature. Instead of the well-made road over the pass which he had promised, the mounts and beasts of burden had to struggle along a track consisting of mud and scree. The Earl breathed with obvious relief when finally a wooden-roofed mountain inn loomed up, which was managed by a sullen-looking man.

Still, the ladies were able to sleep in a bed again after such a long time. The men made themselves comfortable on simple bunks. They were all glad to have a firm roof over their heads.

In the tap-room in which miners and stockmen were squatting with glasses of strong drink, an arrest warrant was nailed to the door.

"Wanted," it said, "Ben Joyce, leader of a gang of escaped prisoners from Perth Jail, who are terrorizing the district. Joyce is thought to have come to Australia a few months ago on an unknown ship. A reward of £100 is offered for his capture."

The little company continued the climb next day with renewed strength. The way became steeper and steeper. The demands made of man and beast grew with each hour and Lord Edward constantly threw worried glances towards the ox-cart in which his wife and Mary were sitting.

Suddenly there was an unexpected halt. The sailor, Murray, who had proved his worth in the crossing of the Andes, had fallen off his horse. Then it was discovered that the animal had simply succumbed to the strain.

"Take my horse!" ordered Lord Edward briefly. "I'll ride with the others in the cart."

"I can't explain the horse's death," growled MacNabbs, who had a wide knowledge of horses, and he was more concerned when, not many hours later, Paganel's horse also fell down dead. "That looks like an epidemic," he feared.

His fears grew to a certainty. Shortly afterwards, Wilson's horse died too. Then the Earl called his friends together for a short council. He wanted to know whether they should break off the expedition.

No, they were all determined to carry on at all costs. Ayrton alone was not completely happy about this decision. Someone ought at least to inform Mr. Austin now, so that he could set sail in the *Duncan* for Twofold Bay immediately.

Captain Mangles objected, "What's the use of that?" And as MacNabbs and Lord Edward also saw no advantage in it, Ayrton did not prevail. He nodded silently, yet one could see by his face that he was rather annoyed.

"It isn't too far to the pass, anyway," Mr. Paganel encouraged the others. "Then we are sure to have the worst behind us."

They did, in fact, all reach the crest without further incident and finally descended by dangerous tracks to a forest of tall bracken. The sky had meanwhile turned dark-grey, and soon sleet began to fall. Within minutes the ground turned into a treacherous, sticky morass. Suddenly the heavy ox-cart sank up to its axles in the mud. As neither the beasts nor the men were able to free the vehicle from its precarious position, Lord Edward declared the day's march ended. He had the tents erected in a narrow clearing. While this was being done the terrible news reached him, "One of the oxen is dead!"

"I've never heard of this disease," murmured Ayrton, with a shake of his head. "Some unknown plant perhaps. I shall see to the feeding myself tonight. I just don't understand it." He tethered the three remaining oxen and the horses right next to his tent and then ran his hands over them in an expert fashion. "Tired, but healthy," he ascertained with visible relief.

Fortunately it had stopped raining and so MacNabbs, who was too restless to sleep, decided to take a little stroll in the middle of the night.

At the edge of the wood he suddenly

The Major crawled very cautiously through the tall grass and soon confirmed that he had not been mistaken.

heard voices. Puzzled, he crept closer. About ten minutes later he returned, extremely thoughtful. Next morning only one ox was still alive, and except for those belonging to the Earl and Ayrton, all the horses were dead too.

"So it's all over," said Lord Edward, deeply shocked. "We shall have to go to Melbourne on foot."

"That would be absurd!" replied Paganel excitedly. "It's not half as far to Twofold Bay as it is to Melbourne. We can be at the coast in four to five days."

"You must mean weeks?" laughed Ayrton harshly. "How do you cross the Snowy River in its swollen state?"

"We build a raft," cried Robert Grant.

"It would be dashed to pieces. Still, it's more sensible to try for the coast than to go to Melbourne. It's just that I think the *Duncan* should make for Twofold Bay now without fail. If a rescue team comes to meet us from there with horses and carts . . . "

"Agreed!" the Earl interrupted him with spirits renewed. "Yet who shall take the news to Melbourne?"

All eyes turned expectantly to Ayrton. "Well," he nodded, "I know the district best. I'll ride via Luckwood. Then I can be there in four days. You must give me the order to Mr. Austin in writing though, in case he doesn't believe me."

"Of course," MacNabbs agreed and turned to his cousin. "Tell Austin to bring a few bottles of whisky with him!"

While Lord Edward set about writing the letter, Ayrton was already packing the most essential luggage for the ride. Things seemed to be going much too slowly for MacNabbs. Impatiently he looked over his cousin's shoulder. "How do you spell Ayrton, then?" he wondered.

"The way you pronounce it, of course."

"No. He may pronounce it as Ayrton. But he spells it: Ben Joyce!"

The bandit fired.

A knavish trick

For a moment the Earl and his party were rooted to the spot. Then a general confusion arose. Only MacNabbs made to hurl himself at the sailor, yet the latter was faster. He leapt back, drew his pistol and fired blindly. Blood welled forth from Lord Edward's shoulder. Lady Helen cried out in horror and bent over her husband. For a few seconds all eyes were fixed on the wounded man.

This was long enough for the criminal to leap onto his horse and gallop away.

Fortunately it was only a grazing shot, and after a few minutes, while Lady Helen and Mary were attending to Lord Edward, Mac-Nabbs called all the men together.

"Let's not fool ourselves," he declared, "we are in a more than awkward situation. Nothing to ride except for one horse, and only one ox for pulling."

"Yet still it's better than being in the hands of these criminals," interjected Captain Mangles. "Anyway, how did you know Ayrton wasn't a quarter master . . . "

"He was that all right, I presume," interrupted the Major. "Yet everything else is a lie. I never really trusted him, and last night when I happened to notice some dark figures nearby, I spied on them. They were bandits who had been following us for some time. It was easy for them to stick to our heels thanks to that clover-leaf which the blacksmith, brought by Ayrton, had fixed to the horse's hoof. I'm sure he was one of the gang too. Well, I heard them laughing about their leader Ben Joyce, who, as honest Ayrton, was killing our animals with poisonous leaves in their fodder in order to render us immobile. Then I knew enough."

"And we have been following a trail which is worthless!" Mary Grant had approached unnoticed. There were tears in her eyes. "This monster just invented the ship-wreck off Two-fold Bay, then! My poor father!"

Captain Mangles put a consoling arm round her shoulder. "The ship-wreck did happen. The message in the bottle proves that. It wasn't hard for Ayrton to bluff us by naming a place and the date of 27th June, after he had heard our tale round the Irish family's table. Only . . . how did he actually get on to the farm?"

"I suppose he wanted to find out about the conditions there and then rob the good people with his accomplices," the Major replied with firm conviction. "But now to us. What shall we do?"

"Go on!" Bandaged, but erect, Lord Edward entered the circle. "Of course, we must inform Mr. Austin immediately. We still have one horse for this purpose."

"A dangerous ride," Mangles reminded them. "Ben Joyce will be lurking somewhere. I'm not afraid of him, so I'll ride!"

"No, Mangles. I suggest we draw lots for this task. What do you think?"

They all agreed, so the Captain fitted in with their wishes. The lot fell to the sailor named Murray. His whole face beamed. "Just let Ayrton come within range of my fists!"

"Nevertheless it might be better if you took my pistol with you!" Mangles gave him the loaded weapon. "Don't leave till it gets dark!"

"That's what I think, too," Lord Edward nodded and turned to Paganel. "Would you please write a few lines in my name to Mr. Austin? Unfortunately, I can't do it myself because of this stupid wound."

Paganel tore a page out of his note-book and accompanied the Earl into the tent where there was a little folding-table.

"To Mr. Tom Austin, Acting Commander of the *Duncan*," Lord Edward began to dictate, while Paganel's gaze wandered absent-mindedly round the tent and finally came to rest on an old newspaper, *The Australian and New Zealand Gazette*.

"New Zealand . . . Zealand . . . land," subconsciously the words went round and round in his head, and "Put the *Duncan* out to sea immediately and head eastwards. Then wait for us on the 37th Parallel in Twofold Bay," he wrote just as subconsciously to Lord Edward's instructions.

Towards evening when the sailor was pre-paring himself for his ride, having first carefully filed off the treacherous clover-leaf from the horse's hoof, it began to pour with rain again. Nevertheless they had all come out of their tents to wish him luck.

"Don't worry," laughed Murray and set spurs to the horse, and in a few moments the dense wood had already swallowed him up.

Yet, before five minutes had elapsed, several shots rang out. Then an eerie silence reigned. Even the noise of the rain seemed to stop. MacNabbs was the first outside. "Murray?" he roared. No answer.

Anxious minutes passed during which the men repeated the cry again and again.

"We must go and look," said MacNabbs finally. "Mangles, Paganel, come along with me!" Then weak cries for help drifted over from the edge of the wood. They all ran there immediately. They found the sailor, bleeding from the hip, lying in a pool of water.

"Ben Joyce . . . the . . . the letter," he murmured in a hardly audible voice, before he lost

Accompanied by the hopes and best wishes of all the others, Murray set out that evening on the dangerous ride.

consciousness.

MacNabbs and Mangles carried him into the camp, where to everyone's relief it was found that the bullet had been stopped by his thick leather belt. Nevertheless, the flesh wound under it was fairly deep. Murray would certainly need nursing for some time.

It was not long before he recovered consciousness and was able to make his report, even if haltingly.

He had suddenly been attacked by five men who immediately started firing. He had been able to knock down two of them before he was flung from the saddle. Fortunately for him, the bandits had thought he was dead. They took possession of the weapon and the horse. Then one of them searched him.

"Have you got the letter?" one of the others had asked. The one who had searched Murray had replied, "Yes, here it is!"

He had recognized Ben Joyce by his voice. "And after that," Murray continued, "I heard this confounded Ayrton, or Joyce rather, crow-ing, 'Now the *Duncan* is ours! You take the way to the coast across the Kemple Pier Bridge, and I'll ride to Melbourne. As soon as the *Duncan* cruises up, I'll let you on board with the others. Then we'll get rid of the crew and clear off across the Indian Ocean. To freedom at last!' Immediately afterwards they rode away."

"What? They want to seize the *Duncan*? Murder the crew?" The Earl put his hand to his head incredulously. "We must prevent that. Sorry as I am, we can't make for Twofold Bay any more. We set off for the south first thing tomorrow morning. We've got a hard journey in front of us."

Not even the Major, who always expected the worst, had anticipated just how hard it would be. Murray had to be carried by two men alternately on a crude make-shift stretcher. Lady Helen and Mary also went on foot as the only remaining bullock would hardly have been able to draw the heavy cart through the rain-sodden ground.

When the totally exhausted party finally

Then they built a second raft.

In the nick of time Mangles and his men seized control of the ship.

reached the Snowy by Kemple Pier, they were struck by a new blow of fate. The bandits had blown up the bridge across the raging torrent. With the courage of desperation the men built a raft. But they could not attempt the crossing until two days later when the rain had abated and the river had settled down a little. While still close to the bank, their craft was dashed to pieces by a rock.

Only with a second, more strongly built raft, was the crossing successfully negotiated. In a whirlpool the bullock, almost all the rations and the weapons went overboard. Only MacNabbs was able to save his rifle.

They finally arrived at Delegate, a small settlement where they acquired horses and a coach. Then they made rapid progress to Marlo on the coast. Lord Edward went straight away to the Telegraph Office and sent Austin a telegram. Two hours later the answer came back from Melbourne, "The *Duncan* sailed this morning. Destination unknown. Lloyd Hampton, Harbourmaster."

A matter of life and death

At this time, everyone became very depressed. Not only were they deeply upset because Ben Joyce and his criminal accomplices had managed to seize the *Duncan*, and probably killed her stout-hearted crew, but also because they had finally realized that the expedition had failed and that there was now no hope of reaching their objective.

Mary and Robert Grant were bearing this thought with admirable composure. They were particularly grateful to Captain Mangles, because he, supported by Mr. Paganel, expressed his unwavering belief that Grant was still alive.

Yet there was nothing else to do but start the homeward journey to Scotland. Even that had its complications: it would be some weeks before they could find a ship going directly from Melbourne to Europe.

Therefore they were all glad when John

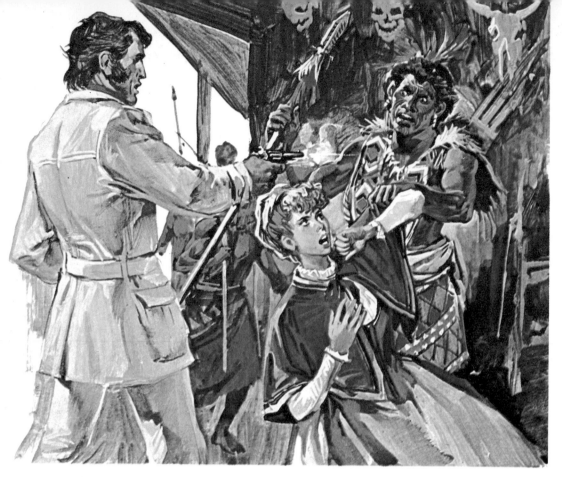

Greedily Kara-tete stretched out his hand towards Lady Helen when a shot rang out.

Mangles discovered the *Macquire* in the harbour, an old slaver, which was destined for Auckland on the North Island of New Zealand.

One day later the *Macquire* was already putting out to sea. It soon turned out that her captain and crew thought more of whisky than of proper navigation. With growing unease, Mangles, Murray and Wilson observed the questionable sailing manoeuvres of the crew. One week later, when they should have long reached port, the *Macquire* was still cruising around Auckland and was caught in a heavy storm, so the three of them took over the command of the ship without meeting any serious resistance. Screaming and shouting, the captain and crew staggered below deck and gathered round a keg of whisky, while Mangles, Wilson and Murray struggled desperately against the storm. Admittedly, they were just able at the last moment to save the hardly manoeuvrable *Macquire* from capsizing. But that night, they were unable to float her off at high tide when she ran onto a sand-bank just offshore, after the sea had grown calmer.

"Tomorrow we shall cross over to the land

in the life-boat," Mangles announced to everyone, "and then we shall have to try to reach Auckland on foot."

In the morning, however, the captain of the *Macquire* and his crew were missing. And the life-boat! No amount of anger or cursing was of any avail. Seething with rage, the men built a raft. In the early afternoon the party left the sinking ship, and with the assistance of a jurymast, rowed for the shore.

When they were half-way there, the life-boat drifted towards them, bottom-up. Empty! "Blind drunk and gone to the sharks. Still, God have mercy on the souls of even these scurvy swabs!" murmured John Mangles.

After some difficulty with the surf, they set foot on the shore and as the storm returned they were glad when Wilson found a cave in which they could spend a reasonably dry night. Paganel was the only one who was still in an imperturbably good mood.

"Today is the 5th February 1865," he announced, as he spread out a map of New Zealand on his knees, "and we are in Axen Bay on the south-west tip of the North Island of

New Zealand." He was silent for a few moments. Then he said significantly, "We're on the 37th Parallel again."

Yet the others were probably too tired. No-one, not even Captain Grant's children, paid particular attention to this part.

Next morning, the weather gradually improved, and when, after a short conference, the castaways set off in a northerly direction, Paganel advised extreme caution.

"The native Maoris are engaged in a bitter war with the English colonial troops," he explained.

The way led through valleys with an enchanting flora, but the ominously precipitous rock walls would not allow them to forget the danger. Finally, a broad river opened up before their marvelling eyes.

"The Waipa," Paganel ascertained with the aid of his map. "We must follow it."

"We'll spend the night here first," decided MacNabbs, and had the tents pitched.

It was a restless night. The echoes of rifle shots from the distant mountains constantly confirmed Paganel's statement about the war. Next day, the last doubts were removed in a terrible manner. On the river a native boat approached, manned by warriors.

The boat landed. The natives stepped out and their chief asked in broken English, "You English?"

"Yes, Englishmen in distress," the Earl confirmed.

"Me King Kai-Kuma." The chief raised his hand and the travellers found themselves surrounded by the Maoris, the points of their spears pointing threateningly towards them. "You my prisoners. British have great Maori-priest Thoaya in power. Exchange you for him."

Without their being able to resist, they were all, including the women, herded into the boat and then began a river journey lasting several days into the interior of the country. Passing lakes with hot springs, through gorges above which volcanoes flared at night, and over rapids, they finally arrived in a valley above which towered an Apah, an old mountain fortress.

In the Maori village, threats and curses were hurled at the prisoners from all sides. It was not until they were enclosed in a strongly guarded hut that they felt safe, for the moment.

Then Kai-Kuma appeared, accompanied by several chiefs, and announced, "Messenger come. Britons have shot sacred Thoaya. You all die for him."

The prisoners were herded into the boat and then began a long agonizing journey into the unknown.

There sat Eliacin Paganel without a care, and he invited his friends to join him in the feast.

"Except woman!" quickly declared another chief and went to seize Lady Helen. "You belong me! Me, Kara-tete, the great . . ."

A shot rang out. Kara-tete fell forwards, dead. The pistol in Lord Edward's hand was still smoking. For a moment no-one could move in the silence that followed. Then from all sides, warriors rushed at the white travellers, and they would probably all have been killed on the spot, had not Kai-Kuma repeatedly called, "Taboo! Taboo!"

Immediately the warriors withdrew. "Taboo" was the age-old magic word which rendered each living creature, each object, each place over which it was pronounced, sacred.

Kai-Kuma regarded the prisoners coldly. "Taboo only till after burial of Kara-tete. Then you living sacrifice for him."

They spent the next few fear-filled hours in a dark cave, consoled only slightly by the thought that Robert and Paganel had managed to escape in the confusion.

The next day, Kara-tete was interred in an enclosed burial chamber on a hill-top. The white prisoners had to watch the cruel ceremony from beginning to end: the entombment not only of the corpse, but also of the chief's wife and slaves who, immediately beforehand, were clubbed to death.

"Tomorrow, you!" proclaimed Kai-Kuma before the miserable captives were driven back into the cave. The only thing left for them was to pray.

Yet in the midst of their deepest despair came salvation: a knocking on the rear-most wall of the cave, scraping, the stone crumbling, a hand, a head, Robert!

He had managed to conceal himself in a neighbouring cave and had succeeded in breaking through the thin dividing wall. The hole was soon enlarged and a few minutes later they all escaped from the cave, raced wildly through the night into the hills, where they lost their way. In the cold light of dawn, they heard the cries of their pursuers. They had run in a circle. In front of them arose the hill where Kara-tete lay buried.

"We are lost," lamented Lady Helen loudly, when from the enclosure a familiar voice called to them. "Why's that? Why don't you come here!"

Sitting in front of the tomb, draped in a Maori cloak, as if it was the most natural thing in the world, was Mr. Paganel. He was eating the fruit and meat which had actually been intended to feed the spirits of the dead on their journey.

"We shall have some peace here for the time being," he explained after they had

166

greeted each other. "Burial grounds are sacrosanct, taboo. And don't worry, I know how we shall get away from here." The Maoris actually did stop at the foot of the hill and contented themselves in keeping a close watch on the fugitives.

Paganel pointed to a block of stone as tall as a man beside the entrance to the tomb. "Can you feel it trembling? There's a little volcano under there. If we can topple the block over at night, there'll be a firework display and also a glowing stream of lava. That'll make the superstitious Maoris lose all their courage." None of them had much hope, but still the men set to work that night. Inch by inch the rock yielded to the combined pressure of their shoulders. Hot steam welled perceptibly from the cracks in the earth which were exposed, and at the very moment when the rock finally toppled over and fell aside, a bright flame shot up from the depths. Stones and clumps of earth were hurled into the air, glowing lava poured across the ground and, with Paganel in the lead, they all ran for their lives down the hillside and into the shelter of the wood.

Long afterwards they could still hear the terrified cries of the Maoris, towards whose village in the valley the stream of lava was creeping like a fiery serpent.

It took three more days of terrible toil before the little group finally came to a flat beach by the sea. They were overjoyed to find one of the big native boats. With this they ought to be able to reach the area protected by the British further along the coast! Yet just when the men, under Captain Mangles' command, had made their first few strokes with the oars, several other boats came racing out of a small inlet to take up pursuit.

"Out onto the open sea. It's better to perish there!" the Earl had just commanded in a quiet voice when they all thought they must be dreaming. On the horizon, the *Duncan* hove into view. "Now we have the choice: to be killed by Maoris or to be killed by Ayrton's gang," murmured MacNabbs.

But, as if by a miracle, Tom Austin and his crew were waving from the ship and a few minutes later the castaways were saved.

Hopes fulfilled

It was quite a long time before Lord Edward was able to ask the question which was in everyone's mind, "What kind fate brought you here unharmed and just at the right time?"

Somewhat taken aback, Tom Austin replied, "Your instructions, my lord." From his uniform pocket, he took out the note which Paganel had written. "Put to sea immediately," he read out, "and wait for us on the west coast of New Zealand at 37° 11'. That was clear enough, wasn't it?"

"Oh, my eternal absent-mindedness!" cried Paganel in mock despair. "Now I remember! When I was writing, the newspaper for Australia and New Zealand was lying on the little table. So I absent-mindedly gave the detail as New Zealand instead of Twofold Bay!"

"God bless your absent-mindedness! Congratulations!" MacNabbs slapped the good-hearted scholar on the shoulder and everyone enjoyed the joke.

"That Ayrton behaved like a madman when we set course for New Zealand, so I had him clapped in irons. Do you want to talk to him?"

"Perhaps we shall now find out the truth about him at last!" hoped the Earl, and had the criminal brought on deck.

Yet Ayrton remained obdurate. Only when Captain Grant's children implored him, and Lord Edward promised to set him ashore with provisions on a lonely island instead of handing him over to the law in England did he confess, "I was the quarter-master on the *Britannia*, but . . . well, I had a row with the Cap'n and he marooned me on the west coast of Australia near Perth. I came across some escaped convicts there. We had nothing to lose, so we joined forces. The *Britannia*? No idea, I only know the Cap'n wanted to plot a course to New Zealand then eastwards round the Horn to Europe."

"That's all that's left for us to do," Glenervan explained to his companions shortly afterwards. "We've gone to great pains to complete the message in the bottle correctly. Unfortunately, we've failed."

This was a painful acknowledgement, above all for Mary and Robert Grant. "I shall not give up," cried the boy. "I shall become a sailor and then look for my father myself."

"Meanwhile, though," Captain Mangles tried to comfort him, "we shall still be sailing along the 37th Parallel for some time yet . . ."

"And set Ben Joyce ashore on one of the islands we see on our journey through the Pacific!" determined the Earl.

As things turned out during the course of their long journey, that was not so easy, because the islands were either deserted rocks or inhabited by hostile natives.

Finally, on the evening of 5th March, a little island-paradise loomed up. "According to the chart it's called Tabor and is not inhabited," said Captain Mangles to Lord Edward.

"Good. We'll cruise around in front of it overnight and tomorrow look for a place to land Ayrton and the most essential supplies."

That night, when the sea was calm and only the noise of the surf on the distant shore could be heard, Mary had a strange experience. "I was standing by the ship's rail and out of the sea I heard my father's voice crying for help," she sobbed. Even Captain Mangles, of whom she was very fond, and who returned her affection, was not able to comfort her.

All the more surprised they were, next morning, when they saw three men on the beach, waving and swinging the Union Jack to and fro.

They immediately lowered a boat, and what no-one had dared to hope became a reality. The men were Captain Grant and his two comrades. Crying with joy, his children embraced him.

"We are situated at the exact spot at which latitude 37° 11' crosses the coast of the island," Mr. Paganel ascertained thoughtfully, somewhat later. "How long we have been searching!"

The rest is quickly related: on 9th May 1865 thousands of people were standing in Glasgow rejoicing as they watched the *Duncan* coming into port. Flags were flying everywhere.

A few weeks later at Malcolm Castle they celebrated the marriage of Captain Mangles to the valiant Mary.

No-one has ever heard any more of the criminal quarter-master of the *Britannia*, Ben Joyce. Nor of his fellow rogues.

Everyone's eyes filled with tears when the three of them fell into each other's arms.

JAMES FENIMORE COOPER

The Last of the Mohicans

JAMES FENIMORE COOPER
The Last of the Mohicans

The Indian scout

"Montcalm is advancing to the south with an army whose heads are as numerous as the leaves on the trees!"

One summer evening in the year 1757 this news was brought by an Indian runner to the British Fort Edward on the Hudson. It conveyed nothing else but that the French, with whom England had been waging a bitter war for the mastery of North America for more than two years, were finally going to fight their way from Canada to their possessions on the Mississippi and on the Gulf of Mexico.

Nevertheless, the report did not worry the Commander of the British Fort, General Webb, very much. It had come from Fort William Henry, which lay about ten miles to the north, on the south shore of Lake George, and was occupied by about one thousand two hundred men under the command of the Scottish Colonel Munro. Webb would only have had to move against the French General with the five thousand soldiers stationed in Fort Edward and with Munro's troops, and he would have been far superior in numbers to the troops of Montcalm.

Yet, instead of a battle which promised to be successful, Webb preferred to wait behind the protective fortifications and merely send out a few companies; in all, one thousand five hundred men, to Fort William, which was already threatened by seige. The fact that he was not sufficiently strengthening Munro against the French superiority, but was weakening himself in a dangerous manner, did not occur to him at all. He had got used to leaving the course of action to the enemy, just like so many British officers of that time.

The French knew how to act. Much more quickly than the British, they had learned how to alter their way of fighting to suit the conditions which were so different from those in Europe. They had also very quickly gained many Indian tribes as allies, amongst them the Hurons in the north, and made sure of the help of experienced settlers and hunters.

Indians were fighting on the British side, too, like the Delawares who had lived for years in bloody tribal hostility with the Hurons. They referred to them scornfully as "Mingos", that is, inferiors.

The Delawares had been forced inland from the Atlantic coast by the whites. They had now, in their turn, quarrelled with the Hurons about the hunting grounds between the Hudson valley and the Canadian frontier, a gigantic forest and lake region which Britain had made secure with countless forts.

For easier communication between Fort Edward and Fort William, which were divided by a densely wooded chain of hills, the British had constructed a road which was wide enough to carry wagons and had many bends because of the climbing nature of the land. Fifteen hundred soldiers were marching north on it the very next morning to the sound of drums and pipes. Fort William lay a good day's march in front of them, because the cumbersome guns and supply wagons allowed them to advance very slowly.

Shortly afterwards, a second, much smaller troop, also left the fort. The young and dashing Major Duncan Heyward had gladly accepted the task of accompanying to Fort William the pretty daughters of Colonel Munro, who, whilst on their way to their father, had spent a few days as the guests of General Webb.

"How long shall we take?" asked Cora, as they rode along the river bank. She was the elder of the two, and in contrast to her blonde sister, had dark hair.

"You will have lunch with your father," was Heyward's firm conviction.

"And the French?" asked Alice, rather anxiously. "Is there no danger that we shall fall into their hands?"

The Major laughed unconcernedly, "They are still a long way off! Pity that I must return today, and so shall not see how they get their heads broken at the ramparts, yet perhaps . . . Ah! Magua is stopping!"

This remark referred to a Red Indian who, up till now, had ridden at the head of the

"That is Magua, the guide whom your father sent to Fort Edward," the Major comforted the two sisters.

little troop. His face was decorated with war paint. Two eagle's feathers were stuck in his long hair. In front of him, on the horse's back, lay one of the typical rifles with which the French occasionally equipped friendly natives.

"Who is that?" asked Alice, with hardly concealed suspicion.

"The scout who brought the news from your father yesterday," the Major comforted her. "He is called Magua, the Cunning Fox, and will bring us to our objective by a short cut which only he knows. Actually, he comes from Canada, but years ago he linked up with our allies, the Mohawks. After your father once treated him harshly, he has proved himself as a loyal and reliable scout and messenger."

"Treated him harshly?" repeated Alice. "Then he is certainly angry with my father. Now . . . now, I like him even less. Perhaps he is thinking of revenge. Do you really trust him, Duncan?"

"Would I put you in his charge if that were not the case?"

As the girl only nodded in agreement to this question, the officer turned to the Red Indian.

"Are we leaving the military road now?"

Silently, Magua pointed into the thicket. Thereupon, Heyward beckoned the servants to come closer, and ordered them to continue following the road to Fort William.

"Only the scout and we three shall take the short cut," he explained to the ladies. "That was agreed with General Webb, because three horses leave fewer tracks behind. It is not quite out of the question even if very improbable, that hostile Indians are already patrolling the forest area. From now on, I ask you to speak as little as possible."

Alice hesitated a moment. "I still don't trust the Redskin," she admitted.

"He is a human being like you and I. What can he do about his colour?" she was reprimanded by her sister.

The Indian threw a short glance at her, and then rode into the thicket. Without asking

"The sun is sinking," said the Indian softly. "Disappearing in the darkness like my people."

any more questions, the three of them followed him.

Only very rarely did a strip of blue sky shimmer through the high roof of the treetops.

As the mighty fir trees were not too close together, the four riders made fairly rapid progress, yet they stopped with a jerk when they heard the clatter of hooves behind them. Magua and the Major went for their guns. Then they saw a more than remarkable man on a sweating, broken down old mare which was followed by a panting foal.

"I've seen him in the Fort," the Major remembered with displeasure. The face of the Indian, which had been sulky before, now became even more sullen. Meanwhile, the man had reached the group. Everything about him was unusual. A much too large head on a lean body, with lanky limbs and conspicuously large feet. In addition, the strange clothing – a bright blue jacket, much too wide, and bright yellow trousers – made him look like a creature from another world.

"Who are you?" growled the Major in a very unfriendly manner.

"David Gamut, a servant of the Lord and psalmist to God's honour and glory. I teach the people to sing songs to the praise of the Highest. Shall I give you a sample?"

"For God's sake, no! That's all we need to bring the savages upon our necks!" Heyward said with horror. "What are you looking for here? Have you been following us, by any chance?"

"Certainly, and the grace of the Lord let me find you in time. But my objective is Fort William, where I want to teach the rough warriors gentle songs. When I saw you setting off this morning, I decided immediately to join you. Well, here I am."

"Then I can only advise you not to be here any more, but to trot back to Fort Edward very quickly," answered Heyward gruffly. "You would only be a hindrance to us."

To the Major's surprise, the two girls showed an interest in the pious man, and when Alice even declared that she would take him under her personal protection, Heyward finally gave way.

"All right, come along, but watch that you don't go yelling out any songs without my permission. Magua, we'll ride on."

The Indian opened his lips as if he wished to protest against the new fellow rider, but then he obeyed the order without saying anything, and the troop got under way again.

Heyward now took up his position at the rear, and more from curiosity than because he feared any danger, examined the forest more carefully. Suddenly, he thought he saw an eye staring at him in the bush, but then he told himself he was being foolish.

"A ray of light flickered on a blackberry for a moment," he consoled himself, and didn't think of examining the bushes more closely. He was still very inexperienced.

In the trap

On the same evening, a weather-beaten white man and an Indian, both of whom were no longer young, were camping beside a raging river. Although only of medium breadth, it had nevertheless cut itself a track with many gorges through the edge of the forest between the two forts. The outstanding thing about the white man was his long-barrelled rifle. The Indian's head was shaved bare except for one short tuft over the centre, his legs were bare and he had black and white paint on the upper part of his body.

"The sun is sinking," said the Indian softly, "disappearing in the night like my people. Yet while the sun's light will shine again, when my son dies, the last of the Mohicans will go to the great spirit."

"Your son still has a rich life in front of him, Chingachgook," said the white man.

The Indian shook his head silently, and strained his ears towards the forest. Now the white man also heard the crackling of branches, and already a powerfully built young Indian was entering the campsite. He was unmis-

takably the son of the old chief.

"The forest is full of Mingos," he reported. "They crawl through the undergrowth like miserable worms, yet now Uncas also hears hoof-beats."

Like lightning, his father and the white man leapt up and seized their rifles. The shadows of two riders came into sight between the tree trunks.

"We are friends of the King!" cried the one wearing uniform.

It was Major Heyward and Gamut, the singer. After they had realized that the white man and the two Indians were not hostile, the officer revealed, "We have gone completely off our course. Our Indian guide has lost the way."

"An Indian who loses his way?" said the puzzled white man. "A Mohawk?"

"Yes. That is to say, he is one now. He was born a Huron."

"Then he will remain false all his life," said

"It is good," replied Magua, then sat down, and appeared to be listening to the forest while the Major continued to encourage him.

175

As quick as lightning, he slid away, and then leapt into the bushes.

the old Indian scornfully. "He has enticed you into this region infested by Mingos and then left you in the lurch."

"No, he is still with us," Heyward contradicted. "Over there, under the trees."

The three of them bent the bushes aside a little, and looked in the direction indicated.

"You have two ladies with you!" cried the white man in astonishment.

"Yes. Do you think . . ."

"No time for talking," Chingachgook interrupted. "Hurons not honest."

"I'm almost convinced of that myself," confessed Heyward quietly. "What shall we do?"

"First take that dog prisoner," growled the white man. "He has not seen us yet, otherwise he would immediately suspect something. Go to him. Tell him that you have met a hunter who will take you to Fort William tomorrow. Get him involved in a conversation and don't mention a word about my friends. They will creep up on him unseen."

"Right," the officer agreed, and rode back into the woods with Gamut. When he reached

the others, he informed them, "We are lucky. Down by the river, I came across a hunter who knows the district. He will come presently and take us to your father tomorrow."

"Is the man reliable, then?" asked Alice. "Or," she made an inconspicuous, but eloquent gesture with her shoulder towards Magua, who was leaning silently against a tree, "is he another one who just has big ideas?"

Heyward, however, acted as if he had not heard the question, and turned to the Indian. "One tree resembles another in the forest. Surely even a fox might not be able to tell one tree from another? Tomorrow, the Cunning Fox will find the trap again, as he usually does."

"Tomorrow, Magua will look for his own trap," answered the runner sullenly. "He does not need the help of the Pale Face hunter."

"What? You want to leave us? And what will you say to Colonel Munro when you stand before him without his daughters? No, Magua, don't act hastily. And think of the reward which the Colonel has promised you. I shall double it out of my own pocket."

"It is good," Magua sat down and seemed to be listening into the forest as he did so.

"Here, eat a piece of meat. I've still got some left," Heyward encouraged him, a little over-zealously, and fumbled around in his haversack until he found a chunk of roast meat. He handed it to the Redskin. "Have that."

At the same moment, he saw the shadow of the young Mohican emerging behind Magua. Yet in a flash, the Huron sensed the danger. He let out a harsh yell, dealt the Major a violent blow, and in one bound leapt into the undergrowth. A shot rang out, but in vain. The Cunning Fox had escaped.

"There's no sense in going after him when it will soon be dark," declared the white hunter who had fired the shot. He gave a hint of a bow towards the ladies, who were clinging to each other fearfully. "My friends and I shall bring you to safety, but we must set off immediately. The whole forest is swarming with Mingos and of course they have heard the shot. Oh, but I haven't told you my name yet. Call me Hawk-

Eye. Right then, pack everything up – we're going on foot. Chingachgook and Uncas will lead the horses. Shhh! What's that? A foal?"

"Mine," confessed the psalmist.

"Take an arrow and shoot it," Hawk-Eye commanded the young Mohican. When he saw the horrified expressions on the faces of his audience, he explained regretfully, "We must do it, as food for the wolves, or do you want them to follow us and betray us by their howling to the Mingos?"

These words brought home to everyone how real the danger was, and that they had no other choice but to obey the hunter's instructions.

Without a word, the two Indians moved through the thicket and just as silently, the others followed. The path led to the river, and then, through almost impenetrable bushes, downstream along its bank. Although night had fallen, they could clearly discern that the river valley gradually narrowed into a gorge, and that the water turned into a raging torrent.

Under a dense canopy of leaves which hung down deeply over the bank, the Indians came to a halt and tethered the horses to the trees.

"Let's hope no-one finds the hiding place," whispered Hawk-Eye. "We shall need the beasts tomorrow." Then he slid down the bank and drew a canoe from a hidden spot beneath the bushes. "Come along!"

Hardly had the two girls and Heyward settled themselves down than the old scout pushed off and steered the boat out into the current. Faster and faster it sped towards a gorge, heading straight for a rocky cliff which divided the river in two. The roaring of the water echoed from the rock walls and grew stronger with each passing second.

Hawk-Eye steered the canoe out into the raging torrent, and then pointed the bow towards a cliff in the middle of the river. There they landed.

They were even sitting in the trees and shooting as soon as something stirred.

"Glenn's Falls," bellowed Hawk-Eye. Presumably it was supposed to sound reassuring, but it had just the opposite effect.

"Shall we be smashed to pieces or do you want us to be dragged into the deep?" yelled Heyward, but almost at the same moment, he breathed a sigh of relief. The canoe was lying alongside a flat spot on the rock.

"Keep quiet and wait until I have fetched the others," ordered the hunter, and was already pushing off again. After a very short

while, he was back with the Red Indians and the psalmist.

"We should be safe here," he stated with satisfaction, after he had tied up the canoe and noticed the questioning faces of his companions. "Chingachgook and I discovered the secret of this rock years ago. You will be surprised."

He had not been exaggerating. To the right and left of the rocky island, the river thundered down into the depths, yet the water had gouged out a cave in its interior with an entrance hidden by bushes above the falls, and an exit above the raging torrent below.

The cave was relatively dry, and Hawk-Eye immediately went to work, preparing a bed for the ladies out of soft branches, while Chingachgook fanned a little fire which was not visible from outside where Uncas was on guard.

"I hardly think the Mingos will find us here," said Hawk-Eye. Then, whilst they were eating, he recounted past experiences so naturally that his confidence gradually transmitted itself to his involuntary guests. Indeed, Gamut finally raised his voice and sang a hymn of thanksgiving.

"How often have I sung this very song," said Hawk-Eye with deep feeling, "in the days

One of them took possession of the canoe.

For some hours they kept the enemy at bay, but when their powder and shot ran out, the end was not far away.

when I was still called Nathaniel Bumppo – Natty for short," and he wished them good-night to hide his feelings. "We must go to sleep – we have a long day in front of us."

Yet the sleep was all too short. A sudden blood-curdling scream came over from the river bank, followed by much howling. Immediately they were all wide awake. "A horse in terror for its life!" said Heyward, who recognized the sound. Then all was deathly quiet.

"The horses have been attacked by wolves," said Hawk-Eye thoughtfully, "but the attackers must have retreated. Why?"

He didn't need to wait for an answer. Suddenly shots rang out from the bank. Arrows whizzed round the entrance to the cave and the war-cries of the Hurons made the very air tremble.

Until late in the morning, the group, which was hemmed in, succeeded in repelling all attacks. Hawk-Eye's long rifle picked off the enemies in the trees and others who tried to swim across. The two Indians and the Major also proved themselves excellent marksmen.

Then both powder and shot ran out, and

when one of the Hurons managed to gain possession of the canoe, deepest despair fell upon those in the cave. Chingachgook and Uncas drew close together and began to speak to each other quietly.

"They are preparing themselves for death," said Hawk-Eye with a shrug of his shoulders. "We shall have to face up to it too." He threw a pitying glance at the two girls. "Perhaps you'll get away with your lives," he said, without much conviction.

Then Cora, unexpectedly, sat up and declared in a firm voice, "We must not give up hope! Please do not contradict me. You, Chingachgook and Uncas, must try to escape by swimming in the current below the falls, and fetch help from Fort William immediately. My father has probably already sent patrols on the way. Don't worry about us, we shall surely be more valuable to the Indians as prisoners and hostages than as corpses. I know that my sister supports my suggestion and I also expect the same from you, Major, and Mr. Gamut. We have no other choice."

An astonished silence followed these words.

"No . . . no," murmured Hawk-Eye, shaking his head. Only when Gamut and the Major urged him to agree, as they knew of no other way of being saved, did he finally withdraw his opposition. "What do Chingachgook and Uncas think?" he asked.

"We shall have to try it," answered Chingachgook resolutely, and the young Mohican, who had listened to Cora's words with secret admiration, nodded. "We must not fail the brave Pale Face Squaw and her friends."

"Hurry up!" urged Heyward.

"Then God be with you and with us!" Hawk-Eye shook hands with everyone before he followed the Mohicans to the exit of the cave, and there carefully concealed his rifle in a crack in the rock.

Uncas had already leapt into the river. Now his father also disappeared into the swirling waters. Hawk-Eye waved one last time, then he also entrusted himself to the foaming mass.

All was quiet on the bank. Apparently the Mingos had noticed nothing.

In greatest danger

It wasn't long before the Hurons came swimming over to the rock. Anxiously, Cora and Alice cowered in the rearmost corner of the cave. Gamut, who had been wounded by an arrow in the shoulder, propped himself up near the exit, moaning softly. The Major had stationed himself behind the entrance with a loaded pistol ready to fire. Branches and shrubs concealed him. Nevertheless, he had little hope that the Indians would not find the cave.

Now cries were to be heard. The Hurons had set foot on the rocky island and were looking for the presumed corpses, above all, for one whose name they constantly called to each other in French – La Longue Carabine. "The Long Rifle!" thought the Major. He had often heard of this famous scout before, who had rendered the British Colonial Army many valuable services, but only now did he realize that Hawk-Eye and the Long Rifle were one and the same person. However, before he could inform the girls and Gamut of this fact, and thus reawaken new hope, Magua's face appeared in the opening. Heyward aimed like lightning. Scornful laughter showed him that his shot had gone astray. He had fired off his last bullet. Now he hurried to the girls and placed himself in front of them, protectively.

Outside, a harsh cry of triumph rang out before the first Indians, with Magua in the lead, cautiously penetrated into the cave. Resistance would have meant immediate death. Silently the prisoners allowed themselves to be taken outside. Immediately a giant of a Huron began to address angry questions to Heyward.

The latter shook his head as if he did not understand, and asked Magua to tell him what the giant wanted.

"Where are the Long Rifle, the Great Snake and the Bounding Elk? Have they suddenly sprouted wings and flown away?"

"No," replied the Major coldly. "The river has carried them away."

This information surprised the Hurons and obviously made them uneasy. After a short exchange of words between Magua and the giant, the latter urged that they should move away immediately. Fort Edward was not very far, and surely the fugitives would find help there.

The prisoners were brought to the bank in the canoe. Cora and Alice were allowed to mount their horses, a sign that the Indians wanted to make rapid progress. Heyward and Gamut, however, had to march into the unknown on foot.

"For the moment, there seems to be no danger to our lives," whispered the officer to the girls. "I'm worried about Gamut, though. His wound seems to hurt him a lot."

Yet the psalmist acted bravely during the following hours. Magua, who constantly threw suspicious glances at the prisoners, rode at the head, and led the troop in a northern direction through the forest with a certainty which was

The cries indicated that the Hurons were setting foot on the island.

the best proof that he had only been pretending that he had been lost the day before.

Finally, the trees thinned out and one could see the view into a small valley where a hill rose steeply in the centre. The giant called a few words to Magua which sounded like an order, and it did not escape Heyward's attention that the Cunning Fox suppressed his anger at the rough tone. Then the Huron chief rode on quickly to the north with the greater part of the troop along the edge of the wood, while Magua led the prisoners and the remainder of the Mingos up the hill. On its plateau, which was surrounded by low trees and dense bushes, he gave the order to stop and have the prisoners tied to the trees.

While the Hurons busied themselves fetching provisions out of their supply bags, the Cunning Fox checked their bonds. Heyward used the opportunity and asked him soft-

ly, "Why do you let yourself be treated by the fat Huron like a mangy dog? Are you not yourself a chief?"

Magua looked at him grimly. "I was one of their chiefs, and they drove me from their wigwams in disgrace, because my mind was confused, and I threatened some of them with death. Do you want to know why my mind was confused?" Heyward had a foreboding of evil, and was silent. "Because the Pale Face had given me fire water, which made me weak and my head confused, and he had me whipped because I did not obey immediately. Colonel Munro forbade the fire water for the Mohawks, to whom I had fled for safety and one of whom I am today. Now the women point at my back and scorn me. The honour of Cunning Fox will be restored only when one of his daughters" – he pointed to Cora, who had been listening with horror – "follows him to his wig-

*The gate was only
opened a hair's breadth,
but they were saved.*

wam and her father, the grey-haired, has to think each day how she serves Magua."

"No!" screamed Alice, even before her sister could say a word. "Let us rather die together!"

"Then die!" roared Magua, and tore his tomahawk from his belt with unbridled anger and hurled it at Alice. It missed her head by an inch. Heyward had no other thought but to protect the beloved girl. Despair lent him unsuspected strength. With one jerk he burst his bonds, but already one of the Hurons was hurling himself upon him, and a knife flashed in his fist. Then a shot rang out. The Indian fell down dead.

Chingachgook and Uncas broke out of the bushes. Somewhere Hawk-Eye's rifle thundered again. Those of the Hurons who were still alive ran away.

"Magua has unfortunately got away as well," growled the old scout with disappointment, after the girls and Gamut had been freed from their bonds. Yet when they wanted to

thank him, he refused to accept. "You must thank Uncas. He found the trail after we had re-armed ourselves from a hiding place in the forest and had fetched my rifle from the rock in the river. Anyway, there's no time to talk now. Fort William is already beseiged by the French. But there will be mist tonight, so we should manage to get into the fort unnoticed. But we must hurry!"

Having been freed from such great danger, they actually managed to reach a small hill in front of the fort without being discovered by Indians. From there, they saw with horror that French troops had surrounded the stronghold from all sides, and on the edges of the wood, countless allied Indians were encamped.

At night, however, when dense mist wafted over the shore from the neighbouring lake, they ventured to break through the lines. It was a foolhardy attempt because the Britons who took them for French shot at them. Then the French, who thought they were Britons shot at them. Finally, when the gate of the

182

fortress was opened a hair's breadth for them, the two girls rushed into their father's arms. Hawk-Eye and the two Mohicans were missing, they had lost their way in the mist.

Secret orders from Fort Edward

Major Heyward was happy to have finally brought his charges safely to their destination, but he was horrified at the fate of the fortress. If reinforcements did not come soon from General Webb, the resistance against the French superiority would collapse in a very short time. Heyward and Colonel Munro hoped Webb had been informed meanwhile about the hopeless position by Hawk-Eye and the Mohicans.

After a few days, even this last hope vanished. The French felt so sure of victory that they sent a prisoner, whom they had apparently captured a very short time before, into the beseiged fort.

It was Hawk-Eye. Angrily he reported to the Colonel that the Hurons had succeeded not only in overpowering him, but also in taking from him a letter which had been sewn into his deer-hide jacket, from General Webb to the commander of the fort. No, he did not know

The greeting between the officers was short but correct and courteous.

The French brought a prisoner, and sent him into the fort.

the contents, but General Montcalm wanted to hand it over to him personally.

"This is a humiliation!" roared Colonel Munro.

But Major Heyward was of a different opinion, and was able to persuade his superior to agree to a conversation with the French.

"Montcalm is a gentleman, and will not do anything dishonourable, nor demand any such thing from us," he added, forcibly. "We must know what General Webb commands."

The next morning, the two Generals met on the open space between the fort and the edge of the forest. As Munro did not speak French, he had taken Heyward along as an interpreter. The salutations were short, but courteous. Then Chevalier de Montcalm spoke about the bravery of the Britons and expressed his regret that there was nothing left for them to do but die, if they wished to continue their pointless resistance.

"Pointless?" Munro said with disgust. "Do you not know that General Webb is advancing?"

Instead of an answer the Frenchman

handed him Webb's letter. Munro and Heyward read it with increasing anger. Webb informed them that he had no intention of diminishing his forces at Fort Edward, even by one single man, and the best thing was for Fort William to surrender to the French. On no account could Munro expect any help from outside.

It took some time before Munro turned to his opponent again. "Your rejoicing was premature. We shall fight to the last man'."

"An honourable point of view," replied the Frenchman. "Yet would it not be more honourable to retain your soldiers for your King and country rather than sacrifice them senselessly?"

"I have never handed over my sword and shall not surrender it to you, either."

"You don't need to. I shall only impose honourable conditions upon you. You may withdraw unhindered to Fort Edward with your arms and colours. We are only worried about the fort, which is of no more use to you."

Munro stepped a little to one side, and conferred with Heyward, who was a very brave but considerably more clear-sighted officer than the old blade was. Several times Munro shook his head, but finally he also submitted to reason.

"We bow to the inevitable," he announced in a husky voice to the Frenchman, who gave a slight bow. "We shall trust your word and leave the Fort tomorrow morning. Armistice with effect from now."

"With effect from now," confirmed Montcalm, and the two commanders parted.

Shortly afterwards, loud rejoicing broke out in the French camp. Around the wigwams of the hostile Indians, however, everything remained remarkably quiet.

"They are unhappy because the capitulation disappoints their hopes of many scalps. I hope that Montcalm can keep them under control," Hawk-Eye said in a worried voice.

"He is a soldier. He will keep his word," Munro answered brusquely. It surpassed his powers of imagination that the 'savages' should not obey the orders of a white man and an officer at that, even if he was French.

It was probably because his mind was stuck in a military groove that Munro, in spite of the dangerous experiences that Cora and Alice had undergone with the treacherous Magua, strictly refused to grant them special protection next day when they formed up ready to march off. They had to walk with the women and children and the baggage train at the rear of the column. Not even Heyward could stay with them. Munro had ordered Heyward and Hawk-Eye to join him at the head of the column. The Major just had time to ask Gamut to stay back and protect the girls.

So the catastrophe came about which had been feared by the guide. Hardly had the women left the gate behind them when, suddenly, Indians fell upon the defenceless women from all sides and caused a terrible blood-bath with their knives and tomahawks, totally unhindered by the French.

In vain Alice and Cora tried to escape. Gamut ran along beside them, singing loudly, with his arms swinging around like the sails of a windmill. For a few moments the Indians gave way in the face of one whom they thought was possessed by demons. Suddenly Magua was amongst them. With a triumphant yell, he swept up Alice, who was on the point of fainting, and threatened to kill her if Cora did not follow him. Almost out of her senses, the girl obeyed.

"I shall stay with you," cried Gamut bravely.

Before the retreating Britons realized what was happening behind them, almost all the women and children were slaughtered. But the French would not allow them to see to their dead and bury them.

The pursuit

Five days later, five men moved cautiously over the scene of the slaughter. They were Hawk-Eye with his Indian friends, a nd two white men who were also dressed as hunters, Colonel Munro and Major Heyward. After an animated argument with General Webb in Fort

Gamut swung his long arms and sang.

Edward, they had been given permission to return to the battlefield to search for possible survivors.

But the Indians had finished off their work when the French moved on after burning down the fort. Desperately, Munro ran to and fro between the cruelly dismembered bodies.

"Where are my daughters? Cora! Alice!" he repeated constantly, but in vain.

"We can't find them, either," said Hawk-Eye thoughtfully. "That makes me hope they are still alive."

This hope was strengthened when Uncas found a scrap of material which came from Cora's veil, and a brooch belonging to Alice. Heyward thrust the piece of jewellery to his breast and breathed heavily.

"They . . . they must still be alive. Tell me I'm right, Hawk-Eye."

"I'm quite convinced of it."

The scout lifted up a piece of wood like a short stick. "Here. This was lying in the bushes. It is Gamut's flute. It seems he has not deserted the girls."

Then he stood up straight and declared, with a determination which showed just how seriously he meant it, "Even if they have taken the girls to the end of the world, we shall search for them and find them. God help those who took them away, and . . . " he made a significant pause, "every Frenchman who comes into my hands from this day on."

Uncas and his father had meanwhile penetrated into the forest. Suddenly they beckoned to the others, and pointed to hoofmarks.

"Indians, almost all on foot. Two white squaws on horses. And here, footprints of drunken Indian."

"Magua," Hawk-Eye realized. Yet when he saw how excited Munro and Heyward were, and that they wanted to follow the tracks, he shook his head vigorously.

"We must keep a clear head now. I guess many Mingos are still patrolling the forest. Besides, it will be dark soon." He pointed to the ruins of the fort. "We shall stay here until tomorrow morning. Then we go out on the lake to the north. Some of the boats are still in good condition. That is safer and water leaves no tracks."

"To the north?" Heyward interrupted. "But if . . . "

Then Magua entered the hut and reared up in front of the prisoner with a cry of rage.

"Magua to north," declared Uncas with certainty. "Over Canadian border where Hurons think themselves safe. White friend of squaws shall see that we cross trail of Magua."

"I hope you're right, Bounding Elk," murmured Munro unhappily, and turned to the scout. "You're in command here. Your experience is greater than ours."

The men spent a restless night. They sometimes felt that someone was creeping round the fort, but in the first light of dawn everything was quiet and nothing prevented them from loading up a large canoe and pushing off from the shore. Thus they began a fairly silent and long journey over the lake which stretched out far in front of them.

"We shall reach the north shore in two days if the Indians don't catch us first," declared Hawk-Eye.

They saw how justified this provision was when, a few hours later, the boat was fired upon from a little island. Immediately afterwards several canoes put out from the shore but the five friends aimed well, and after three attackers crashed mortally wounded into the water, the Indians gave up the pursuit.

During that night, which the men spent on a small island, they had to ward off an attack. On the following day, however, they were undisturbed and reached the north shore of the lake in the evening. They hid the boat in the reeds and immediately set out. It was already fairly dark when Chingachgook suddenly raised his hand in warning, and the others heard the panting of a horse.

Cautiously, they crept up to the spot from where the noise had come. They had great difficulty in suppressing a cry of astonishment. On a small clearing, several horses were grazing without any sign of a guard.

"There . . . I know those two," Heyward said excitedly. "They are the horses on which Cora and Alice left Fort Edward. We had to leave them behind before we reached Fort William."

And while he and Uncas caught the

horses, Hawk-Eye nodded to the Colonel encouragingly. "We are on the right track, then, and not too far from Magua's camp. Until now it was important for him to advance quickly, but now he feels safe and has simply left the horses behind. The Indians here in the north still have no real love for horses. They still prefer to walk on their own two feet if it is at all possible."

Uncas led Cora's horse in front of them. "Young squaws not hurt. Uncas will set free daughters of Grey Head."

Munro nodded to him gratefully, and impatiently urged that they should set out. Chingachgook and Hawk-Eye, however, shook their heads.

It would have been pointless to try to continue during the night, but early the next day they were forcing their way through hilly country, partly covered by woods and partly by tall grass. At this stage, the two Indians were particularly cautious, and kept a constant look-out in all directions. Hardly any tracks could be seen now, and yet Chingachgook suddenly stopped in front of a dip in the ground, at the end of which bare rocks towered up, and said softly, "Camp of Huron dogs not far now."

Without making any sound, the five men now crept through the undergrowth until they reached a place from where they could look down. Not far away, in the valley in front of the dark wood, a lake glistened; it had numerous beaver lodges. On the shore stood a tall figure which, in spite of the coloured painting on face and body and the feathers in its hair, did not look much like an Indian.

Suddenly, Hawk-Eye laughed softly to himself. The twitching on the faces of the Mohicans also betrayed their amusement. The guide was already drawing himself up to his full height and waving to the figure. He was at first taken aback, but then came towards them with long strides and arms flailing. It was the psalmist, David Gamut.

"The Lord does not desert his own," he called, while still a long way off, and it took

The bear paced along beside the two of them as if it were quite natural.

some time before the mutual astonishment had abated sufficiently for Munro to ask, "How are my children?"

"They are well," Gamut reassured him, and reported that Alice was guarded by Huron women in the nearby village. Cora, on the other hand, had been brought to a different tribe. Were they Hurons too? He didn't think so, as he had seen that their delegates had a tortoise as a totem sign.

"A tortoise?" Chingachgook repeated with surprise. "So they are Delawares." Then, without giving any explanation, he asked the singer to continue.

There wasn't much more to say, the latter maintained. Just that he was busy, admittedly without any success so far, teaching the Indian children hymns. Nevertheless, his skill in singing had had the effect that he was fairly kindly treated by the Indians and could move around completely freely.

"Perhaps they think I am mad?" he asked, harmlessly.

At the very moment when Heyward discovered the joyful girl, he heard a rustling behind him.

"Perhaps," Major Heyward agreed. "And I shall turn that to my advantage!"

The others looked at him uncomprehendingly, whilst he declared resolutely, "The Indians are in awe of madmen, so I shall play mad as well, and go into the camp with Gamut!"

"That is more than madness!" the old Colonel gasped, and even Hawk-Eye looked thoughtful. Yet the officer could not be persuaded to give up his plan.

Contrary to expectation, the two Mohicans also supported him. Then Hawk-Eye gave way as well. With his cheeks and forehead painted with colours which Uncas had with him, Heyward set off with Gamut on their dangerous undertaking. The village consisted of numerous huts with mud roofs, and the Major felt extremely uncomfortable in his disguise when, surrounded by children, he and the singer approached the largest house in front of which stood many braves. Gamut stepped inside and

*His voice died away in a helpless gurgle.
The bear's grip was merciless.*

sat down quite naturally. Heyward copied him silently. Just as silently the braves followed and sat round them in a circle. After an ominous silence, Heyward declared to them in French that the Great Father in far away France had sent him to his red children to enquire as to their welfare and heal such as were sick.

The suspicion in the faces of the Indians disappeared. They nodded approvingly, and one of them, obviously a chief, fetched out a long stemmed pipe and lit it. But before the smoking ceremony was over a loud cry arose outside. The braves and Heyward and Gamut stepped out into the open. A party of Hurons were bringing a prisoner. It was Uncas.

It was difficult for Heyward not to betray himself. He returned with the braves to the hut into which Uncas was also led. In the short scuffle, the Mohican succeeded in whispering to him quickly, "The others are free."

The Hurons still didn't know whom they had actually taken prisoner. They only knew that it was an Indian from the large family of the Delawares who were friendly to the British. He only answered their questions with mockery or scornful silence.

Anxiously, Heyward looked around for Gamut, but the singer was nowhere to be seen.

However, the officer had no time to worry about his disappearance. Suddenly Magua entered the hut and reared up before the Mohican with a cry of rage.

"That is the Bounding Elk. Tie him to the torture stake."

The Hurons leapt up with surprise and talked in excited confusion. They congratulated each other on their catch, and then took Uncas to an open place where they bound him to a stake.

"Begin your death song," mocked Magua. "Tomorrow you die."

Without having recognized Heyward, the Cunning Fox finally withdrew. Then the officer heard a voice behind him which brooked no contradiction.

"My eldest squaw is very sick. Come with me and heal her, white medicine man."

It was the chief. Whether he liked it or not, Heyward nodded, and followed him into the dusk.

A daring plan

The track led to a rock wall at the end of the village. Suddenly Heyward felt something against his leg and heard a deep growl. To his

horror a large bear was trotting along beside him. But when he saw that the chief paid hardly any attention to the animal, he also felt easier in his mind. He remembered that in many tribes the medicine men liked to disguise themselves as bears. Finally they stood in front of a door in the rock wall. The chief unbolted it. Behind it, a weakly lit cave opened up which was divided by rugs into several rooms. In the foremost lay the sick squaw, surrounded by howling women, and in one corner singing in a loud and solemn voice sat Gamut.

It was not difficult for Heyward to persuade the chief that they should leave him alone with the squaw, who was possessed by an evil spirit. Without hesitation he and the Indian women withdrew. The bear, however, remained and growled threateningly when Gamut whispered to the Major, "Alice is at the back of the cave."

Hardly had the door been closed from outside than the bear drew itself up to its full size and took its head off. Underneath appeared the laughing face of Hawk-Eye.

"We haven't much time," he whispered. "I was lucky enough to be able to knock out the medicine man just outside the village. No-one has noticed yet that another person is playing his part. Now listen. Look for Alice immediately. I shall guard the door while you look. Then, we will decide what to do next."

Still completely confused by the unexpected turn of events, Heyward hastened to the next room. But at the same moment he found the joyful girl, he heard a rustling behind him. As quick as a flash, he turned round. Scornfully, Magua stood in front of him and hissed, "You are cunning, Briton, but no cunning will save you and that Mohican dog . . . "

His voice died away in a helpless gurgle. The bear was throttling him. Unconscious, he sank to the ground.

"Quickly now," commanded Hawk-Eye from under his mask. "Wrap the girl in those blankets from the sick woman whom you can't cure now anyway. Carry her out and tell the Indians it is the patient you are taking into the fresh forest air so that she may recover completely, and where she must stay alone until tomorrow morning."

Even while he was speaking, he bound and gagged the Cunning Fox, and then helped the Major to wrap Alice up in the blankets.

"Pick her up in your arms, and now, go."

Although Heyward's knees were trembling, everything went off much more easily than he had feared. He told the chief, who was waiting outside, to guard the cave. No-one must enter it until tomorrow, because the evil spirit which had possessed the woman, was locked in there. If it escaped, the woman would die.

The Indians moved aside shyly, when the supposed medicine man walked slowly towards the nearby forest carrying his burden, and the bear moved clumsily along behind him. When the three had gone far enough from the village, Hawk-Eye stopped. They set the girl free from the blankets, and then the guide explained, "Now do exactly what I tell you. Keep straight on for the north, until you come to the lodges of the Delawares. Ask them for shelter. They will not refuse you. I must go back to the Huron village and help Uncas."

The Hurons had, as yet, no inkling of the events in the cave. Everything was quiet in the village. The only noise was a soft singing from a ruined hut, which stopped immediately when the bear appeared in the entrance.

The singer was Gamut. He was about to break forth in a song of joy when he realized who the bear was.

But Hawk-Eye quickly put his hand over Gamut's mouth. "Where is Uncas?"

"They have taken him back to the council hut. A dozen young braves are guarding him."

"You must help me. Will you?" And as the psalmist nodded resolutely, Hawk-Eye told him of his plan, which was particularly dangerous for Gamut.

"Let's go," was all the latter said. "My life lies in God's hand."

The unsuspecting guards allowed the one "who was protected by the Great Spirit" to turn them out of the council hut because he and the medicine-bear wanted to cast a spell upon the prisoner. As soon as they were alone, Hawk-Eye cut through the Mohican's bonds and handed him the bear skin. He himself took Gamut's clothes and spectacles. The singer sat down in front of the stake. Uncas and Hawk-Eye were able to leave the village without being stopped. When the Hurons realized the deception, the two were long since in the forest at the place where the scout had hidden their weapons. Once more, they heard the penetrating cry in the distance.

"Now they have found Magua!" laughed Hawk-Eye, "but no Alice!"

Magua's revenge

It had not been hard for Magua to convince the Hurons that the fugitives could only have fled to the Delawares. They also discovered now, for the first time, that Long Rifle, who was so famous for his bravery, was amongst them. Thus, a troop of braves, thirsting for revenge, followed the Cunning Fox to the camp of the Delawares.

But he was clever enough to leave the men at some distance behind him. He, who had once been an exile, now enjoyed a certain repu-tation amongst the Hurons again. He hoped, by virtue of this respect, to be able to accomplish his demands without a battle which might have doubtful results.

As a sign of his peaceful intentions, he rode with arms outstretched between the tents, and only stopped in front of that belonging to the chief. The latter greeted him formally, and welcomed him as a guest. Magua was well acquainted with the ceremony. It would have been very bad manners to have started to discuss the purpose of his visit immediately.

The Delawares offered him food, and only after the meal did the chief remark, incidentally, "We last saw our brother when he went off to win scalps in Fort William."

Magua immediately took up the cue, and enquired whether the white prisoner was too much trouble for the Delawares. He was perfectly willing to take her back again.

The chief shook his head, "We are glad to have her."

Magua sensed the refusal, and took good

With a cry of rage, Magua was going to hurl himself at the young Mohican.

care not to repeat his request. First, the atmosphere had to be more favourable for him. Thus he began to talk about the great victory at Fort William in general terms. Then he spoke about the great booty and when he saw that the eyes of his audience lit up greedily, he explained, "Even in these days, I did not forget my friends and I have brought along presents for you."

He stood up in order to go out to his horse, and returned with several leather bags, which he opened one after the other.

When he had spread out the loot: pieces of clothing, blankets, toys, crockery, all of which had been the property of the British women and children who had been so savagely butchered, he nodded to the braves, "Pick out what you like."

Immediately the Delawares threw themselves upon the presents. Skilfully the Cunning Fox saw to it that the chief gained the most valuable piece. Whilst the men were contentedly examining their new possessions, Magua began to speak again.

He praised the courage of the Delawares, whose fathers and forefathers before them had made all enemies tremble. They, and many other red men, had only been driven by the white men out of the land which belonged to them alone. But the Great Father of the French had taken them up as his children, even if at the present time they had not dug up the hatchet against the tribes who were fighting on the side of the hated British. The Hurons knew that the Delawares first needed peace in order to recover from the terrible losses which they had suffered in their battles with the white men. Contentedly, Magua saw that his audience was nodding approval. Then he continued with his voice raised, "Naturally, the white chief who calls himself Montcalm, regrets that he must do without the help of the brave Delawares for the moment. All the more is he able to treasure their unshakable loyalty. Can the Delawares therefore risk coming under the suspicion that they give shelter to British spies?"

Now the audience became visibly uneasy, and the chief asked with astonishment, "Which

Old Tamenund listened to the voice.

mangy dog has carried this lie to my brother? Tell me his name, and we . . . "

"Have you not strangers amongst you?" Magua interrupted him, and confessed immediately how impolitely he had behaved. "My anger at the falseness of the British, who have gained your hospitality by underhand means, made my tongue run away with my good sense."

"Strangers have sought shelter with us," the chief confirmed. "They had lost their way."

"Does my brother really believe that La Longue Carabine, the Long Rifle, loses his way?" retorted Magua. "You have taken the leash-dog of the British into your midst. What will the Great White Chief say to that?"

"The Long Rifle?" The braves only suppressed their excitement with difficulty, and the chief repeated, disbelievingly, "What will he say?"

Magua poked the fire while it was still hot. "Bring the dogs here," he cried. "Ask them. You will see how they begin to whimper because we have seen through their lies."

"We shall ask them." The chief pointed to a few braves. "Fetch them."

While the men hastened away, all the male members of the tribe gathered together upon a

sign from the chief, on an open place in front of his wigwam and formed a circle. Finally, the strangers were led into the middle of it.

Cora and her sister led the way, followed by Heyward and Hawk-Eye. Their faces were calm and composed, even if, in the case of the girls, very pale. Silently, the four looked around them.

"Strangers, who are our guests," the chief declared in the silence. "You are accused of having deceived us and of creeping into our midst like treacherous snakes. We shall hear your accuser and shall hear your words on the matter, and the Great Spirit shall help us to pass a just verdict."

The four of them had already seen the Cunning Fox and they guessed that their fate now hung on a silken thread. Heyward was especially worried about the two girls, and it was Cora who whispered to him bravely, "I am not afraid."

"That's good. We must not give up hope," Hawk-Eye nodded to her and her sister encouragingly. "Besides that, your father and Chingachgook will certainly not remain idle. But . . . Quiet, they seem to be starting now."

After a short introductory speech, the chief walked with some of his assistants to the hut next to his own, and entered it with them. Then they returned slowly. In their midst they led, respectfully, a white-haired old man, and finally helped him, with a moving display of attention and love, to a soft seat padded with many skins.

"That can only be Tamenund," said Hawk-Eye softly. "He is at least a hundred years old and is respected for his wisdom by friend and foe alike. I feel happier now that I know that he will pronounce the judgement."

The old man looked down to the ground with his tired eyes, but announced with a weak hand signal that he was ready to listen.

The chief now recited in a loud voice how first, a white man and a girl had come to the Delawares and had asked them for hospitality and protection as they were being pursued. The two of them had done nothing to harm the Delawares so they were welcomed. A little later, a white hunter had then appeared, and had asked for food and drink and somewhere to sleep. He was called Nathan and had been wandering around lost in the forests. The law of hospitality had made it the duty of the Delaware to take him in as well. Yet the Great Spirit had had a watchful eye on his children, the Delawares, and had sent them a brave red brother and chief to open their eyes and let them see how very evil spirits had struck them with blindness, so that they had been hospitable to British spies and sworn enemies of the Delawares and Hurons. The hunter, who had called himself Nathan, was in reality, the Long Rifle.

The chief fell silent as the old man had slightly raised his head and beckoned Magua to him. He looked at him searchingly. "Who are you? With what voice do you speak?"

"I am a friend," replied Magua, and added with pride, "a chief of the Hurons. My voice is obeyed by many."

"But the Mingos are not yet the lords of the earth," the old man retorted, and his face grew stern.

Magua was startled. "I only demand justice. Give me my prisoners."

Slowly, Tamenund sank back and announced, after a short silence, "It is right that you have your prisoners back. Take them, and leave us immediately."

Magua had achieved what he wanted. Triumphantly, he turned round and seized Alice. Yet before he was able to stop her, Cora threw herself down on her knees in front of the old man, and implored, "Do not believe this liar. We have never done anything to you, and even if you do not believe the words of an unfortunate white woman, then at least let the young Indian speak, whom your sons have captured as well."

"No," Magua had to confess, quivering with rage. In answer to Tamenund's further questions, he had to confirm, just as angrily, that the prisoners had been set free.

Yet now came the question which not only Hawk-Eye had been fearing all the time.

"And the dark girl? What about her?"

"Yes. The sacred totem of the tortoise."

"I entrusted her to the Delawares. They have guarded her for me," said Magua scornfully. "She was my prisoner from the beginning, and now I demand her back."

Tamenund turned to Uncas. "For once the Mingo is speaking the truth," the latter had to confess.

"Then take her, Huron, and go to your own people."

At Tamenund's words, Hawk-Eye had to forcibly restrain the Major from attacking Magua, while Alice and Cora fell sobbing into each other's arms.

Triumphantly, Magua stepped over to the two girls, and pulled Cora to him. "The Grey Head had Magua beaten like a dog. Magua has never forgotten this shame, but now the Grey Head must always think that one of his daughters is Magua's servant."

No-one prevented him from leaving the circle with the girl, but when he carried the motionless girl to his horse, Uncas raised his voice. "The laws of hospitality force us to let you go, but you must know, Mingo, that as soon as the sun sinks there will be war between us. We shall drive the Hurons out of their stinking holes like rats, and you will lie whining before me on the ground, and curse the day you were born."

In a shrill voice which could be heard far

across the valley, Magua answered with the terrible war-cry of the Hurons, swung his tomahawk several times, and then rode off as slowly as possible to emphasize the mockery.

Tamenund pricked up his ears, and Magua hastened to assure him, "A renegade dog who has sold himself to the British."

"I want to hear him," decided the chief, and with hardly suppressed rage, Magua had to watch them fetch Uncas.

Tamenund looked at him for a long time with his half-blind eyes. "You have the proud bearing of a Delaware. Why have you cut yourself off from your people and joined the British?"

"Should I whine for the crumbs of the French like your braves here?"

A murmur ran through the ranks of the Delawares, which was only stilled when Tamenund pronounced the judgement. "You shall be tortured to death."

Two braves seized the bound Mohican in order to take him away, yet the latter shook them off with a powerful twist of his body. As he did so, his leather shirt tore open and exposed his chest.

The braves bounded back, then seemed to freeze with amazement, and one of them said in a voice full of awe, "The sacred totem."

"Yes. The sacred totem," repeated Uncas in a loud voice and stepped in front of the old man. "Hear me, revered father. I am Uncas, the son of Chingachgook, and we two are the last in whom the blood of the Great Tortoise flows. It supports the world, and on its shell stands your tribe. We have not gone with our people because we were not allowed to leave the graves of our great chiefs unguarded. Therefore, no-one has the right to call us traitors, certainly not this howling coyote from the brood of the Hurons."

The old man rose, trembling, embraced him, and announced with a wavering voice, "Yes, I hear the voice of our fathers, speaking from you, and I thank the Great Spirit that he has answered my prayers and brought back the last chief of the Mohicans, the son and grandson of the Tortoise, to our camp fire. Cut his

bonds, and show him all honour."

Full of hatred at this unexpected turn of events, Magua stared at Uncas and the tortoise which was tattooed upon his breast. While the bonds fell from the young chief, he tried to drive the white girl who had been promised to him, out of the circle of the Delawares.

Yet with one leap, Uncas was at Hawk-Eye's side, "Never was this man Magua's prisoner. He is my friend, and has never killed one of us. He has only declared war on falseness, and for that reason the Mingos tremble at his name and fear his long rifle. It was he who saved the white man there, the squaw and me from the camp of the Hurons and who has made a mockery for all time of the Mingos and their Cunning Fox who should be better called a blind and sleepy skunk. Ask the coyote how he was overcome by a bear who was no bear."

With a cry of rage Magua went to throw himself upon Uncas, yet a hand signal from Tamenund brought him back to his senses. The Delawares would have killed him immediately.

He seized the unfortunate girl by the arm.

196

The "Long Rifle" did all honour to its name.
Heyward also fired ceaselessly.

"Was the Long Rifle your prisoner?" asked the old man.

"No," Magua had to confess, quivering with rage. In answer to Tamenund's further questions, he had to confirm, just as angrily, that the prisoners had been set free.

Yet now came the question which not only Hawk-Eye had been fearing all the time.

"And the dark girl? What about her?"

"I entrusted her to the Delawares. They have guarded her for me," said Magua scornfully. "She was my prisoner from the beginning, and now I demand her back."

Tamenund turned to Uncas. "For once the Mingo is speaking the truth," the latter had to confess.

"Then take her, Huron, and go to your own people."

At Tamenund's words, Hawk-Eye had to forcibly restrain the Major from attacking Magua, while Alice and Cora fell sobbing into each other's arms.

Triumphantly, Magua stepped over to the two girls, and pulled Cora to him. "The Grey Head had Magua beaten like a dog. Magua has never forgotten this shame, but now the Grey Head must always think that one of his daughters is Magua's servant."

No-one prevented him from leaving the circle with the girl, but when he carried the motionless girl to his horse, Uncas raised his voice. "The laws of hospitality force us to let you go, but you must know, Mingo, that as soon as the sun sinks there will be war between us. We shall drive the Hurons out of their stinking holes like rats, and you will lie whining before me on the ground, and curse the day you were born."

In a shrill voice which could be heard far across the valley, Magua answered with the terrible war-cry of the Hurons, swung his tomahawk several times, and then rode off as slowly as possible to emphasize the mockery.

Bloody victory

Again and again, Duncan Heyward looked towards the edge of the forest in the west, where the sun gradually approached the tree-tops much too slowly for his impatient state of mind. Hawk-Eye tried to cheer him up. "Haven't you noticed how Uncas looks at Cora with secret admiration? You can be sure that he will do everything to free the girl."

Almost at the same moment as the sun began to sink behind the trees, the young chief

As if paralysed, Hawk-Eye and the Major had to watch the battle to the death on the rocky ledge without being able to interfere. They would only have endangered their friends' lives.

emerged from his wigwam. He was stripped to the waist so that the sacred tortoise on his chest was visible to all. The war paint glistened on his face. In his right hand he swung a tomahawk. Slowly he strode up to a fir tree whose trunk had already been stripped of bark by young braves.

He came to a halt in front of the tree, and then, with all his strength, cut a deep notch in it. Immediately the Delawares broke forth in loud cries. One warrior after the another began to dance round the trunk, swinging his tomahawk and also driving the shining steel into the wood.

"The braves are announcing with these blows that they will follow Uncas," Hawk-Eye explained to the Major.

Eventually, a grating sound came from the trunk. One more blow and it toppled over, and with much splintering, crashed to the ground.

That was the time that they should march off to battle. Uncas was now the undisputed leader. He indicated a troop of young Delawares who should follow him, and allotted about twenty braves to Hawk-Eye.

His plan was to attack the Huron village from both sides of the valley simultaneously.

Heyward attached himself to Hawk-Eye's group. Silently the march proceeded through the forest, which meanwhile had become dark, but it was not very long before the first shots were ringing out.

"Of course, the Hurons know we are coming. We must reckon on their reconnaissance parties everywhere in the forest," whispered Hawk-Eye.

Yet not until the first light of dawn did the attackers meet with more serious resistance. Countless hand-to-hand battles were fought. The death screams of Hurons and Delawares echoed through the undergrowth, but irresistibly the Delawares approached the valley in which the village lay.

Sheltered by a dense screen of tree trunks, Hawk-Eye and Heyward looked at the huts in front of which only braves were moving around. The women and children had long since left the village and hidden themselves in the woods.

"The resistance has not been very strong so far," said Heyward thoughtfully.

Hawk-Eye took aim, then shot. A cry from the village. Then he nodded, calmly. "The Hurons are only fighting half-heartedly. They obviously have little desire to fight a war which they did not want and for which they only have Magua's ambition to blame. Don't forget that Magua has already been exiled by them once before."

Just after Hawk-Eye had spoken, they suddenly saw Magua standing in the midst of the Hurons, yelling and gesticulating at them wildly.

"We must attack before he urges them on any more." Hawk-Eye gave a sign with his left arm to the impatiently lurking Delawares. "Forward! Drive them into the gorge. Uncas will be there any moment now."

Heedless of the danger, the scout and Heyward stormed forward at the head of the Indians. Hawk-Eye was holding his long rifle by the barrel and swinging the butt. The Major now relied on his pistols. Unerringly he fired to right and left, yet always kept one eye on Magua. The latter, without retreating one step, was firing shot after shot from several rifles

which he had loaded beforehand.

As soon as he had emptied the last barrel, he took one leap out of the circle of the Hurons surrounding him, and ran to the base of the cliff.

"After him. He is making for the cave. He is bound to have hidden Cora there," cried Hawk-Eye but Heyward was already on the heels of the Indian.

An arrow hit him in the shoulder. He stumbled, pulled it out and ran on, but the momentary pause had been sufficient to allow Magua to disappear through the entrance.

"We've got him now," Heyward heard Hawk-Eye shout behind him. "Be careful."

The warning was unnecessary. Nothing stirred in the cave. It was empty. "Damn!" cursed Hawk-Eye. "This is impossible. He must . . . " Then he discovered the rear exit. Burning with rage, he stormed out.

A narrow cliff path wound its way upwards. Magua could be seen quite high up already, roughly pushing the defenceless girl in front of him. He was accompanied by two Hurons.

In desperation, Heyward raised his pistol. "There's no point," Hawk-Eye roared at him. "Much too far." And already he was taking aim

Praying silently, and then singing movingly, David Gamut paid his last respects to the dead whose cruel fate he had tried to prevent at the last moment.

with the long rifle, but even he did not dare to shoot. He could too easily have hit Cora.

Magua had now reached a small ledge. Triumphantly he looked around him. At this moment, Uncas emerged on the rim above him, and on the cliff alongside, a giant figure reared up. Between its long arms it held a huge boulder, and even before Uncas could fling himself at Magua, the giant hurled the boulder and hit a Huron who disappeared into the depths, screaming horribly.

"Gamut! He has finally woken up," cried Hawk-Eye incredulously.

But the very words died on his lips in horror, and Heyward moaned, "For Heaven's sake."

Uncas had jumped down onto the little ledge but had missed Magua, and before he was able to stand upright and swing the tomahawk at Cunning Fox, the second Huron had plunged his knife into the heart of the girl, who sank silently to the ground. The Mohican yelled his despair and beside himself with rage, smashed the murderer's skull. In doing this, he forgot his arch-enemy for a moment and turned his back on him. Cold-bloodedly, Magua struck. Uncas was dead instantly.

Magua's victory whoop rang out short and cruel to the horror-struck pursuers below. He turned to the path, slipped, caught at a root and hung for seconds above the abyss . . . then, Hawk-Eye's bullet hit him. But even in falling, even in death, hatred and triumph were reflected in his face – the pride of the victor.

Deep mourning reigned next day in the village of the Delawares. The bodies of Uncas and Cora were laid out a few yards from each other, according to Indian custom. Silently Chingachgook kept the death watch beside his son. Inconsolably, the old Colonel sat at the feet of his butchered child. For hours, the psalmist stayed beside him, deep in prayer.

When the time came for the final farewell, Hawk-Eye drew the last Mohican to his feet, held his arms, and said, so loudly that all could hear it, "Even now, Chingachgook, you are not alone."

Then the wavering voice of Tamenund rang out tremulously over the graves. "Go back to your huts, my children. The anger of the Great Spirit at his red sons still lasts. For how long, only he can say. That will be when the time of the red man comes again."

HERMAN MELVILLE

Moby Dick

My first name is Ismael. Everyone calls me that, as my surname is irrelevant, as is the fact that I ought to have remained a teacher. But having tried it, I am overcome with rage, I can't stand being hemmed in a room any longer, and I have to feel freedom around me to seek the open sea. Just as a simple deck hand, for apart from the fact that I could never afford a passenger cabin, I don't give two hoots for position and authority. I leave that gladly to the Admirals, they have more brains.

Admittedly, as a mere sailor you have to do all sorts of things and be ready to jump when you are told, as well as risk your neck now and again. However, the main thing is that the pay is right!

Now the time had come round again, and I had to feel a ship's planks under my feet again. And as I had never seen a whale although I had heard so much about these mighty creatures and the adventure of their hunt, I wanted to join a whaler. So I went to New Bedford, where I arrived one icy cold Saturday evening in December. However, I was unlucky: the post boat for Nantucket had just set sail and I had to wait until Monday.

Nantucket is on an island in the Atlantic, which is still part of the US State of Massachusetts. Since the first of the white whales ever to be captured was landed here, it has belonged to the whale hunters. The Indians had once set out in canoes from Nantucket to hunt these giants of the oceans, now ships followed them right into the South Seas and into Antarctic waters.

Come what may, I had to look for lodgings. Somewhere cheap, to match my scant resources. Down by the harbour I found a place. It was called 'The Whale Fisher' and the fact that the landlord bore the ominous name of 'Peter Coffin', did not trouble me. Today, however, I ask myself whether this name should not have served as a warning.

I entered the bar via a cold, badly lit hallway, which was adorned with hunting gear, whale bones and a soot covered oil painting of a ship going down in a storm. It was packed full of seafarers sitting at roughly planed tables; they were drinking beer and noisily recounting true and fabricated stories. The landlord stood behind the bar and I asked if he still had a room free.

"No vacancies!" he replied regretfully, "no . . . that's to say . . . " he rubbed his nose, "if you don't mind sleeping in a big bed with a harpooner? A respectable fellow of course."

"I'll take it!" I said quickly, since I wanted to get on to a whaler, and the acquaintance of a harpooner would not do me any harm. "Which one is he, out of those people there?"

"None of these. He's in the town, selling his head."

I thought I had misheard. "His what?"

"His head. But it won't be so easy, it's so

smashed." The landlord shrugged his shoulders nonchalantly, as though he were discussing the most natural thing in the world. He obviously wanted to have me on!

"Don't give me that!" I stated energetically. "Your fairy tales . . ."

"Fairy tales? Are you slow or something! I am talking about a shrunken head! He brought twelve back with him from the South Seas and eleven of them were already embalmed. Well, there are enough people with peculiar taste. But the broken one . . . well it's not my worry," concluded Mr. Coffin, "and you, the best thing you can do is get in your bed, don't you agree?"

And how! I was more than happy to let him lead me up a steep staircase to the first floor, where he opened the door and said, "Here you are!"

The room was small, the fire in the grate was dead, but apart from that everything was fine. I nodded, looked over at the taut seaman's bag next to the unusually wide bed, undressed and crawled shivering under the covers.

Although I was dog tired, I could not get to sleep. I rolled over backwards and forwards restlessly, and when I heard heavy footsteps approaching in the corridor about half an hour later, I was immediately wide awake. That must be the harpooner.

Indeed the door swung open and in its frame stood a real giant. In his hand he held a candle, whose restlessly flickering flame made him look even more threatening. Between the fingers of the other hand a shrunken head was swinging by its hair.

The giant examined me briefly, then taking no notice of me, he entered the room, placed the candle on the floor, knelt down next to the sack, his back towards me, opened the bag and placed the gruesome head inside out of view. As if spellbound I followed his every move. I scarcely dared breathe as he slowly pulled a seal skin pouch and a tomahawk from the bag. And now he turned towards me. God what was that? His brow, cheeks and chin looked as though they were burnt, covered with deep scars and marks.

Seeming not to notice me, the man removed the beaver skin hat from his head. In the middle of his bald shaven head grew an erect, oiled crest of hair, just like a cockscomb. Yet, only when the giant uncovered the top half of his body, did I know for sure his skin was naturally so dark, and what looked like scars, were tattoos. My room mate was a South Sea Islander, a savage, perhaps even a cannibal, a man eater.

I was becoming frightened. He now took out a small wooden figure from the pouch and placed this idol in the grate. This did as little to reassure me as the small fire he was kindling with wood shavings. Over the flames he burnt a piece of ship's biscuit. He rubbed the ashes over the figure, whilst he moved his lips, without making a sound. When the sacrifice was over he put the idol into the pouch and then placed this in the bag.

I had pulled the covers right up over my nose, not letting this tattooed being out of my sight. His next moves reduced me to trepidation. He picked the tomahawk up from the floor and approached the bed. And then something remarkable happened, that left me so astonished I forgot my fear for a few moments: he took the handle between his lips and with the flame from the candle lit the ostensibly sharp blade. This immediately produced a thick cloud of smoke. Like a slowly disappearing cloud it rose to the ceiling. The savage was smoking his tomahawk!

As I had at that time never seen such pipes and did not realize that they were quite common amongst Indians and Islanders, I cried out loudly in terror, when the giant suddenly, without removing the supposedly deadly weapon from his mouth, threw himself backwards at full length next to me on the bed.

It may have been that without this scream he would have continued to take no notice of me. But I had only screamed once and as if compelled, I continued.

With a start the other jumped high in the air, sprang from the bed and roared, "Damn. What is matter?" His huge arms were round my trunk and as I tried desperately to extricate myself from him he continued bellowing, "Quiet. I kill you . . . I kill you." And threateningly he raised his tomahawk.

I managed to fall out of bed. "Help. Help. Mr. Coffin!" I pushed my way out yelling shrilly. "Quickly! Quickly!"

The savage followed me. "Who you are?" he gasped. "Who, who? I kill you!"

At this point the door flew open. The good Mr. Coffin burst in, dressed in his night shirt and carrying a lantern. "What the devil is going on here?" he scolded and looked at me. "Stop screaming at once. Everything is quite all right. Queequeg won't harm a hair on your head for sure."

"And you say so, do you?" I said, getting angry. "And why did you conceal the fact that he's a cannibal?"

"What? Didn't I tell you that he dealt in heads? That should have made you think . . . no." The landlord turned towards my room mate and looked at him reproachfully. "Stop it now, Queequeg, this man is a guest, do you understand? He is sleeping here."

"I understand, is sleeping here," grumbled Queequeg. He sank back onto the bed and busied himself with his tomahawk pipe again. Pulling strongly on his pipe he produced stinking clouds of smoke which rose thick and heavy to the ceiling. Undecided I reflected on what I ought to do. The landlord was still in the room.

"And what do you think, Mr. Coffin?" I snapped furiously." Should I suffocate here or be set on fire?"

He moved his lips without making a sound.

Mr. Coffin nodded. "Now, Queequeg, put your pipe out!"

My room mate agreed, though somewhat resentfully. He wrapped himself up tighter in the covers just as resentfully and turned his back on me disdainfully. For my part I just behaved as though he did not exist. Mr. Coffin left satisfied, and fearlessly I fell asleep.

The next morning when we awoke, we had got used to one another just enough to exchange a few words. Thus I learnt that Queequeg wanted to join a whaler as I did. I asked whether we should try together? Queequeg, who by now did not seem wild and frightening any longer, nodded enthusiastically, "We good friends, Ismael!"

So on the Monday we travelled to Nantucket together on the post boat. During the relatively stormy crossing I learnt Queequeg's story. Nothing too exciting, he thought. I, on the other hand, think that it is very well worth writing down.

Queequeg's home was on one of the many islands in the middle of the South Seas, that cannot be found on any map. It was called Rokovoko. His father was chieftain of the tribe, his uncle high priest. The son of such a distinguished family can expect a pleasant life, but Queequeg had another future planned. He wanted to get to know those far away lands from where ships strayed in to Rokovoko now and again. They were mostly whalers. They merely stocked up with water and fresh provisions

on the island or repaired storm damage, before they weighed anchor again.

One day Queequeg rowed after one of the ships as it sailed off, clambered aboard and despite the curses of the captain and the crew could not be made to return. He would rather have been killed. Thanks to his obstinacy he was allowed to stay and he learnt quickly to handle the harpoon very adeptly, unlike almost any other whaler. Over the years he had killed quite a number of whales.

I must emphasize here how much the life and the greedy peoples of these so-called Christian lands disappointed him. Long since, he has had to bury for ever the dream of his youth: to teach his people the supposed achievements of the white people.

"So you don't want to return to Rokovoko any more?"

Queequeg shook his head, "Not yet, only when worthy, to take throne from father. Now still catch whales. Then when soul clean again, go back to Rokovoko. Perhaps soon."

Soon? In a year, in two, in ten? The sea has her own time. I remained silent, as the ship was already entering Nantucket harbour.

At first sight Nantucket seemed to consist only of a bare rock, without a tree or shrub and down below, a mass of grey sand, upon which just as little grew as on the rugged stony beach. As this impression was not altered even by a second look, there was only one thing that the people on the island could do, instead of looking on the land — look more at the sea. It was all right this way. The harbour made her rich, the whole island lived off the sea.

Even in the inn "The Fish Kettle", where we found a lovely room, they knew what seafarers needed. We noticed that at the excellent and ample meal.

Before we fell asleep I said to Queequeg, "Tomorrow we'll have a look round the harbour for a ship."

"You go. I no go," grumbled Queequeg.

"You . . . I not. What kind of nonsense is that?"

Yojo, the wooden idol that Queequeg trailed about with him in the sack, had told him that he should stay at home and allow me to look for a ship alone, revealed my tattooed friend. "And when Yojo says that, then Queequeg listens. You go, I no go! You speak with captain. I no speak. You alone decide, Ismael!"

I blew out the candle. "Okay, I'll go. Goodnight." I set out for the harbour bright and early. I soon learnt that three whalers were docked by the pier and they were obviously wanting to sail shortly as, judging by their hulls that lay deep in the water, they were laden with provisions for at least two or three years. Two of them did not feel quite right to me, but the third, the *Pequod,* aroused my curiosity immediately.

Up to now I had flattered myself that I knew more or less every kind of ship. But I had never seen one like this before. The *Pequod* was not all that large, but she was impressive. The first look told me that here was a ship of the 'old school', without all that frippery that is so fashionable today. The hull was wide yet not bulky. The pitch on her sides glistened in the morning sun. Threatening like a cannon, the bowsprit towered sloping up to the sky. The masts stood erect, as is only proper, the bridge and the deck structure revealed the work of the best shipwright. But the most striking features were the rigging and the helm. The ropes did not run through iron hoops, but through rings made from whale bones, and in place of a spoke wheel the gigantic lower jaw of a sperm whale served as a helm.

This ship was used to winning. It seemed to abound immediately with strength. And yet she exuded something like a mysterious melancholy, which I could not shake off.

Without much reflection, I mounted the gangway and proceeded to the bridge. However, it was empty. I looked around further for someone. Then I discovered a collapsible cabin in front of the main mast. It no longer surprised me at all that instead of being made from boards it was made of slab-like whale bones. Nevertheless seated in it, on a stool made from a whale skeleton of course, was not a whale but a person in blue uniform with gold braiding. His weather-beaten face was full of wrinkles. He looked at me with clear and not unfriendly eyes, when I asked, "Are you the Captain?"

"Let's suppose I am. What do you want?"

"To be taken on!"

"Aha. And how often have you been on a sloop full of water?"

"Never," I had to admit.

"Then you've no idea about whale hunting?"

"Not yet. But I'm young and strong enough to learn. I've been on merchant men and . . ."

"Merchant men!" broke in the man in blue with horror. "God save us! A right royal trickster. I suppose you've been pilfering in the Officer's Mess and been thrown overboard? Or was it a pirate ship maybe? No normal sailor volunteers for a whaler. Out with the truth!"

"I just want to see the world."

"See the world! And have you seen Captain Ahab, who commands this ship?"

"Ahab? I thought . . ."

"Thought. Thought. I'm Captain Peleg, I'm just the owner of the *Pequod*. Me and my companion, Captain Bildad, whom I'm waiting for here, we only deal with the equipment and crew. That's something completely different from the hunt. Wait till you see Ahab. Then perhaps you will realize what you want to let yourself in for. The Captain has only got one leg."

"Does that mean that a whale tore the other one off?"

"Tore off, pulverized, ate." Peleg suddenly rolled his eyes in a frightening manner. "And do you know who? The biggest, most dangerous and malicious whale that ever . . ."

He broke off in the middle of the sentence, his anger subsided and he looked at me quietly again. "Well, have you enough confidence to throw a harpoon? Yes? Good. And then if necessary, to jump on the whale's back and finish him off once and for all?"

"If it's required and really necessary, of course!"

Peleg nodded contentedly. "All right, you can stay. Here." He fanned my nose with a sheet of paper. "Sign! As your share you will get, let's say, a

One day Queequeg rowed after one of the ships as it sailed off and clambered aboard.

"Are you mad?" gasped Peleg.

bled Peleg.

Bildad put in again, "I'll soon fix that. Bring your friend along with you, Ismael."

When I returned on board with Queequeg, Captain Peleg threw up his hands in horror. "What, a cannibal? We hadn't bargained for this, anything like it, had we Bildad?" As the thin man shook his head energetically, Peleg continued in a rage, "We're having no heathens on this ship. Or should the fellow be baptized like a good Christian or what?"

"And what of it?" I replied boldly, while Queequeg, unmoved, remained silent. "My friend is more Christian than Christian."

"Whoever believes that will be saved, but he surely doesn't know what a whale looks like. Does he?" Peleg stepped towards Queegueg. "Can you use your harpoon, man eater?"

With a start my friend sprang on to the ship's side and pointed to the water with the tip of the harpoon. "You see little drops of pitch on waves? Good, little like eyes of whale. Watch."

And just then he hurled the harpoon with a mighty thrust, like a dart it sped a good fifteen metres from the ship and hissed right into the middle of a drop of pitch, which was scarcely as big as the palm of your hand. Then he pulled it back silently with a rope. Peleg stared incredulously for a few seconds, first into the water and then at Queequeg, before his voice cracked as he said candidly, "I'll give you your due, the whale would be dead. Damn! Here, Quickquack . . . what an idiotic name . . . here, the contract. A harpooner with a ninetieth of the spoils. I hope you know what that means, you cannibal. Nobody in Nantucket up to now has ever got that much. Clear?"

We returned to the inn in good spirits. We had to wait there until the *Pequod* was ready to set sail. At the end of the jetty there was a scarecrow of a man standing in our way. He stared us right in the face and croaked,

"Have you sold anything on this ship?"

"If you mean the *Pequod* . . . " I retorted.

"What else? You've just sold your souls, yes?"

"Our souls? What sort of twaddle is that?"

The scarecrow spread out all his ten fingers and said cursing, "Yes, yes whoever sells himself to Ahab, sells his body and soul to him. And that's the honest truth, though you weren't to know."

"Queequeg, did you hear that? This fellow does not seem to be quite all there to me!"

"I'll show you who's not quite all there! You or me? Me, because I don't want to go on the *Pequod*, or you, because you really do? I can see it, you rush to Ahab . . . may God be with you, sailors . . . and when you get on board, tell the others not to wait for me. May heaven have mercy on your souls."

The scarecrow wanted to go. But I pulled him back, "Hey, you prophet of evil. Who exactly are you anyway?"

"Me . . . " the lifeless eyes seemed to look

seven hundred and seventy seventh from the spoils. Agreed . . . "

"Hang on a minute." A strong voice resounded unexpectedly behind me. I turned round. A taller, thin man, wearing a stove-pipe hat and with a pince nez perched on his nose, approached us. Captain Bildad, as I assumed. "One moment," he repeated, "that is too little, Peleg. The sailor will get a three hundredth share."

"What? Three hun . . . are you mad?" gasped Peleg.

"Me? You are, you old skinflint."

It rested on Bildad's decision. "What's your name?" he wanted to know as he faced me.

"Ismael."

"Very nice. You're hired. Will you sign?"

"Thank you, sir." And then I came out with, "I have a friend, an experienced harpooner. He wants to come with me!"

"So? And what share is he expecting?" grum-

through me, "I'm called . . . Elijah."

Elijah, that was indeed also the name of a prophet, wasn't it? As it occurred to me, I have to admit that for a moment I was overcome by a peculiar feeling, like some sort of premonition of impending doom. But I threw such thoughts off and laughed. "In fact, a poor lunatic, Queequeg."

Two days later the *Pequod* was ready to set sail. Even before dawn Queequeg and I hurried through the thick mist to the harbour. As we approached the pier, I was taken aback and said, "Look there are some people going on board already. Come on, Queequeg, we must hurry."

"Hang on," a voice resounded near us. I recognized Elijah. His eyes were glowing this time. "Destinations please, travellers? Are you getting on board?"

"Mind out," scolded Queequeg.

I too was angry. "Yes, on the *Pequod.* We've already told you that, Elijah. Or have you something

against that, eh? Don't delay us any longer now, please!"

The old man tottered behind us. "Did you see the sailors who've just gone on deck?"

"We're not blind you know," I shouted imperiously at him.

"Then wait and see if you can find them," he tittered.

As he had obviously a few screws loose, we did not let him bother us any further and we simply left him standing there. "Good luck," he cried after us through the mist. "I won't see you again . . . not before the Last Judgement . . . no, not before!"

We were finally on board. We looked around bewildered: nothing stirred, every hatch was tight, apart from the fog lamps there was not a single light.

Odd, from the pier I had quite clearly . . . shaking my head I followed Queequeg, who opened the door to the lower deck. "The others will already be

Two days later the Pequod *was ready to set sail.*

below," I thought, as we descended. As still as a graveyard everywhere. No, not quite; the sound of snoring rose from one corner. We investigated. An old sailor was in a deep sleep there.

"But, where are those who came on board before us?" I exclaimed. Or had I just imagined them in the mist? Yes, mists can be deceptive and . . . nonsense, Elijah had seen them too! Now, yes, what did he say? Then wait and see if you can find them . . . Good God man, Ismael, don't start to go crazy now. I made a desperate effort and pursued Queequeg to the capstan.

There was nothing for it but to wait.

As it became light, the crew finally arrived in dribs and drabs. Even Captain Peleg and Captain Bildad appeared and could be found going about their business here and there. As there was nothing as yet for Queequeg and I to do, I lounged idly over the deck. I hoped to catch sight of Captain Ahab. I hoped in vain.

"The Captain is staying in his berth," I heard Mr. Starbuck, the First Officer, say to Bildad.

"Okay," cried Captain Peleg immediately, "then we'll set sail." He turned to the bridge, although Bildad was the pilot and ordered, "To the capstan, weigh anchor!" And at the same moment, as quick as a flash, he gave me a kick in the behind that sent me stumbling to the windlass. "Did you lounge about with your hands in your pockets in the merchant navy?" he roared. "Or did the bogey man do your work for you?"

Good God, he was right. There is more than enough to do, when a ship is being manoeuvred out of harbour. Without grumbling I set to work with the others.

When the *Pequod* had at last reached the open sea, Peleg and Bildad disembarked. They were sad, we could see it in their faces. We gazed after them for a long time, as they rowed towards the disappearing coastline and waved to us now and again.

But in front of us lay a deep blue heaven, the endless sea, that for the next three years was to be our home.

Captain Ahab had still not put in an appearance. Mr. Starbuck assumed the command in the meantime, a strict but fair man. He came from Nantucket and was in his thirties. His energetic face and his muscular form betrayed the fact that he had grown up on the sea. He had already proved himself brave and above all prudent on many whale hunting trips.

The Second Officer, Mr. Stubb, was an entirely different sort. You never saw him without his pipe in his mouth, he always gave the impression that he considered whale hunting about as dangerous as sparrow hunting. For him it was a job just like any other. The Third Officer was a carefree, young, rosy faced lad, by the name of Flask. He had obviously given no thought to what a voyage round Cape Horn and what three years cooped up with men on a ship would demand from him. He consi-

dered himself simply a born whale hunter. Indeed he was certainly very able.

After the officers there were no more important people on board than the three harpooners. I certainly do not need to waste any more words on Queequeg. But the other two demand a description.

One of them was called Tashtego and he was an Indian. He had dark hair and his eyes were also just as dark, his thick set body was muscular and he was as agile as a cat. Nobody quite knew what destiny had driven him from the woods in Canada to Nantucket and whale catching, all that time ago. Daggoo on the other hand, the third harpooner, had, whilst still a youth, smuggled himself aboard a whaler in some African port or other, as a stowaway. He was a gigantic negro, as black as coal and wore large gold rings in his ears. These harpooners had one thing in common; that self assurance that commands respect from people who are used to looking the huge beasts of our earth in the eye.

Nantucket was already several days' sailing behind, but not for one moment had Captain Ahab appeared on deck. I only heard his loud and powerful voice from time to time, when he gave commands from his cabin. Even when I was not on watch I scarcely let my glance stray from the deck. I was consumed with the thought of finally seeing the man of whom such incredible things were told and to whom, for better or worse, we had relinquished ourselves.

And so when I did see him, it was totally unexpected. It was dawn and the *Pequod* was sailing peacefully with a following wind. I scrambled up to the bridge, to relieve the watch. As was usual I also glanced at the quarter deck. And there he was!

My breath seemed to freeze, the sight frightened me so much. This man looked like somebody out of another world. He looked as if he had been roasted on a fire and pulled out from the embers at the last minute. Motionless as if cast in bronze his huge form stood out against the pale yellow horizon. Beneath his greying hair began a deep, whitish scar, that ran from his brow down across one half of his face, disfigured his neck and chest and disappeared under his shirt. He reminded me of a lone giant tree, around which a storm was roaring, without being able to fell it. He stood there with his legs slightly apart, but only one leg was covered in the trousers of his uniform. The other was fixed like a column into one of the precisely matching holes in the deck planks. It was not a wooden leg, but a whale bone. And now I also knew what the many holes in the deck, from bow to stern were for. They provided a rest for Ahab's artificial leg everywhere, a secure hold where ever he wanted to stand. Yes, indeed he was a tree, but one who somewhere in Japanese waters a whale had laid low. But Ahab had not taken to his bed. He had never once left his ship. He had picked himself up again. And since then defied stubbornly and courageously all the dangers of the seven seas.

Immediately, I felt physically conscious of the savage resolution and the iron will of this man, from whom indeed nobody could escape.

The Captain only remained in his place for a short time. But as long as he was standing to the aft of the deck like a statue, not one of us, neither officer nor hand, dared utter a single word. Everyone got on with his work in silence, and we only breathed out after Ahab had returned to his cabin.

From then on he came on deck every day at the same time and scoured the horizon in silence, before he disappeared again. We gradually became used to this apparition.

As the *Pequod* finally approached the warmer waters on the Equator from the cold northern seas, our morale improved visibly. And strange as it may sound, even Ahab seemed to become more human. At least his face did not seem quite so austere any more, so repulsive, when he looked silently out to sea. Sometimes you could even think he was smiling.

One day, we had then been sailing for several weeks, totally unexpectedly the order came, "Everyone on deck!" The Captain had something to say to us.

We assembled in front of the bridge and did not quite know what awaited us. Ahab was already standing in front of the main mast staring out on to the water. Suddenly he began to walk up and down, without honouring us with a single glance. We began to feel rather stupid and superfluous.

However, he stopped, looked directly at us and asked in a loud voice, "What are you to do if you see a whale?"

"We are to sing out!" we roared with relief.

"Good and then what?"

"Then we hunt after him in the boat until he is senseless."

"And then what do we sing out, young men?"

"The boat is asunder, the whale is our plunder!"

Ahab nodded several times approvingly; our roaring seemed to be music to his ears. As it died down, he turned his face towards us again. "Those of you who have already been on watch are aware of my orders. Be on the look out for a white whale! No other, only a white one counts! And now look carefully. What's this?" He threw his right arm high into the air; sparkling between his fingers was a gold coin. "Correct, sixteen dollars in pure gold. Mr. Starbuck, a hammer and chisel please!" The First Officer brought the tool and rather devoid of understanding we looked on as Ahab first cut a notch in the mast and then with a mighty blow of the hammer drove the coin deep into it.

"Take heed!" he now cried. "Whoever is the first to report the sighting of a white whale with wrinkled brow and sloping jaw and three holes in its tail fin, the gold coin shall be his!"

"Hurrah." Our voices broke out in excitement. "Hurrah! We'll fight him all right!"

"Captain, are you speaking of Moby Dick?" asked Tashtego.

Slowly Captain Ahab laid his hand on the point where the spears crossed.

With a movement of his hand the captain bade for silence again. "A white whale," he repeated as if in a fever. "Keep your eyes open then. Keep your eyes open!"

"Captain," Tashtego stepped forward. "Are you speaking of Moby Dick by any chance? That damned monster, that just before it dives always stretches its tail high out of the water?"

Ahab winced, "What are you saying, Tashtego? Moby Dick? Have you already seen him then?"

"Even met him," Daggoo thrust forward. "He blows gigantic fountain!"

"And have harpoons broken off in back, three, four, Captain, yes?" Queequeg ascertained publicly.

Ahab went up close to the three harpooners. His face was glowing, the white scars in his face had become deep red with excitement. "You know him?" His voice trembled. "Yes, that's him! The tail, the gigantic fountain, the harpoons! There is only one Moby Dick!"

As if spellbound we listened. Even now, as the First Officer asked reflectively, "Moby Dick? But . . . wasn't it him who smashed your leg, sir?"

Angry at having his conversation with the harpooners interrupted Ahab moved round and called to Starbuck, "How do you know that?" He did not wait for the answer. "Yes, it's right, this fiend has maimed me." He clenched his fists. "I have him to thank for my misfortune, this fishbone instead of a leg! But I've sworn bloody revenge on him. And if I have to hunt Moby Dick to the ends of the earth . . . I'll find him, he will not be safe in any corner of the seven seas . . . and you, young men, are going to help me. We will hunt Moby Dick! That is your duty!"

"Yes, Cap'n! Yes! Yes!" we roared spiritedly, infected by Ahab's fanaticism.

"God will bless us for it," said Ahab solemnly. "Smutje!" he yelled immediately after that. "Bring rum, and enough for everyone! And . . . eh, Mr. Starbuck, what's the matter with you? You're pulling such a face, as if . . . Are you afraid of Moby Dick perhaps?"

The First Officer's face coloured up, he straightened his shoulders. "Afraid? You know well enough that I'm not frightened of hunting Moby Dick. But . . . because, I think, it is our duty to kill as many whales as possible and to bring their meat, their oil, their blubber and the spermaceti home. If we help you with your personal vendetta for revenge and only hunt Moby Dick . . . how many full casks do you think we will return with?"

Ahab grew pale as death, his eyes flashed dangerously. "Vats of blubber? You ask about blubber, when it concerns my seeking reparation?"

"Moby Dick is an animal. You're acting as if he were a person!" After these words from Mr. Star-

211

buck there followed a long silence. Ahab looked at the First Officer imperviously. It was clear to me that the Captain felt mortally wounded, although I could not quite see why.

"Mr. Starbuck," Ahab's voice rang out again, though tired, as if in ruins, "you can't understand. Moby Dick is neither man nor beast, he is . . . he is a nightmare. He has a hold over me as if I am in a brass cage chained to him. And I, Starbuck, I must . . . must break loose, I must break his sinister power . . . I hate this feeling, to be chained up . . . I will vanquish Moby Dick . . ." He was still only whispering, then suddenly he roared, "Where's the rum?"

Smutje placed a large jug in front of him.

"Everyone here," commanded Ahab. And as we stood in a circle around him, he looked at each of us individually, before he reached for the jug next to him, "Drink! And pass it on!"

The jug went round. And with it went Ahab's imploring gaze from man to man. Then he gave a sign with his hand, "Men, keep your eyes open day and night! I would however ask the officers to cross their spears in front of me in the old whalers' custom!"

Was I mistaken or did Starbuck, Stubb and Flask hesitate for a moment? But they did as they were bid. Slowly Ahab laid his hand on the point where the spears crossed and thrust them against one another strongly. The ceremony was over.

Peleg and Bildad waved after us for a long time.

Now he turned to the harpooners, "Pull the iron hooks off the shafts. Good . . . look, they are hollow like steel goblets! Now I'll fill them with rum . . . " He took each individual barb and filled it up from the jug. "So, now drink them dry! And swear that you'll not be happy again, until all of these barbs are buried deep in the flesh of Moby Dick. Death to the Beast! The heavens will bless our hunt for him!"

"Death to Moby Dick," we roared fanatically, whilst the harpooners emptied their strange goblets.

Yes, even I, Ismael, had roared with the others, had sworn against Moby Dick, although an undefinable fear wrang at my breast as I did so. This fear of something inevitable roused animosity and hatred against the white whale within me and eagerly I listened to every word that my comrades said about him.

Only a few people had really seen Moby Dick, and those who had hunted him could be counted on your fingers. Many legends arose about this strange whale. One however seemed to be perfectly true: he had brought bad luck to all those who had ever come face to face with him, to most even death. Almost everyone who had dared to throw a spear or harpoon at him, became the victim of the terrible wrath and the malicious intelligence with which Moby Dick counter-attacked. Split spears, smashed boats, maimed sailors and some bodies mutilated beyond recognition carry the marks that Moby Dick has left behind, sometimes high in the North and then again deep in the South.

Nobody knew where the white whale stopped. Completely untraceable, he appeared apparently everywhere, then nowhere. Perhaps he was even immortal?

No wonder that Moby Dick haunted the minds of all whale hunters. However, even the most gruesome reports of his lust for blood had not been able to deter anyone from doing battle with him. There were resolute men, perhaps like the Captain, who did not even surrender as Moby Dick tossed the boat into the air as if it were a toy, so that the crew of three plunged headlong into the water. Two of them were dragged into the deep immediately, the other, who was the helmsman, got on to the back of the whale. In a helpless frenzy, he clung on to the shaft of the harpoon that projected from the smooth back and drove the bare blade into the monster.

Moby Dick let out a dreadful noise, he reared vertically, high out of the water, shook the man off him like an annoying insect and brought his tail fin down on him with a mighty blow. From that moment the man had only one leg. The man was Captain Ahab.

As if by a miracle the ill-fated man survived the duel, after the crew had managed to pull him on board in spite of the mountainous sea.

The *Pequod*'s return journey took months. Even before Cape Horn she had to tack the winter storms for several months, before she eventually reached her home. It was a depressing voyage during which Ahab had enough time for the unextinguished fire of hate against Moby Dick to burn in his heart. Moby Dick had not only disfigured his body, he had wounded Ahab's pride. The Captain roared with rage on his sick bed, he behaved like a madman for days on end, and several times the officers seriously considered whether, both for his own safety and that of the ship, it would not be better to chain him. However as the *Pequod* sailed slowly in peaceful waters, Ahab's attacks of delirium subsided. Day by day he became calmer and soon he was back on the bridge again. He gave his orders concisely and wisely, nothing in his face betraying the thoughts that raged behind his brow and consumed his innermost being like fire.

And yet Ahab had changed. Everyone on board sensed it, although he seemed just as composed as before. From what he did and said, there was no mistaking that he now had only one goal: revenge on Moby Dick. The white whale for him had become quite simply the embodiment of evil, to kill him was to rid the world of one of the worst ills. It was a hatred that did not abate with time, rather, on the contrary, it grew year by year almost to a pathological madness.

Since the day Ahab, as a cripple, manoeuvred the *Pequod* into Nantucket harbour, he has lived only for his revenge. For forty years he has sought Moby Dick on all the seas in the world, he has eagerly searched for every captain who has encountered the whale, and in his cabin he has accumulated maps on which he has marked the proven and unproven routes of Moby Dick, without ever again, up till now, having encountered him.

It did not bother Ahab that year after year he had to take doubtful companions on board, because the *Pequod* had long since become distasteful to normal sailors. He hired men without papers, deserters, savages from the Islands, and it was all the same to him what they had eaten. The wilder the hoard, the better. Only those who had nothing more to lose and so feared neither death nor devil, would not be afraid of Moby Dick either!

On a gloomy sultry afternoon, those who were off duty were lying about idly around the deck, when suddenly we were all startled by Tashtego's long drawn out cry. He was seated high up in the crow's nest and pointed excitedly to the stern. "There! There! There they blow! Not far. A couple of knots!"

Everyone rushed to the bulwarks. Indeed in the distance rose a high frothing fountain, and right beside it another and then another.

Ahab came out of his cabin and roared, "All hands on deck! Man the boats!"

The helmsman guided the *Pequod*, so that we could let the boats down into the water on the lee side. We worked as though in a fever, everyone wanted to be the first to reach the whales.

"Where are they coming from then?" someone or other shouted suddenly.

In helpless frenzy he drove the bare blade into the monster.

Behind Ahab stood five men, who were complete strangers to us: three Indians, that's what they looked like to me, a Chinese, and an Arab wearing a large white turban. They followed the Captain in silence to the fourth boat. "Ready, Fedallah?" he asked the Arab.

Quite a few seconds elapsed before we recovered from our surprise. "Stowaways . . . It's better, don't trouble yourselves!" Mr. Starbuck whispered to us admonishingly. Then we loosed the ropes and seized the oars.

"Separate the boats!" thundered Ahab. "Get a move on, Mister Starbuck! Faster, Mister Stubb! Not so slow, Mister Flask!" He stood erect at the helm of his boat, the tawny men in front of him lay ready with all their power at the oars.

Even Starbuck, Stubb and Flask now urged the crew on to their boats with curses, pleas and oaths. Queequeg and I were in Mr. Starbuck's crew. We rowed like wild men, but Ahab's boat darted away from all of us. Ahab's crew moved the oars in such regular motion, they might have been attached to them. Fedallah sat right at the front, he was obviously Ahab's harpooner.

All the boats approached the first whale. However, he sensed the danger immediately. He turned on his side, raised his tail high momentarily and disappeared under a frothing wave crest into the depths. Disappointed we held the boats close together for a short time, then slowly we increased the gap between us and waited for the same or another whale to appear. It might have been minutes or even hours that went by. The first and third officers were becoming restless. Mister Stubb on the other hand was smoking his pipe calmly.

"There!" cried Queequeg then. "Whale! Row! Row!"

Suddenly the air seemed to change into a cloud of steam, I thought I could feel a quivering, and then, not far away at all, clearly under the surface of the water, I saw the whales!

"After them!" cried Mr. Starbuck, and immediately all the boats gave chase. The oars groaned, the officers at the helm roared, the boats chased through the waves, we were still thinking only of the whales and did not notice at all that the sea was swelling more and more, or how the mist was becoming thicker . . . now, Ismael, you are having the adventure that you have wished for so much!

No, I had not wished for this. In the mist we had not only lost sight of the other boats, but the whales as well, and the storm was advancing!

Mr. Starbuck kept calm and roared over the wind, "Set the sail! And row! Row! All is not lost!"

And, in fact, all of a sudden, all three of the monsters appeared at the same time just in front of us. As if in a fever we rowed towards them.

"Queequeg! Let him have it!" cried our helmsman.

Queequeg threw the harpoon, but before it reached the whale's back, a violent thud made our boat shudder, we flew headlong over the sides. Next to me, above me, underneath me, the sea was frothing, a huge shadow appeared before me. The whale! But he did not take any notice of me at all, but swam away. Merely away.

Now I caught sight of the boat. It had remained intact, it was just full of water. I managed to pull myself up on the side. All the others managed to save themselves too. Dripping wet, we all took our places at the oars again. The water came up to our knees. Gusts of wind roared away over us, the waves were lashing higher and higher, to add to the mist, night fell.

"No need to get agitated," asserted Mr. Starbuck calmly and tried to light an oil lamp. Contrary to expectation he managed to do it and passed it to Queequeg. "Hang it on the helm and keep it high! The others will certainly be looking for us."

Throughout the night Queequeg stood erect and unflinching at the bow. However, not one of us held out any hope that the paltry, miserable light could bring deliverance. We froze and stared ahead whenever, despite the damp, our eyes did not briefly fall shut from exhaustion. The day finally broke, the storm subsided and the sea calmed. But in vain we looked for the *Pequod* and the other boats. Only the mist stood before us.

Suddenly Queequeg held his left hand to his ear, his body became taut. We hardly dared breathe. More and more clearly we could hear an all too familiar groan and roar. And then the silhouette of the *Pequod* rose out of the mist like a primeval giant coming towards us at full speed. We roared like madmen, rowing for our lives, Starbuck threw the helm around . . . too late . . . we managed to jump into the water at the last minute, just before the *Pequod* rammed the boat.

The crashing and grinding was still ringing in my ears, when activity broke out on the *Pequod*. "Hold on!" cried someone at the rails, life lines clattered down, rope ladders followed, after just a few minutes we were all saved. Even our boat, which was upside down in the sea, was brought on board. As I was recovering from the shock, wrapped tightly in blankets, I wanted to know more precisely from Queequeg, "Is that actually right, do whales overturn boats?"

Queequeg grinned patiently, "Capsize boats? It's often so, Ismael!" I had certainly let myself in for something big, I realized, unfortunately too late. And what will it be like some day when we encounter Moby Dick? In an attack of melancholy I tapped Queequeg on the shoulder, "Well, I had better make my will now! You are to be solicitor, executor and sole beneficiary, Understood?"

Queequeg grinned again, but pleased this time, "Okay, beneficiary, but what you got?"

"Nothing," I grinned back.

Weeks and weeks passed by, during which we crossed the hunting grounds in the Azores, the Cape Verde Islands and the mouth of the La Plata. We came through storms and day long doldrums. We had not caught a single whale. But we experienced something sinister.

In the middle of a moonlit night, we heard Fedallah cry out from the top look out, "Whale! There blows a whale!"

Although, according to old seaman's superstition it is unlucky to hunt at night, we all rushed on deck immediately and unleashed the boats. Ahab sailed the *Pequod* at full speed in the direction that Fedallah had indicated. However the whale no longer blew, the sea was calm and motionless. Had

Fedallah been mistaken? No, the watches contested vehemently. They both insisted that they had seen the high spout quite clearly.

Some days later, again shortly before midnight, Fedallah again sang out 'a whale'. Again we gave chase immediately . . . and exactly as before, in vain. As the same thing was repeated for a third night, nobody doubted any longer that a whale was deliberately making fun of us. Just making fun, some of us realized eventually. We were convinced that the whale wanted to lure us with its brief nightly fountains deeper and deeper into more dangerous waters, so that he could then destroy us. Every one of us knew who we meant by this mysterious whale. Moby Dick!

Finally we set course to the east around the Cape of Good Hope. Good God, we needed hope as there was a hurricane blowing not far from us, the like of which even the oldest sailors on the *Pequod* had never before experienced in these parts. God was merciful, we survived even this storm and managed to get south east into calm waters.

One day, as I had watch, high in the Crozett Islands I saw a white sail flashing on the horizon. It was the *Albatross*. She was on her homeward journey after almost three years of sailing. The two ships approached one another rapidly. Judging by her appearance the *Albatross* had been through a lot. The sail was in tatters and had only makeshift repairs, rust ate into the iron work and mussels and

All boats approached the first whale. However, he sensed the danger immediately. He turned on his side quite slowly, and suddenly . . .

algae covered the hull from bow to stern.

Standing on the bridge was the Captain and two watchmen. Dishevelled hair and beards framed their hollow cheeked faces, their clothing hung from their thin shoulders in shreds.

The *Albatross* came so close that we feared she would graze us. Without moving, the three men stared over at us vacantly.

"Ship ahoy!" cried Ahab. "Have you seen the white whale?"

The Captain of the *Albatross* went to take hold of a battered megaphone. But it slipped from his hands, clattered on to the deck and from there fell into the sea. At the same time a mighty gust of wind caught the sail and the ships were driven together.

The crash drowned the words the Captain was shouting to us.

"Did you see that?" asked a startled sailor, who was standing next to me by the rails. "He had only just mentioned the white whale, and the megaphone just slipped into the water!" "And the gust came from a clear sky!" murmured another.

Meanwhile Ahab was obviously reflecting whether he should be rowed over to the *Albatross*. However, he decided to roar through his megaphone, "This is the *Pequod*, on a long journey round the earth. Tell the ports that they are to send our post to us in the Pacific. And if in three years we have not returned, then they are to . . . " Then he fell silent. Only now had he seen what had just

Slowly the ship approached.

befallen us.

Attracted by the slops that had been thrown overboard, we had been escorted for days on end by large shoals of fish. Their slender bodies shone dimly in our sail line. However, where the waves behind us crossed with the wake of the *Albatross*, the shoals turned abruptly and followed her. "Are they leaving me alone?" Ahab broke out loudly and visibly perplexed. But he regained control of himself immediately, turned with a jolt to the helmsman and ordered, "Set course hard-a-port. On further round the world!"

A light breeze was driving us on a north easterly course towards the island of Java, when one morning while the sun was burning through, Daggoo, from his place in the crow's nest, saw something huge and white appear from the sea and then disappear again immediately. Shortly afterwards the water frothed up again.

"White whale! There, white whale!" he sang out, his voice cracking.

Immediately we were all overcome with hunting fever. Faster than ever before the boats were lowered into the water. Ahab and his dark skinned crew were the first again. We did not give ourselves any time to think. We rowed as fast as our oars could take us, and suddenly a white iridescent mass raised itself up from out of the sea a few yards in front of us. Millions of bubbles danced and burst in the sunlight, and several slimy arms groped over the crown of foam. Before we had even recovered from

our amazement, the monster disappeared below. "I wanted to meet Moby Dick," scolded Mr. Starbuck. "Not you, you damned beast!"

"What was that?" shouted Mr. Flask from his boat.

"A giant octopus! Whoever encounters one, it is said, never sees his home again. Or so they say!" the First Officer shouted back.

Captain Ahab, who had of course heard everything, remained silent. Signalling with his hand he ordered the return to the *Pequod.*

However Queequeg asserted, "Where big octopus, whale not far!" He was right!

The next day the spout from a whale who had just appeared glistened high in the distance. We jumped into the boats again. And this time luck was on our side. On the calm sea we were able to get quite close to the monster. It noticed us too late. Before it could turn in flight Mr. Stubb had hurled the harpoon into its tail. "Slacken the rope, Tashtego!" he yelled at the same time. "Be careful! Hold on tight!"

"Aye! Aye!" roared Tashtego and threw the second harpoon. It stuck fast behind the whale's head. The monster reared up, the rope tightened, with a jolt he dragged the boat forwards and pulled it faster and faster behind him. It seemed to be flying in a whirlwind of froth and foam over the waves, water spumed overboard and as the strength of the whale finally flagged, all hands were dripping wet from head to toe.

218

Mr. Stubb finished the whale off with several blows of his lance. Once more it opened its gigantic mouth helplessly, then the animal rolled on to its side, the lighter belly was showing, the water round about was coloured blood red.

Loud cries of jubilation broke out on every boat, although a hard stretch of work lay ahead of us; we had to pull the ton weight of booty, which next to our boat looked like a swimming island, over to the *Pequod*. Sweat ran out of our every pore, until we finally were able to secure the whale next to the sides on hooks and ropes.

For the days that followed, we were all busy dealing with the whale. There was not even one bit of this giant animal that was not worth something somewhere. Firstly the body was hauled on board with several windlasses. It was so heavy, that for several moments we feared the *Pequod* would overturn and capsize. But finally this task was accomplished.

Now it was Mr. Stubb's turn again. With a blade like a drop-keel he cut off the gigantic head, which was then hung on well secured ropes, so that it was easily reached on all sides.

First came the extraction of the teeth. There were forty-two. Next the metre long jaw bones were sawn up like wooden laths and put in piles. We collected the oil and fats in large vats, the brain was shifted to the galley.

Meanwhile others were already working on the trunk. They cut it into metre long strips and threw these past the hatches down into the hold. Waiting down there already were the blubber extractors with spoon-like blades on poles. They had to remove the precious fat between flesh and skin. The best pieces of flesh from the tail were kept by Smutje for a celebration roast. Finally only the skeleton was hanging in the ropes. "Into the sea with it!" ordered the First Officer. "And then scrub everything down!"

The bone frame smacked the water. Immediately the water around bubbled with small

Even before we had recovered from our surprise, the monster dived under.

This time we had the
head of a particularly
large whale hung
out over the side,
and we were pleased
with the spermaceti.
Then it happened . . .

predators, who tore off the last shreds of meat.

Just a few more words on the head of the whale seem necessary to me. It has a dual value for the hunter. One because of the bones, to which the teeth also belong and then also for the soft parts. The tongue is held to be a delicacy by connoisseurs, opinions differ on the taste of the brain. However, they are unanimous generally on the spermaceti, as the watery clear oil in the cartilage hollows is called. The highest prices are paid for it and so every whaler is very careful that not one drop is lost.

As many whale heads are too heavy to be pulled on deck and hung up there, they are left to hang on a frame by the side. Then, through a hole in the skin on the head, the oil is scooped out as from a vat by a sailor. It is a very laborious and dangerous task, as the man stands barefoot on the slippery swinging head, mostly not even secured by a rope, whilst he lowers a bucket on a line into the hole. The full bucket is pulled on board by helpers, at the same time they pass an empty bucket down to the man bailing the spermaceti out, so that he can carry on working without interruption.

Now one day, we had the head of a particularly large whale hanging over the side and Tashtego was already ladling out the eightieth bucket full of spermaceti, and then the accident occured.

A breaker dashed against the gigantic head and drove it on to the ship's side. Tashtego lost his balance and plunged headlong through into the whale's skull.

"Man over board!" yelled Daggoo first, whilst we were still staring at the blood red hole, as if petrified, into which our comrade had disappeared. And then right away, presumably due to the hefty jolt caused by the rush, the ropes broke, the whale's head with the Islander inside it fell like a log on to the surface of the water and sank slowly into the depths.

But someone acted, Queequeg. He tore the whale knife from his belt and jumped behind the skull into the water, that was something. We held our breath in trepidation . . . the seconds, the minutes lasted an eternity. "Blasted spermaceti!" I thought. "Is the stuff really worth the lives of valiant men? And even more such a good friend as Queequeg?"

"Ah! Ah! Ah!" Daggoo suddenly shouted for joy and pointed to a crown of a head between the crests of foam.

We scarcely dared trust our eyes, before we all cried out loudly in jubilation. Just a few metres from the ship's side, Queequeg was swimming with one arm. The other he held around fast to the motionless Tashtego. Minutes later we had pulled both of them on board. Queequeg recovered relatively quickly. After some time the one he had saved came to. Only then did we besiege Queequeg with questions, as to how he had managed to save Tashtego.

Queequeg did not make too much fuss about it.

"Man over-
board!"
Daggoo's cry
resounded.

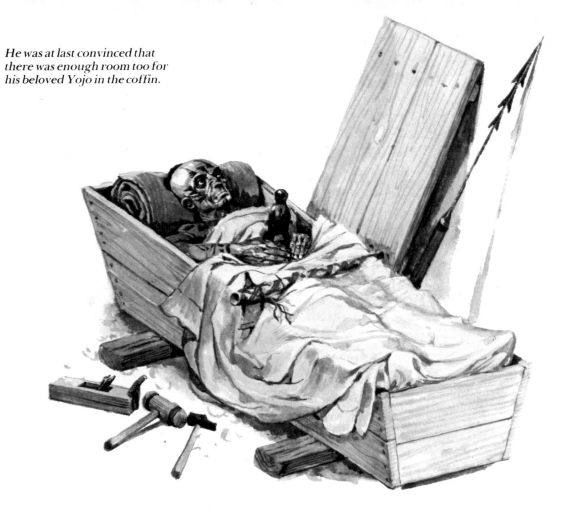

He was at last convinced that there was enough room too for his beloved Yojo in the coffin.

He said that because of the large fat content the skull would sink slowly. Luckily for Tashtego, as Queequeg then had enough time to cut an opening through the thick skin, in the place where he thought the injured man's head was, and from which he could pull out the already unconscious body.

A quite outstanding feat, which I too would have taken for a sailor's yarn had I not witnessed it with my own eyes.

I must admit that immediately after the accident, not entirely inhuman thoughts were stirred within me. Could there have been a more beautiful and honourable death for a harpooner, than to travel to the bottomless depths of the ocean, in the head of a whale, the proudest and cleverest of sea creatures, surrounded by the precious spermaceti?

All the casks of oil and spermaceti in the hold were washed down thoroughly twice a week. This soaking kept the wood and joints water-tight. First of all sea water was laboriously pumped up in long hoses, and then later, just as laboriously pumped out from the hold.

Whilst we were cruising by Japanese waters, small flecks of oil appeared on the water as we were pumping out. One of the casks must have been leaking, perhaps even a few were. That meant that

we had a devilish hard job to tackle. We had to shift each cask in turn in the suffocating vapour of the hold, in order to find the one or the ones that were leaking.

We toiled hour after hour deeper and deeper down into the ship's belly and only when we were right over the keel did we discover a broken cask. But it was already too late for Queequeg.

The poor fellow had already inhaled so much of the polluted air and the poisonous stench, that he suddenly collapsed and thereafter lay in his hammock for days on end between life and death. He grew visibly weaker, and when he was hardly able to speak any longer, he summoned the ship's carpenter.

"Build canoe for corpse," he whispered. "When dead then let me swim in canoe, not throw corpse to fishes! Canoe, yes? So is custom on Islands."

"You mean a coffin, man. So custom with Christians," growled the carpenter. He took measurements carefully with his yardstick and went about his work.

It was a handsome coffin, made from thick planks nailed and jointed solidly, and my sick friend nodded weakly when he saw it. He was however only satisfied, when in accordance with his wishes,

The carpenter grumbled first, yet he set himself to work all the same.

we had laid him in it to try it out. He satisfied himself at last that there was also ample space for his beloved Yojo, that wooden idol, and for a few hens as food for the journey into the heathen underworld. Amidst the mocking of a few onlookers we were finally able to stow Queequeg back in his hammock. Others may well laugh, but he did mind whether the fishes gnawed at his corpse or whether he set out on his last journey in a respectable canoe.

To the surprise of us all, from the day that the coffin was completed Queequeg began to get better rapidly. "How can that be?" I wondered happily, as at last after a long time he leant next to me by the bulwarks.

"Not to die yet, still something to finish," he replied tersely and mysteriously.

The *Pequod* was now sailing in the Equatorial zone and was approaching the waters in which, according to Ahab's calculations, we could run into Moby Dick at any moment.

Now one morning there was a terrible accident. A horrible scream made us suddenly raise our eyes up to the look-out. We looked up just as the sailor, who should have relieved the watch above, plunged head first into the sea. Had he been taken ill? Had he fallen out? No time for questions . . . the life-buoy had already been loosed at the stern. The

injured man appeared . . . we threw the buoy, an empty cask, made watertight with pitch, that could easily carry a man. But it did not carry the half conscious man, he was so desperate he was clinging on tightly. "Damn! The wood is dried up and is soaking up full of water like . . ." I was not listening any more to what my neighbour was saying, I just saw how the buoy sucked the drowning man down into the deep . . . as the first of Moby Dick's victims? Ahab allowed us no time to ponder. "We need a new buoy!" was all that he said about the incident. Mr. Starbuck turned to the carpenter. But he shrugged his shoulders in sympathy "There isn't a single empty cask on the whole ship any more."

The First Officer reflected for a moment and his face lit up. "We've got the coffin haven't we?"

"A coffin for a life-buoy, sir?" The carpenter shook his head in refusal. "That does not please me at all, no . . ."

"Nonsense!" the First Officer interrupted him. "On with the lid, nails, pitch, so it'll be really unsinkable, clear?"

"No," grumbled the carpenter, but he set to work without further protestations.

On the following day the *Rachel,* an old whaler out of Nantucket, crossed our course. Almost her entire crew were standing at the bulwarks. The

223

Ahab remained up there for a long time.

Pequod slowed down and Ahab, cupping his hands, shouted over to them, "Ahoy, *Rachel*! Have you seen the white whale?"

"We have!" someone answered. "And have you sighted a whale boat?"

"No!" Ahab looked as though he wanted to dance for joy. Impatient and excited, he waited for the boat that was bringing the Captain of the *Rachel* to board us.

"Ah, it's you, Gardiner!" Ahab hardly took time to greet him. "Well, tell me more! Where is Moby Dick? You haven't killed him already, have you?"

"We've hunted after him," reported Captain Gardiner. "But he got away. With one of my boats in tow. That happens when you don't cut the harpoon rope quick enough." Ahab nodded, unimpressed. "Your boat will soon turn up again."

"I hope so, we have been looking for it for two days already. My . . . my youngest son is on it. So young, only twelve years old. Help me, Ahab! As seaman to seaman I beg you. Forty-eight hours only . . . two ships see more than one . . . I'll pay you any price . . . we must save him! Please, Ahab, your answer cannot be no!"

Tears were in the old man's eyes. However, not a muscle flinched in Ahab's face.

"Say yes, sir!" urged Mr. Starbuck softly.

"An end of it!" Ahab's voice rang cold in refusal. "I'm sorry, Gardiner," he explained sternly, "it's not on. As it is I have already lost much too much time. Goodbye and good luck! Mister Starbuck, escort the Captain off the ship. In three minutes we'll be sailing on!"

He turned round curtly and thudded into his cabin. Silently, accompanied by our embarrassed looks, the desperate father took leave of our ship.

For a long time I watched the *Rachel* getting smaller and smaller. She was a picture of despair and misery. A sign for us? I wondered instinctively.

For days we saw nothing but the wide endless sea and the grey sky above. Yet we all had the feeling that Moby Dick could not be far off. Ahab was completely certain of this. From early morning until late in the evening he hardly left his place on the quarter deck and he scoured the horizon constantly. Unremittingly he called upon the watches in the crow's nest to kindly keep a better look out. He was in a real frenzy over the meeting with Moby Dick and hour by hour he grew more impatient.

Finally one day we had to hoist him in a basket to the top of the main mast, far above the crow's nest. He remained up there for a long time, the wind blew his hat away, which, as every traveller knows, means bad luck, and we heard him say several times through his teeth, "I'll earn the gold coin myself . . . I'll be the first to see him!"

Then we met the *Delight*. The ship was called this, but there was nothing of delight about her appearance. A huge hole gaped in her starboard, right above the water line, which had been repaired more badly than correctly. The boats also showed signs of damage.

"Ahoy! Have you encountered the white whale?" was Ahab's first question again.

"Look at the hole!" roared the other Captain. "He hit us!"

Ahab yelled, "Did you kill him then?"

"The harpoon for this murderer must be forged first!"

"Must it?" Ahab let out a piercing laugh. "I . . . look here . . . I have the very harpoon here in my hand!" He held the weapon up high, that had been forged from the best steel by the ship's smith. "It is tempered in blood, and I will thrust it into the heart of Moby Dick!"

"Pray to God that this demon doesn't eat your heart!" the oath came back. "Here , in this sack lies one of our men. We are just about to bury him. Only him. We have not yet found his four companions from the boat. Moby Dick has taken them with him into the depths."

Ahab did not show the slightest sympathy. "Up helm. Windward!" he ordered. The *Pequod* leaned slightly to the side and changed her course.

From aboard the *Delight* the sack with the dead sailor slipped off a plank into the sea. The splash was still ringing in my ears when the Captain of the damaged ship yelled over to us, "Are you sailing away as we pay our last respects to our dead? Sail on, but do not forget your ship is already a floating coffin!"

One day the blue of the sky seemed to fuse with the blue of the sea and the warmth of the sun's rays soaked pleasantly through the skin. At the same time a light, cooling breeze was blowing; and colourful birds, from God only knows where, flew over the waves and buzzed round the *Pequod*. On this day Captain Ahab leaned out over the bulwarks and breathed in deeply.

"This wonderful air! And how the sea sparkles like magic!" he said, lost in thought, to the complete surprise of the First Officer who was standing nearby.

Ahab did not expect an answer. Reflecting, he continued, "On a day just like today I killed my first whale. I was eighteen at the time, a green harpooner. That's over forty years ago. What years! Full of unfulfilled hopes, deprivations . . . only whaling . . . when I tot it up, not three years all together on dry land. Do you know what that means, Mister Starbuck? No fruit, no fresh vegetables, no crusty crisp bread. Always only salted meat, dry biscuits, fish. And no family. Even if I were married. My poor wife . . . a widow is better off. For me, Starbuck, the ship is everything. House, home, family. Now is that any kind of life?"

The boat turned. Immediately next to the bow the gigantic head appeared.

Ahab was silent for a few minutes and the First Officer preferred to remain silent too.

"No, it's no life," Ahab said at last. "But I cannot, I will not give up. I must stand by my oath. And you, Starbuck, you must take charge of the *Pequod*, when we eventually meet Moby Dick. No, no objections. A man like you must stay on board!"

In the middle of the night Ahab came on deck and inhaled the salty air, examining it. "There's a whale nearby!" he asserted. And all at once we too thought we could smell the blubbery odour that sometimes emanates from whales.

Ahab ordered almost all of the sails lowered. Silently and slowly now the *Pequod* glided on further, whilst above us one after the other the stars went out and dawn fell. Again our captain was hoisted up the main mast.

Scarcely was he up, when he yelled, roared, cried out in jubilation, "There! There he blows! Yes, a white hump . . . It's him! Moby Dick!" We all rushed to the bulwarks in order to get a better view. And in fact just about a mile away, a frothing jet rose into the sky and a massive white hump shimmered above the waves.

"He blows! And how he blows!" repeated Ahab. "Bring me down!" Barely had he stood on deck, his thin face deep red, he asked, "Now, who saw him first?"

Tashtego lay his hand on his chest, "Me, sir. With you."

"Not quite, my good man. Not with me, after me! I have always known that I'd be the one . . . Look! Moby Dick blows again! Stand by three boats. On with the chase!"

Straight afterwards the boats cast off from the *Pequod*, slowly they rowed over the almost motionless sea to the whale, who seemed to be taking no heed of them whatsoever. A swarm of birds circled above him. In his back were three broken harpoons. Suddenly, as if he had just been waiting until the boats were near enough, he vaulted out of the water, and made an elegant diving curve back and disappeared with the speed of lightning back under the surface.

"Did you see that?" cried Ahab, bent far out over the side and stared, as if possessed, into the unfathomable depths. At almost the same moment Tashtego pointed into the sky in terror, "There! Birds flying over Ahab. Bad omen!"

The Captain continued to look down. Out of the darkness a light speck shimmered and grew bigger and bigger.

"Over here! Row! row!" There was no longer need for Ahab's command, the men in his boat had also recognized the danger and were ready at the oars and Fedallah turned the helm around. The boat turned . . . then suddenly next to the stern the gigantic white head of Moby Dick appeared. With a terrible grunt he opened his huge jaw, pulled his head back slightly, hurled himself forward as quick as lightning and lunged at the bow with his terrifying jaws and smacked them together.

We could hear crunching and grating, we could see screaming men taking flight to the stern and how, in vain, Captain Ahab tried to thrust the harpoon into the body of the beast. Finally, helpless in rage, he snatched out with his bare hands towards the lower jaw, but slipped and at the same moment as all the men disappeared in a frothing eddy, he plunged overboard. The last to go in was Fedallah, who up to this point had stood upright at the helm. The white whale curved his back into a high ridge, stretched and began to swim in ever-decreasing circles round our comrades, who were swimming for their lives.

Mr. Starbuck recognized the deadly danger. At full speed he steered the *Pequod* between the white whale and the shipwrecked men so that the two other boats could venture forth and save them.

By the time we had all men on deck again, Moby Dick had slowly swum away from us. His huge hull ploughed through the sea like a fully rigged ship, millions of white bubbles formed a stringlike trail that gradually became ever swifter, before he finally disappeared under the water and continued on his journey.

Only now did Ahab inquire, "Everyone on board? Good then listen carefully: the gold coin is still fixed in the mast, although it actually belongs to me. But, whoever sings out Moby Dick on the day that I kill him, shall have it. And I promise you, no one will go empty handed. After our victory I will share out gold ten times the value of this coin amongst you!"

Before we had really understood his words he turned and did not say another word that day.

Early the next morning we heard the cry from the look out, "He blows! Moby Dick in front of the bow!"

"Yes, blow then, damn beast!" roared Mr. Stubb. "We know the devil's in you!" And Captain Ahab cursed, as immediately after, there was nothing more to be seen. He was still cursing when Moby Dick appeared majestically and we, as if by instinct, broke out into loud hurrahs. Suddenly the whale reared straight up out of the water at its full size. Gleaming white, like a demon from another world, he seemed to stand in the air before he sank back into the stormy swelling waves.

"He is looking at the sun for the last time!" sneered Ahab. "Mister Starbuck, take over the bridge. And the others lower the boats immediately!"

Those of us from Mr. Starbuck's crew had to stay on the *Pequod* too and watch the hunt from there. Hardly had Moby Dick spotted the three boats than he went to attack, swimming right between them and lashing out wildly on all sides with his tail fin. Although the boats were tossing about as if in a hurricane, several harpoons hit the whale. The pain increased his rage. His untraceable, lightning-fast movements tangled the harpoon

We could hear
crunching and
grating, as all
the men
disappeared in a
frothing eddy.

A jolt went through Ahab's body. With clenched fist he made threats out to the sea and cursed.

lines together in knots, Ahab's boat threatened to be pulled into the deep, he managed to sever the rope at the last minute. It sped back . . . a cry . . . Mr. Flask's boat crashed into the second, both crews flew defenceless into the water.

Ahab wanted to go to their help immediately, but Moby Dick dashed against the side with all his force, the boat overturned . . . as it righted again, it was empty. And now for the first time the whale seemed to be really raging. He swam through the capsized boats, crashed his head against the side and lashed the sea into a maelstrom of foam and froth and boiling waves.

Again Mr. Starbuck steered between them. Nothing seemed to unnerve him. Deliberately and calmly he then pushed the whale to the side.

This time it took quite a long time to get all the men, the damaged boats and also finally the equipment that was bobbing around, safely on board. However, Moby Dick slipped proudly out of our view, like a victor. The ropes from the harpoons that were stuck in his back, he dragged behind him like trophies. He had left wounds, bruises and sprained shoulders behind. Our courage, the courage of a mortal enemy, he had not managed to break.

Only when Ahab was leaning on Mr. Starbuck's shoulder did we see that his whale leg had been broken off into a small stump.

"Are you hurt, sir?" asked the Second Officer, shocked.

Ahab shook his head contemptuously. "I do not give in so quickly. Especially not . . . the devil, where's the whale?"

"Up and away, sir!"

"Away? Hoist the sails! We must find him again! Give me something for a prop . . . yes that broken lance there is all right . . . Am I mistaken, Mister Starbuck? Is someone missing? All men on deck."

We fell in for roll call. Ahab had not been mistaken. Fedallah's place was empty. We looked disbelievingly at one another, staggered.

"He must be there!" asserted the Captain obstinately.

We scoured the ship from top to bottom. In vain. Mr. Stubb turned finally and hesitatingly came out with the dreadful suspicion, "As the severed line coiled back quickly, it seemed to me . . . as if it had wound round a man, before he plunged into the sea." Ahab's face became numb like a mask, "I . . . I severed the line. I have . . . delivered him up to Moby Dick." A jolt went through his body. With clenched fist he said threateningly to the sea, "Moby Dick! Moby Dick! And if I have to chase you ten times round the earth, I . . . do you hear? . . . I will kill you! Kill!" Then he turned to us again, "Now calm down, young men. And do not worry yourselves, because we have lost Fedallah. These things happen. But if you are still superstitious, then you must also believe that everything that is doomed to perish, appears three times. Ah, you didn't know that?" His eyes lit up. "Moby Dick appeared yesterday, and again today. Tomorrow on the third time, he will perish!"

We nodded, dumb and confused. And we could hardly sleep that night. Restlessly we listened to the hammering and sawing on deck, where our comrades were again repairing the boats and equipment.

A pale dawn hue announced the third day. Ahab already stood on deck and stared expectantly up to the top mast. But the sailor up there only shook his head again and again.

Hours followed, which tugged at our nerves and in which Ahab crossed the *Pequod* aimlessly, changing his direction this way and that. Restlessness drove him to and fro. Finally we had to hoist him up in his basket. Motionless he persisted up there, until suddenly far aft the now well-known and for this reason the no less terrifying jet spouted.

"Moby Dick!" roared Ahab. "Today is the third time! The last time. Come here . . . come here!"

Only minutes later the boats were in the water. And I, Ismael, had to take Fedallah's place on Ahab's boat with him. Was I proud of this show of trust? No, the excitement that I felt within me was of another kind. Anger, impotence, fear . . . I do not quite know what it was. I only knew that Ahab's excitement was much more intense. His whole body trembled, his bushy eyebrows quivered as in a fever, and as we wanted to jump into the boat, he remained standing in front of Mr. Starbuck and said with uncharacteristic emotion to him, "He has come for the third time . . . It's here, as though the waves are pulling me irresistibly to him. Starbuck, give me your hand!"

The First Officer stood with tears in his eyes. "Captain . . . ," he began, yet Ahab was already shouting, "In the boats!"

We rowed hard and fast. Sharks were following in our wake. For whom where they waiting? For

The line had twisted like a noose around Ahab's neck.

Moby Dick? Or for us? Ahab stood like a statue at the bow with his harpoon under his arm. The sea was calm, but suddenly there was a flurry of foam and there was Moby Dick!

Numerous harpoons and lances projected clearly from his massive white body. It was obvious the many and deep wounds hurt him. Otherwise the wild movements, with which he threw himself over the waves, before he shot into the depths again, leaving behind a boiling heavy sea, could not be explained.

"Get ready to attack!" Ahab had barely cried out as Moby Dick already drove high between the three boats and, raving, lashed around them with his gigantic tail.

Ahab's harpoon hit him, but slid off at the neck and whilst the Captain, cursing, was still pulling in the rope, almost at the same time Mr. Stubb's and Mr. Flask's boats were hit with such a mighty thud that their bows were immersed deep under water, and, quick as a flash they filled and keeled over

We rowed so that the oars bent as Moby Dick was preparing to swim under our boat from the stern. Only at the last minute were we able to dodge the deadly blow. Like a mountain of white primitive stone the shimmering back slid past at our port.

Ahab thrust his harpoon high, but his arm froze as if paralysed. And we too were gripped by cold terror at what we saw. Behind the huge hump of the head, entangled in harpoons, broken lances and torn lines hung the gruesome silent corpse of Fedallah, the dead eyes directed at Ahab, as if in accusation.

By the time we had half recovered from our shock the white whale was a long way out of throwing reach and was rapidly getting further and further away.

"Hoist the sails! After him!" roared Ahab.

We gave chase immediately, whilst to our rear the *Pequod* fished our shipwrecked comrades and the two overturned boats out of the water.

"Mister Starbuck, follow us slowly. Slowly!" cried Ahab over to the ship. "And order the best look-outs on the top mast! Yes, the best! Queequeg, Tashtego and Daggoo. Understood!"

"Aye aye, sir!" he shouted back.

Amidst Ahab's incessant and impatient urgings we approached the whale surprisingly quickly. The chase over three consecutive days and the many wounds had exhausted even him and sapped his original strength.

The distance between ourselves and him grew smaller and smaller. Ahab wielded his harpoon high again, the sinews of his arms stretching. With all his force he threw the steel and at the same time sent wild curses after it. This time the harpoon hit the whale with full might. The hooked barbs bore directly deep behind the head into the neck, and disappeared right down to a short stump.

In a steaming cloud of spray and mist the giant body vaulted out of the bubbling foam, a lash of its tail struck the bow. The boat stood firm, but three oarsmen were catapulted overboard by the blow. We were able to rescue two immediately, before the sharks came. The third swam too far off. We had not enough time to get him, as he cried out so frantically for help. Moby Dick came straight towards us at full speed. Like the wall of a house his terrifying skull rose before us out of the foaming waves.

"Row! Row for your lives!" Still shouting Ahab seized a new harpoon. Yet before he could throw it Moby Dick quite suddenly changed course.

Ahab grew pale. "He's seen the *Pequod*! He's attacking her! No . . . that he cannot! After him! Quickly. Quickly!"

We gave our last, we rowed until our lungs burst, but the white whale was quicker.

Our comrades on deck seemed unable to move. Thunderstruck, aghast with horror, they stared as if paralysed at the oncoming fate. As the gigantic skull lunged full against the starboard side, the air shook with the blast that was like a thousand cannon. Men, equipment, boxes whirled past each other, sliding, rolling, thundering over the splitting sides. Cries resounded in our ears. Mortally wounded, the whole ship was grinding and groaning, and although she was only just barely leaning, she began to sink faster and faster.

Up to the last minute Queequeg, Tashtego and Daggoo, our brave harpooners, stood fast in the top masts. Only when it reached the main mast did the sea swallow them up.

"My ship! The *Pequod* is going down without me!" The wail of Ahab's voice was even louder than the raging and roaring of the sea. Like a madman he seized the harpoon and hurled it at the white murderer, who was swimming away unhurriedly. It stuck in the root of his tail.

Now Moby Dick took flight. But he was so exhausted and consequently so slow that the harpoon line did not tighten. It hung there loosely. Ahab bent to pull it in . . . at the same moment the boat rolled, the sea around us began to bubble, to turn . . . for God's sake, I realized, we were being pulled into the wake of the sunken ship! . . . Dimly I now saw that the line had shot in the air and had twisted like a noose around Ahab's neck, and then Moby Dick suddenly shot forward. Like a great black bird on the line, the Captain flew high in the air, carried away by his mortal enemy, the white whale . . .

Then the water closed in over us all, the sea pulled and sucked us all into the depths. We, the last of the *Pequod*, followed our ship into the everlasting night . . . only the sharks were witness to the tragedy . . . and the world would never find out how Captain Ahab and his men met Moby Dick and were beaten by him.

Never? How then is everything described here so precisely? Because someone indeed survived the horror: I, Ismael.

I was sitting at the stern. As the gurgling eddy took me, the main force of the vortex was already broken, the sea spat me out again as the only survivor. Sharks encircled me, without attacking me. Several gulls circled above me and then I saw something black. Its length appeared near me: the life buoy. I pulled myself up on to it, what should have actually served my good Queequeg as a coffin. Now he had had to travel to the fishes without his 'canoe'. Instead it was carrying me, his young friend, back to life.

That is to say, that it was indeed my carefree youth that gave me hope to travel back into life, although my situation told me that there was little to hope for.

Moby Dick had lured the *Pequod* far off the routes that were frequented by whalers at this time, and no-one could conceive that there should be anyone else as mad as Captain Ahab.

Ahab! I should think more about him than my pitiable state. How would he and Moby Dick get on with one another now; now that they could no longer be parted from each other. Even in death the white monster took the man with him, who alone amongst all whalers on the seven seas had defied him. And still in death this man had to see how his ship and his men became victims of a crazy hunt, his hunt.

Yes, he, Ahab had us all on his conscience! Even me! Or not just him alone! Had we not all rejoiced!

Had we not all roared, "Death to the white whale!" as though he were also our personal enemy. And are we to call a man mad because he stuck to a goal he had set himself in spite of all danger, all his life long? And when in his eyes this goal was the destruction of evil, personified by Moby Dick?

Remarkably I lost all sense of time and hours. I was so wrapped up in the craziest thoughts of the past, I did not think of the future.

I think I was still dreaming, I saw Ahab, my comrades and, again and again, Moby Dick . . .

And I saw the brave Queequeg, who had now travelled into the depths without 'canoe', bequeathed defenceless to the sharks and other fish. Would he or would he not perhaps cleanse his soul?

I thought of old Elijah too. Why had I scorned his warnings? Did he really know that the *Pequod* would only sail out of Nantucket once more and then never again?

Thoughts, thoughts . . . yes, I was still only dreaming . . .

After two days, strong arms pulled me out of the water. I could barely open my eyes any more. But before I completely lost consciousness from weakness and happiness, I recognized my rescuers. They were the men of the *Rachel*. They were still looking for their comrades, but instead of them they found one whose comrades likewise would never return. Me.

What should have served my good friend, Queequeg, as a coffin was now giving me hopes of survival!

MARK TWAIN

The Adventures of Tom Sawyer

MARK TWAIN
The Adventures of Tom Sawyer

Aunt Polly's punishment

"Tom!" No reply. "Tom!" Silence.

Aunt Polly glanced around and hissed, "You little rascal, just wait 'til I get hold of you . . ."

She heard something gently rustling behind her, turned round and just caught the young boy slipping out of a large cupboard. "Oh yes," Aunt Polly said furiously, "I might have known it. What were you doing in there?"

"Nothing, Aunt dear," replied Tom, but she had already seen Tom's filthy hands, which were sticky with marmalade, and grabbed her cane.

"Oh, Good Heavens, over there, Aunt, turn round quickly!" shouted the boy.

Aunt Polly turned round but Tom ran off like a rabbit, leapt over the garden fence and was gone. The old lady stood for a second or two, then began to laugh helplessly.

"By golly, it seems I still don't know him," she cried. "I ought to, after all the tricks he's played on me!"

That day Tom had played truant from school, and passed the time in quite a different way. Of course he got home at the proper time to help Jim, the little Negro, collect the wood.

Or to put it a better way, he came home at the right time to tell Jim all about his adventures, while his friend had to work away for both of them. Now Sid, Tom's younger stepbrother, had already done his work. Sid was a quiet and calm lad and did not get on anyone's nerves . . . except Tom's. He was always top of the class and fancied himself in the role of Aunt Polly's telltale; that is, telling her all about Tom's misdemeanours.

Two minutes after the sight of Aunt Polly's cane had prompted Tom to take to his heels, he was sauntering through the streets, practising a new way of whistling. Suddenly he stopped dead. In front of him stood a boy who had recently moved into the village, and who was a lot bigger than Tom. The two boys weighed each other up. When one of them moved, so did the other. Then they looked at each other, without saying a word. After a while, Tom said, "You looking for a fight?"

"Just try it!"

"Your cap looks stupid."

"Well, take it off me then; you're a coward if you don't dare."

"So are you."

They went on threatening and watching each other for a while, until Tom marked out a line with his foot and said, "I dare you to cross this line."

He had hardly finished speaking when the other boy had already stepped across. A few seconds later, both of them were rolling around the ground, clawing at each other like rabid cats. They tore each other's clothes, pulled each other's hair, scratched each other's noses, boxed each other's ears and splattered each other with mud, all quite honourably. At length Tom forced the other boy to submit. The latter toddled off muttering vulgar threats, and when he noticed that Tom was looking the other way, he picked up a stone and threw it at him. Tom immediately took up the chase, but the stranger managed to reach his house and bolt the door behind him. Tom

"Aha, Tom," teased Ben, "she's lumbered you today then!"

roared after him, "Don't be surprised when we settle this later!" then set off home, where Aunt Polly was waiting to settle her unfinished business.

It just happened that the next morning was a glorious summer's day. Aunt Polly pressed a bucket of paint and a long-handled brush into Tom's hand. He had to paint the long, wooden fence. Tom groaned, dipped the brush in the paint, daubed it over one plank, dipped it in again, painted another and another. Then he sat down cheerfully on the pavement. Jim came through the garden gate with his bucket. He was going to the well to pump some water. Tom would willingly have swapped places with him, but Jim would not be persuaded. Aunt Polly's instructions were clear: Tom had to paint the fence alone. Angrily, Tom went back to his work and thought of the many splendid things he had planned to do that day which were now impossible. There seemed to be no solution until escape came in the form of Ben Rogers, who, out of all the boys in the village was the one who was most afraid of Tom's mischievous tricks. When Tom saw him appear at the end of the street, he had a brilliant idea. He went on painting as if he were thoroughly enjoying the whole thing.

"Aha, Tom," chortled Ben, "she's lum-

bered you today!"

"What do you mean, lumbered?"

"Don't give me that, you know what I mean. You can't tell me you're enjoying that."

"Sure, I'm enjoying it. Why shouldn't I? A boy of my age doesn't get a chance like this every day."

Suddenly the affair took on a whole new twist for Ben Rogers. As he chewed on his apple, he listened and followed the artist's every move with growing attentiveness. Then he pulled himself together.

"Tom, may I have a little go?"

Tom thought for some time, then shook his head, "No, Ben, I'm sorry, but I'm not allowed to. Aunt Polly is frightfully fussy about her wooden fence. It's got to be painted in a very particular way and there's nobody else in the whole village she can entrust it to."

Ben did not give up, first he offered Tom half, then the whole of his apple as a swap, until Tom (seemingly reluctantly) gave way and handed him the brush. Tom sat down in the shade and watched Ben doing the job for him. He did not lack additional helpers either. From time to time a friend would pass by, to pull Tom's leg, and stayed to work. So when Ben could not do any more, Tom had already given Billy Fisher permission (in exchange for a kite),

The girl looked at Tom and threw him a violet over the garden fence.

and when Billy came to an end, the brush went to Johnny Miller (in exchange for a dead mouse, which had threads attached to it so that you could swing it around). Thus the brush went from one boy to another.

By four o'clock in the afternoon, Tom had built up a small fortune, and the fence had received three coats of paint. What is more, Tom had made two important discoveries: in order to talk a person into doing something, you must make them believe that the work is difficult, and secondly, work consists of what you have to do but enjoyment is what you're not obliged to do.

Aunt Polly could hardly believe her eyes when she saw the immaculate fence and had no choice but to let Tom go out to play.

On his way home, Tom went past Jeff Thatcher's house. There was a very pretty girl in Jeff's garden. She had blue eyes and blond hair and for a moment he forgot Amy Lawrence with whom he imagined himself madly in love. He began to make boyish faces at her to attract the attention of this newly discovered angel. The girl looked at him, tossed a violet over the garden fence and went back into the house. Tom beamed, picked up the flower, opened his jacket and held the flower against his heart (or rather, against his stomach – for anatomy had never been his strong point).

Tom Sawyer as a paragon, and the dung beetle in church

On the next day, a Sunday, there was Sunday School. Sid had already learned his lesson days before. Tom, however, just did not see himself learning five short verses from the Bible by heart. His cousin, Maria, had really smartened him up. He wore his best suit and had to put on shoes as well. Then they all three set off. Sunday School lasted from nine o'clock until half past ten, and was followed by a church service. At the church door, Tom managed to take a friend to one side quickly. For a stick of liquorice and a fish hook, he managed to get a little yellow ticket. The yellow ticket was not just any old yellow ticket. For every two Bible verses learnt by heart, a pupil received a blue ticket. For ten blue tickets, he got a red ticket, ten red tickets were worth one yellow ticket and ten yellow tickets won the pupil a Bible. This did not often happen, because ten yellow tickets represented two thousand Bible verses learnt by heart. Tom did not know one, but thanks to his brisk business with swapping things, he had collected a good number of tickets.

On this particular Sunday, events did not turn out in the usual way. While lessons were in progress, Judge Thatcher and his family turned up unexpectedly at church with an older man. Mrs. Thatcher was holding a pretty blond girl by the hand: Tom's latest idol. The older man was the County Judge, perhaps the most important local personality that the pupils had ever seen. Mr. Walters, the Sunday School teacher, became extremely flustered and started giving orders left and right. The librarian and lady teachers tried to attract attention and started treating some boys sweetly, who had been slapped just a few minutes before. There was only one thing lacking to make Mr. Walters' ecstasy complete: the chance to present a Bible as a prize and show off a model pupil. He waited tensely for one of his boys to put their hand up. Of course there were boys who had amassed a considerable collection of tickets, but not enough for a Bible. And now as the Sunday School teacher saw his hopes disappearing, Tom Sawyer came forward with nine yellow tickets, nine red and ten blue tickets in his hand. Mr. Walters was so amazed that he almost lurched over the pew, since he had certainly not expected this achievement from Tom. But the tickets were there and they were genuine.

He handed him the Bible and introduced Tom to the Judge, who said, "You've done well, young man!" Then he started on a long, boring speech on the importance of learning Bible verses by heart, none of which Tom could understand. Finally the Judge asked, "No doubt you can give me the names of two apostles, Tom?" Silence. "Well then, tell me the names of the first two to be appointed." Tom went beetroot red, and looked down, which was his usual practice on such occasions. Mr. Walters gasped. When he had pulled himself together, he tried to cheer up the embarrassed pupil, "Come on Tom, answer up, don't be afraid." A lady teacher also felt obliged to intervene, "I'm sure Tom will tell me. What are the names of the first two apostles?"

"David and Goliath."

Mr. Walters, the Sunday School teacher, presented Tom with a Bible and introduced him to the Judge.

The shaggy dog sat down, right on the dung beetle, then leapt up and ran about yelping.

Everyone stared. Fortunately it was already half past ten and the church service was beginning. The sermon was yet again too long for Tom and in order to while away the time sensibly, he pulled a small box out of his trouser pocket, while Aunt Polly was not looking. The box contained a particular treasure: a fat, black dung beetle. He set the beetle free and it promptly nipped his index finger. In his fear, Tom flicked it headlong into the aisle, and other people, uninterested in the sermon, amused themselves by watching the little creature struggling across the floor. The whole business, which had been harmless up to this point, became more complicated as a large shaggy dog, with a drooping tail and long muzzle, looked forlornly round the church and walked in. He saw the beetle, wagged his tail and sniffed round it. When he had had his fill of sniffing, he sat down . . . right on the dung beetle. He immediately leapt up and ran round the church yelping. Like a woolly comet·he raced up and down the nave spinning on his own axis. The congregation had the utmost

difficulty in not bursting out laughing and Tom told himself that there was something rather nice about a sermon which offered a bit of variety.

Tom and Huck try out a remedy for warts and become witnesses to a murder

Monday arrived – always a sad day for Tom because it meant school. He desperately sought an excuse to escape this fate and he decided on terrible toothache. He woke Sid up with a fearful roar. Sid fetched Aunt Polly who simply laughed at him. Tom quickly pointed to one of his teeth, which he said was aching dreadfully. It was actually loose. He had little success, however, because Aunt Polly decided to pull it out. Aunt Polly's method of extracting teeth was certainly different. She tied one end of a piece of thread around Tom's tooth, and secured the other to the bed post. Then she put a piece of burning coal in her shovel and made as if to

Aunt Polly thrust a shovel containing red hot coal in Tom's face, and in a trice the tooth was out.

thrust the lot into Tom's face – in an instant, the tooth was out, and dangling on the end of the thread by the bed post.

Tom's performance was rewarded. He aroused the envy of his school friends, because from now on the gap in his teeth made him the undisputed champion at spitting.

On his way to school, for that is where he was now heading, albeit late, he met Huck Finn.

Huck Finn was the laziest boy in the district; disapproved of by all the mothers, for their children simply adored this lawless, coarse, rough and idle lad. Perhaps, however, this was because Huck just lived independent of everybody. Sometimes he would sleep on a door step, sometimes in an empty barrel. Nobody made Huck go to school or church and he obeyed nobody but himself.

"Hello, Huck," said Tom, "what have you got in your hand?"

"A dead cat, what does it look like?"

"What are you going to do with it?"

"Stupid question. Don't you know that dead cats are an excellent remedy for warts?"

Tom was so astonished and disgusted that his jaw sagged. Then he pulled himself together and said, "Really? But there must be better ways . . ."

A discussion on warts and the best way to treat them developed. Huck insisted that his method was the best and Tom wanted to know every detail.

"Well," said Huck, "you get yourself a dead cat and go to a cemetery at midnight. You look for a freshly dug grave where somebody wicked has been buried. When the bells chime twelve a devil will climb out of the grave, or maybe two or three. You can't see them, you only hear a whispering and rustling. As soon as the devils carry away the evil man's corpse, throw your cat and say, Devil catch the corpse! Cat, catch the devil! Warts, catch the cat! Straightaway your warts will be gone for ever."

"Have you tried it?"

"No, but old Mother Hopkins gave me the tip."

"Then there must be something in it 'cos she's supposed to be a real witch. When are you

"Hello, Huck," said Tom, "what are you holding?"

going to try it?"

"Tonight. I've heard they'll be fetching Hoos William's body tonight, and nobody is more evil than him."

"Can I come too?"

"Sure, if you don't get the heeby-jeebys."

"Heeby-jeebys – that's a laugh!"

The two boys went their own ways after Tom had swapped his newly-extracted tooth for a coin which Huck had found in the wood.

***

Shortly after eleven o'clock, Tom awoke with a start and heard the crash of a bottle against the woodshed. As quick as a flash, he got dressed and quietly opened the window. He climbed out of it and shut it again. Huck was already waiting for him with his dead cat, and half an hour later they were entering the cemetery.

"Huck, do you think the dead people like us being here?"

"No idea, but I bet Hoos William's spirit can hear us talking."

Tom seized Huck's arm.

"Shh!"

"What is it?"

"I can hear something."

The two boys listened intently in the quiet air. A sound of whispering voices came from somewhere.

"Over there," whispered Tom.

Three vague figures approached through the gloom, swinging an iron lantern, and Huck thought he could see will-o-the-wisps.

"No," he said eventually, "that's not the devils. I heard that old drunk Muff Potter's voice."

"Yes, and the other voice is Injun Joe's. I'd have preferred the devil incarnate."

Then they fell silent for the three men had reached the fresh grave and were standing only a few steps away from them.

"Here it is," said the third voice, and by the glow of the lantern the boys recognized Doctor Robinson.

Joe and Muff began to dig. The Doctor put the lantern on the ground and sat down on the roots of a gnarled elm. The two boys crouched behind a gravestone, about three metres away. For some time the only noise in the quiet air was the sound of the shovels scraping. Then a spade struck against the coffin. Joe and Muff threw down their tools, hoisted the coffin out, opened the lid, got out the body and dumped it roughly on the ground. They fetched a small barrow, laid the corpse on it and covered it with a blanket. Then they tied the whole thing up. Muff took out a sharp knife, cut off the cord, and turned round abruptly to the Doctor. "We've got this far," he said. "Either you double our money or the corpse stays here."

"That's right," said Joe.

"What does that mean?" the Doctor protested and got up. "I paid you in advance."

"Yes, and that's not all you've done," said Injun Joe and approached the Doctor. "Five years ago you drove me away from your father's kitchen when I asked for some food. When I swore I'd get even with you, your father had me locked up. Do you really think I'd forget something like that? It's time to settle our accounts, and now I've got the upper hand." He was threatening the Doctor with a fist in his face. The Doctor suddenly grabbed Joe's arm and threw him to the ground. Muff brandished his knife and shouted, "God help you if you hurt my friend." Then he grappled with the Doctor and soon the two men were rolling on the ground. Meanwhile Joe had staggered to his feet. His eyes flashing, he snatched Muff's knife and crept round the two combatants, looking for an opportunity to strike. All at once, Robinson managed to break loose from Muff. He stood up, seized the heavy coffin lid and smashed it down on his opponent. At the same instant, Injun Joe drove the knife up to the hilt into the Doctor's breast. He reeled and fell on Muff's motionless body.

The clouds blotted out the moon and in fear and panic, Huck and Tom disappeared into the darkness.

"Now we're even," murmured Joe and put the knife in Muff's right hand. Then he sank down in exhaustion onto the empty coffin. After a few minutes, Muff regained consciousness and his hand closed on his knife. He sat up and glanced around confusedly.

"Good Heavens!" he said quietly. "What happened?"

"It's a really stupid business," Joe replied. "Why did you kill him?"

"Kill him? I didn't kill him!"

"Well, you just listen to me."

Muff trembled and his face was as white as the moon. "I should never have got drunk, I was plastered, I just didn't know what I . . . I didn't mean to . . . I just don't know anything any more."

"When he hit you with the coffin lid, you got to your feet as quick as lightning and jammed the knife into his breast. Then you fainted again."

"What a mess, and all due to that cursed rum. Joe, promise me you won't give me away, we're friends aren't we? Please keep your mouth shut." Poor Muff dropped to his knees and gazed beseechingly at the real murderer.

"Muff," said Joe, "you've always been a good chap, I won't give you away."

"I'll never forget this, Joe," sobbed Muff.

"That's enough – just don't get caught."

Muff went off, first at a jogging pace, then as fast as he could run. For a long time the Indian gazed after him and said to himself, "What a fool he is! He's forgotten his knife. Still, when he remembers it he'll be so far away that he won't dare to come back here alone."

Smitten by lover's grief, Tom decides to become a pirate

After their desperate escape, Tom and Huck crouched behind the old tannery, gasping for breath.

"What now, Huck?" stammered Tom.

"If Doctor Robinson's dead, Joe'll be hanged."

"And what are we going to say?"

"Are you mad? Just imagine what'll happen if Joe managed to escape the gallows. He'd kill us as surely as we're standing here. No Tom, there's no question of that. We'll have to swear to forget the business once and for all."

He bent down, picked up an old piece of

Doctor Robinson sat down on the stump of a gnarled elm while Joe and Muff began to dig.

243

wood and scratched the following words on it with a pencil, 'Huck Finn and Tom Sawyer swear they'll keep quiet about this secret. May they drop down dead if they don't.' Then they both pricked their thumbs with a needle and signed the document solemnly in blood.

***

The next morning everyone was talking about the brutal murder in the cemetery. Muff's name cropped up frequently because people had recognized his knife beside the corpse.

The teacher gave them the afternoon off and Tom could not resist the temptation of joining the long procession of people making their way to the scene of the crime – the cemetery. He met Huck among the eager spectators, who revealed their interest by shrieking in a mock terrified way. Both boys shuddered as they espied Injun Joe's face in the crowd. Then the crowd surged forward. Some were shouting, "There he is! There he is!" "You murderer, Muff." "You should be hanged, Muff."

The people moved to one side as the Sheriff led Muff by the arm. The poor drunk stood in front of the body of the murdered man, broke into tears and pressed his hands to his face. He turned to Joe and begged, "Tell them Joe, tell them I didn't know what I was doing." Then Tom and Huck listened horrified to the liar's description. When he had finished, the people started to applaud. Yet the boys were too frightened to expose Joe.

This terrible secret and the gnawing at his conscience because he had not told the truth, gave ·Tom many bad nights. Even Sid remarked, "You're thrashing round in bed like a propeller, and I can't sleep."

During these harrowing days, Tom often went to the prison to visit Muff and take him something. These small gifts mostly comprised something to eat and salved Tom's conscience somewhat.

But these were not the only worries that Tom had to bear. In addition to all this, he also had romantic problems. Becky Thatcher, the

Tom and Huck made a vow in writing that nobody would hear of their secret.

They captured the raft without hesitation, and Tom took command.

blond angel with whom Tom was madly in love, did not deign to look at him. And all because Tom had mentioned Amy Lawrence's name while speaking to Becky. Amy was Tom's previous girl friend. Becky was seized with jealousy and ignored him from that moment on. Tom grew sadder from day to day, and was so depressed that Aunt Polly treated him with tablets and juices, to restore his cheerfulness. (It is worth noting that Aunt Polly did not stop grumbling when Tom was well. However, this is a good example of how contradictory adults can be.)

Nothing was of any use. Tom felt desperate, without friends and neglected by everyone. As he was playing truant again and wandering aimlessly along he came to a decision: if nobody loved him, he might as well run away and lead a life of crime. While he was brooding thus, he bumped into Joe Harper whose state of mind was not a great deal happier. His mother had whipped him because she suspected him of wolfing down a cup of milk, which Joe had in fact never laid eyes on. He was convinced that his mother could not stand him and would be happy if he disappeared for ever.

The two miserable boys started to make new plans. Joe had firmly decided to die as a hermit of hunger, cold and pain. Tom could not persuade him that a life of crime had considerable advantages over this. So they compromised and agreed to become pirates. Huck was also invited to join the project and he agreed instantly. Where the Missouri was a nautical mile wide, lay an isolated island, which seemed ideal as a meeting place. The island was called Jackson Island and the boys chose it as their robbers' den.

They met at midnight on the riverbank and each revealed his new name. Tom was called 'The Black Avenger', Huck, 'The Red-Handed' and Joe, 'The Terror of the Seas'. Tom had brought a large leg of bacon, The Terror of the Seas had some dried fish and The Red-Handed had an iron pan, a packet of tobacco and five corn-cobs which would do for pipes (he was the only smoker of the three pirates). An abandoned raft, made of tree trunks, lay in the river. This was their first capture. They made short work of taking possession of it and Tom assumed command. Joe stood at the front, Huck at the back. First of all they rowed, then they drifted with the current. Tom saw his sleepy village in the distance, thought about Becky and wished that she could see him now – a heroic seafarer, struggling against the stormy waves.

At about two o'clock the raft ran up on a sandbank, about two hundred yards away from the island, and the boys had to wade back and forth several times until they had carried all their possessions to land. They lit their camp fire next to a tree stump and fried the dried fish in the iron pan. The pirates felt so well that they decided to turn their backs on civilization for ever. Then tiredness overwhelmed them and they lay down in the grass. When Tom awoke the following day, he was confused at first. He rubbed his eyes, looked around and then remembered where he was. Joe, Huck and Tom caught a lot of fish, devoured them for breakfast, explored the island, bathed, ate the bacon, and lay in the grass, chatting. Suddenly, however, a sullen boom disturbed this idyllic existence.

"What was that?" whispered Joe.

"Let's go and see."

They all leapt up and ran to the bank from which they could see the village. They parted the bushes and peered out over the water. A small ferryboat was about a mile downstream and a few boats bobbed about her. Then came that sound again. A jet of white steam burst from the ferryboat's side.

"I know," exclaimed Tom, "that's the rescue crew, looking for the drowned."

"That's it," said Huck, "they did that last year. They shoot a cannon over the water, to make it rise."

Then the pirates fell silent. Suddenly Tom clasped his head and cried, "Do you know what? We're the ones who have drowned."

And this was the case. After the three boys had disappeared, the abandoned raft was discovered five or six miles away, and the conclusion was reached that Tom, Huck and Joe must be drowned. Now a crew had started a search for their bodies.

✳✳✳

The boys went to bed early that night. Tom waited until the others were fast asleep, then got up again and ran off towards the sandbank. A few minutes later he set about trying to swim across the river. Soaking wet, he reached his village in the middle of the night, ran through the deserted streets and climbed over the back fence of his garden. He quietly approached the house and glanced through the window into the brightly lit bedroom. A sort of crisis headquarters was installed. Aunt Polly, Cousin Maria, Sid and Joe Harper's mother sat beside the bed, by the door. Cautiously, Tom opened the front door, crept into the hall and up to his room, where he could squeeze unnoticed under his bed.

"Basically," Aunt Polly was just saying, "he wasn't a bad boy," and tears came to her eyes, "just a bit irresponsible and mischievous. He was good-hearted, more so than we are." Mrs. Harper agreed with her. "That's like my Joe. He was always up to every kind of mischief, but as unselfish as he could be."

"I hope Tom's better off where he is," said Sid, "but if he'd been better in some ways . . ."

"Sid!" interrupted Aunt Polly shocked, and Tom felt deeply satisfied. "Woe betide you, if you say another word against Tom!" Then she turned to Mrs. Harper. "You know, I don't think I can go on without him. He was such a comfort to me, in spite of all the worry he caused me."

The two women carried on talking in this way and Tom really did not know whether to feel flattered or full of remorse. Hidden under the bed, he could not fail to hear all this praise, and began to have a much better opinion of himself.

Mrs. Harper took her leave and went away. Aunt Polly, Sid and Maria said their prayers and went to bed. When everything was quiet in the house, Tom slipped back out from the bed, kissed his Aunt gently on her cheek and ran off. It was high time he returned to the island. Huck and Joe were already thinking that he had betrayed them and renounced the whole pirates' life.

Tom described his night-time adventure to his friends, and since they were vain, they all imagined themselves heroes.

Their enthusiasm for the wonderful island existence began to fade with time, however. The pirates went looking for turtle eggs, fished, bathed and played around in the water, but somehow the lustre had gone. Boredom set in. And with boredom came regrets and homesickness. Joe Harper was the first to show it; he was so depressed that he could not control himself any longer. Huck felt saddened too and Tom was uneasy. He remembered his secret and was conscious of a desire to confide in his friends. Joe stood up and declared, "Friends, I'm giving this up. I want to go home. It's vile here."

"No question of that," countered Tom, "just think of the fabulous fish and places to swim – you won't find those at home. It'll all get better."

"Firstly, I don't care for swimming if there's nobody to forbid me, and secondly, I want to go home."

"Oh, the poor little cry-baby," said Huck insultingly. "He wants to go home to his Mummy's porridge."

"Yes I do, I do want to go home to my Mother and if you had one, you'd want to go home too."

Tom turned to Huck, "Let's leave the poor little baby alone. The poor little boy wants his Mummy. We'll stay here, just the two of us, eh, Huck?"

Huck glanced downwards and started to stutter. "No, Tom, actually I wouldn't mind . . . I'd like to get away from here too. Come on, Tom, let's all get going."

Tom remained obstinately rooted to the spot and watched the other two walk off. When he realized how alone he was, he wanted to go with them and torn between pride and stubbornness, he ran after them. "Stop a moment, I've got something important to tell you!" he shouted and when he had caught up with them, he shared his secret with them. The disclosure was so important that Huck and Joe were persuaded to go back on their decision and to stay on. After a sumptuous meal of turtles' eggs and fish, they decided to smoke

the pipe of peace and it was of no matter to them that this was an Indian rather than a pirates' custom. Huck made three pipes out of the corn-cobs and shared them out. The smoke and the tobacco gave Tom a painful throat but he did not show this and said, "If I'd only known how easy it is, I'd have started smoking long ago." Joe agreed with him. But after some time both boys felt an ominous rumbling in their stomachs. "Must go and look for my knife," said Joe and disappeared into the bushes. "I'll help you," said Tom and jumped up too. Huck found them later, sleeping in the wood and there were sure signs that smoking the pipes had not agreed with either of them.

The dead boys return

On Sunday at half past ten the Sunday School lessons were over. The little bell tolled for the

Hearing so much praise, Tom, who was hidden under the bed, began to feel happier.

After they had eaten, Huck shared out the corn-cob pipes.

dead. This was the day when the solemn funeral of Tom Sawyer, Joe Harper and Huck Finn was to take place. The church had never been so full. As Aunt Polly, Sid, Maria and the Harper family entered the church, a murmur of sympathy went round the congregation. "I am the Resurrection and the Life," said the minister and began a funeral oration in which he praised so intensely the good characters and excellent manners of the missing boys, that many people present, who had hitherto thought the opposite, broke down and started sobbing.

A few seconds later, there was a rustling at the church door. The pastor looked up and appeared to be stunned. One after the other, the congregation rose and turned towards the door. The 'dead' boys walked in, Tom at the head, followed by Joe and Huck. Pandemonium broke loose in the church: kisses, embraces, prayers, joy, tears of happiness and impatient questions all came the boys' way.

This chaos ended with the congregation singing a hymn of thanks.

***

It had happened exactly as Tom had planned their return – to attend his own funeral with Huck and Joe. His plans had come to fruition. They had become real heroes.

Tom's behaviour had altered. Gone were the skipping and somersaults. He moved more positively, as befits a hero who knows he is in the public eye. His new opinion of himself was so inflated that he thought of becoming independent of even Becky Thatcher. The glory was enough for him, he would live for glory and that would last him a lifetime. So he ignored Becky in school. In fact he went further. He had a lively conversation with Amy Lawrence, who had been a stumbling block in his relationship with Becky. In an unnaturally vivacious voice, Becky was talking about a picnic for the last day of the holidays and was inviting all her boy and girl friends. Everyone wanted to go, only Tom and Amy made no move to accept. That was too much for Becky. "I know how I'll get you," she thought and furiously sat down next to Alfred Temple, the boy Tom had fought in the street. "I wouldn't have minded if it were anyone else," thought Tom, "but that idiot . . ." He thrashed about in the air with his fists as if he were coming up against his rival.

At midday Tom stamped discontentedly home and although Becky waited for him to return, it was in vain. She realized how unhappy she was. She left Alfred Temple sitting with a puzzled expression on his face. He began to realize that she had only played up to him in order to spite Tom. Alfred had always hated Tom but this bitter experience made him swear that he would make Tom's life difficult. He went back to the empty classroom, and took hold of Tom's exercise book. In the book was the homework for that afternoon, albeit incomplete. Alfred quickly sprinkled a little ink from a bottle over the book, shut it, and put it back again. Becky was just going by the window and saw this mischief. At first she was full of

The 'dead' boys walked in, and the congregation stared.

sympathy and was going to alert Tom, but then she thought back to the business of the invitation to the picnic and resolved to keep quiet. But she went further; when Tom got back to the school yard and went to speak to her sensibly, she turned her head away and said scornfully, "I don't want to be bothered with you, Master Tom Sawyer." Then she walked off. At that moment, Tom wished she had been a boy so that he could thrash her.

Meantime something else had happened. Becky had hurried back to the classroom and found herself alone there. She went up to the teacher's desk and saw the key lying in the drawer. She glanced round and made sure that she really was alone, opened the drawer and seized the book. The most fascinating thing about this drawer was this mysterious book, which Mr. Dobbins the teacher used to get out from time to time. He would study it attentively, and then carefully replace it in the drawer. Nobody in the class knew what sort of book it was and what was so intriguing about it. Now Becky had an opportunity to find out. 'Ana-

tomy' was written on the cover; a word which meant nothing to Becky. She turned over and saw an illustration of a naked man. Then Tom walked into the classroom. Hastily, Becky slammed the book shut but in her hurry, she ripped the page showing the naked man in half. She threw the book back into the drawer and turned the key, then burst out crying partly from anger and partly from shame.

"Shame on you, Tom Sawyer! You were spying on me! Oh heavens, what shall I do. You're bound to tell the teacher and I shall be whipped, I know I will be."

In a few minutes the room was full. The teacher came in and wanted to see the homework. When he opened Tom's book, Tom took his beating without any fuss. Since he treated school things in such a slovenly manner, he really did not know whether he had spilt the ink or not. Becky remained quiet.

An hour went by and then Mr. Dobbins took the famous book out of the drawer. When he discovered the torn page, he began to walk round the class, in a tense, excited way. He

looked at his pupils with such a dangerous glint in his eye that even the most innocent started to quake.

"Who tore my book?" he asked loudly. Silence. Then the teacher began questioning each child individually. Ben Rogers, Joe Harper, Amy Lawrence, Grazia Miller and so on. It would soon be Becky's turn and her face was getting whiter and whiter. She would not have been able to lie to him. Suddenly Tom jumped up and shouted, "I did it!" His school friends stared at him in horror. Tom went up to the desk and received his second beating. It would have been worth a hundred floggings to get Becky's surprised, grateful and admiring glances however.

✳✳✳

And so the last school day arrived, but a most painful business took place on the very last day.

The pupils had to sit a written examination in front of their parents, the school authorities and the local dignitaries. Then their teacher walked to the blackboard and drew the outline of America for the geography exam. His hand was trembling and he made a sad job of it. As his pupils giggled, he rubbed out the sketch and began again, but the second map was much worse than the first. The pupils' giggling grew to a shameless roar and it was not only caused by the drawing. Over the classroom was the garret and in the ceiling was a small trap-door directly over Mr. Dobbins' head. Down through this hatch a cat came suspended by a string and with a rag tied over her jaws to keep her from mewing. Seconds later the animal landed on the teacher's head and clawed desperately at his hair. As if controlled by a ghost, the string was once again pulled, the cat rose up and Mr. Dobbins' wig went too. What was left was a gleaming bald pate and the general laughter of all those present. Thus the boys had once again been avenged for his tyranny.

Tom did not deserve his beating, but Becky kept quiet.

Joe, the murderer, escapes from court

The regular village routine was thoroughly stirred. The trial against Muff, the accused murderer, had begun and Tom was reminded of many things which he had hoped to suppress a long time ago.

"Huck, have you told anyone about the business?" asked Tom.

"No, on my word of honour. You know that we wouldn't be alive if that got out," Huck replied.

"Yes, yes, I know but I feel so sorry for Muff. He may well be a good-for-nothing, but he'd never hurt a fly. He even gave me half his fish once."

"And he mended my fishing rod. If only we could help him!"

The two boys went to the prison and pushed some tobacco and matches through the bars to Muff, but this did not ease their consciences – the drunk was so grateful to them that they felt even more miserable. Tom went home in low spirits. For the next few days, Tom hung round the court-room, drawn by an almost irresistible impulse to go in. Huck felt the same but they both studiously avoided each other. By the fourth day, all the villagers were convinced of Muff's guilt, principally due to Joe's evidence; he was a Crown witness. The day came when the verdict was to be pronounced. The entire village flocked to the court. Witness after witness entered the court-room. They all spoke of Muff's strange behaviour which they had noticed the day after the murder. One thing was striking: Muff's Counsel remained silent and gave the Prosecuting Counsel a free hand. When public dissatisfaction began to make itself heard around the court, the Defending Counsel got to his feet and said, "I call Tom Sawyer." All eyes were fastened wonderingly on Tom, but he stepped forward to the

The cat swung upwards, taking Mr. Dobbins' wig with it.

stand with a firm step and took his oath, submitting himself to interrogation.

"Tom Sawyer, where were you on the night of the 16th and 17th of June?"

Tom gulped. "At the cemetery," he said quietly, and Injun Joe's bronze face grew pale.

"Were you anywhere near Hoos William's grave?"

"Yes, sir."

The Indian started.

"Were you alone or was anyone with you?"

"Somebody was with me, sir."

"You don't have to tell us your companion's name. Just tell us what you were doing in the cemetery."

"I was carrying out a test for warts using a dead cat."

"For warts?"

"Yes, to get rid of warts."

The tension in court relaxed and here and there laughter was heard, which the judge rebuked straightaway.

"Child, just tell us exactly what happened in the cemetery."

With a hesitating voice, Tom began to describe what he had seen. He became so overwhelmed with his own description, that after a few sentences, his words just poured out. "While the doctor lifted the coffin lid and Muff Potter fell," said Tom, "Joe jumped with the knife and . . ." Injun Joe, at that moment, burst through the crowd, lurched at the window and disappeared.

✳✳✳

Tom was once again the glittering hero, coddled by the old and envied by the young. Muff Potter received as much affection as formerly he had curses hurled at him. Tom's days were days of splendour but his nights were seasons of horror, for Injun Joe haunted his dreams. Huck was in the same state of fear, although because the murderer ran out of court, he had been saved the ordeal of testifying. Tom, however, had told the Defending Counsel everything, including Huck's name.

Muff's gratitude was a small comfort to both boys and somewhat alleviated their tense anxiety, but Tom knew that his nightmares would haunt him until he saw the murderer hung.

A reward was put on Injun Joe's head and a detective came up from St. Louis. He sniffed around and said, "I'm on the right lines!" But you cannot hang the 'right lines' for murder, so the detective went home at the end of his inquiries, which did not amount to much. Tom felt just as insecure.

Tom and Huck go hunting for treasure in a haunted house

Tom looked for some new adventure to take his mind off his anxiety. There comes a time in every boy's life when he is seized by the desire to go treasure hunting, and Tom was filled with that desire. He looked for Huck. The two boys agreed that the haunted house was the only place to look. This house was some way from the village, in a small valley where nothing grew and nothing much survived. They were somewhat reluctant to break in at night, in case they came across ghosts, so decided to begin their search the next day.

This was a Saturday and they arrived at the haunted house with shovels and picks. As they stepped into the dark, eerie house, they would have rushed home instantly, but then they pulled themselves together and carried on investigating. They walked into a large room. It was totally derelict and grass was growing between the floorboards. Plaster was peeling off the walls, the old fireplace was caked with dirt, there was no glass at the windows, the staircase had half crumbled away and there were cobwebs everywhere. They wanted to look upstairs yet they hesitated for they would have had no means of escape from there, should an emergency have arisen. They dared each other, however, and put their tools in a corner and crept upstairs. The first floor did not look any more comfortable, everything there was in the same state of decay. The large cupboard in the corner looked as if it might hold something, but to the great disappointment of the boys it was empty. They were feeling braver now and decided to try their luck

*When the murderer heard the evidence against himself,
he lurched out of the window.*

digging. They were just about to go back to
their tools, when Huck grabbed Tom's arm.
"What was that?" he whispered, pale with terror. Footsteps rang out on the ground floor.
Someone must have come into the house. The
two boys lay on their stomachs and peered
through the knot holes in the floor boards of
the room. Two men were standing there, and
they did not look very trustworthy. Huck
thought he recognized one as an old deaf and
dumb Spaniard, who came into the village
from time to time. The other man, who was
dressed in rags and had a beard, was a total
stranger.

"No, I don't like it, the whole thing is too
hot!" he whispered.

"Too hot?" said the so-called deaf and
dumb man. The boys were very surprised at
this. "What a fool you are!"

This voice filled both boys with a terrible
certainty, it was Injun Joe's voice. The discussion that the men had about their mysterious
plans became more and more violent; they
talked about revenge and 'Number two' and a
cross.

"And what do we do with the swag?" asked
the bearded man.

"We leave it here as usual. I'd strain myself
trying to carry six hundred and fifty dollars'
worth of silver away."

253

Joe and the bearded man were surprised by the priceless hoard.

"All right, but I'd like to bury the bag."

"Yes, you're right," said Joe and he knelt down in front of the chimney, lifted up a hearth stone and felt around for a bag full of coins. When Huck and Tom saw this, they forgot their fear. The treasure exceeded their wildest dreams.

But this was not the end of the affair. When Joe was getting the bag out, he noticed something hard in the hole under the hearth stone. He used the pick which the boys had left, and to everyone's surprise, brought up a wooden box. He smashed the rotten wood with one blow and bright gold coins scattered everywhere. "Gold!" roared the scruffy man. "This must be the gold the Murrel gang left here. I've often heard that story."

"Just a minute," hissed the Indian, who had suddenly thought of something. "How did this pick and these shovels get here? I'm going upstairs for a moment."

Huck and Tom were suddenly jolted out of their dreams of the gold, they lay still and

waited. The footsteps creaked nearer and nearer. Then suddenly there was a crash. The staircase had collapsed under the Indian's heavy weight. He struggled to his feet and called back to his companion, "We'll leave it. What difference does it make if somebody was here? We'll leave and take the gold with us." The two men disappeared with the precious box. Tom and Huck picked their way over the ruins of the staircase, vastly relieved, and ran home.

✳✳✳

For several nights, Tom was tormented by what had happened at the haunted house. But in the meantime, it was the desire for gold rather than fear which caused his restlessness. One day he poured his heart out to Huck.

"Where do you think they took the gold?"

"No idea. Do you remember they mentioned a 'Number two' but who knows what that means?"

"Perhaps it's a house number?"

"No, it can't be, there aren't any house

numbers in the village." Tom thought and thought, then suddenly he leapt up and shouted, "I've got it. It must be a room number!" And he ran to one of the two village guest houses. He reported back to Huck half an hour later. In the better of the two inns, he learned that room number two was regularly occupied by a young lawyer. In the other, he had more success. Room number two was occupied by an unknown guest, who always locked his room behind him. The young innkeeper said that he had seen the light on again last night.

"That's the one we're after, for sure," said Tom and was very proud of his detective work. "I know what we'll do. The room has a back entrance by the old brick store. We'll get hold of a few keys and have a go at that lock."

And that is what happened. Tom tried the doors and Huck stood guard at the brick store. Tom was gone for some time and Huck was frightened that he would find him with a knife in his stomach. Tom suddenly ran up and whispered, "Run for your life!" Huck ran like an arrow. When they reached the slaughter house at the end of the village, Tom gasped, "It was awful, Huck, almost as if I'd stepped on Injun Joe's hand."

"He wasn't there?"

"Yes, he was lying fast asleep on the floor, with a patch on one eye. There was a bottle beside him and he was as drunk as a lord, otherwise he'd have woken up."

"And where was the box?"

"I didn't see it. Anyway we might as well forget it all while Joe is in the room. The main thing now is to stand guard every night in front of the room, until we see him leave. Then we can grab the box and push off."

"I think we should divide up the work – I'll stand guard and you look after the rest."

So from then on Huck stood guard at the brick store night after night.

A rescue team searches for Tom and Becky in the cave

While Tom was waiting to start his mission, Becky Thatcher had returned from her summer holiday. She had decided to have her picnic on Sunday and Tom had resolved to go along. He therefore found himself being pul-

Tom went to the door, Huck stood guard.

led in two directions, and spent the night waiting for Huck's signal. He would have loved to get his hands on the treasure that night so that he could impress Becky the following day. But no signal came from Huck. Between ten and eleven o'clock the next day, a small group of children gathered in the Judge's house, all ready to be off. Since the outing might finish very late, Mrs. Thatcher allowed Becky to stay overnight at Susanne Harper's house, as she lived near the ferry landing on the river bank. A ferry boat had been chartered for the party, and this was to take the group three miles down river to a small wood.

The children romped around energetically and after a sumptuous meal, somebody suggested going into the cave. Armed with candles they moved towards the cave, which was really more of a grotto, with several tunnels leading off it. All the children knew it but nobody had dared to go further than the entrance. However, they felt braver as they were in a crowd and they ran through the dark passages shouting, hiding in niches, and leaping out at each other. Then, tired and hot they straggled back, one by one, to the entrance. It

had grown dark outside and the ferryboat was ringing its bell to call everyone for the return voyage.

Huck was already on guard. Clouds were gathering in the sky. By half past ten the village was deadly quiet. At eleven o'clock the tavern lights were extinguished. Huck moved from one leg to the other, his courage weakening. He would have liked to have dropped the whole business and gone to bed. Then he heard a noise. The back door was quietly being closed. Then two shadows brushed by Huck, so close that they could have touched him. One was holding something in his hands. "The box!" thought Huck and decided to follow them. First the two men followed the path to the river bank, then walked along the street which led to Cardiff Hill. When they had passed the quarry, they stood in front of the entrance gate to Widow Douglas' grounds.

"Wait 'til the lights are out," he heard Injun Joe say.

"Do you think we ought to go ahead with this?" the other man asked.

"Sure, I'm not missing the opportunity, before I leave this country for good. Anyway

Nobody had ever dared to go further than the entrance to the cave.

he had me whipped in front of the whole village. Now he's passed on, I'll settle the score with his old wife."

Huck perspired. Now everything was clear to Huck; when Joe talked of revenge, it was not on Tom and himself. He gingerly stepped backwards and holding his breath he ran as fast as he could, past the quarry to the Welshman's house. (He was called this, although he was a villager, because many years ago he had arrived from Wales.) Huck knocked on the door and shouted, "Huck, Huck Finn's here, let me in!" "Huck Finn?" floated out from inside, "hardly a name to open many doors." At last the door was opened and Huck stepped inside. "For heaven's sake," whispered Huck, "you mustn't tell anyone anything, but the old Widow has been so good to me . . ." Huck poured out the details of what he had seen. Minutes later the old man and his sons armed themselves and ran with Huck towards the Widow Douglas' house. Huck waited on the hill and hid under a boulder, listening for the action. When he heard shots, his spirits fell and he ran back home. The following day he met the Welshman, who told him that both the gangsters had got away but left a package behind. But Huck's joy was swiftly transformed to disappointment when he heard that it contained tools. The questions concerning the whereabouts of the treasure remained unanswered.

The two figures crept past Huck with their box.

***

The next day Mrs. Thatcher met Mrs. Harper at the door of the church. "My Becky must have got back tired to death," said Mrs. Thatcher. "Is she still asleep?"

"Your Becky?" replied Mrs. Harper, astonished.

"Yes," said Mrs. Thatcher, shocked. "Didn't she spend last night with you?"

"No, she didn't!"

Aunt Polly came up excitedly.

"My Tom didn't come back. Is he at your house, Mrs. Thatcher?"

"No, and I'm looking for my Becky too."

At last it was confirmed that neither had returned from the picnic. Inquisitive people gathered around the three women and offered advice on what to do. When a young man suggested that they might be wandering round in the cave, the women completely lost control. Mrs. Thatcher fainted and Aunt Polly burst into tears. Five minutes later preparations were being made for a rescue team. Two hundred men set off for the cave with horses and boats. The village seemed deserted in the afternoon.

The night passed without news. The first bulletin came in the morning, "Send more food and candles!" The first party of exhausted men came back before midday. The others were sticking it out. Three days and nights of anxiety and fear went by, but there was no sign of the children. The only person who knew nothing of all this was Huck, who was lying in bed in Widow Douglas' house, with a high temperature. He asked many times for Tom, but Widow Douglas nursed him tenderly and replied, "Don't talk, child, get some rest, you are very ill!"

***

"Didn't my Becky sleep at your house last night?" asked Mrs. Thatcher in dismay.

Meanwhile Tom and Becky had been wandering round their labyrinth. They were driven ever onwards in the hope of discovering a stalactite cavern, which had fascinated them in the cave. Behind the cave, two walls led up to a steep rocky staircase. Tom was immediately seized with a need to explore. He scratched a sign on the wall so that he could find his way back, then the two children stepped into the darkness, making their way aimlessly through twisting passages and came to a marvellous underground spring, which glittered with crystals. Further on they saw a huge vault which appeared to be supported by pillars, formed by stalactites and stalagmites joined together. Thick, black clusters of bats hung from the ceiling, and when they were frightened by the light of the candles, they began darting wildly. Tom took Becky's hand and pulled her into the first tunnel on the left.

They walked along a twisting path and discovered an underground lake, which stretched away into the darkness. Before they got to the bank they resolved to have a rest. As they stood there the clammy, deep stillness struck the children for the first time. They then realized they could no longer hear the other children's voices. Becky, smitten with anxiety, said, "Tom, shouldn't we go back?"

"Yes, I think it would be better."

But the way back was not so easy to find. They entered a tunnel and walked along side by side in silence for some time, hoping to find something they recognized. Then Tom said, "There's no doubt. This is the wrong way." Then, since even he did not know which direction to go, he tried turning off at random. He began to shout, but his cries echoed in the empty passages and died away into quiet snig-

"For Heaven's sake, don't give anything away," said Huck to the Welshman.

The underground spring was glittering with crystals and gems.

gering sounds. Becky was so exhausted that she gave in and fell asleep. When she awoke, she laughed aloud, then the seriousness of their situation struck her. Silently they ate the remaining food. They then walked aimlessly and hopelessly onwards.

Tom and Becky spent many hours in this stone and crystal cavern. On the fourth day they woke up hungry and desperate. Becky became increasingly depressed.

Tom, on the other hand, grew determined. He wanted to explore some side tunnels, so they set off again. After a few yards, the small passage led into a large split in the rocks. Tom moved forwards. Behind a thick lump of rock, a hand holding a candle suddenly appeared. Tom gave a shout of joy, but the hand belonged to Injun Joe. Tom stood there,

paralysed with fear. The Indian started then took to his heels and disappeared into a tunnel. Tom was puzzled that Joe had not recognized his voice, but the echo must have made it unrecognizable. Tom decided that Becky was to know nothing of this, and he went back to the girl who had gone to sleep again.

The murderer eats bats and starves to death

Tuesday evening and the villagers were still hopeful that the two children would return. But no news came from the cave. Most of the rescue team had gone home, the men had given up hope. Mrs. Thatcher lay in bed in the depths of despair, and very ill. Aunt Polly was

259

Tom stood there, paralysed with fear as Injun Joe appeared from behind a rock.

so depressed that her grey hair had turned white.

Everyone went to bed, helpless and dejected. Towards midnight, the village people were torn from their sleep by a violent peal of bells. "We've found them, we've got them back!" somebody shouted. In seconds the streets were full of people in nightclothes, who were almost delirious with joy. People ran down to the river blowing hunting horns and banging iron pans.

They surrounded the open coach in which the children were being carried and walked with Tom and Becky to their doors. Aunt Polly and Mrs. Thatcher were overjoyed.

Later on a number of people stopped by Aunt Polly's house to find out the details of what had happened. Tom lay in glory on the lounge sofa describing his adventures, which he naturally embroidered, so that they ended up considerably exaggerated. He told how he

left Becky alone to search for a way out. He found salvation in the second side tunnel. Right at the back he saw a crack in the rocks, pushed his head out and saw the large river. He went back for Becky and guided her to freedom. Some fishermen who were passing in their boat, noticed the children and picked them up. They gave them some food and then brought the missing children back to the village. Yet the affair which provoked so much excitement was not over. On the following day, Tom learnt about the shooting at the Widow Douglas'. Meantime the body of Joe's accomplice was fished out of the river. He had apparently drowned whilst escaping.

Tom was allowed to visit Huck two weeks later, Huck having not yet totally recovered. On his way to the Welshman's house, he stopped off to see Becky. Judge Thatcher assured Tom that the dangers of the cave would be eliminated once and for all. "We've had an iron door with a triple lock put in front of the entrance, and I've got the keys." Tom grew pale.

"What's the matter, Tom?" asked the Judge.

"Oh, Judge," stammered Tom, "Injun Joe's in the cave."

***

They found Joe when they opened the heavy door. He lay dead on the floor. Tom was considerably upset by the news, because he knew from his own experience that Joe must have suffered enormously. Joe's knife lay beside his body, broken in two pieces. Seemingly, he had tried to open the door with it. Other clues indicated that Joe had eaten candle stumps and bats, then starved to death.

***

After Joe's funeral, Tom took Huck to one side. "They're both dead now, but where's the treasure?"

"I've been wondering that too. I heard that the police searched room number two, but found nothing except rum."

"Huck," whispered Tom, "the gold was never in that room, it's in the cave!"

Huck's eyes gleamed with excitement. The two boys set off immediately for the cave, and slipped through the hole in the rocks on the river bank. They found Joe's hiding place, a small wooden chair and the remains of a meal. Also a cross, which had been scratched into the rock. "Do you know something, Huck? Apart from the number two, Joe mentioned a cross. I reckon we ought to dig here."

They quickly grabbed their shovels. About one foot down, they struck wood. There were boards which covered a deep hole in the rocks. Right at the bottom, beside a sack of gun powder and two guns lay the treasure box.

"Tom, we're millionaires," yelled Huck and ran both hands through the glittering piles.

***

The precious hoard provoked fresh excitement in the village. The box contained some twelve thousand dollars' worth of gold. The local paper marked the event with a four column spread, with thick black headlines and biographies of the two heroes. A marked change had taken place in Aunt Polly's house. Tom had now become the unrivalled favourite. Everyone, especially Judge Thatcher, treated him with great respect.

Huck was also seen in an entirely different light. Widow Douglas adopted him because she was so grateful to him for saving her life. His new-found riches lifted him into high society,

They surrounded the open carriage and embraced Tom and Becky.

"We're millionaires, Tom," shouted Huck and ran his hands through the glittering piles of gold coins.

whether he wanted to go or not. Brushed and combed, clean, well-dressed and well-shod, he was passed round from house to house. He had to go to school now, as well as to church, and eat respectably with a knife and fork.

Huck bore all this quite heroically for three weeks. But one day he simply disappeared. Widow Douglas searched for him in despair. In the end Tom found his friend, in an empty barrel behind the wine distillery. Huck had returned to freedom and sat comfortably smoking his little pipe.